# GENTIAN HILL

*Also by Elizabeth Goudge*

*Novels*

ISLAND MAGIC
A CITY OF BELLS
THE BIRD IN THE TREE
THE CASTLE ON THE HILL
GREEN DOLPHIN COUNTRY
THE HERB OF GRACE
THE HEART OF THE FAMILY
THE ROSEMARY TREE
THE WHITE WITCH
THE SCENT OF WATER
THE DEAN'S WATCH

*Anthology*

A BOOK OF PEACE

*and available in Hodder Paperbacks*

ELIZABETH GOUDGE

# GENTIAN HILL

HODDER PAPERBACKS

*The characters in this book are entirely imaginary and bear no relation to any living person*




| | |
|---|---|
| FIRST PUBLISHED | 1950 |
| FOURTH IMPRESSION | 1960 |
| HODDER PAPERBACK EDITION | 1965 |
| SECOND IMPRESSION | 1966 |
| THIRD IMPRESSION | 1970 |

Printed and bound in Great Britain for
Hodder Paperbacks Ltd.,
St. Paul's House, Warwick Lane,
London, E.C.4
by Hazell Watson & Viney Ltd.,
Aylesbury, Bucks

ISBN 0 340 00855 5

FOR

HELEN

# NOTE

This story is a retelling of the legend of St. Michael's Chapel at Torquay. Built in the thirteenth century it was in existence until not so many years ago, and until the beginning of the nineteenth century any foreign vessels dropping anchor in Torbay, and possessing Roman Catholic crews, sent them on pilgrimage to the Chapel. The legend as it has come down to us is as Dr. Crane tells it in Book I, Chapter X, its elaboration is my own invention; though the story has come to me so vividly from this bit of country where I live that I have hard work to believe it is not true.

The village where Stella lives is now called Marldon, derived from Mergheldon, the Hill where the Gentians grow, and as I have been guilty of taking some liberties with it I have called it Gentian Hill. I have given it a Vicar at a time when it did not possess one, but was served from the parish church of Paignton. The Chaplain of Torre Abbey is also an imaginary character. Weekaborough Farm is an invention, though I have imagined it standing roughly where Lower Westerland Farm is now.

It is quite true that a living child, clasped in her dead mother's arms, was taken from the water after the wreck of the *Amphion*. The wreck of the *Venerable* is also historical. The tower room at Cockington was at this date as I have described it and was probably at one time used as a priest's hiding-place.

# *BOOK I*

# THE FARM

# CHAPTER I

## I

ON a clear August evening, borne upon the light breath of a fair wind, the fleet was entering Torbay. The sight was so lovely that the men and women in the fishing villages grouped about the bay gazed in wonder, and stilled the busyness of their lives for a moment to stand and watch, shielding their eyes with their hands, trying each in their own way, consciously or unconsciously, to imprint this picture upon their memories so deeply that it should be for them a treasure while life should last.

Since England had been at war with Napoleonic France the fleet was often in Torbay. Admiral Hardy in the *Victory* had known the bay well. Admiral Rodney had sailed from Torbay to the Battle of the Saints. Three times in one year the Earl of St. Vincent had anchored in the bay; and Nelson had visited him here. Yet none of these stately comings and goings had had quite the unearthly beauty of this quiet unobtrusive arrival of two ships of the line and four frigates, just at the penultimate moment of the most glorious sunset of the year.

The last light of the sun was streaming over the rampart of green hills to the west, brimming the leafy valleys with liquid gold, then emptying itself in a sort of abandonment of glory into the vast domed space of sky and sea beyond. There were ripples on the water, and a fragile pattern of cirrus clouds above, and these caught the light in vivid points of fire that were delicate as filigree upon the fine metal of the gold-washed sea and sky. There was no sound anywhere. Voices were stilled upon sea and shore and the white gulls with their gold-tipped wings floated silently. The half-moons of golden water, swung and withdrawn so rhythmically by the ebbing tide, creamed soundlessly upon the golden sand, and the tiny sound of the ripples lapping against the jetties and the hulls of fishing boats was lost in the great silence. Into this vast peace, this clear light, sailed the great ships, and for the one unforgettable moment seemed to gather beauty to them as the sun gathers the dew.

Each oak hull, so cumbrous yet so beautiful in motion, was aglow from the ruddy gleam of the copper sheathing just above the waterline to the lemon yellow of the lower gun decks. The painted poops, the gilded stern works and figureheads, the glazed cabin ports, winked and sparkled, yet the bright hulls were almost eclipsed by the soaring beauty of the raking masts, and the swell of the great sails that caught the gold light in their curves as delicately as flowers do, yet had so terrible a strength. Flags fluttered from each foremast, mainmast and mizzen, and in the wake of each ship the white foam shone like snow.

The moment passed, the streaming light was withdrawn behind the hills, the colours flared for a final moment of glory, then dimmed. Gently, with slight headway on, the great ships passed each to her anchorage and were presently at rest. Evening fell, there were lights here and there upon the ships, scattered lights on the shore, faint lights in the sky, and still the silence was unbroken and the peace profound. Those on shore saw phantom ships upon the sea now, and those on board saw phantom white villages gleaming along the shore, and after the habit of human kind each man yearned to be where the other was, and saw in the place where he was not his heart's desire.

Mr. Midshipman Anthony Louis Mary O'Connell, on board the leading frigate, was no exception to the rule. At the moment he was enduring the punishment meted out to midshipmen who sleep on watch. He was lashed in the weather rigging, his arms and legs widely stretched, his head burning, his body shivering from the bucketful of cold water that had been emptied over him, every nerve in him stretched to what felt like breaking point, and in his heart black rebellion, fury and despair. For he had been treated with the most shocking injustice. Spread-eagling was the correct punishment for the offence he had committed, and he would have endured it with stoicism had there not been added to it the "grampussing," the sousing with a bucket of cold water; for that, though also a recognised punishment for falling asleep upon watch, was not meant to be employed in conjunction with the other. Either spread-eagling, or grampussing, but not both, was the rule of the navy. But upon this ship there was no justice. It was a bad ship. There were not many bad ships in the British navy, but there were some, and this was one of them. In fact, in the opinion of Mr. Midshipman O'Connell, it was not a ship at all but the deepest pit of hell. It had the devil for captain, fiends for officers and an army of rats for seamen. He tried to ease his position a little and a pain like red-hot fire shot up his spine into the back of his head. He groaned and cursed softly but fluently. He had been in the navy for exactly eight weeks and in all the misery of those weeks he counted only one thing upon the credit side; he had learnt a vocabulary which for richness, flexibility, scope and power surpassed anything hitherto dreamed of by him. He had always liked words and they were now the only comfort that he had.

Nothing in the fifteen years of Anthony Louis Mary O'Connell's life until he entered the navy had prepared him for the hell he had had to endure these last two months. He had been brought up in the cultured and queenly city of Bath by an aristocratic and autocratic Irish grandmother, a devout Catholic, a lady of impeccable taste, not wealthy but moving in a society where a fashionable wig was held of no account if the mind beneath it was mediocre, and where the dinner guest with a violin under his arm was more welcome than one with a pocketful of gold. Lady O'Connell had known Dr. Johnson. She had drunk a dish of tea with Mrs. Delany and been on terms of intimate friendship with Fanny Burney. Anthony, the only child of her only child, another Anthony who had married a French wife, lived with her in France and died with her at the beginning of the Terror, was to Lady O'Connell the reason for existence. It was the very intensity of her devotion that had made her give him a softness of upbringing that was about the cruellest thing she could have given him. He was like his father; sensitive, clever and highly impressionable. The elder Anthony had been sent to Harrow, fallen under the influence of a brilliant agnostic master and lost his Catholic faith. He had gone to Oxford and developed so fine a palate for expensive wines and so passionate a devotion to the cards that the competency left him by his dead father melted into thin air almost at once. Sent upon the Grand Tour by an obliging uncle he had lost his heart to a French girl, deserted his mother and her country for his wife and her country, and eventually, by a foolhardy act of courage had quite unnecessarily lost his life. When his baby son was brought to Lady O'Connell by royalist refugees she vowed that nothing of this should happen to the second Anthony. The evil influences of school and university should not be allowed to touch him. She had him educated at home by private tutors and she watched every friendship, every contact, with a jealous eye, and smashed it as soon as she fancied any danger in it. In some ways Anthony's education was not altogether disastrous, for he was well taught, he had an eager mind and was not lazy, and so managed to learn a good deal without the stimulus of competition. He was musical, and his grandmother's friends were men and women from whom it was possible to catch much loveliness of mind and manners. . . . But nothing at all in his early training fitted him in the very least for what befell him when Lady O'Connell died.

She had visualised all the dangers she could possibly think of for Anthony except that one danger of her own death before he had reached maturity. She was a healthy woman, and never thought of death. She had imagined she would live till ninety, like her mother before her. Instead she had died suddenly at the age of seventy, and the guardianship of Anthony had devolved upon her nephew by marriage, Captain Rupert O'Connell, the son of the obliging uncle who had sent the elder Anthony upon the Grand Tour, a man whom she had set eyes upon only once or twice in her life.

To do Captain O'Connell justice he did the best that he could for the almost penniless Anthony. He took him on board his own ship and made a midshipman of him, thereby putting him in a fair way to earn his livelihood, with eventual promotion and honour if he had it in him to attain them. Having thus established Anthony he took no further notice of him; though in that perhaps he was wise, for any show of favouritism would only have made the boy's lot more wretched than ever.

And his lot was so wretched that it could hardly have been worse. Persecution was the fate of any greenhorn of a newly joined midshipman, but the fact that Anthony was the cousin of a hated captain was a good excuse for giving him an extra dose; the brutalities of the captain could be revenged on Anthony. And then there was his seasickness, which he could not manage to surmount. And there was the ridiculous array of his Christian names, including the Mary that was borne by all the Catholic O'Connells in honour of Our Lady; he had tried in vain to keep them hidden. And there was the rosary that he had been taught to wear always round his neck, and stubbornly refused to abandon; not that it had really meant anything to him until now, but he was damned if he was going to take it off and chuck it overboard because of the taunts of a handful of dirty-mouthed, hard-fisted brutes who had no conception at all of the obligations of gentlemen to the traditions of their race.

And lastly there was the misfortune of his age. Had he been younger he would have been one of the "younkers," little boys of eleven and upwards who slung their hammocks in the gun room, messed by themselves with the gunner to cater for them and keep their clothes in order, were taught by a schoolmaster or the chaplain and enjoyed a certain amount of shelter and protection. But he was just too old to be a "younker," he was the youngest of the "oldsters" and must mess and sleep with the senior midshipmen and the masters' mates in a pestilential den below the waterline, in the after-cockpit. The things that he saw, heard and endured in the after-cockpit were enough to turn the reason of a boy to whom vice and brutality had until now been nothing but names whose exact meaning he had not bothered about. Yet he endured somehow. There was a stubbornness in him that he had not known that he possessed, and was thankful to discover; for he knew that he was not naturally courageous. He held on to decency as a drowning man holds to a spar, and vowed that he would while he could. When he couldn't, what then? But he did not consider that question often, for what happens when a man can no longer endure is not that man's responsibility. It would have been easier if he could have got some proper sleep, something better than the feverish snatches that were all that the din and stench of the after-cockpit allowed. He had slept on watch at last; and so here he was lashed in the weather rigging.

The punishment lasted for two hours; but he could swear that he had been here for four. The pain in his back and head was such that he shut his eyes lest he should be sick; he had discovered that you were less likely to be sick if you didn't watch the motion of the ship. He lost consciousness for a moment or two perhaps, and returned from it to that state of semi-nightmare with which he was now so familiar, in which the horrors he had seen passed and re-passed against the darkness of his closed eyelids. The day the whole ship's company had been lined up to see a poor fellow flogged at the gangway; and he had died. The wretched sailors racing mast against mast when sail had to be made or shortened, with the captain cursing at them from below because the best they could do was not good enough; and then the flogging of the last man down. The day when one man, in terror of the flogging, lost his footing and fell. These pictures, actually seen, and others that were painted for him by his too active imagination. He had not yet been in action and shrank from it with dread. He thought he would show himself then for what he was, a coward. He imagined and pictured all the ways in which he might be put to the test, and fail. All his life he had been afraid of so many things, of noise and pain, of death, above all of being shut up or imprisoned in any way. It was partly his claustrophobia that made him hate life at sea so much. The ship was like a prison and the after-cockpit a prison cell. . . . One could not get out. . . . And this was his life, now, for ever, this imprisonment and fear and pain. Much better to die. Open your eyes, you fool, don't look any more. . . . But he couldn't. They seemed stuck. . . . Open them, you fool. Better be sick than watch any more.

With a struggle Mr. Midshipman O'Connell opened his eyes, gazed, blinked, caught his breath and gazed again. Drowned in his misery he had not known that the ship had entered the bay. He had opened his eyes just at that moment when men on shore, looking out to sea, had seen the ships caught up in that golden moment of perfection; he, looking towards the land, saw a scene that he would not forget while memory remained to him.

He saw the hills sweeping around the bay and the wooded valleys brimming with gold. He saw the sheeted gold of the sky behind the hills and the streaming light. And just opposite him he saw a fishing village built beyond the golden water in a green cup in the hills; a small place, peaceful and perfect. He supposed this was the village they called Torquay. Beyond a half moon of sand was a green field, then a low stone wall. Behind the wall half a dozen white-walled cottages stood in gardens full of flowers, the smoke curling lazily up from their chimneys. To the right of the cottages a stream flowed beneath a low stone bridge, crossed the meadow and lost itself in the sea. Anthony guessed that the white-walled house next to the bridge was an inn, for he could just make out the swinging signboard. Just beyond the bridge and the inn, to the right, was the slipway of a ship-building yard, and then the harbour with a row of neat little houses beyond it. There were a few fishing boats and one larger ship anchored in the harbour and around and over them the gulls were wheeling.

Anthony stared, his eyes aching, his heart beating. Would they be allowed to land? He knew that except in exceptional circumstances sailors were not allowed to go ashore when a ship dropped anchor in harbour; the risk of desertion was too great. But he was a midshipman, an officer. Surely the officers would be allowed shore leave. He began to imagine to himself what it would be like. . . . He was in the liberty boat, gliding nearer and nearer to that loveliness. He was climbing up the flight of steps against the harbour wall. He was on firm land again, free at last of seasickness. He was crossing the bridge, drinking a glass of milk at the inn, walking in one of the flower-filled gardens. He was following the stream up into the wooded valley behind the village, where it was cool and quiet, following the stream to the house up there, the old thatched house overgrown with ivy, in a valley musical with the sound of running water, with the purple hill behind it, and inside——

A sharp pain shot through his right thigh. It was only a good-natured slap dealt him by the young lieutenant who had come to take him down, and who was unfastening the ropes round his legs, but it happened to light on one of the many bruises with which his body was covered. "Come along down, Mary my girl, you've had your two hours."

"Sir!" gasped Anthony. "Will we go ashore—I mean—the officers?"

"Damn your eyes, and who may you mean by the officers? Not you, Mary. Not little girls who sleep on watch. And next time you start nodding you know what it will mean—laid on a gun and given a dozen with the colt."

The lieutenant assisted Mr. Midshipman O'Connell from the rigging, dropped him, not unkindly, face downward on the deck and departed on his own affairs. Mr. Midshipman O'Connell stayed where he was for a while, sick and dizzy. He heard eight bells ringing and knew he had missed supper, but the state of his inside being what it was, and the ship's food being what it was, he did not feel this to be a disaster. But he badly wanted a drink. There was drinking water down in the after-cockpit—if he could get there. Eight bells. He had to turn in now, until midnight, when he had the middle watch. It was hell in the cockpit but there was water there—grog too if he was lucky—and if they let him alone he could lie still in his hammock. He dragged himself to his hands and knees and crawled a little way, then pulled himself to his feet with the help of a handy stanchion, and at last got down to the orlop deck and along to the after-cockpit and the midshipmen's mess.

The dingy place was not more than five feet high and twelve feet square and into this space was crowded a table, used by the midshipmen for their meals and by the surgeon as an operating table when the ship went into action, the midshipmen's chests, their hammocks and themselves. The reek of the bilges below, mixed with the smell of rancid butter and putrid cheese from the purser's storeroom nearby, was horrible, and coming into it Anthony wondered dully, as always, how he would endure it for four mortal hours. But the noise was worse, for the elder gentlemen were getting round the table for their nightly rum-drinking and the younger ones were tumbling into their hammocks. Anthony's entry was the signal for the usual jeers and catcalls, but apart from that he was not tormented tonight; brutal though the population of the after-cockpit might be on this ship they knew when a man had had enough. No one helped him sling his hammock, or got him a drink, and his struggle to do these things for himself was the subject of much merriment; but when he had accomplished them he was let alone to sleep if he could.

And astonishingly, in spite of his aching limbs and splitting head, after an hour or so of misery he dropped into a queer, feverish sort of sleep; awakening from it suddenly to find himself in the most peculiar state of mind.

A grown-up would have recognised it as a subtle form of temptation, very apt to attack one during a wakeful hour of the night, when vitality is at its lowest. Because it suddenly seems impossible to go on, values are abruptly turned upside down. To endure, that perhaps a mere half hour before was the right and obvious thing to do, is now presented to the mind as simply ridiculous; escape, that would have seemed despicable a little while ago, now seems to be the only sane course of action. The experienced man knows that it is not impossible to go on because one thinks it is, that you can always go on in some manner while the power of choice remains. This sudden reversal of the values is a temptation to pre-ordain the moment when a man can no longer make his choice and his responsibility for what happens next must be laid down. Faced with it the experienced man once more chooses to come to grips with the impossible and finds it possible.

But Anthony was not experienced and to him it seemed perfectly simple. He was not aware of any temptation. His mind was absolutely clear. He had endured as long as he could and now he was going to get out.

## 11

Five minutes later, before any doubts had had time to obtrude themselves, the middle watch was called and he fell out of his hammock, fully dressed as he had dropped into it, and staggered up on deck. It was a still night, and a slight sea mist had crept up after sunset, so that he could tell the whereabouts of Torquay only by the gleam of lights still burning in the inn, and the harbour lanterns. No more perfect night for escape could have presented itself; the dim glimmer of light was sufficient to guide him but his body in the water would not be seen. He knew exactly what he was going to do. His mind had that extraordinary lucidness that comes sometimes at the peak of fatigue, just before bewilderment comes down like a woolly blanket and smothers thought. The middle watch, with the ship at anchor in home waters in fine weather, was a routine affair. The officer of the watch on the poop, the sentries and helmsman at their appointed places, were peacefully inattentive. As they were at anchor, with no danger threatening, the boatswain's mates who usually walked round with their starters to tickle up any man who looked like falling asleep, were absent. There was no sound but the lap of the water against the ship's side and the occasional cry of "All's well" from a sentry. Anthony, with another midshipman, kept watch upon the forecastle.

He waited patiently, alert and attentive to his duty, until the very last hour of the watch when vigilance was relaxed to the minimum and he found himself with no eye upon him. He took off his short dark blue coat with its brass buttons, his nankeen waistcoat and black silk neck-handkerchief, and stowed them in a corner with his three-cornered hat and his dirk. Then wearing nothing but trousers and frilled white linen shirt, his thin heelless black shoes stuck in his pockets, he crept down the main hatchway to the deck below, and down again to the lower gun deck. It was such perfect weather that the gun-ports were open and he was so thin that it was not hard to slip through one of them, cling by his fingers for a moment, then let go.

He had thought that he had so short a distance to fall that there would not be much splash, but the noise he made seemed to burst in his ears like the explosion of a carronade. Yet when he came up choking with sea water and panic he heard no shouts behind him and guessed that if anyone had heard the splash they had thought it was the cook chucking out rubbish, for work in the galley started round about four o'clock. Reassured he struck out instantly for the shore, guided by the glimmer of the harbour lanterns. He was a good swimmer and he had not thought it would be difficult, yet now he had his second moment of panic, for his stiff aching limbs were like lead. Then the panic passed;

drowning or that village, it did not really matter which; either was escape.

He got there and clung more dead than alive to an iron ring in the harbour wall, beside a flight of steps. Then somehow he got on the steps and crawled up them. Though it was still dark he remembered the lie of the land from his vision of the village the evening before, and he made his way along the harbour to the shipbuilding yard. There in the lee of a half-built fishing smack he wrung the water out of his trousers and shirt as well as he could, put on his soaking shoes and lay down to wait for dawn.

It came quite soon, with its inevitable quickening and reassurance, and that interpenetration of light and sound and scent by each other that one seems to notice only in moments of deep peace. The crying of the awakening gulls, the soft slap of the sea against the harbour wall, the running of the stream, the sound of an opening door and a voice singing, a church clock striking the hour, made a music that was a part of the growing pearly light. There was a faint scent of seaweed, of baking bread, and that indescribable fresh smell of the dawn compounded of dew-drenched flowers, wood-smoke and wet fields. That too was a part of the music and the light, and all of them together were like a personal presence coming to him, and wrapping itself about him like a cloak, so that for a few moments he ceased to be aware of the shivering of his body and felt a glow all through him, the warmth of a fresh beginning and a new day.

It passed and he was shivering again, but the reassurance remained. He came cautiously out into the open and looked about him. The whole world, now, was sparkling with clear light, and he had to shield his eyes against the dazzle of the sun rising like a ball of fire out of the sea. His Majesty's ships, resting in painted glory upon the sparkling water, looked unearthly in beauty; who could have guessed that their loveliness held such misery? His reassurance was suddenly shattered, for they seemed to be all eyes, searching for him. He looked quickly away from them to the white cottages in their flower-filled gardens, the stream slipping like a silver ribbon under the stone bridge and across the field, the green hills and the wooded valleys. He saw now that the valley up which he had imagined himself walking, following the stream, was not unpopulated. There were white houses of a most genteel appearance among the trees. He realised that this was a bigger place than he had thought; almost the beginning of a fashionable watering place. He would not dare go up among those formal houses in search of his ivy-covered one, for they looked just the sort of homes that might contain naval officers on leave, and bedraggled though they were his midshipman's frilled shirt and nankeen trousers were perfectly recognisable to a knowledgeable eye; and the floggings delivered to captured deserters had been known to kill them. Somehow he must get food, but he would beg it from poor folk who, if they recognised him, would be less likely to give him away.

Smoke was curling up now from the chimney of the inn, and it was from its open doorway that there floated the delicious smell of baking bread, and the sound of a man's voice singing, very beautifully, to the music of a guitar. It was not an English voice. He guessed there must be a foreign seaman there, and looking round he was not surprised to see a small Portuguese privateer anchored among the English fishing boats. These little piratical ships of the allies nosed their way about the world in an extraordinary way, and this one, judging by her battered appearance, had had some rough handling from storms or the enemy, and had put into harbour to refit. Sailors in a foreign port were notoriously open-handed; they'd share their breakfast with him. It seemed crazy, perhaps, not to get right away from the village before he tried to get food, but without something to eat he knew he'd not get anywhere.

The cob-walled, whitewashed inn stood in its gay garden just beyond the stone bridge, and the swinging sign proclaimed it "The Bird in Hand" by a motto painted on the board.

> "A bird in hand is better far
> Than two birds in the bushes are."

Dizzy and sick, with such a singing in his ears that he could scarcely hear the music of the guitar, Anthony leaned in the doorway and looked in. Half a dozen bronzed seamen, gold rings in their ears, bright handkerchiefs bound round their heads, were sitting about the table munching bread and bacon, washing it down with copious draughts of ale. The singer, a young man, had finished eating but wetted his whistle between each song. Their shirts were clean, their faces shaved, and they seemed in high good humour. The kitchen had a sanded floor and brightly burning fire, and a fresh-faced woman was busy about her morning's work as though she liked it. There was an air of warm festivity about the scene, the invitation and friendliness of a great occasion, and letting go of the door jamb Anthony fell plop into it as a gasping fish falls off the gunwale of a boat into the reviving water.

When he came to himself again he was lying on the settle by the fire, the woman bending over him with a glass in her hand. "Drink it up, love," she advised him, and clinked the glass against his teeth. He gulped down the fiery stuff and presently sat up and rubbed his knuckles in his eyes, smiling sheepishly. "Soaked through and hungry," diagnosed the woman. "Sit there and dry off, boy, and eat a good breakfast." She brought him bread and bacon and hot milk and he did as he was told, gratefully aware of the kindly concern of the men about the table and the motherliness of the woman, that were like balm after the brutality of the past weeks.

"One of you?" she enquired of the men. "Been off on the spree by himself? He's got his heathen beads round his neck, poor lamb." Anthony's shirt had come undone and she could see his rosary. Coming to him with another slice of bread she picked it up and dropped it again with kindly contempt. The Portuguese seamen, scarcely understanding her, shook their heads but smiled companionably at Anthony, and he noticed that they were all wearing their rosaries. Apparently this festival, into which he had fallen headlong, was a religious festival. He smiled back as he munched, making himself one with them in whatever it was that they were celebrating.

"It's a queer thing, how it goes on," said the woman. "For hundreds of years, now, not a Popish ship comes into Torbay but some of the seamen must be landed to go and do their heathen antics in St. Michael's chapel. You don't know why you do it, and neither do we, but so it goes on. Some sort of pilgrimage. They give thanks, they say, but I doubt if they know for what."

"Escape," suggested Anthony timidly.

The woman looked at him thoughtfully. "They do say that chapel was built by a sailor who'd been saved from drowning in some storm. But I don't know the story rightly. Some sort of an old legend. Hundreds of years ago it was and I've no time for such nonsense. Have a bite more, boy? You can twist your tongue round a bit of English it seems. What's your name?"

"Anthony." He still spoke softly and timidly, and the name was unfamiliar to her.

"Zachary," she repeated. "Odd, now, to have a good old English name fastened on a poor Popish foreign lad."

He did not correct her. Zachary, he thought, would be as good a name as another for him to be known by in a new life. Anthony was dead. Now he was Zachary. The men got up, and he got up too, for it seemed that he was one with them in this pilgrimage.

The woman came to the door to show them the way. "Cross the bridge over the Fleete and go along Cane's Lane," she said, "and up over the cliff by Ladybird Walk, and then you'll see Torre church and St. Michael's chapel. You can't miss them."

III

The little party crossed the bridge and made their way along the lane beside the stone wall, past the five white houses standing in their bright gardens. The Portuguese sailors were merry, singing and laughing and chattering to each other. They leaned over the walls of the gardens and picked sprays of tamerisk and fuchsia and stuck them behind their ears. One of them flung a posy to Zachary, who was sticking to them like a forlorn disreputable dog, trying to keep their comforting bulk between himself and the sea; for now that he was out in the open again there had come upon him once more that horror of the eyes of the ships. The food and kindness at the inn had put new strength into him, but he still felt dizzy in the head and heavy about the feet, as though a bushel of mud was clinging round each of his wet shoes, and it was with dismay that he realised that there was no way round under the towering rocky cliff that enclosed Torquay upon the south, they had to climb up over it by the pathway that their hostess had called Ladybird Walk. Yet he still continued to follow the others, for he had no idea in his head now except just to go where they went.

The path climbed steeply upwards, bordered by rocks and gorse bushes, and stunted rowans clinging wherever they could find a foothold of earth. Zachary was too occupied in dragging himself up to look about him as they climbed, but when they reached the summit of the cliff he stopped with the others and sat down on a rock, his head in his hands, to get his breath. All about him he heard guttural exclamations of delight, and presently he stood up and looked about him.

It was incredibly beautiful. He could see the whole glorious stretch of the bay, and the green and wooded hills piled about it, and to the west high peaks of purple moorland, sharp and clear against the sky. Between the bay and the distant moors he could see the rise and fall of hills and valleys patterned with green pastures, harvest fields, copses and orchards, and could guess at the peaceful villages, farms and churches folded among them. He thought with an aching heart of those quiet farms. He knew little of country life; Bath and the misery of the past few weeks was all that he knew; but he thought that if he could only get to one of these farms he would be safe there, and have peace. Some farmer would surely give him work; it couldn't be difficult to learn to plough, and milk cows, and shear sheep. He would make his way inland he decided, when this pilgrimage was over. He would leave it until later to see if the ivy-covered house really existed.

Then he tore himself away from the thought of the quiet farm where he would find sanctuary and looked down to the scene below them to the south. He could see a beautiful house, with about it what looked like the ruins of some great abbey, surrounded by gardens and orchards, and parkland where deer were feeding, the whole bounded upon the east by a strong sea-wall.

Between the abbey and the cliff-top where they stood were two hills.

The one nearest to them was low and green and tree-covered, and among the trees were a few small houses and an old grey church, with sheep feeding in the churchyard. It must have been the bell of this church that Zachary had heard before, for now it tolled out the hour, clear and sweet, the voice of the bell joining itself to the bleating of the full-grown lambs.

The other hill was rocky and precipitous and built upon its summit was the Chapel of St. Michael, the goal of the pilgrimage. Gulls circled about it and it was so old and weatherworn that it looked a part of the rock upon which it towered, and strangely lost in the midst of the peaceful pastoral landscape. It would have looked more at home, Zachary thought, on a rock in the middle of the sea. Yet it was a fitting shrine to have been built by a seaman who had been saved from death in a storm, and a fitting place of pilgrimage for other seamen who were holding their lives in their hands in days of peril. For though one might forget, on this golden August morning, with the painted battleships apparently asleep there on the painted sea, that half the nations of Europe were at war, and England fighting for her life, one remembered it when one looked at that chapel. It had a look of vigilance about it, of endurance. It might have been St. Michael himself, standing with drawn sword to keep watch over this lovely land.

Silently the little company filed down the steep path to the green valley below, skirted the hill where the church stood among its trees, and came to the foot of the limestone precipice up which they must climb to reach the chapel. It was a steep climb, but the feet of many pilgrims had made a path and there were rocks and bushes to give handhold. The thirteenth century building at the top was a strange, bare little shrine. There was no door in the arched entrance, no glass in the narrow windows. The floor was of rough rock and sloped steeply upward from west to east. The walls were three feet thick and the barrel-vaulted roof was composed of small stones. A little of the original plaster clung to roof and walls, and there was a plain piscina in a niche in the south wall, to show that once there had been an altar here, and two empty niches in the north wall, with what looked like a fleur-de-lys carved in the stone between them. The solid little place looked now less like a shrine built by man than a cavity hollowed out of the solid rock by wind and rain as a refuge for all storm-battered creatures. The storm of a few nights past had evidently swept through it, for it was fresh and clean. And it had the compelling power of places that have been used for prayer, and nothing but prayer, for generations.

The seamen filed reverently in through the archway in the north wall and knelt upon the rough rock, giving thanks for whatever deliverance it was that had left their ship so battered but themselves unharmed, and for a little while there was no sound but the click of their beads, the crying of the gulls who circled about the chapel and the beating of their wings. Zachary knelt just inside the door and took off his rosary. His beads slipped through his fingers but his weary mind was a blank, he gave thanks for nothing in particular, prayed for nothing in particular, merely stayed himself upon the fact of the safety of this place. Looking out of the narrow windows he could see only the sky and the gulls; he could not see the ships and their searching eyes could not see him. He was safe from them in this impregnable cell of stone, high up in the sky upon this rocky precipice.

Revelling in this blessed sense of safety he did not go away when the other men did but stayed where he was just inside the doorway, his eyes shut, his beads still slipping through his fingers. "Holy Mary, Mother of God, pray for us sinners now and at the hour of our death." The mechanical repetition of the words soothed him, but he was hardly conscious of saying them. The words that he heard seemed to be spoken by the chapel itself, by the rock floor, the stout walls and the stone roof. "The Lord is my fortress, my rock and my defence." Each stone cried out in triumph, but the triumph had a biting edge, as though the words were cutting into his spirit, so that gradually, as the triumph continued the pain of his bruised and aching body seemed mysteriously transferred to his soul. What had he done? The question repeated iself, mingling with the voices of the stones, until he faced it. Deserted. Run away. Found refuge in flight instead of in—what? Some impregnable fortress that existed as the core of quiet at the centre of whatever whirlwind of fear or pain. His lips moved, the beads slipped through his fingers and his face was still, but there was a sudden turmoil of defiant shouting in his soul that tried to shout down the mounting accusation of the voices of the silent stones. "I couldn't do it, I tell you. It was not possible. Flesh and blood could not endure it. I tell you I could not do it."

But the stones were not silenced, and suddenly the chapel was no longer a place of refuge but the thing that he dreaded most of all, a prison. The walls were closing in on him, coming nearer and nearer. They'd get him in another minute, hold him in their hands of stone, take him prisoner for ever. . . . He must get out! Get out! . . . He opened his eyes and scrambled to his feet, and then for the first time realised that he was not, as he had thought, alone in the chapel. A white-haired, white-faced man in black was kneeling in prayer before the place where the altar must once have been. He must have been there all the while but Zachary, coming in behind the other seamen, had not seen him. He stood still, breathing fast, his queer panic increased by the sight of that still figure. Then the man turned his head and looked at him. It was a look of infinite kindness but Zachary in his panic did not see the kindness, only the almost stonelike whiteness of the face. It was as though the chapel itself had taken human shape, with hands that would hold him and keep him here. The power of movement returned suddenly to his legs and he bolted out of the door and round the corner, keeping close to the outer wall, for if he detached himself from that for a moment the eyes of the ships would see him. At the landward side of the chapel, where its bulk stood between him and the sea, he leaned against the wall, away from the windows so that the man inside could not see him. He stood there with his limbs shaking and the sweat streaming off him until the normal worldly outlook upon things, which he was accustomed to call sanity, slowly returned to him again.

"Fool!" he said to himself. "Crazy fool! Feverish and crazy. You got away from that damn ship only just in time. Get inland and find that farm. Right inland. It will be safe there."

He let himself down to the gravel and rested for a little, his eyes upon the coloured lovely distance of the folded hills. It was warm here in the sun and strength came back. Presently he got up and began to climb down the rock.

## CHAPTER II

### I

WHEN she was grown-up Stella smiled sometimes when she heard people speculating as to what was their first memory, and seldom able to identify it with certainty. She was in no doubt about her first memory, nor her second, and she knew they had come into her possession on the same day—September the 22nd, 1796, when she was two years old. They were strongly contrasted, and perhaps that was why they had affected her so deeply. The first, though mercifully vague, was none the less dreadful in its terror, and visited her again and again through her childhood, in nightmare or fever, a memory of noise, fire, the grasp of thin arms round her that hurt with the agonising tightness of their grip, then the blackness of water closing over her head. The second was merciful and beneficent; deep silence, starlight shed upon a quiet garden, air that was light and cool upon scorched skin, and then the arms of Mother Sprigg about her, not hard and tight like those other arms but steady and comfortable like Mother Sprigg herself.

"Am I your own girl, Mother?" she asked suddenly when she was ten years old. They were sitting together before the kitchen fire, alone except for the cat Seraphine asleep in her basket with her kittens disposed around her. The candles were lighted and the fire burned brightly, for though it was only the beginning of September the evening was chilly, and Stella was sewing her sampler while Mother Sprigg stitched at her patchwork quilt. It was a fine evening and they had not pulled the curtains, outside the sunset spread a sheet of pure gold behind the beautiful motionless shapes of the old orchard trees, and there was no sound except the whisper of the flames on the hearth, the ticking of the grandfather clock and the soft click of Mother Sprigg's flying needle against her thimble. Stella's needle did not fly and so it did not click. It went slowly and laboriously in and out of her sampler, pursuing painfully the bloodstained path of duty, and now and then ceasing work altogether while Stella sucked her finger and then sprang yet another question upon poor Mother Sprigg.

"Bless the child!" she cried now, and dropped the quilt on her lap. Generally she managed to go on stitching while grappling with Stella's thirst for information, though at times her rosy face puckered with the distress of the intellectual effort, but this question brought her to such a complete full-stop in household activity that Stella gazed at her in round-eyed astonishment. Only once before had the little girl seen her sit like this, quite still, with her plump hands folded upon the work in her lap and her eyes gazing into the fire, and that had been when Father Sprigg had been gored by the bull, and Doctor Crane had sent her out of the bedroom and down to the kitchen to wait for his verdict. It had been a merciful thing, Stella had thought at the time, that father had got better, or mother might have got stuck like that, gazing into the fire, for ever and ever. She had known instinctively then, as children do, that that would always be mother's way with trouble; not outcry, just stillness. Had she said anything wrong? She stretched out a slim brown hand, the beads of blood on the pricked finger sparkling in the candlelight like tiny rubies, and laid it on the work-hardened fat red hands clasped in Mother Sprigg's lap. "Mother?" she queried tentatively.

Mother Sprigg gave her head the sudden accomplished jerk which shook her spectacles (required for close work only) from the bridge of her short button nose to a little lower down, and gazed over the top of them at the child on the stool beside her.

"What makes you ask, love?" she whispered. Yet even while she asked, she knew. The child was old enough now to notice the contrasts; the graceful hand lying on her own clumsy one was only one of many.

"I remember that I came from somewhere else to here," said Stella. "It was quite different."

"What do you remember, child?" asked Mother Sprigg.

"Noise, a fire and black water, and arms that hurt," said Stella in a quick whisper, as though anxious to get it over; and then, slowly and with great sweetness she said, "and after that, Mother, it was quiet in the garden, and your arms were comfortable."

All her life Stella would never be exuberant with her thanks; she would just say what it was that you had done for her and leave it at that; but the fact that she knew exacly what it was would give to her plain statement of fact a remembered value far outweighing all the muddled emotionalism in the world. Quiet and comfort. In years to come Mother Sprigg would recall that she had given that to the child Stella, and would feel again the touch of the slim hand on hers, and remember that there had been more true affection in it than in the hugs and kisses of a more exuberant child. She would know then that she had given Stella, and had called forth in the child, things of worth, and would be glad.

And now her momentary distress passed suddenly in the knowledge that if this question had to come it had come in a good hour. They were alone, and quiet, with the child old enough to be told the truth, yet not old enough, she thought, to feel that distress that only experience of suffering can quicken.

"No, you are not my own girl," she said. "Though the Lord knows you are as dear to me as though you were. Nearly eight years ago, love, you were brought here as a little thing of two years old. Sitting here before the fire, I was, like I am now, patching a shirt, and feeling a bit anxious because father was not back from Plymouth. 'Back at eight o'clock on Wednesday, Martha,' he'd said to me, but the grandfather had struck ten and still I sat there stitching. It was a still night and the strokes of the clock had fallen loud and heavy, like a bell tolling. I was jumpy, I don't say I wasn't. There was an invasion scare that year, and every day we were expecting a landing of the French, and every day the troopships were going off from Plymouth with men and guns for Ireland, for they didn't know where that blackhearted scoundrel Bony would strike, there or here. It was to see Bill his soldier brother set sail on the frigate *Amphion* that your father had ridden to Plymouth. There was to be a grand farewell party on board and your father had ridden off on the Tuesday before it was light, all in a taking because he'd overslept himself and he feared he'd be too late for the grand doings, and too late he was—by the mercy of God."

"Why, what happened?" asked Stella.

"The *Amphion* blew up, love, with wives and sweethearts and little children of the men all on board. They say a light was dropped by a gunner who was stealing ammunition. A terrible thing it was. Three hundred men and women and children lost their lives, your father's brother among 'em. Your father, riding through Plymouth, heard the explosion, and when he reached the Hoe they were taking the bodies from the water. Your father, he did what he could, and worked as hard as any. One poor young woman whom he helped to take from the water he never forgot. He said she was beautiful, even in death. A sailor had held her up and kept her from drowning but she'd died while he held her—shock, maybe, or some injury—I don't know. She wore a green gown and there was a gold locket round her neck, and her arms were locked tight round the body of her child."

"Me?" whispered Stella.

"Yes. . . . Your father, when he saw you, lost his head. You see, love, we'd had a little girl who'd died at just about the age you were then, the only child we ever had, and your father had grieved over the loss and couldn't seem to get over it. When he saw you there, and a couple of rough chaps unclasping your dead mother's arms from about you, he just snatched you away from them and picked you up in his own arms. One of the men said, 'The child's dead,' but though you were wet and cold like a little fish he knew you were alive. He was in such a taking he didn't answer the man, he just made off with you, without a with-your-leave or a by-your-leave. There was an inn nearby, and he took you there and had the good woman look after you, while he went back to help with the rescue work and see what had become of his brother. . . . He was not among the saved, was poor Bill. . . . And the next day, you being as fit as a fiddle by that time, and no one seeming to know a thing about you, he wrapped you up in his cloak and rode off home with you. Hour after hour he rode through the twilight and dark, knocked nearly silly by the shock of it all, but you were good as gold all the way and never cried."

Stella laughed suddenly, her clear happy laugh that was a delight to all who heard it. Mother Sprigg decided that it was as she had hoped, though the child was tender-hearted and sensitive she was too young as yet to realise the tragedy of the story.

"Weren't you startled, mother, to have father ride home with me like that?"

"You could have knocked me down with a feather," declared Mother Sprigg, gaiety springing up in her to answer the laughter of the child. "I heard Bess trotting in the lane, and I ran out of the house and down through the garden to the gate. 'Here you are, mother,' says father, and he leans down and dumps you in my arms. You'd been asleep but you woke up then and looked about you; at the garden and up in my face, and then you cuddled down comfortable and went to sleep again. The next morning you were up with the birds and behaving as though you had lived at Weekaborough Farm from the day you were born."

"And no one ever tried to take me away from you?" asked Stella.

"No, love. Of course I sent your father back to Plymouth at once, to make more enquiries, for it was nothing but baby-stealing, the way he'd walked off with you, but he couldn't find that you'd any relatives. No one seemed to know who your poor mother was. There was nothing in her pocket but an embroidered handkerchief and your little coral, and nothing in her locket but a curl of dark hair, and a scrap of paper with something written on it in a foreign language that no one could make head or tail of. Your father saw her buried decently, and then he put the handkerchief and the coral and the locket in his pocket and rode off home as fast as he could to tell me you were ours for keeps, our own girl—Stella."

The child was sitting now with her pointed chin cupped in her slim hands, staring at the fire. She spoke no word of pity for her real mother; it seemed that just now it was the woman beside her with whom her thoughts were busy.

"Mother, was your little girl who died called Stella?"

"No, love, she was called Eliza after my own mother. But your father, being clean besotted about you, must needs choose some fanciful name for you. Star-bright eyes you had, he said, when you first looked up at him, and the starlight was bright on your face when I looked at you that first time, so Stella it had to be, though the name don't go well with Sprigg to my way of thinking. 'But what matter?' said your father. 'The maid will be changing my name for another as soon as she's husband-high, and meanwhile she's my Stella and my sprig of mischief, born on the first of June with candles in her eyes'."

"And why should I have candles in my eyes because I was born on the first of June? And how do you know that I *was* born on the first of June?" demanded Stella. She had an accurate as well as an imaginative mind. She delighted in the fantastic provided it was based upon a fairly reasonable hypothesis, like a pretty flower with solid roots in the earth, but she did not like it just fluttering down from nowhere.

"There's no knowing what day you were born, love, but you seemed just over two years when you came to us, and the first of June, 1794, was the Glorious First, when the fleet sailed into Plymouth Sound with six captive French battleships, and in each house a lighted candle was set in every pane. All night they burned, pretty as a picture. Your father saw the sight, and he never forgot it. 'Like all the stars fallen down from heaven,' he said it was; till the dawn came and put them out."

" 'Night's candles are burnt out, and jocund day stands tiptoe on the misty mountain tops'," said Stella in a voice that suddenly became curiously deep and mature for a child.

"Eh?" asked Mother Sprigg with sudden sharpness. "Have you been reading some old book again?"

There were few things that made Mother Sprigg angry, but one was to have Stella browse among Doctor Crane's old books. The doctor was the best friend they had, and he had taken upon himself the business of Stella's education, but he and Mother Sprigg differed a good deal as to what was, and was not, education. Reading, writing and elementary arithmetic were all the child needed to learn of the doctor, Mother Sprigg maintained; this combined with the arts of housewifery that she herself could teach her was all the education required by a farmer's daughter. Doctor Crane disagreed; the education required by an individual, he maintained, was just exactly all the knowledge the individual could possibly assimilate. Stella agreed with him, and let loose among his books she assimilated at a good pace, keeping her knowledge hidden from Mother Sprigg as much as she could. Yet Mother Sprigg always knew when she had been reading the doctor's books because quite unconsciously she would quote little scraps from them in that startlingly unchildish voice. Then Mother Sprigg would scold. She didn't know why she scolded; unless it was because Stella's thirst for knowledge seemed to hold some sort of unexplainable threat that frightened her; and she always scolded when she was afraid.

Stella, her chin still cupped in her hands, did not answer. She was always silent when scolded, but there was no sullenness in her silence, merely a smooth shining determination to go her own way from which scoldings slithered to oblivion like water off a duck's back, accomplishing nothing whatever. Mother Sprigg sighed in irritated frustration, then laughed as Stella lifted her face from her hands, hitched her stool nearer, and looked up at her adopted mother with the countenance of a merry elf, the laughter running over her face like light and both her dimples showing. And that, too, was typical of Stella. Her own way once insisted upon and secured she was swift to dispel any smallest hint of unpleasantness, and Stella sweeping away unpleasantness was like the sun bursting out through the clouds; one could not greet it with anything but forgetfulness and a lightening of the heart.

The sudden intrusion of Doctor Crane into the real business of the evening was now as though it had never been, and Stella's laughter vanished too, even as her previous queer maturity had vanished. She was just a loving serious little girl as she laid her hand on Mother Sprigg's knee and said gently, "*You* are my mother." Then it seemed that she put from her also the story for which she had asked, for she smoothed her skirts, looked at her pricked finger, sighed, sucked it, then replaced her thimble and began once more to sew her sampler. Mother Sprigg too picked up her quilt, adjusted her spectacles, and chose a hexagon of crimson velvet with a sigh of relief. . . . It was over, the question and the explanation she had been dreading for so long, and it had all passed off very well indeed. . . . But what an unaccountable little soul she was, this beloved Stella. Mother Sprigg did not quite know how she had expected the child to take the story she had had to tell, but not somehow as calmly and quietly as this.

II

The farmer's wife and the elfin child were a delightful contrast as they sat there together in the quiet of the autumn evening, in the mingled light of sunset and candlelight and firelight, before the broad hearth of the beautiful farmhouse kitchen. Mother Sprigg was in her fifties but she had worked so hard all her life that she looked older than her age. She was short, round and stout, with a red weather-beaten face, and plump toil-worn hands. She had no beauty to commend her apart from the sweetness of her smile and the kindliness of her round brown eyes, but she carried with her wherever she went that aura of almost heavenly motherliness which so often shines about a woman who has borne only one child, and in losing it has become mother to all the world, more wonderfully than about the mother of a dozen. And she was a comfortable person, her comfortableness such a perfect blend of commonsense, unselfishness, capability and a complete absence of either physical or mental angularities, that like her motherliness it had become with the years so excellent a virtue that now it seemed hardly of this earth. And it was the same with her neatness and cleanliness. Being neat and clean was not with Mother Sprigg just not being untidy or grubby, it was a quality raised to such a pitch of perfection that it seemed more spiritual than physical, as though her spotless aprons and shining well-scrubbed countenance were a visible sign of invisible grace. She had her faults, of course, a hint of jealousy and possessiveness in her love, a sharp tongue at times when deliberate stupidity or sluttishness offended past endurance, but her failings were all on the surface, and one knew her to be sound and sweet right through like a ripe nut.

Though she cared nothing for fashion she had an eye for line and colour, and the gown of homespun Dartmoor wool which she wore was well-cut, of an exquisite shade of lichen-dyed beech brown, and the folds of the voluminous skirt fell beautifully about as she sat very upright in her straight-backed chair. Her apron and fichu and mob-cap were of the finest lawn, and white as snow.

And she knew exactly how to dress the elfin Stella. The child's short-sleeved, high-waisted gown was made of green gingham, fresh and crisp, and supplied with a voluminous hanging pocket, but no frills except the small white one round the neck. She wore a diminutive white apron tied round her waist but no mob-cap or ribbon on the head of dark curls cut almost as short as a boy's. Frills and furbelows did not suit Stella, for she was not a very feminine child. She was tall for her age, with small bones and a beautifully shaped little head set rather proudly on a long slender neck. She had none of the normal plumpness of childhood, and her swift graceful movements were those of some wild woodland creature, a fawn or gazelle, rather than of a little girl. Her small heart-shaped face was thin and brown, with little colour in the cheeks, and she had a straight arrogant little nose, a short determined upper lip, a cupid's bow of a mouth and a very dainty but very purposeful pointed chin. Though her face was so thin there was a dimple in each cheek, her dark grey eyes were star-bright with a direct gaze which was sometimes quite difficult to meet, and her lips coral pink and with always a hint of laughter in their delicate curves. She had, for so young a creature, a most astonishing elegance. Doctor Crane and her doting foster-parents thought her a beautiful child but the village folk called her downright plain. She played very little with the other children, for they did not like her. They said, with injustice, that she gave herself airs. This she did not do, but she did not speak their language nor they hers and so she was shy and aloof with them. She grieved and puzzled over this sometimes but try as she would she could not bridge the gulf of their unlikeness. And so she remained, unknown to anyone, a little lonely.

III

Outside the birds were silent and the light grew dim, and the orchard trees seemed to Stella to step more closely about the house, gathering in like men-at-arms to protect them against the perils of the night. The candle flames and the flames of the burning apple logs, having it all their own way now, seemed to breathe and grow like living creatures and slowly and triumphantly the grand old kitchen came into its own. By day the business of the farm filled it with bustle and clamour, and the bright gay world outside the windows challenged attention, and soon there would be the weight of dreams and darkness on its life, but this pause between the one and the other, between the day and the night, the work and the sleep, was its hour. Stella, looking up, saw the kitchen and recognised a friend coming towards her. The kitchen, to her, was the face of the house, that expressed its personality more accurately than did the walls and roof and chimneys that she thought of as its body, and at this hour the face smiled and she knew as much as she would ever know about Weekaborough Farm, the rugged, strong old creature that was her home, her fortress and her friend.

The kitchen was the living-room of the farm, for they scarcely used the small panelled parlour upon the other side of the flagged hall. It was a large room, roughly square, but with many nooks and bulges, like a cave, two wide mullioned windows with deep window-seats in the long west wall, and one smaller one to the south. The walls were whitewashed and the whitewashed ceiling was crossed by strong oak beams with iron hooks in them for the hams and bunches of herbs to hang from. The furniture, the huge kitchen table, the tall dresser, the settle and the straight-backed chairs, were of oak, shiny and black with age. The stone flagged floor was snowily white from centuries of scrubbing, and under the kitchen table were the pails of water that were kept filled from the big well in the yard.

But the greatest glory of the kitchen was the fireplace that filled nearly the whole of the north wall and was almost a room in itself. It was so deep that there was room for seats on each side, while across the opening in front was a sturdy oak beam with a little red curtain hanging beneath it. The wood fire never went out, winter or summer. Each morning Father Sprigg, always the first downstairs, would rake the ashes together, put on fresh dry wood and blow up the sparks with the bellows. On each side of the fire were firedogs to hold the spits for the roasting, and swinging cranes for the pots and kettles. Delicious smells were creeping out now from the fireplace; onion broth cooking in the pot that hung from one of the cranes and apples roasting in a dish placed under the outer ashes of the fire.

All the crannies and bulges of this enchanting cave-like room had unexpected things in them; the bread oven in the thickness of the wall, underneath its fascinating little arch, the grandfather clock, Mother Sprigg's spinning wheel, the warming pans, secret cupboards filled with home-made wines (and in the very secret cupboards, under the fireplace seats, and in recesses made by removing a few stones from the wall, something even stronger), shelves piled with pickles and preserves, brass candlesticks and Toby jugs. The window-seats in the west wall lifted up and inside one of them Stella kept her sampler, and her few treasures, and in the other Mother Sprigg kept her workbox and the current patchwork quilt. Stella had no workbox and the lack of it was the one and only grievance of her life. She longed for one with little compartments in it, and an emery cushion and a real silver thimble. But Mother Sprigg said that until she could sew a bit better she must be content with her tiny hussif and brass thimble. Stella was quite sure that if she had a workbox, and a silver thimble, she would immediately sew beautifully.

But though the irregular shape of the great kitchen made one think of a cave there was no suggestion of damp or darkness, the sun streaming in all day saw to that, and later the light of the fire that never went out. And there was plenty of colour in the kitchen with the blue willow pattern china on the dresser, the scarlet rugs on the floor, the scarlet window curtains, and always baskets of apples and plums in their season, golden marrows, and pumpkins in their striped jackets of yellow and green. Beside the hearth a door opened on to the passage that led to the dairy, stillroom and larder beyond, and a door in the east wall led to the stone-flagged hall and front door. On windy days the kitchen could be draughty and the smoke of the fire might swirl into the room, but Mother Sprigg and Stella were inured to draughts and smoke, just as they were inured to the perpetual talk and racket of farm men and neighbours coming and going all day long. That was all part of the stuff of daily living, of the unceasing toil that made the background of their life. . . . But in this twilight hour the doors were shut and the smoke went where it should, up the chimney to the stars that one could see quite clearly when one peered up the great shaft from below, there was no coming and going, and in the quiet the house unveiled its face and smiled upon them.

"I wish it lasted longer," said Stella.

"What, love?" asked Mother Sprigg.

"Just you and me sitting here talking and sewing, with Seraphine and the kittens, and the house loving us."

"Weekaborough Farm," said Mother Sprigg softly. "Your father, he was born and brought up here and he's never left it for more than one night at a time. And I came here as a bride thirty-five years ago and I've never left it for a night and I don't suppose I ever shall."

"I shall," said Stella decidedly. "I shall go to all sorts of places all over the world. But wherever I go Weekaborough kitchen will always be in the middle, like the hub of a cartwheel, and all the roads and seaways will be spokes leading back home."

Mother Sprigg looked at the child sharply. Here was another of the contrasts; this adventurous roving spirit of Stella's was a thing she could not begin to understand. And the child's strange way of talking, always catching hold of one thing and setting it down in the middle of another, like a cartwheel in the middle of the kitchen, a most unsuitable place for it in Mother Sprigg's opinion, made a body's head go round. Yet, apart from her adventurousness, which caused her to go dashing off now and then to goodness knew where in a most disconcerting manner, she was a good little maid who never went roving until she had finished the work which it was her duty to do, and never put things in unsuitable places except in her conversation; and she was to Mother Sprigg the dearest thing in all the world.

# CHAPTER III

I

A MAN'S heavy footsteps in the hall, and a hearty hail, warned them of the approach of Father Sprigg. The quiet hour was over and it was time for supper and bed. They rolled up their work and put it away, and while Mother Sprigg bustled about setting the table Stella flew out into the hall and precipitated herself, as from a catapult, into the arms of Father Sprigg. Her foster-father was the only person in the world with whom she was exuberant, and that not because she loved him best (she loved him dearly, but not best) but because Father Sprigg himself was so exuberant that it was next to impossible to be anything but exuberant with him.

He was like a great genial wind that slaps people so boisterously upon the back that even the most precise among them are obliged to break into a run, and skip and clutch their hats. He was six foot tall, and broad to match, and though he was sixty years old he was only slightly bent about the shoulders after half a century of hard toil. He had a weatherbeaten countenance surrounded by a fringe of grizzled ginger whisker, and blue eyes that were like two bright windows beneath the ginger eyebrows that came down over them like a thatched roof. His head was bald except for a ginger fringe that surrounded its vast shining expanse as his whiskers surrounded his face. He had kept all his teeth and was a mighty trencherman. He had the choleric temper that goes with ginger hair, touchingly combined with a vast patience and a superb courage, so that though his language in the face of disaster was enough to make all the godly within miles fear for his immortal soul his method of dealing with it would have commended itself to the greatest of the saints. Moreover he was a very wise man. He was a great bee-master and a fine shepherd and what he did not know about bees and sheep was not worth knowing; indeed in no single brand of husbandry did he know less than the most knowledgeable of his men. When he had stepped into his father's shoes Weekaborough Farm had been on the brink of disaster; in ten years he had made it one of the most prosperous farms in the countryside. He was an indulgent and loving husband and father, a just if severe master, a good patriot and a good Christian; but a farmer first and last and all the time, paying attention to family, country and God in that order and only at what he considered the proper hours, at meal time and bed time, at the appointed meetings of the South

Devon militia, at evening prayer and Church on Sundays, but not allowing either of the three to interfere with the serious business of his life.

He was always a well-dressed man but like his wife he paid no attention to fashion. His various suits of clothes, his Sunday, wedding or christening suit, his funeral suit, his hunting pink, his fair and marketing suit, his militia uniform, were all made of fine cloth, well-tailored, with suitable waistcoats, but several of them had belonged to his father, and of them all only his uniform was less than twenty years old. These garments were kept so carefully in the great oak press in the best bedroom, were so tenderly brushed and pressed before and after use by Mother Sprigg, that they never wore out. And neither did the series of smocks that he wore on ordinary week-days, exquisitely embroidered by his grandmother, mother and wife in succession, for they were hand-sewn from such stoutly woven material that no amount of rough weather or rough usage seemed able to harm them. Each of these garments was a work of art, and the wearing of them for farming labour would have filled a modern woman with horror. Mother Sprigg, perpetually washing and ironing them only to have them perpetually dirtied and rumpled again, did not feel that way. To her husband and herself their work upon the farm was not just something they were obliged to do to make a living, it was life itself, a prideful thing in which they gloried, and without realising that they did so they endowed it with an almost religious pageantry and ceremonial. Beautiful garments were dedicated to the labour, age-old festivals were interwoven with it, each branch of it had its own especial ritual that must not be departed from by a hair's breadth. And the particular garments and festivals and rituals had their flowering times at particular seasons, just as the corn and fruits of the earth had theirs, with all of it linked to the rhythm of the turning world, the waxing and waning of the moon's light and the sun's heat, the sweep of the rain and the wind, the fall of the snow and the dew.

Of this glorious unity Father Sprigg seemed somehow the human personification. When you looked at him you were conscious at once of so many virtues, so much comeliness and wisdom and strength, and all of it so well integrated and so finely balanced, that no one could wish for him that he should have more or less of anything than made up the fact of him. Even his choleric temper, like the hot sun of harvest, was not a thing that one could wish away, so excellent was the use to which it was frequently put. For there was no meanness in Father Sprigg. He frequently went too far but he never stopped too short. He might, all in the day's work and with no more personal animosity than that of the hurricane or the avalanche, crush you to powder, but he would never stick pins of sarcasm into you of aforethought malice, or defraud you of the smallest iota of what he thought was yours.

Upon the sensitive Stella, with her love of life and adventure, this elemental quality in Father Sprigg took strong hold. She leaped into his arms in much the same sort of way as she would sometimes fling herself down into the meadow grass and lie with arms outspread and cheek against the warm earth; both places gave her a satisfying sense of oneness with all that was. It was Father Sprigg, everyone thought, whom Stella loved best; they did not know that where she loved most deeply the little girl made least display of emotion.

"Hey, lass!" said Father Sprigg, receiving the impact of the small creature upon his bulk as though she were of no more weight than a sparrow. "Steady, lass, you'll have me over!"

This was a mighty joke with them. Laughing, Stella leaned her cheek against Father Sprigg's smock, enjoying the scent of wood-smoke that clung to it. The wood-smoke was one of the best of the autumn smells, almost as good as the blackberry smell, and the smell of pumpkin jam. Then she leaned over Father Sprigg's arm and peered at the shadows beyond him. "Hodge?" she whispered softly, stretching down a hand. A cold nose touched her palm and then a warm tongue caressed it. The dog Hodge was present and she sighed with relief and satisfaction. Hodge was one of her dearest on earth, but he was a mighty warrior and she was always afraid that some day an enemy even mightier would prove too powerful an opponent even for his considerable prowess. But once more he was safe within the walls of their stronghold and she need not worry about him again until the morning.

A sudden delicious smell of onion came through the crack of the kitchen door and all three entered precipitately, to find Mother Sprigg ladling the broth into the big brown bowls on the table. Seraphine was stirring in her basket and Madge the dairymaid was coming through from the dairy with the butter and cheese and a big blue dish of clotted cream. Solomon Doddridge the ploughman had come in from the back when Father Sprigg entered from the front and was now sitting in the seat within the fireplace, to the left of the fire, that was always his by right, his knotted hands on his knees, his short clay pipe sticking out at the side of his mouth. Of the several who worked on the farm he and Madge were the only two who actually slept in the farmhouse, and with Father and Mother Sprigg, Stella, Seraphine and Hodge, made up a household compactly knit together in a loyalty that had never been expressed in words, but of which each was so unconsciously aware that they acted upon it, and in the case of Seraphine traded upon it, with just the same certainty with which they trod the solid earth and knew, without considering the matter, that it would not give way beneath them.

Old Sol did not know how old he was, could not remember when he had been born, had no idea whether he had been christened or no, knew nothing whatever about himself except that man and boy he had worked at Weekaborough Farm, eaten there, slept there, and would die there. He may at one time have remembered more about himself but he did not now, for though he did not know his age it was obviously a good age; he remembered Father Sprigg being born, and remembered that even then he had left his youth behind him, and had a twinge of rheumatism now and again. He was now bent almost into the shape of a hoop with the rheumatics, and when he stood up leaning on his stick he reminded Stella of the old mulberry tree in the walled garden, whose main bough would have grown right down into the earth again had it not been propped up by a forked stick. Indeed old Sol was now much more like a tree than a man. His legs and arms were like brittle old branches, his face was brown and seamed like bark and the stubble of grey beard upon it was like the lichen that grew over the oldest of the apple trees. His voice, after so many years of exposure to bad weather, was nothing but a raven's croak, and a complete absence of teeth made articulation difficult. Yet his dark eyes were bright as a robin's, his sense of humour was a perpetual delight, and incredible though it seemed he could still guide the plough, and still, with his ploughboy as counter-tenor, provide the deep notes of the beautiful mysterious chant with which the Devon ploughmen animated their teams. Indeed without the chanting of Sol the Weekaborough oxen refused to plough at all; if the chanting ceased they stopped dead in their tracks, together with the seagulls wheeling behind the plough; that chant seemed to set them all in motion as it was said the singing of the stars kept the whole universe swinging on its course.

There was no mystery about the origins of Madge. One of many children she had been sent to the poorhouse on the death of her parents as a child of ten, and twenty years ago had come to Weekaborough Farm and had worked there ever since. The first kindness she had ever met with had been shown her by Father and Mother Sprigg and she was devoted to them and Stella. She was a freckled, buxom, snub-nosed creature who laughed a great deal, sang at her work but said very little. No one had ever been able to teach her to read, write, or subtract two from five without disaster, but in the arts of the stillroom and the dairy she had not her equal in the whole of the West Country.

Seraphine was a sleek tabby of an unusually domesticated appearance. Though three stable cats were kept to deal with the outside rats she was the only house cat. She was supposed to deal with the inside mice but she was so busy rearing kittens that she seldom had time to attend to them. No cat ever had as many kittens as Seraphine. Upon the first day of her arrival at the farm as little more than a kitten herself, Father Sprigg had happened to read aloud the command "Be fruitful and multiply," at evening prayers, and it seemed that she had taken it very much to heart.

It is difficult to do justice to the dog Hodge. Eight years ago a very noble and aristocratic hound of the name of Agamemnon had strayed from one of the great houses of the neighbourhood, Cockington Court, and gone for a little outing on his own. . . . It was an exceptionally lovely spring and the great gentleman had felt restless. . . . Pacing along a flowery lane in the neighbourhood of Weekaborough Farm he had espied through a gate Father Sprigg and his sheepdog Gypsy, inspecting the lambs gambolling in a field of daisies. Gypsy was an exquisite creature with melting dark eyes, a plumy tail, feathered heraldic feet and long black silky hair everywhere upon her body except upon her chest, where it was creamy white. Happening to glance over her shoulder just at the moment when Agamemnon was looking through the gate, her melting eyes met his, and Agamemnon was undone. The story of Cophetua and the beggar-maid repeated itself and Hodge was the result; at least one of them, for the other four were drowned.

It might have been thought that the offspring of so handsome an aristocrat and so beautiful a beggar-maid would have been a lovely creature, but unfortunately such was not the case, for Hodge had showed no discrimination as to where he put what. The creamy waistcoat handed down to him from his mother he wore not upon his chest but upon his back, where it looked odd upon the smooth brown body that was his paternal legacy. He had his father's stature and moved with his father's dignity, but it consorted oddly with a ridiculous plumy tail and the long soft ears that flopped upon each side of his great domed forehead. His eyes were his father's, tawny and somewhat stern, but there was great sweetness of expression about the mouth. He had a character of the utmost nobility; he was wise, brave, loving, loyal, patient, chivalrous, and fastidious in his personal habits. He had only one fault; he was an incorrigible fighter. Mercifully his chivalry did not permit him to attack an animal smaller than himself, so that as he was a large dog his battles were not as frequent as they would have been had he been smaller, but he could not see a dog of his own size, or larger, without attacking it, and now in his middle age, his body was marked all over with the scars of old wounds, one ear was torn and one eye permanently half shut. These mementoes of past conflict, superimposed upon an appearance that at the best of times had been eccentric, had given to Hodge a slightly rapscallion air that was wholly out of keeping with the nobility of his character. He was therefore sometimes misunderstood by those who were not intimately acquainted with him. But not by Stella. She knew, better than anyone else, the sterling worth of Hodge.

They talked little as they ate their supper, for they were all tired after a day of hard labour that for the adults had started at four o'clock in the morning. What little talk there was concerned some vagabond who had come to Father Sprigg in the orchard, asking for work.

"Never seen such a scarecrow," said Father Sprigg. "Looked as though he hadn't the strength to dig a sack of potatoes. A good-for-nothing scoundrel, to my mind."

"Couldn't you have given him work, Father?" asked Stella pitifully. She hated to think of even a good-for-nothing scoundrel being turned away from Weekaborough Farm. "Or food?"

"No," said Father Sprigg shortly. "Escaped from the press gang or a prison camp from the looks of him. I've no mind to get myself into trouble with authority."

"Did Hodge think he was a good-for-nothing?" asked Stella.

"Hodge was not there," said Father Sprigg. "Hodge had gone with Sol to bring the cows home. And isn't my judgment as good as Hodge's, I'd like to know?"

Stella opened her mouth to say that in her opinion it was not, but Mother Sprigg cut her short. "There, love, hold your tongue and sup up your broth."

Stella did as she was told, for Mother Sprigg's onion broth was the especial flowering of her genius and it would have been sacrilege to have partaken of it otherwise than in reverent silence. . . . As well as the onion and stock she put oats into it, cloves, a bayleaf and fresh milk. . . . And the apples were baked to a white froth and the clotted cream was the colour of buttercups.

Mother and Father Sprigg, Stella and Madge, sat at the table, with Hodge and Seraphine one on each side of Stella's chair, expectant of the tit-bits which she always managed to smuggle down to them, but old Sol stayed in his chimney corner with his bowl of soup upon his knee. His methods of absorbing nourishment were all his own and it was thought better that he should put them into practice in comparative privacy. But he listened to the little that was said, and now and then his low appreciative chuckle rumbled from the chimney corner. That chuckle was one of the distinctive sounds of Weekaborough, like Madge's singing, Hodge's deep bell-like bark, the striking of the grandfather clock, the click of Mother Sprigg's needle against her thimble, the ring of Father Sprigg's heavy boots upon the stone floors, and the rustle of the wind in the apple trees. In years to come, when she was away from Weekaborough, Stella would remember these sounds, and her recollection would harmonise them into a piece of music that would sing like a lullaby in her ears and take her straight back to the farmhouse kitchen. She scarcely realised now, of course, that she was exceptionally happy and beloved, but she glowed like a rose as she sat there in the soft candlelight and ate her apples and cream.

II

When supper was finished Mother Sprigg, Madge and Stella quickly removed the dishes while Father Sprigg, sepulchrally clearing his throat, walked with heavy deliberate tread to the dresser, took the Book from inside the willow pattern soup tureen that was never used except to hold the Book, carried it back to the table and laid it down carefully before his chair. There he seated himself, took off his spectacles, polished them on his scarlet handkerchief, readjusted them on his beak of a nose, wetted his finger and slowly turned the pages until he found the pressed carnation that marked the place. Mother Sprigg, Madge and Stella re-seated themselves about the table with hands reverently folded in their laps, and Sol in his chimney corner cupped his right ear in his hand.

The only books at the farm were the Bible and the family Prayer Book, and Father Sprigg read one chapter of the Bible aloud to his household every evening. He worked solidly through from Genesis to Revelation, taking the difficult words with the same courage with which he took a five-barred gate in the hunting field, charging as fast and furious as his own bull through the more indelicate passages of the Old Testament, happy in the New Testament with the parables of sowing and reaping and harvesting and with the shepherds in the fields, but making his way through the last chapters of the gospels with stumbling tongue, his ears scarlet with distress, humiliated by his inability to read such a story as it should be read, but shirking nothing whatever from the first page of the Book until the last.

What his wife and Madge and Sol made of it all, what he made of it himself, it would have been difficult to say; perhaps to them it was mainly a soporific before bedtime, to him one of those duties which from generation to generation fall to the master of the house and must be performed with constant patience.

But to Stella this nightly reading was glory, enchantment and anguish. Sitting there so demurely, her eyes cast down, her hands folded, she gave no outward sign of her excitement; but the blood drummed in her ears at the old tales of adventure, of battle and murder and sudden death. She was one of the trumpeters who blew their trumpets about the walls of Jericho. She stood with the watchman on the tower and saw the cloud of dust whirl up in the distance and heard him cry aloud the dreadful tidings, "The driving is as the driving of Jehu the son of Nimshi; for he driveth furiously." She held her breath while that splendid wicked woman Jezebel painted her face and tired her head and looked out of the window to greet her murderer. She mourned with David over Absalom, "Would God that I had died for thee, my son, my son." She listened with Elijah to the still small voice that came after the whirlwind and the fire, she gazed upon the mighty Seraphims with Isaiah, she was with Daniel in the lions' den and with Ruth she wept in the harvest fields so far from home.

The New Testament she could hardly bear, so great was her rage at what they did to Him. She could scarcely enjoy the Baby in the manger, the wise men with their gifts, the little children coming to be blessed and the sick folk to be healed, because of what was coming. This King crowned with thorns instead of gold and helpless on a gallows had a kind of royalty and power that she dared not as yet even try to comprehend; she was just sickened and infuriated. She was not much cheered by the Resurrection stories; to her they were ghost stories and they scared her. She had a feeling, now and then, that the part of the Bible which now so frightened her would one day come to mean more than all the rest of the Book put together, but that time was a long way off yet. She recovered herself in the Acts and the Epistles, though that was about all she did do, the story-telling there being upon the meagre side, but in the Book of Revelation she was at home again; a child once more in this fairy land of magical beasts and a city built all of jewels.

But all through the Book, even in the dreadful parts, the language would now and then suddenly affect her like an enchantment. The peculiarities of Father Sprigg's delivery worried her not at all. It was as though his gruff voice tossed the words roughly into the air, separate particles of no great value, and immediately they fell again transmuted, like the music of a peal of bells or raindrops shot through with sunshine, and vista beyond vista of unobtainable beauty opened before the mind. It was a mystery to Stella that mere words could make this happen. She supposed the makers of these phrases had fashioned them to hold their visions as one makes a box to hold one's treasure, and Father Sprigg's voice was the key grating in the lock, so that the box could open and set them free. But this metaphor did not take her very far. That transmutation in the air still remained as unexplainable as the sudden change in herself, when at the moment of the magical fall her dull mind became suddenly sparkling with wonder and her spirit leaped up inside her like a bird. She wondered sometimes if the others felt the same. She had never looked to see if their faces changed when the brightness fell from the air; but she did not suppose that they did, nor hers either. And they did not say anything; but then neither did she. This was probably one of those many queer experiences that human beings could not speak of to each other, because though words could be formed into a casket to hold visions, and could be at the same time the power that liberated them, they seemed of very little use when one tried to use them to explain to another person what it was that they had set free. Words were queer things, Stella decided, to be at once so powerful and so weak.

For the past ten days Father Sprigg had been wading through Deuteronomy and Mother Sprigg and Madge had dozed a bit. But not Stella. There had been Og the King of Bashan, the last of the giants, and his vast bedstead. And then there had been the Ammonites who dwelt in the mountains and came out against you and chased you, as bees do, and you returned and wept before the Lord. Og had stalked through Stella's imagination, and the Ammonites had buzzed through it, for days. And now to-night, in the eleventh chapter, the tossed words sparkled and fell and the brightness was with her again. "It is a land of hills and valleys, and drinketh water of the rain of heaven. A land which the Lord thy God careth for; the eyes of the Lord thy God are always upon it, from the beginning of the year even unto the end of the year."

It was her own West Country that Stella saw, with its round green hills dotted with the sheep and the streams winding in and out between them, and down in the sheltered valleys the orchards and ploughed fields of rose-red earth, the homesteads and the old grey churches. She saw the sun and rain sweeping over the land, and the great arc of the rainbow in the sky, and it was as though the earth lifted itself to drink of the sun and the rain, and even as she watched the corn sprang green in the furrows, the orchards frothed with blossom, and the perfume of many flowers and the singing of a multitude of birds rose up like incense to the God Whose eyes, looking upon it, had given life. There was a reverse side to the picture, a terrible one. If God were to weary and glance away that would be the end of light and life; darkness and chaos would come again. But then God did not weary. From the beginning of the year until the end of the year the light of His eyes streamed down and the life of the earth streamed up. Dazzled, Stella saw the light and life meeting, mingling, looked again and saw her familiar countryside slowly transformed by the union, saw it become another country, the same yet different, the symbol becoming the actual, the shadow reality, the dream the fact of the promised land.

The brightness faded and for the first time she looked at the others. It was old Sol whom she looked at first and his attitude had changed. He was leaning sideways, to bring his ear and cupped hand close to Father Sprigg's voice, and he had lifted his head a little, as a man does who looks at a distant view. Then she looked at Mother Sprigg and Madge. Mother Sprigg was dozing and Madge's face wore the curiously vacant look that it always had when she was not engaged in the active work that was her life. Then she looked back again at old Sol and this time, feeling her gaze, he looked at her, and he smiled and she smiled. So old Sol saw things too. Of course. She ought to have known. That chant with which he kept the oxen moving so rhythmically had made its way into this world from another country.

Father Sprigg closed the Book and they all bent their heads while he repeated the Lord's Prayer. "Amen!" said Father Sprigg in a voice like a thunderclap when he got to the end. Then he let out a great gusty sigh of relief and profound self-satisfaction, inflated his chest and squared his shoulders. Once more he had performed an uncongenial duty creditably and the mingled feelings of martyrdom and virtue that it gave him was pleasantly inflating to the ego. Mother Sprigg rubbed the sleep out of her eyes and intelligence dawned again in Madge's face as she got up to set the table for breakfast.

Stella jumped to her feet like a Jack-in-the-box, once more right back in the middle of this world. "Seraphine! Hodge! I'll put them out," she said. Though these favoured animals slept in, they had to be put out for a few moments before bed, and this ritual always followed immediately upon the ending of family prayers. Picking up Seraphine, and with Hodge at her heels, she darted through the door to the left of the fireplace, and down the passage beyond, past the doors leading to the larders, china closet, stillroom and dairy, to the open back door. Here she sent Seraphine spinning out of her arms into the cobbled yard beyond, gave Hodge a vigorous push upon the haunches (neither animal resenting this treatment, which they suffered nightly) and dashed to the china closet and seized a bowl and plate.

Then she flew to the dairy and half filled the bowl with milk, dipping a little out of each full jug in a cup so that it should none of it be missed. Then she went to the larder where she was occupied a little longer, extracting a bit of something from every dish that stood there and piling it all up on her plate. After that she carried plate and bowl very carefully out into the yard and hid them in the dark shadows behind the mounting block. As she did so she heard a low chuckle behind her, smelt a whiff of tobacco and knew that old Sol was there, waiting to shut the back door. . . . If he knew what she did every night he never gave her away. . . . She returned to the back door, stepping now very demurely and with her head held arrogantly high. "Hodge?" she called to the shadows by the well in the centre of the yard. "Seraphine?" They reappeared and followed her in. The arrogance left her abruptly as she passed old Sol. "Goodnight, Sol," she whispered, and gave a little airy jump, light as a bird's, and left on his cheek a touch so soft that he did not know whether she had kissed him or caressed his cheek with a fingertip. He growled affectionately and she was gone, arriving in the kitchen slightly breathless, but having been absent for so short a time that Father Sprigg was still winding the clock, Madge setting the table for breakfast and Mother Sprigg lighting the bedroom candles for Stella and Madge. . . . She and Father Sprigg and Sol would not go to bed just yet, they would sit for perhaps another hour before the fire, talking over the affairs of the farm. . . . Stella kissed them goodnight, took her candle and went out into the hall, Hodge at her heels. Since he was a puppy he had slep on a rug in her bedroom, a proceeding of which Father and Mother Sprigg highly disapproved, but Stella ignored their disapproval with that quiet, sweet obstinacy of which she was a past mistress and against which they were powerless.

Going upstairs to bed was one of the things which Stella enjoyed. There was a special savour about this moment of leaving the ground floor of the house, where the work of the day had taken place, with its attendant hurry and worry, and perhaps misunderstandings and sorrows too, and mounting up away from it all like an angel into heaven. She was sorry for people who lived in small cottages, sleeping on the same floor where they worked, who could not enjoy this lovely slow ascension to restfulness and peace.

She went up the old oak staircase very slowly, pretending she was an angel, enjoying the contrast between her stately progress now and the bustle of a few moments back, and the further activity that would come before she slept. The candlelight gleamed on the polished stairs and the dark panelling on either side. Ahead of her there was a window with a deep windowseat, where the staircase widened out on either side to the passage that ran the length of the house, and through it she could see the sky powdered with stars. The night was so still that when she stood at the head of the stairs to listen she could hear no sound except the rustle of a mouse in the wainscot. Hodge came beside her and leaned his head against her thigh. They stood motionless for a full five minutes, and silent except for a few snorts from Hodge. Stella was no longer thinking of anything in particular, she was just absorbing the starlight and silence and letting it sink down inside her to liberate that deep peace in which her being was rooted like a tree. Adventurous spirits tend to grow arid with too much activity but Stella had early learned how to refresh hers. So had Hodge. He did it through his nose and the smell of starlight was to him particularly refreshing. When Stella suddenly swung round and scurried down the passage he lingered for a final sniff before he turned and padded after.

## CHAPTER IV

### I

STELLA's room was a closet opening out of the big bedchamber where her foster-parents slept, and she had to go through their room to reach it. She thought this best bedchamber a most imposing place with its big tent bed hung with maroon curtains, its beautiful tallboy, and bow-fronted chest of drawers of shining mahogany. Her own little closet was dainty as the inside of a flower or seashell for Mother Sprigg had made white muslin curtains for the small bed, and a patchwork quilt of pale soft colours. Father Sprigg himself had made the dressing chest, the little chair and the stool for the ewer and basin, and painted them pale green. There were flowered curtains at the windows and the plastered walls were white. The only notes of bright colour in the room were the gay rag rug upon which Hodge slept and Stella's hooded scarlet cloak hanging on a peg behind the door.

She made no attempt to go to bed, instead she put on her cloak and opened the window. It was a dormer window that opened like a merry eye in the thatch that roofed the farm. The thatch was old, hillocky in places, and sloped away beneath the window at an incline that was no steeper than that of a hayrick, and just as easy to climb. Stella climbed it almost nightly, for she could climb as well as run with remarkable agility. And so could Hodge. From the moment when he first learnt to stagger he had been following Stella wherever she went, and she went to such extraordinary places at times that throughout the years he had been slowly adding to the natural powers of a dog those of many another creature too. Besides climbing like a squirrel he could now in company with Stella wriggle like a worm, leap like a toad and roll up into a ball like a hedgehog. Such was their accomplishment that whatever they did they seldom got caught.

They got out of the window and stepped nimbly down, digging their toes into the strong old thatch. Where the roof ended a wistaria, almost as old as the house itself, grew out of a flower bed in the yard below, its branches lying like great knotted ropes against the farmhouse wall. Stella, going down feet first, found it as easy to negotiate as a ladder. Hodge, going down nose first, found it harder, but Stella kept one hand gripped upon the scruff of his neck, and he managed.

They reached the yard in no time at all and retrieved the plate of scraps from behind the mounting block, carrying it to the far end of the yard where Daniel the yard dog was lying in his kennel waiting for them, his chin resting on his extended forepaws and his eyes very bright. As soon as he saw them he shot out of the kennel to the full extent of his chain and in a moment he was wolfing up the contents of the plate as though he had never had a good square meal in his life. Like all the animals at Weekaborough Farm he was in actual fact adequately fed and cared for, though not pampered, but he always had an insatiable appetite and always looked a sight. You could feed him with everything in the larder, you could brush him till your arm ached, you could bath him daily and still he would look like nothing on earth. He was black and rusty, all his bones showed through his skin, his legs stuck out at extraordinary angles, his tongue hung untidily out of the side of his mouth and his long ragged tail perpetually tripped him up. He wore a permanent worried frown upon his forehead and his ears flapped in the wind like signals of distress. He had arrived at Weekaborough Farm three years ago as a puppy, conveyed thither by Hodge, who had found him somewhere, picked him up in his mouth and brought him home. He was not much use, and seemed a little wanting in the head, but he was affectionate and well-meaning and everyone was fond of him.

While he ate, sweeping the food untidily into his mouth with swirling movements of his long tongue, his ragged tail rotating like a windmill in the rear, Stella and Hodge watched him with a look of humble apology in their eyes. Class distinctions were abhorrent to them. It did not seem right that there should be indoor and outdoor dogs and cats. Why should Hodge and Seraphine sleep indoors, petted by the family, while Daniel and the stable cats were not allowed to set foot across the back door step. Daniel's frightful appearance and slight mental deficiency were not his fault, and the stable cats would have been just as sleek as Seraphine had they had her advantages. It just was not right, and as soon as Daniel had polished off the last scrap of his meal Stella knelt down on the cobbles besides him and gently pulled his distressful ears and smoothed his worried frown. "Never mind, Daniel" she whispered, "to-morrow I will take you for a walk." He never seemed to understand what she said to him, as Hodge did, but he could recognise the promise of something good in the tone of her voice, and he went back inside his kennel the wrong way round, so that his tail could poke through the hole and rotate outside, which was always with him a sign of happiness.

Stella fetched the bowl of milk from behind the mounting block and carried it carefully across the yard to the stable door, which Hodge opened for her by standing on his hind legs and lifting the latch with his nose. The stable was never locked, and neither was the back door of the farmhouse. They both opened into the yard which was fortified on the north and south by the stables and the house and to the east and west by great walls, and had strong doors in the east wall that were secured at night by the trunk of a tree laid across iron bars. The yard had been built in this way so that in time of war all the cattle could be driven into it and kept safe.

The stable by night was an enchanted place, dim and mysterious, its daylight russet and gold and brown overlaid by the silver moonlight shining through the small high unglazed windows that gave upon the outside world. The moonlight transmuted the colour so that it was no longer colour but the phantom of it, knocking at one's heart with a sort of sadness, like that spectrum that sometimes encircles the moon with the faint echo of an April rainbow. The shadows were deep, soft as velvet, not hard like the daylight shadows. The sounds were muted, breathings and rustlings that seemed to lie as lightly upon the silence of the night as did the moonbeams upon the velvet shadows. The scent of the hay in the mangers was a sleepy smell, and the smell of the clean and healthy beasts, whom Stella could dimly see there in their stalls, was good and wholesome.

At Weekaborough Farm they had a couple of oxen, Moses and Abraham, for the ploughing and for drawing the sledge carts used at harvest time, two little agile Devon pack horses, Shem and Ham, one dun and one red, and Father Sprigg's beautiful old mare, Bess. Stella knew them all intimately and loved them well, but she did not stop to talk to them now for they were tired after the hard day's work and she was pressed for time, she just looked affectionately at their gleaming flanks and swinging tails and went on down to the empty stall at the far end where the stable cats slept, and where at this hour they were always eagerly waiting for their milk. She could see their eyes shining like emeralds in the shadows and as soon as she came to them they ran to her and began weaving round and round against her legs, pushing against her, purring loudly, whiskers protuberant, tails aloft, soft paws planted with a steady rhythm that kept time with the organ hum of their vibrating vocal chords. The church band in full blast, drum, tambourine, clarinet, serpent, hautboy, tenor viol and double bass all sweeping together into the Old Hundredth, always reminded Stella of the stable cats beholding milk. In both cases it was as though body, instrument and spirit were so coordinated by delight that the body was not so much making music as being music; you couldn't tell where one began and the other ended, it was all one thing.

She set the bowl down on the floor and there was instant silence, as there was in church when they had shouted Amen and sat down for the sermon. The cats sunk their chins into the milk and absorbed in silent ecstasy. Stella, with Hodge alongside, her left hand resting lightly on his back, stood regarding them. They were called Shadrach, Meshach and

Abednego and they were a sorry crew, scarred by many battles. Stella had named them, as she had named all the animals at Weekaborough Farm, drawing her inspiration from her beloved Old Testament. Shadrach was black, and had lost the tip of his tail. Meshach was ginger and had lost an ear. Abednego was black with what was intended to be a white patch under the chin, but try as he might he couldn't get at it with his tongue to give it a washing and it remained of a neutral tint. He was always trying, poor soul, and had a permanently cricked neck in consequence. They ought to be indoor cats, all of them, Stella thought compassionately. Why should they have to live outside, fighting rats and getting all dirty and torn. Cats were not meant to live outside, ratting, they were meant to live inside, mousing. It just wasn't fair. She did what she could to make it up to them, but still it wasn't fair.

II

The most extraordinary sensation went up Stella's left arm, a queer prickly sensation that reached her brain as a sudden feeling of panic. The hair upon Hodge's back was rising beneath her hand and he gave a loud growl deep in his throat. She looked at him. His head was raised and his eyes were fixed upon the small window high up in the wall above the manger, one of the windows that gave upon the outside world and through which the moonlight shone. A man's head had come between them and the moonlight, held in the square of the window as in a picture frame. Stella had a sudden impression of a thin face, wild and dark, and then she was so frightened that everything was suddenly blurred and she could not see any more; but she could still hear Hodge's low growl and feel his stiff hair beneath her hand. But she did not cry out, for she was a brave little girl. She stood quite still, fighting her panic; until the mist cleared, the dark face came back, and she could put a name to her fear.

"Bony," she whispered.

It had come at last. The French had landed. She had grown up with the fear of invasion a permanent dark background to the happy life of the farm. The English Channel, the only barrier between England and her enemies, was only a few miles away. All her life she had never gone to Church without seeing the pikes stored there in readiness for invasion. She had watched men drilling, Father Sprigg among them, and had heard tales of the dreadful press gangs. From the farm windows she could see Beacon Hill, where was one of the great bonfires that would be lit when the French came, flashing the news in fire across the country. . . . There was always a man there, watching the sea. . . . She had been only a small child during that winter when the enemy transports had been waiting at the ports to carry thousands of soldiers across the Channel, but she could remember the great friendly storm that saved them, and the thanksgiving in the Church. But the worst invasion scare had been only a year ago. They had said then that one-hundred-and-fifty-thousand Frenchmen were assembled at Boulogne, and that Bony had selected Torquay as the best landing-place. Father Sprigg had left home altogether then, for the South Devon militia were guarding the batteries along the coast, and arrangements had been made to send all the children and old people away to Dartmoor. She had watched their biggest wagon being got ready for the journey and had seen Mother Sprigg going about white-faced and tight-lipped and Madge crying. . . . But still it had not happened. . . . And now it *had* happened, on this quiet September night when everything had seemed so safe and happy. That dark face up there was a Frenchman's face, and soon an army of them would be battering at the closed doors of the stableyard, and the great tree trunk that barred it would give way before the onslaught, and they would all be killed.

As suddenly as it had arisen her fear died. As panic had come to her from Hodge so now he gave her reassurance. The hair on his back lay down again and his growls subsided. His head was still lifted to the window but his tail was wagging.

"Dammee!" croaked an indignant voice above her. "All that milk fed to a lot of mangy old cats! And me so empty that my stomach is flapping loose and sticking to my backbone." He paused, visited by a certain delicacy at this point. She was quite a little girl, he suddenly perceived. "Why aren't you in bed?" he finished, his hoarse croaking voice ending in a sudden squeak.

The squeak betrayed him. He wasn't a man at all, let alone a Frenchman, he was only a boy, an English boy whose voice had not yet finished breaking, a dirty disreputable English boy with a sunburnt face, wild bright dark eyes and lank dark hair tossed untidily on his forehead.

"Why aren't *you*?" retorted Stella with spirit.

He laughed, his white teeth flashing in his dark face. "Well, you see, my bed is the lee side of a haystack and I don't have to go to it if I don't want to."

"How did you get up to that window?" demanded Stella, thinking of the high wall outside, going up sheer from the lane.

"Climbed the wall," said the boy. "Plenty of crannies in it. Thought I might get through and find something to eat. But the window is too small."

Stella noticed that his hands, holding to the windowledge, were white and bloodless. He was clinging on with fingers and toes like a monkey and she felt respect for one whose acrobatic powers equalled her own; and even surpassed them; she did not believe that she could have climbed that wall. Beside her Hodge was swinging his tail faster and faster, and she knew his judgment of character to be unerring.

"If you don't get down your fingers will go numb and you will fall," she said. "Drop down into the lane again and I'll bring you out something to eat."

"Will you? Or will you bring the farmer out on me? He's sent me packing once already. Next time he'll collar me for the press gang."

The boy looked at her, his dark eyes searching her for the truth. She did not answer, but for a few moments she looked back at him, her glance clear, unwavering and a little scornful because of his question. Then she looked down at Shadrach, Meshach and Adebnego, whose pink tongues were patiently pursuing the last drops of milk round and round their empty bowl, and bending she gently caressed their heads, just as she always did each night, and picking up the dirty dilapidated Abednego, held him for a moment against her breast. The face of the boy at the window crumpled like the face of a child who is going to cry, then he abruptly disappeared. The little girl had been loving the cats just as she always loved them every night, making no special display for his benefit; but all the words in the world could not have told him more clearly how passionate was her concern for all the vagabond creatures who were outside the warm bright circle of love and home. She'd not betray him. Not she. She'd die first. From that moment he loved her.

III

For the second time that night Stella and Hodge raided the larder, and this time Stella was afraid their thefts were noticeable. Mother Sprigg was a generous housekeeper and the inroads made for the benefit of Daniel and the cats made little impression on the plenty of the larder, and she never seemed to notice them. But Stella did not see that she could fail to notice this time, with a huge wedge of pigeon pie gone, a hunk of bread and cheese and a couple of apples. But she would abide the consequences. That boy outside, right outside, more outside even than Daniel and the cats, had got to be fed.

She went out into the yard again, carrying the loaded plate and a jug of milk from the dairy, and crossed over to the barred door. Here she set the food down on the cobbles and considered the problem before her. How was she to get the trunk of the tree lifted out of position? It must be done somehow, for she could not get to the front door without either climbing back up the roof to her room, which would be impossible with both hands occupied, or passing through the kitchen where Father and Mother Sprigg were sitting. Her foster-parents were kindhearted, but during these last dangerous years the country people had had so many unpleasant experiences with mutineers, spies, deserters and escaped prisoners that now they gave scant encouragement to any unknown vagabond. It was the yard door or nothing, and Stella went to it with a will, bending down and getting her back and head beneath the tree trunk. Hodge did the same and together they heaved and strained until there was no more strength left in them. But they did it. The tree trunk lifted off the iron bars at last and Stella eased it to the ground without too much noise. But she felt sick and dizzy when she had done it, with the blood drumming in her ears and her breath coming in painful gasps, and it was all she could do to pull the great door open. But she did this too, and picking up the jug and plate again made her way out into Pizzle Meadow, that bordered the yard upon the north, and through which a cart track led to the gate opening upon the lane that ran along behind the stables and was the western boundary of Weekaborough Farm.

Pizzle Meadow, inhabited by the Weekaborough pigs, was a pleasant place, dotted here and there with old cider apple trees, and with a stream running through it. Stella hurried along the cart track to the high padlocked gate and the thick thorn hedge, and after standing on tiptoe to put the plate and jug on top of one of the strong old stone pillars that supported the gate on either side, she climbed up it, dragging Hodge after her, and fell off the other side into the grass that bordered the lane. She did not usually fall off the gate like this, she usually climbed both up and down with the agility of a monkey, but she was still dizzy after her struggle with the tree trunk.

Strong bony hands lifted her and set her on her feet again, and for a brief moment their grip reminded her of her first memory, her mother's arms holding her so tightly, and her heart constricted with sudden pain, so that she was more breathless than ever.

"Why didn't you call?" demanded the boy. "If I'd known which direction you were coming from you could have handed me the grub through the bars. You need not have gone falling on your nose like that."

"Someone might have heard," panted Stella. "And hereabouts—since the mutiny and everything—they're scared of strangers."

The boy was still holding her, looking down at her, his hard hands gripping her arms above the elbows. "And aren't *you* scared of strangers?"

"Sometimes. But not of you, after the first minute when I thought you were Bony. I knew you were all right. Hodge told me."

For a moment he shifted his gaze from her to Hodge, standing beside her slowly swinging his tail, and they exchanged a long appreciative look, as man to man. Then he looked back at Stella again. The moon was so bright that he could see her face as though it were day. She was very flushed, the hood of her cloak had fallen back from her short tumbled boyish curls, and there were beads of perspiration on her forehead.

"You're all in a lather," he ejaculated.

"It was lifting the tree trunk and opening the gate," said Stella.

"And you such a little 'un!" he murmured. He picked her up, carried her to the old oak tree that grew near the gate and sat her down where the knotted roots made a comfortable armchair for a small person. Then he fetched the plate and jug from the top of the pillar, walking in a queer sort of way as though he were lop-sided, and as though the ground beneath his feet was red-hot, and sat down beside her, Hodge lying near them. But starving though he had professed himself to be he seemed in no hurry to eat. He set the food and drink at his feet and looked at them much as David must have looked at the cup of cold water that they brought him in the cave. But he had more commonsense than David. His tribute of denial, though offered up with all his heart, was merely momentary, and having offered it he turned to Stella, said "Thank you," gently, and then fell upon the pigeon pie like a wolf.

Yet a well-mannered aristocratic wolf. Had Stella been older she would have gazed at this most unusual vagabond with bewildered speculation. But the world to Stella was still so full of surprise that all the ordinary happenings of life seemed as wonderful as fairy tales, and conversely fairy tales did not seem anything out of the ordinary. Everything and everybody was so surprising that something or somebody a bit extra surprising did not put her out at all. Besides, though she had never seen anyone in the least like this boy, she was completely at ease with him. She felt, for the first time in her life, a sense of likeness with another human creature, and a sense of safety; not so much physical safety as the safety of understanding that comes between those who are two of a sort. Though she loved Father and Mother Sprigg so deeply she had never felt with them this particular feeling of safety. The gulf that yawned between her and the village children was only a crack between her and Father and Mother Sprigg, but it was there. Between her and this unknown boy it was not there. It was very odd. Turning to look at him she had the queer feeling that she was turning to look at herself. . . . Yet she was quite sure that she did not look like this. . . . She hoped she didn't for he was almost as much of a fright as poor old Daniel. That, she supposed pitifully, was because they were both outside people.

He was tall and his tattered shirt and torn trousers fluttered on a body so bony and thin that set up in a field he would have done very well as a bird scarer. But here the likeness to a scarecrow ended; indeed, a discerning grown-up, looking again at this boy, would have dismissed the analogy and thought instead of a tall reed shaken by the wind or a terrified unbroken colt galloping to the sea, but not of anything so static as a scarecrow. Even in comparative stillness, body, mind and soul absorbed in pigeon pie, a sensitiveness and grace were apparent in this boy. The grace at present was clumsy, but it had a thoroughbred air. The sensitiveness showed itself now in a stubborn defensiveness of expression and restless movements; set free from adversity it might have been a thing of smooth and responsible beauty. The physical contrasts were striking. The untidy dark hair fell over a broad low forehead, the skin very white where it had been shielded from the sunburn that tanned the rest of the face. The dark eyes were sombre beneath heavy dark eyebrows but the nostrils of the thin aquiline nose flared like those of a startled horse. Though the lips could set obstinately, laughter transfigured them to gentleness. His hands had broken nails and calloused palms but they were finely shaped. One could not see his feet for they were wrapped in bloody mudcaked bandages of torn rag. He finished eating and wiped his fingers delicately on the grass upon either side of him.

"Have you a handkerchief?" he asked Stella.

She fished a delicate little square of cambric out of her pocket and gave it to him and he blew his nose loudly and satisfyingly.

"That was almost worse than anything," he said.

"What was?" asked Stella.

"Blowing my nose in the air."

"Old Sol, our ploughman, never has a handkerchief and he does it beautifully, like this," said Stella, and she gave an exhibition; a serious and charming exhibition, quite without vulgarity.

"It needs practice," said the boy. "Would you mind—please—may I keep your handkerchief?"

There had been no pathos about him until now but in the shy pleading of his question it showed for a moment. Then it vanished as she nodded and smiled, and laughing he stuck the handkerchief in his pocket.

"My name is Stella Sprigg," said Stella. "What is your name?" To her, as to all children, names were tremendously important. Your Christian name, joining you to God, your surname linking you to your father. If you had both names you had your place in the world, walking safely along with a hand held upon either side. If you had neither you were in a bad way, you just fell down and did not belong anywhere, and if you only had one you only half belonged.

"Zachary," said the boy.

"Only Zachary?"

"Only Zachary."

"Just a Christian name?"

"That's all."

Stella looked at him with concern. Only God had hold of him. He was lop-sided. She had noticed it in his gait when she first saw him walking. Then she remembered that but for Father and Mother Sprigg she would have been lop-sided too, for her nameless mother had died. This memory deepened her feeling of oneness with Zachary and she put out a small hand and laid it on his knee.

"Do you know where you come from?" she asked wonderingly. The name Sprigg and the name Weekaborough were inseparably connected in her mind. She came from Weekaborough because she was a Sprigg. She was unable to visualise anyone without a surname coming from anywhere.

"From the moon," replied Zachary promptly. "Haven't you seen me up there?"

Stella dimpled delightedly. She loved moonlight, and when she had been smaller and in need of a playmate she had often wished that the man in the moon would come down and play with her.

"Zachary Moon," she said with pleasure, and felt she had got him a bit better supported upon the other side. Zachary put his hand on hers that lay on his knee, carefully and gently, as though it were a small bird. Then he turned her hand over and put their two palms together, as though they were the two halves of a shell. "I come from the moon and you're a star," he said. "Quite right, isn't it, that we should see each other first at night." Then he lifted her hand off his knee with a light gesture, as though he tossed back the captive bird to freedom. "But not right that you should be out of your bed so late."

He got up clumsily, still as though the ground were red-hot to his feet, and picked up the bowl and plate; and he'd polished off his meal down to the last drop and the last crumb, just as Daniel and the cats did. Then he held out his free hand. "Come on, Stella. I'll help you over the gate."

He was very grown-up suddenly, and Stella felt chilled. But she got up obediently and put her hand in his, and they walked along silently, Zachary with his lop-sided gait, Stella light and airy as a fairy's child. Hodge loped along behind. When they reached the tall locked gate Zachary helped the child and the dog to scramble over and then passed over the bowl and plate. "Thank you," he said. "I haven't tasted a meal like that since I left the moon. Good-bye, Star. Good-bye, Hodge."

There was a flat finality in his tone and Stella felt dreadful; like one half of a bi-valve shell being detached from the other half. "No, Zachary!" she pleaded. "No!"

Her chin only just reached the top of the gate. She propped it there, her hands laid upon the bar one on each side. Hodge thrust his head between the bars below and whined distressfully. Zachary looked from the little pointed face and the row of small fingertips to the furry countenance below, as though memorising them.

"No what, Stella?"

"No good-bye," said Stella.

His face grew sombre. Looking up at him Stella saw it with queer dark shadows on it, like the moon. He caught his breath sharply, as though he were going to say something more, but he seemed to change his mind, for his face set hard and without another look at her he turned away and was hidden by the thick thorn hedge. Stella did not call after him, for she knew that set look on a man's face. Father Sprigg looked like that when he had been telling her stories and had suddenly had enough of it, and put her down off his knee and went off to the milking. She never ran after Father Sprigg at those times for she knew by instinct that men do not want women with them all the time; they keep certain compartments in their life for them, and do not want them overflowing into the wrong ones.

Yet as she walked slowly homeward through the meadow, Hodge beside her with his tail between his legs, she stumbled several times because she was crying. It was for Zachary she was crying. She was sure that neither the place that he had come from, when he had stepped into that moonlight magic hour that had enclosed them both, nor the place to which he was going when he left her, were good places. . . . And he could have stayed here if Father Sprigg had not sent him away. . . . He was like the bedraggled bird who once flew in from the outside darkness when snow was on the ground, circled about the lighted kitchen and then flew out again, and though she had cried out for pity he was gone so quickly, and the frozen dark outside was so immense, that there was nothing at all that she could do about it.

IV

But Stella was a child who scarcely ever cried, and by the time she had reached the great gate into the yard she had rubbed the tears out of her eyes and had complete command of herself and the situation. Hodge's tail, too, as sensitive to her moods as a compass needle to the magnetic north, had trembled uncertainly back to the perpendicular. But they were tired, both of them, and they could not lift the tree trunk and get it back into position. "It's no good, Hodge," Stella gasped after ten minutes fruitless struggle. "We can't do it."

Hodge snorted exhausted agreement. It took a good deal to beat them, but they always had the sense to know when the moment of defeat had arrived and not to waste strength in futile struggle. They left the tree-trunk there on the cobbles and putting the plate and bowl behind the mounting block again, to be rescued by Stella in the morning, they tackled the climb back up the thatch to Stella's bedroom window. It was harder than usual tonight, but they managed it, and fell in an exhausted heap upon the floor.

"Hush, Hodge!" whispered Stella, for a line of light showed beneath the door and there was a murmur of sleepy voices from the big bedroom. They must have been gone a long time, for Father and Mother Sprigg were in bed already. Sometimes Mother Sprigg looked in upon Stella when she came up, but evidently tonight she had not done so, and as she quickly and silently undressed Stella thanked heaven for her luck. Of course, in the morning, with the pigeon pie gone and the tree trunk not in its place, something or other was bound to happen, but it was a comfort not to have it happening tonight. She wanted peace and silence tonight. A great flood of feeling had been for hours dammed up just behind the happenings of the evening routine and then behind the adventure of Zachary; but it would have to come free now and submerge her.

She slipped into bed, lay down and shut her eyes. Hodge usually slept at the foot of her bed, but tonight he came and lay down close beside her, so that she could put her hand down over the edge of the bed and touch his soft head. It comforted her to do this. Touching Hodge she could imagine herself a small ship safely tied up to a bigger one; feeling, like harsh black water, might swirl about her but she would not be torn away.

Her mother, her real mother, in her brave green gown. Against the flood of dark water she saw her dead face as clearly as though she looked on a picture; and it was white and shadowed, like Zachary's when he had said good-bye. Mother Sprigg had thought her too young to feel grief at the story told her, but there she had been wrong. Stella was old for her age beyond Mother Sprigg's understanding, sensitive beyond her understanding, and loving too, and possessed of love's supreme power of dissimulation for the sake of the beloved. "You are my real mother," she had said. Not by a word or a look had she then, would she ever, let Mother Sprigg know that she found any lack in her motherhood. Yet at this moment she longed for the arms of her real mother as she had never longed for anything yet, and recoiled from the horror of her death with that instinctive understanding without benefit of experience that is both the blessing and the bane of the imaginative.

She shivered with cold and fatigue as she lay flat in her bed, staring at the square of moonlit, starlit sky that was her window, yet the sweat ran down her body and soaked her nightgown, as though she had a fever, and tired though she was she could not shut her eyes; the lids seemed glued open. She was her mother, dying in the cold water, trying desperately to save her child. She was Zachary, hungry and thin, his feet wrapped in blood-stained rags. She was both of them coming from an unknown darkness, going back to the darkness again. By being them she tried to comfort them, just as she tried to comfort Daniel and the stable cats by going to them night by night to share their outlawry. But it wasn't much use, she thought. She could only be them for a little while between darkness and darkness. She could not follow into the outside darkness because she did not know anything about it. She wished that she knew, for though it was dreadful being them, it was much worse not being them. She began to cry again, but without sound, the difficult tears trickling out of the corners of her eyes and making stiff scorching tracks down the side of her face until they dripped off on to her pillow. Daniel and the cats had claimed her sympathy, but not more than that, for though their condition might have been bettered it was not really very bad, but now her compassion had been pierced and set flowing; it felt as though her life's blood were running away.

This must be stopped, thought Hodge, or she'd bleed to death. He knew all she was feeling; the touch of her hand on his head conveyed it. He jumped up on her bed (a thing he had never done before) and wedging himself in between her and the wall lay down beside her, his cold nose against her ear. . . . A tear dropped on it and he sneezed irritably. . . . Suddenly she began to laugh, a strangled laugh choked by sobs, but still a laugh. The wound was staunched for the moment. Hodge was funny; warm and comforting and funny. She turned over on her side towards him and flung an arm across his back. Her eyelids, that had been so painfully stuck open, fluttered and closed, and soon she was asleep.

## CHAPTER V

### I

Stella woke up abruptly next morning, awakened by some sound beneath her window. It was still very early, with the light of the September dawn entering her little room in the slow conspiratorial way she loved, as though night was still on guard and it had to creep in very secretly lest it be caught and turned back again. It was a grey light, for the shadow of night had fallen upon it as it passed by, but there was a gleam both of silver and gold in the grey, as though it held a sunbeam dusted with starlight beneath the veil of shadow. Stella watched in delight for a moment, her desolation of the night before forgotten while she watched the light that in some way that she did not understand was an extension of the loveliness that she had known in sleep.

She could not remember where she had been in her sleep but the words "not yet, not yet," seemed to be saying themselves in her mind, as though she had nearly got somewhere but had been turned back; but the dawn light that had been more successful than she, and slipped triumphantly through night's fingers, held a reassurance of eventual arrival that took all bitterness from the return and left it saturated with the same peace that she had known in that far place. Then the noise that had disturbed her came again and she was wide awake, remembering last night's desolation, facing today's difficulty, yet not bruised between them because that timeless loveliness lay between the harshness of the one and the other and held them apart by its greater power.

The noise was Father Sprigg in one of his mighty rages, bellowing at Old Sol down in the yard below. "Maundering, twily old dotard!" shouted Father Sprigg, relapsing into gentler language after a stream of profanity that had echoed like thunder round the yard. "Addle-pated old numbskill! Going to your bed leaving the yard door all abroad, and the countryside alive with mutineers and vagabonds. And I'd told you at supper there was one about. No thanks to you, old scoundrel, if the women-folk are not murdered in their beds. There's the best part of a pigeon pie gone as 'tis, and the mistress all of a galdiment to think of a thief in her larder. I'd take a whip to your shoulders if you weren't such a rattling old bag of bones that you'd fall to pieces at a touch, an' not be worth the burying, you vinny old deathshead!"

"No call to be so tilty, Master," said Old Sol equably, as Father Sprigg paused for breath. "Poor soul o' me! Whoever left the door abroad 'tweren't I. Madge and I, we closed un an' barred un same as always. If the pisgies tumbled the bar down that ain't my fault; I done my duty, same as I always done it, man an' boy these fifty years an' more——"

"Fags!" interrupted Father Sprigg violently. "Pisgies, is it? I'll not stand here and listen to such vlother. I'm a patient man, Sol Doddridge, but I'm a fore-right man, and neglect of duty puts me so out of temper——"

A jerk of Sol's thumb upwards checked him. Stella was leaning out of her window and calling, "I did it, father! I did it!"

"Eh?" ejaculated Father Sprigg, red-faced, perspiring, almost throttling himself as he choked upon his wrath. "*You* left the door abroad, poppet?"

"Yes," said Stella. "It wasn't Sol, it was me. I took the bar down and then I couldn't get it up again. I took the pigeon pie too, and milk from the dairy, and gave them to that ragged boy."

Both men gaped up at her in astonishment and Father Sprigg took out his handkerchief and mopped his forehead.

"I'm strong," explained Stella. "Hodge helped."

Hodge was standing up on his hind legs beside her now, his furry face framed beside hers in the little window. Father Sprigg blew out his cheeks, exhaled the air in a long whistling breath of bewilderment, turned and brought a hand like a large ham penitently down on Sol's shoulder. If he was quick in his wrath he was equally quick in making amends if he found himself mistaken. "A little maid like her!" he ejaculated with admiration as Stella withdrew from the window to get dressed.

But his admiration had evaporated by the time they met again at breakfast and his anger was smouldering once more. If Stella ever did such a thing again he'd turn her upside down and spank her, big girl though she was, he declared between mighty mouthfuls of porridge, and it was no idle threat either, he meant what he said. Had she not those damned stable cats to pamper, and that vinny bag of bones, Daniel, a fool not worth his keep and kept only to pleasure her, but she must go wasting good vittles on some dirty scoundrel who might have murdered them all in their beds? He paused to stick a hunk of bread into his mouth and Mother Sprigg carried on where he left off. Stella had never seen her so annoyed. Had she not told Stella time and again that she must never speak to strangers, especially disreputable strangers? She might have come to some terrible harm and if she had it would have been entirely her own fault, and a just punishment for as flagrant an act of disobedience as Mother Sprigg had ever heard of in all her days. Here Madge and Old Sol murmured agreement and shook their heads sadly. Seraphine, presiding over her kittens beside the fire, had her back turned to Stella. Only Hodge, sitting beside her chair and pressing his head hard against her knee, was on her side.

But Stella went on placidly eating her porridge and was not disturbed. She knew perfectly well that all this disapproval was caused by nothing but love. If there had been no danger to her in what she had done they would not have been so angry. But she did not say she was sorry because she was not. She knew she had done perfectly right to feed Zachary Moon. She knew that the inside people must always help the outside people. But she was sorry that she could not say she was sorry because she could see that her silence was exasperating Father and Mother Sprigg worse than ever.

"She shan't be spanked this time, Father, since you say not," said Mother Sprigg, "but punished she must be. It's her morning for going to the doctor for her lessons. She must bide at home; both to punish her and to keep her safe from that scoundrel, if he's still about."

Stella looked up quickly, dropping her spoon, wounded to the quick. Her lessons with Dr. Crane were the most precious hours in her week, and Mother Sprigg knew it. The face she turned to her foster-mother was white and set hard. Mother Sprigg was jealous of her lessons, afraid of them for some reason, and now she was using this necessity for punishment as an opportunity to stop Stella learning things. It was not fair. The little girl got up, went to the cupboard under the windowseat where she kept her treasures and came back with the ruler that Dr. Crane had given her.

"Father," she said, standing in front of him, "please, I do not want to give up my lessons. If mother does not wish me to be out in the lanes by myself Sol will come with me to the village; you said yesterday he must take Bess to the blacksmith. And Dr. Crane will bring me back in his gig before he starts his rounds. Please, Father, instead of keeping me in will you whip me instead. Please will you whip me just as hard as ever you can." She laid the ruler beside his plate and held out her slim beautiful little hands, palm upwards, considering them. "My left hand, please, Father, because I shall want to hold my pen in my right." She put her right hand behind her, out of harm's way, and held out her left. "Hard, please, Father."

Though it was an age when corporal punishment for the young was highly esteemed he had never whipped her yet; he loved her far too well. But now, meeting her unflinching look with one of deep respect, he picked up the ruler, swung round in his chair and gave it to her good and hard until her little palm was scarlet, and the ruler, not designed for corporal punishment, broke in his hand. Then he flung it into a corner, swore, and rising left the room as near tears as Mother Sprigg had ever seen him.

"Soft," said Mother Sprigg. "That's what he is. Soft. Sit down at once, Stella, and finish your breakfast."

She was very upset. Not only had her authority been openly flouted by Father Sprigg and Stella but Stella had shown her, as never before, just how much her lessons meant to her. But she could not go on being angry with her darling child, and when Stella had gone upstairs to fetch her cloak she followed her into her little room with a pot of ointment and a bandage. "My love, my love," she murmured, as Stella held out her hand, with white weals across the palm, the skin broken and the hand bleeding in one place. "Poor little maid! He gave it you as hard as though you were a mutineer needing the cat."

"I asked him to," said Stella.

Her hand was hurting badly but she was glad that it was. Zachary had had bloody bandages round his feet and she was glad that she had a bloody bandage too, even though it was only slightly bloody. But he and her mother came a little nearer to her because she was not quite as comfortable in her body as she had been this time yesterday. Then she lifted her face to Mother Sprigg and they kissed and hugged each other. "Of all the people on the farm I love you best, Mother," said Stella. "I love you very much. I love you best——" Then she paused, truth compelling her. "After Hodge."

Then she was out of the room and down the stairs, leaving Mother Sprigg laughing. What a ridiculous little maid it was! Only a child, after all, a child who would stay with her and be her own babe for a long time yet, in spite of this dratted book-learning.

II

During the day Stella and Hodge were frequently parted, for Hodge had often to attend Father Sprigg upon the farm. "But Daniel must come with me," said Stella to Old Sol, as he led Bess from the stable. Sol growled and grumbled. Daniel, whirling and twirling and tangling himself up in his chain, wailed like a banshee in the desperation of his anxiety. "Yes," said Stella firmly. "I promised him."

Stella's firmness was a thing against which Old Sol was powerless. He untied Daniel, who immediately raced around the yard like a creature demented, upsetting two buckets of water which Madge had just drawn up from the well, and then lifted Stella upon Bess's back. Then they left hastily, through the yard door into Pizzle Meadow, leaving the buckets to be dealt with by others.

Stella forgot all about her smarting hand in the delight of being enthroned on Bess. The old horse, lacking a shoe, went slowly and gently through the meadow. She was a magnificent creature, still able, in spite of increasing years, to carry Father Sprigg's weight in the hunting field and put up a very creditable performance there. Yet she had no arrogance and even had she not lacked a shoe she would have gone gently with the child upon her back and lame Old Sol walking beside her. Such was her nobility of character that she put up patiently with Daniel, who was whirling about them barking shrilly, meaning well but perpetually underfoot in the most irritating way. Beautiful weather always went to his weak head.

It was lovely in Pizzle Meadow on this perfect September morning. Up in the far corner a spring, the Pixies' or Pisgies' Well, that had given the meadow its name, bubbled up beneath an old hawthorn tree and from it ran a small stream that crossed the field, fed the trough in the centre of it, and then disappeared underground again where it mysteriously fed the well in the centre of the yard and the duck pond in the orchard. In spring a mass of white blossom covered the hawthorn tree and the few old cider apple trees that grew in the grass, and forget-me-nots and primroses bordered the stream, but Stella thought it was just as lovely today with the berries clustered thickly on the hawthorn branches, deep crimson against the blue sky, and golden leaves floating gently down from the apple trees. Most of the apples had been taken to the cider press but a few still lay in the grass, and the black pigs were rooting happily among them.

Sol opened the gate and they went through into the lane beyond, that led steeply up the hill toward the village. Stella wondered if Zachary had come this way last night, and she looked lovingly at the old oak tree among whose comfortable roots they had sat together. The leaves had begun to turn very early this year and the oak tree was already crusted with gold, and in the thick hedge below the hips were scarlet and the sloes had a purple bloom upon them and were all ready to be gathered for Mother Sprigg's famous sloe gin.

The old stony, rutted lane had sunk with each succeeding generation more and more deeply into the earth between its steep banks, and they could see little of the surrounding country until they had nearly reached the summit of the hill. There they stopped so that Sol, completely winded, might get his breath, and looked back the way they had come. Down below them was spread out a scene so lovely that the rosy colour came flooding up into Stella's face, as it always did when anything delighted her. Even Old Sol grunted appreciatively and Bess stood still as a statue with Daniel just for a moment quiet and attentive beside her.

Weekaborough Farm lay in the valley below them, backed by low round hills, with Beacon Hill shouldering up into the sky behind like a friendly protecting giant. Somewhere beyond Beacon Hill an old castle, Berry Pomeroy Castle, was built upon a hill in the woods. Stella could not see it but she knew it was there, and greeted it in her mind. To their right they looked through a break in the hills across a wide landscape of woods and fields to the splendid rampart of the moors rising against the western sky, while to the east, seen through another break in the hills, was the sea. The colours, the turquoise of the sea, the buff and emerald of the harvest fields and meadows, the green and gold of the woods and copses, the purple and russet of the moors, the clear blue dome of the sky, glowed through the silver haze of autumn sunlight like the colours of an opal, vivid and warm yet so soft that one felt invigorated and yet stilled at the same time.

Weekaborough Farm itself seemed to Stella, who loved it so much, to be the central point of the loveliness. She could see the whole of it there at her feet, dwarfed by distance and yet having the visionary quality of all things seen far off, so that the tiny domain that she could have picked up in her hands awed her as it never did when she was down there and a part of it. . . . Home. . . . It showed you its face when you sat quiet within it at that moment when day was passing to night, but it could only reveal its spirit, its eternal meaning, when you stood at a little distance, just turning to leave it or just returning to it, seeing it at that transition moment when a larger world was claiming or releasing you. It was always at these transition times, it seemed, when for a moment nothing owned you and you owned nothing, that you saw things so very clearly.

The awed moment passed and she saw the details with delight; the white thatched farm buildings, with the garden to the south gay with autumn flowers, the big orchard to the west and the vegetable garden and the walled garden where the bee-hives were to the east. Besides Pizzle Meadow several fields and two round green hills where sheep and cattle were grazing also belonged to Father Sprigg. One of the hills, Bowerly Hill, to the south of the farm, was crowned by an old wind-twisted yew tree that Stella loved very much, and the other, Taffety Hill, upon whose summit they were now, had a copse of nut trees and thickets of blackberry bushes. This kingdom was surrounded by a great rampart of earth flanked with stones, one of the Danmonian fences, old beyond memory, that divided the property of one man from that of another. . . . Dr. Crane had told Stella that the word Devon came from the word Danmonian, meaning deep hollows, and the Danmonii, of whom she was one, were the dwellers in the glens. . . . Father Sprigg's fence was a grand one, eight feet wide at the base, and nearly as high, narrowed at the top to four feet and covered with coppice wood, oak, ash, birch and hazel. These fences gave shelter from the winds and kept the cattle from straying; and nowadays they were saying that they might soon be put to what was perhaps their ancient purpose of giving protection against an invading army. . . . Men, hidden with their muskets behind these fences, would be in a strong position.

"But they won't come!" Stella cried suddenly. "Sol, say they won't come!"

"Let 'em come!" growled Sol savagely. "Let 'em come, an' us'll show 'em. Us an' Them."

At the mention of Them Stella began to tremble. She was a brave little girl but she was dreadfully afraid of three things, thunderstorms, rats and Them.

A few moments ago Sol had taken from his pocket a curious-looking wooden object, about the shape and size of a large bay leaf, with a long string fastened to one end which he twisted about his finger. Now he began to whirl the thing round and round. For a moment nothing happened, but Stella, knowing what was going to happen, set her teeth, shut her eyes and put her hands over her ears. For this was Sol's bull-roarer, a possession that had come down to him from his father before him, and to him from his father. Many Devon country boys possessed these ancient instruments for making uncanny, terrifying noise, but Sol had prolonged his passion for the thing right on into old age. It was the medium through which he expressed deep feeling. When another man would have played a fiddle or written a poem Sol swung his bull-roarer.

The noise started as a low whirring, with a strange sharp tone thrilling through it, but became louder and louder until it was like the roar of a mighty rushing wind. It was a dreadful and almost hellish noise and always seemed to Stella to darken the world, as though the wings of demons were sweeping overhead between her and the sky. It was that she might not see Them that she always shut her eyes while Sol swung his instrument in evocation. Dr. Crane had told her once that the bull-roarer was to be found in many countries of the world and was used as a sacred instrument in connection with heathen mysteries. It had been so used in ancient Greece. . . . And in England, long ago.

"What heathen mystery is Sol thinking about when he swings his bull-roarer?" Stella had asked.

"He has forgotten," the doctor had answered.

"Who does he mean by Them?" she had asked.

"He has forgotten," the doctor had said.

The terrifying noise died away, the dreadful presences, the ancient defenders of the land, passed away with it, Sol pocketed the bull-roarer and Stella, shuddering with relief, took her hands from her ears and opened her eyes. Bess and Daniel had remained perfectly placid throughout. They were as perfectly at home with Them as Sol was. It was only Stella who was afraid.

Sol turned abruptly and opened the gate that closed the lane behind them. The lane here cut through the rampart of the fence, and when they were through the gate they had left Father Sprigg's land.

The lane led downhill again to the village of Gentian Hill, lying in a secluded valley. This valley was another little kingdom all to itself, quite different in character from Weekaborough, for there was no break in the hills which surrounded it through which one could see the moors or the sea, and through which the fresh winds could blow, so that the trees were not bent by the winds as in the Weekaborough valley, and the flowers came out earlier and were more luxuriant. In hot weather it could be very sultry down in Gentian Hill, and in wet weather, when the stream that ran down the side of the village street overflowed, it was often flooded.

But it was a beautiful village, surrounded with orchards, its thatched cob cottages set in gardens packed tight with flowers, the low stone walls that surrounded them cascading with green ferns. The beautiful old church with its tall tower crowned the knoll that gave the village its name, and gentians grew in the churchyard. Grouped about the church were the Church House Inn, the Parsonage, Dr. Crane's house, the forge and the village shop, and this part of the village was considered highly respectable. But there was a secondary village, separated from Gentian Hill proper by a hill crowned by a small dense wood, Hangman's Wood, that was not so highly esteemed. There a group of very old cottages lurched drunkenly in the midst of gay untidy gardens, surrounding an old inn with bulging walls and dilapidated thatch, and a gaudy painted sign showing a scarlet-hulled full-rigged sailing ship breasting a purple sea. But in spite of the brilliant swinging sign the inn was never called the Ship Inn, but Smoky-house, and the whole gay, disreputable group of cottages was known briefly as Smoky.

The people who lived at Gentian Hill had mostly lived there for generations, and seldom left their homes, but the Smoky people were a shifting population, sometimes here and sometimes not. The Excise men always had their eyes on Smoky, and so had the gamekeepers of the neighbouring estates. Gentian Hill always spoke with patronising disapproval of Smoky but never gave it away. There were certain homes in Gentian Hill where a Smoky man in trouble knew he would not be refused a welcome and a hiding place, and few among the more well-to-do cottages whose secret cupboards had not got their hidden store of French brandy and tobacco.

But not all the cottages in Gentian Hill were well-to-do. In an age when the wages of an agricultural labourer were barely enough to keep his family and himself alive, the whitewashed cob walls and thatched roofs of some of the cottages hid a poverty that Dr. Crane, who dealt with its results, was careful to keep hidden as far as possible from his pupil Stella. He knew her to be abnormally sensitive, unusually compassionate, and he was admitting her only gradually to knowledge of the suffering of the world.

III

He lived alone in his creeper-covered dark little house, waited on by his old sailor-servant Tom Pearse and by no one else. He had been a naval surgeon for most of his life and had a hearty distaste for all female society. He did not dislike women when they were ill, provided they were genuinely ill, for then in his view they were no longer women but suffering bodies, and for suffering bodies he had a compassionate sympathy that made them almost sacred in his eyes. And at Stella's age they were hardly women yet but merely children; though he would never himself have put the word "merely" before the word children, for he worshipped childhood even as he worshipped the starry heavens, the wind-swept corn, untrodden snow and all things healthy and fresh.

Highly paradoxical was the love of this strange old man, for he gave with equal passion to the ideal and to its opposite, to the whole thing and to the broken thing that had fallen by the way. But for careful people, those who could not leap for fear of the falling, who kept their windows shut against fresh air and guarded minds, hearts or purses against the possibly painful inroads of truth and compassion, for the evasive, the plausible, dawdlers and the self-absorbed, he had nothing but a contempt so biting that few patients subjected to it called him in again. Not that he cared. He preferred a small practice now that he was getting old. And there were plenty of the other sort about. For one malingerer, he'd say, you'd meet fifty who carried pain like a banner, and for one skinflint there were a dozen who'd give you their last penny and never let you know there wasn't a pocketful where that one came from. But he liked to catch 'em young, and batter their minds and hearts wide open with whatever tool came readiest to his hand. He had caught Stella very young, and was mercilessly beating her mind into shape with all possible speed, before domesticity submerged her altogether. But her heart he tried to touch not at all, because for some reason or other she had been born with a wounded heart. In his opinion it was salves that she needed for it, not a hammer.

Stella parted with Sol at the doctor's gate and with Daniel leaping around her ran up the paved path between the bushes of rosemary and lavender to the open front door. Here she paused, gripping Daniel's collar.

"Come in, can't you," shouted the doctor impatiently from the shadows within. "Don't dawdle. If you think that mind of yours is already sufficiently well informed to permit of dawdling upon the threshold of education, then say so, and I'll waste no further time upon you, but if——"

"I've got Daniel," interrupted Stella, who was no more afraid of the doctor than she was of Father Sprigg, for if the rage of the one was as invigorating as a sou'wester the irritation of the other had the bracing quality of one of his own tonics. "I don't know what to do with him."

"What in the name of thunder made you bring that great gangling ninny of a beast to a lesson on the death of Socrates?"

"I had to. I promised."

"Then bring him in and tie him to the table leg."

Stella towed Daniel over the scrupulously scrubbed flags of the dark little hall to the open door of Dr. Crane's study. Only in the worst weather were any of his doors shut; his passion for hospitality was only equalled by his passion for fresh air. The study was as clean as the hall, but mercifully not quite so dark and bare. It was stone-flagged, the walls completely lined with books. An old table of Spanish chestnut stood in the centre of it, with two beautifully carved chairs pulled up on either side. The one with its back to the window, the doctor's, had no cushion, but the one facing the light was comfortably supplied with a couple of them. Patients and pupils, and many who came to consult the doctor about problems other than physical or intellectual, sat in this chair, and while they poured their troubles into the comforting depth of his comprehending silence he watched their faces in the soft light that shone through the spotless muslin curtains draped in the window, and learned more from the shadows round the eyes and the play of expression about the mouth than he did from the flow of confused words, tumbling about his ears. Yet he listened attentively while he watched, quick to detect alike the hesitant truth and the glib evasion, and impatient though he was by nature he never interrupted until the last word had been uttered. He knew how a flow of words, like a flow of blood, can wash away poison.

The room had an Adam mantelpiece and a basket grate filled with fircones. Pipes and tobacco jars and medicine bottles were piled on the mantelpiece, and over it hung an engraving of one of the doctor's three heroes, Lord Nelson, with whom he had once been shipmates. His writing-desk was in one corner of the room and in another corner was a big locked cupboard containing his drugs, bandages and splints. An engraving of Shakespeare and another of the bust of Socrates, his other two heroes, hung over these. He had no surgery, he lived, studied, taught and healed in this room, but on the other side of the hall was a dining parlour that served as a waiting-room for his patients. He never dined in it unless he had guests, he ate at his study table surrounded by his books, and studied while he ate. His hunger for knowledge gave him no rest, it was at once his bane and his joy.

He glanced up from the great tome he was reading when Stella entered, pointed to the chair opposite and was at once engrossed again. She tied Daniel to the table leg and sat down to wait patiently till he got to the end of the paragraph and was free to attend to her. "Never stop in the middle of a paragraph," he had said to her once, "for any reason whatever except the dire need of another or your own sudden death. Finish one thing as completely as possible before turning your attention to the next, even though the next be invasion by the enemy, and allow other people to do the same. A divided allegiance leads to woolly-mindedness, and that to senility of the intellect at an unnecessarily early age. You have been warned, Stella. I shall not speak again."

And he had not needed to speak again. Stella never interrupted him, and even on the day when a wasp had stung her on the cheek she had gone steadily on to the end of the passage of Shakespeare she was reading before asking if she might fetch a raw onion from the kitchen to rub on the place. She had received no commendation for that act of heroism. It was Dr. Crane's opinion that a desire to be praised for doing her obvious duty was a typical feminine failing, and he did not encourage it in Stella.

While he read to the end of the paragraph Stella sat still and upright in her chair and studied him lovingly. She could not see his face very clearly, sitting with his back to the light as he was, but the window behind him threw his rugged old head and the huge breadth of his shoulders into splendid relief. Though he was nearly seventy his rough iron-grey hair was still thick and plentiful, receding only on the temples, and he wore it neatly brushed back and tied in a queue in the nape of his neck. The hot suns of his seafaring life had burned his skin mahogany colour and the endurance of many things had seamed it as though it had been gouged with a bradawl. He had a huge domed forehead, a large ugly broken nose twisted slightly to the right, and dark penetrating eyes beneath bushy white eyebrows. His jaw was aggressive but his mouth was mobile and sensitive. He was always scrupulously clean-shaven and his large yet delicate hands well tended. His well-cut shabby clothes were well-brushed and the voluminous stock that he wore twisted round his throat snowily white. He had a few little vanities; an eyeglass on a watered silk ribbon, a bunch of fine old seals attached to his watch-chain and always a fresh flower in his buttonhole. Seated, his large head and broad shoulders and long arms gave the impression that he was an unusually tall man but when he stood he was seen to be very short. He was bow-legged to the point of deformity and slightly hunchbacked. As a young man he must have been painfully grotesque but as an old man his very infirmities seemed to add to his impressiveness, adding their witness to that of the steady grandeur of his face that here was a man who had won the battle against enormous odds.

He reached the end of the paragraph, shut the book and looking up met the direct and loving glance of the child opposite. Some, meeting his eyes, dropped theirs. Others, aware of the revealing light upon their faces, stirred uneasily. Stella did neither. She had nothing to hide. The light seemed to reflect back from the still, lovely little face as from the surface of some pool pellucid to its depths. The old man's face twisted suddenly. God, how he loved the child! To keep her just as she was, unsullied and happy, he would have given his surgeon's skilled right hand. Happy? But she was not happy. Though she was smiling now, both her dimples showing, she was not the same Stella that she had been when she came to him last. There were no candles burning in her eyes. There was a new maturity in the thin brown face, a wistfulness about the mouth that had not been there before. Some new experience had come to her. She had been told of some past sorrow, or met some present adversity in the person of another, and being what she was she had lived in that past or been that other. He said nothing. It was not his way to win confidence by questioning but only by the unspoken invitation of his vast compassion. But he abruptly abandoned any idea of saying anything whatever about the death of Socrates. He had been taking her gently through carefully chosen passages of the Phaedo but he would not tell her today of the death of that "most noble, meek and excellent man." Instead he shut the open book in front of him, screwed in his eyeglass and looked at her comically. "Like a history lesson in the gig, Stella?"

Delight rippled over Stella's face. Now and then, for a great treat, if he had a patient to visit at a distance or some business to transact in one of the neighbouring villages, he would take her with him and as they drove along he would talk of the history of this lovely land and tell her the legends connected with the houses, the churches, wells and bridges that they passed. He was a born story-teller. So was Stella. It was their mutual love for story-telling that had first made her his pupil.

IV

Three years ago, leaving the farm one evening after a visit to Mother Sprigg who had been taken with a sudden and alarming colic, he found the little Stella standing at the gate of the flower garden gazing up at the stars. It was already cold and dark and had the house not been in a turmoil she would doubtless have been sent to bed an hour ago, but she stood there with her cloak held loosely about her, apparently neither lonely nor afraid, completely absorbed in the glory above her. "There's the Great Bear," she informed him. "I've made up a story about him. Shall I tell it to you?"

He expressed eagerness to hear the story and she told him a gay little tale that delighted him. Then she pointed to another glorious light and asked, "What's that one?"

"That's the hunter Orion," said the doctor. "The Great Bear keeps an eye on him, you see, for fear of being attacked. Those are Castor and Pollux. They were two brothers famous for their love. Zeus, to make their memory immortal, placed them among the stars."

"Are there lots of people and animals in the sky?" she asked.

"A great many," he replied. "Come and see me one of these days and I will read you a story about a man called Trygaeus who made an expedition to heaven and found that we all become stars when we die."

Then he had told her to run in out of the cold and had gone home and thought no more about it. But next day, when he had just got home from his rounds and was sitting down to hot tea and buttered toast in his study, there was a knock at the door. Answering it, he had found Stella and Hodge on the doorstep, her red cloak shining like a poppy in the dusk.

"Got a pain?" he enquired.

"No," said Stella. "I have come to hear about Trygaeus."

She had remembered the name perfectly correctly. Dr. Crane put in his eyeglass and had a good look at her. He had always been fond of her as a taking little thing but now he perceived her to be a lady of quality.

"Who brought you?" he asked.

"Hodge," said Stella.

"But you've not been here before. How did you find my house?"

"I asked the way at a cottage," said Stella. "Now, please, may I come in and hear about Trygaeus?"

He sent his servant Tom Pearse to tell them at the farm that she was safe, brought her and Hodge into the candle-lit study and fed them on tea and buttered toast. They both of them ate daintily, spoke little but were quite at home. Afterwards he pulled his two chairs close to the fire, and with Hodge at their feet and the "Pax" of Aristophanes open on his knee, he and Stella made with Trygaeus the journey to heaven and back again, having there a good many adventures with the shining spirits that perhaps owed more to the imagination of Dr. Crane than to that of Aristophanes. The encounter with those seven little girls, the Pleiades, for instance, was certainly not in the book. Stella laughed as the story unfolded and when it was over she had a good many questions to ask. "Who is the moon?" was one of them.

"The identity of the moon has never been quite certainly established," Dr. Crane told her seriously. "The people of India say he is a very noble hare, who lived such an exemplary life upon earth that when translated to the sky he became a very great light indeed. The Eskimos say the moon is a girl, we say he is a man, an old man carrying a bundle of sticks."

"I think he is a boy," said Stella. "A boy not much bigger than me carrying a bag full of toys on his back. I wish he'd come down and play with me. Do the star people ever come down to the earth again?"

"About that, too, I lack certain information," he told her. "But I should think it quite possible." Then he resettled his eyeglass, looking at her thoughtfully. From her last remark he guessed her to be a lonely child. Mother Sprigg had told him that she did not get on very well with the village children, and that an attempt to send her to the village dame's school had not been successful and had had to be abandoned. She learned too quickly and easily, and the other children had teased her because of it.

"That's another language, not English," said Stella, laying a slim brown hand on the book still open on the doctor's knee. "What is it?"

"Greek," replied the doctor.

"Say a bit," commanded Stella.

He was a passionate classical scholar and he said a bit as perfectly as he could.

"I like that language," Stella told him. "Please, sir, will you teach it to me?"

He took her home that night and demanded of Mother Sprigg that Stella become his pupil. He was so determined that Mother Sprigg, still feeling weak after the colic, was unable to argue with him and gave in without having given the plan her mature consideration; a circumstance which she afterwards regretted.

But Stella and Dr. Crane never had any regrets. From that day on there began between them one of the most perfect of human relationships, that of teacher and disciple from whose mutual love of learning has blossomed a love for each other as purged of selfishness and passion as any love can be; for they demanded nothing of each other, the teacher and disciple, except a mutual devotion to the mutual goal.

## CHAPTER VI

### I

STELLA put on her cloak again and untied Daniel from the table leg, while Dr. Crane went to tell Tom Pearse to put in the horse. Ten minutes later, having told Old Sol at the forge to expect Stella home when he saw her, they were trotting through the village bound for the sea. Stella's face was pink with pleasure. Though she lived only a few miles from it she seldom saw the sea except in the distance. The market town to which she was taken occasionally was inland, and Father and Mother Sprigg had no time for pleasure trips. They were so much a part of the beauty that surrounded them that they never regarded it objectively. The distant roar of the sea on stormy nights, the sea wind blowing in at their open windows, was as much a part of them as the breath of their bodies, but to go to the sea just to look at the sea would have seemed to them sheer idiocy. But Stella had been born with the gift of wonder, and the fact that something was a part of herself did not prevent her from contemplating it with awe and delight; there were times when herself seemed to herself the most astonishing thing of all.

Used as she was to the slow-moving pack horses and wagons of the farm, Dr. Crane's gig seemed to Stella as near flying as made no difference. The seat, suspended from curved springs by leather braces between the two great wheels, swung excitingly, and Aesculapius, the doctor's fine grey gelding, went at a brisk pace. The doctor, in a many-caped brown overcoat, with his tall beaver hat cocked at an angle and his eye-glass in place, drove well, and Stella, sitting very upright beside him in her scarlet cloak, was delightedly conscious of being part of a very smart turn-out indeed. Daniel, on the floor between them, his nose just poking out from beneath the plaid rug that covered their knees, rent the air with his shrill whimpering of excitement and scourged their legs with his tail, but otherwise behaved well. Hodge, had he been with them, would have kept perfectly still and not made a sound, but then Hodge was a gentleman and Daniel was not.

They passed through the village, the doctor acknowledging the friendly greetings of the villagers with his whip raised to the brim of his hat, and slowed down as they came to the steep rutted lane that led up through Hangman's Wood, named from the gallows that until only a few years ago had stood at the crossroads not far away. It was really a beautiful wood, oak, ash and birch all growing thickly together, with beneath them a dense undergrowth of blackberry and hazel bushes, yet it had a sinister reputation and after dark was said to be a haunt of footpads. But today it looked beautiful with the sunlight falling on the gold of the turning oaks and the slender silver stems of the birches, and the blackberry bushes gemmed with scarlet leaves, and from the safety of the gig Stella could marvel that anyone should ever shun such a lovely place.

They breasted the hill and were out in the open again, bowling along between green meadows to Smoky. Stella was never allowed to go to Smoky by herself, and the sight of its gold and white cottages, lurching with so abandoned and yet so gay an air in gardens ablaze with dahlias, with the brightly painted inn sign swinging in the wind, thrilled her to the marrow. Here too the doctor had his friends. A little old woman, hanging out washing in a cottage garden, smiled at him, and a red-bearded giant of urbane yet disreputable appearance, wearing a sea-man's trousers and tattered shirt and lolling in the doorway of the inn, waved his clay pipe in the doctor's direction and called out a greeting. This time the doctor took his hat right off to both of them, without a hint of mockery in his deference. "They say Granny Bogan is a witch, but she's a brave woman," he explained. "And of all the scoundrels of my acquaintance, and I know a good many, George Spratt is the one I'd choose to have with me in a tight place."

They were driving now very slowly down a lane with high banks crowned with gorse bushes and storm-twisted oaks that arched over their heads, but so steep that down below, between the grey lichened branches, they could see the sea, pale blue and aquamarine, soft as silk, with golden lights upon it. Then the lane took a turn to the left and flattened out a little, taking the curve of the hill, the bank changing into a low stone wall, and the whole stretch of Torbay was spread out below them. Dr. Crane stopped the gig. "Take a good look, Stella," he said gently. "I have sailed from one end of the Mediterranean to the other but I have never seen any sight as beautiful as this. To my mind the Bay of Naples can't touch it, nor the coast of Corsica, nor Crete. Keep still. Take a good look."

The coast swept in a great half moon about the gleaming sea, from the rocks beyond Torquay to the amethyst coloured heights of Berry Head above the ancient port of Brixham. It was so clear today that they could just make out the tall old houses of Brixham climbing the rocky cliff behind the harbour, and the splendid hulls and towering masts of two frigates riding there at anchor, with sails hanging loose to dry. Torquay looked a fairy-place that you could have picked up in your hand. The group of cottages close to the sea, grandly called the Strand, the shipbuilding yard and the harbour, stood out clearly. Now that the fleet was so often in Torbay they were building neat little houses for the officers' wives inland from the village, but these were hidden among the trees. The lovely little place was encircled by seven hills, Warbury, Waldon, Lincombe, Peaked Tor, Park Hill and Beacon Hill. In the deep and lovely valleys between the hills the birds sang so riotously in the spring-time that it seemed the hills themselves were singing.

Coming round the bay from Torquay, sandstone cliffs and pasture land edged the sea with a ribbon of red and green, and in the fields between Torre Abbey and the sea the deer were feeding behind the strong sea wall that George Carey of the Abbey had built to protect his land. Stella could just see the Abbey among its trees, with Torre Church and the Chapel of Saint Michael looking down upon it from their hills. The hamlet of Livermead had its ancient jetty running out into the water in the centre of the bay, just where once upon a time a forest had been submerged by the sea. Stella was always thrilled by the thought of this forest, and sometimes when she was awake at night she would tell herself stories about it. . . . She wondered if there had been a little chapel in the forest, like the chapel of St. Michael above the Abbey, and if on stormy nights you could hear the bell in its belfry ringing. . . . In Torre Abbey sands you could still see the roots of trees at low water, and to this day the fiishermen would bring up the antlers of deer in their nets.

From the cluster of cottages that was Livermead two lanes wound through fields and coppices, one to Cockington and the other to the village of Paignton to their right. Paignton was much older than Torquay and looked upon the lovely little place with its flowery Strand as a mere upstart. Paignton was famous for several things, its cabbages, its beautiful fifteenth century church, and the Palace of the Bishop of Exeter standing in a great meadow beside the church, with sheep cropping the turf beneath its windows. Some people said Miles Coverdale, Bishop of Exeter, had made his translation of the Bible there; but whether he had or not it was a place of tranquillity and peace; and so was the old harbour, with thatched cottages clustered about it.

"The sea looks so gentle," said Stella at last. "You wouldn't think, would you, that it could turn black and cruel and drown people?"

The doctor looked at her keenly, then touched up his horse and they moved on down the lane.

"Where are we going?" asked Stella.

"I've a patient to see at Torre Abbey," said the doctor.

"Torre Abbey!" cried Stella. It was the greatest house in the neighbourhood, greater even than Cockington Court. It was to Stella as though he had said that they were going to Windsor Castle. "Is Sir George or his lady ill?"

"They would not call in this country sawbones if they were," laughed the doctor. "Nothing so grand as that, my honey. They've a footman who once upon a time was shipmates with me. He's ill and suffers from the delusion that I'm the only man who can put him on his feet again. I was useful to him once before, when we were both with Nelson in the *Agamemnon*, and he was blown sky high at the siege of Bastia. I doubt if he's ever got over that, poor fellow."

He paused. He never spoke to Stella of the horrors of war, but he had done so this time with a purpose, for after what she had said about the sea he had hazarded a guess at what had saddened her.

"Is it very dreadful to be blown sky-high?" she asked in a clear, strained voice.

So his guess was right, and she had been told about her mother. He looked at her anxiously. Her face looked pale against the background of the shimmering sea and the blue sky and he was extremely angry. She had been told much too soon. He had many times asked Mother Sprigg not to tell her until she was at least twelve years old, but Mother Sprigg, jealous of his influence over Stella, had always replied obstinately that she was the best judge as to when Stella should be told what. He said nothing until they had reached the bottom of the hill and were jogging along the lane that led through meadows and woods to the Abbey, and then he said, "So you know about your mother, Stella?"

Stella nodded, aware of his compassion inviting her confidence and glad now to give it. "I asked Mother Sprigg. Somehow I felt that I wasn't really Mother Sprigg's daughter. . . . I could remember other things. . . . And so I asked."

"And when you heard about your real mother you felt unhappy, did you?"

"I did not feel so bad at first. But afterwards, when I'd seen Zachary Moon, and he'd gone away again, and I'd gone to bed, it all seemed real." She fumbled a little desperately for words. "As though I was them. Only it was worse when I couldn't be them."

"Who is Zachary Moon?" asked the doctor.

Stella told him all about Zachary; not about him seeming like the other part of herself, for she could not find the words to explain that part of it; but the actual story part. The doctor had trained her to tell a story well and she did not leave out anything from the rising of Hodge's hair beneath her hand to Zachary limping away into the night.

"Away into the darkness, like your mother," said the doctor gently, when she had finished. "To somewhere outside the life you know about where you cannot follow them or be them any more. And it is worse, is it, not to be them than to be them?"

Stella looked up at him, nodding, wide-eyed with amazement that he should understand so well. He rubbed his broken nose, wondering how best to help her. "I think I know how you feel, my honey. If you know what is happening to people you can *be* them in your mind and can keep them company. But when they have gone to some place where you don't know what is happening to them, you can't. But you don't have to know just what people are doing and feeling to be of assistance to them Your own life seems to you like a very small lighted room, with great darkness all round it, and you can't see out into the darkness and know what is happening there. But light and warmth from your room can go out into the darkness if you don't have the windows selfishly curtained, keep a brave fire burning, and light all the happy candles you can. Do you see what I mean?"

Stella nodded slowly. "Yes. You mean my mother will be happier if I'm happy?"

"That's what I mean. And this Zachary Moon, and all other misfortunate vagabonds, will feel more valiant if you are keeping your courage up. You may think that sounds fantastic, but it's the truth. Were you whipped for feeding the young scrounger?"

Stella had not known that he had noticed her bandaged hand. But of course he had noticed. He always noticed everything. "I asked Father

Sprigg to whip me instead of keeping me away from lessons. He didn't want to do it, but he did."

The doctor nodded approval of both Stella and Father Sprigg.

"But Zachary isn't either a vagabond or a scrounger," she went on.

"What is he then?" asked the doctor. He was feeling his way to some knowledge of this Zachary, who was so mysteriously the boy from the moon whom the little Stella of three years ago had wanted as her playmate, and had used the words vagabond and scrounger as a draw.

"He was ragged, but you could see that he wasn't used to being that way, and he asked me to give him my handkerchief because he was not clever at blowing his nose without one, the way Old Sol is. And he only asked for food because his stomach was sticking to his backbone and he just had to ask for it. He didn't ask for money; scroungers always ask for money. And when he ate it wasn't like Sol and Madge eat, or even Father Sprigg, it was like, well, the way you eat." She surveyed him thoughtfully, then nodded. "Yes, he was like you."

"What, with a broken nose and an eyeglass and a wrinkled countenance?"

"No, not like you to look at." She puzzled over it, then pounced upon the resemblance. "You could trust him. Hodge knew it and stopped growling and wagged his tail almost at once, but I think I'd soon have known it, even if Hodge hadn't been there. You know how one feels with people like you and Zachary—safe."

The doctor took off his hat in acknowledgment of the prettiest compliment he had ever been paid by a lady; and he considered that he now knew enough about Zachary to enable him to keep his eye open for that unfortunate young gentleman, for whose acquaintance he found himself increasingly eager. Abruptly he changed the conversation. "Now, my honey, no more grieving. Whatever your mother suffered it's over and done with long ago. She's happy where she is and will be the happier for your happiness. And as for this Zachary, he appears to be an exceptionally gifted young gentleman, perfectly able to possess himself of a meal and a handkerchief when required, and will undoubtedly fall upon his feet sooner or later, and I've told you how to be useful to him in the meantime. . . . There's the Abbey. Have you ever heard the story of its building?"

Stella looked up, shaking her curly head, candles in her eyes again at the prospect of a story. They were now in the fields where from above they had seen the deer feeding, and the road wound under oaks and beeches, stalwart giants of trees who were yet bent all one way by the wind from the sea. To their right they could see through the trees the strong wall that kept back the sea when the winter storms were raging, and to their left and ahead of them was the Abbey embowered in trees, the more modern manor house surrounded by the old monastic buildings; the gatehouse, the old barn, the tower and ruins of the church, with orchards beyond and then the Chapel of Saint Michael keeping watch over it all upon the hill beyond the orchard. . . . That chapel drew Stella especially, almost as though it belonged to her.

II

"Once upon a time," began the doctor in the approved style, "in the days of Richard of the Lion Heart, a man and a girl lived in these parts and loved each other. He was Hugh de Bruière, the descendant of a Norman knight who had settled here after the Conquest, and she was Lady Hester, of the House of Ilsham, who lived in an old castle over there beyond Torquay. They promised to be faithful to each other and then he went away to the Crusades and she sat in her bower at the castle at Ilsham, looking out to sea and telling her beads for his safe return. But de Bruière was not the only man who loved her; there was another fellow, de Pomeroy, who lived in Berry Pomeroy Castle in the woods beyond Weekaborough Farm, a fellow who was not trustworthy like Zachary Moon. He had gone to the Crusades too, with Hugh de Bruière, and a year later he turned up at Ilsham, having been entrusted by de Bruière with a message for Lady Hester. But he did not give the message. Instead he told a long cock and bull story of de Bruière's death at the hands of the Saracens, and the Lady Hester believed him. Then he made furious love to her, and a year later they were married."

"Well!" exclaimed Stella indignantly, "you'd have thought she'd have had the sense to know he was lying, wouldn't you?"

"Telling her beads so often, and looking at the sea so long, must have addled her brains," said the doctor, finding what excuse for her he could. "Doubtless a feather-pated girl at the best of times and easily persuaded. Well, as I say, she married de Pomeroy, but on the wedding night a ship sailed into Torbay and dropped anchor, a boat was lowered and a knight came ashore."

"Hugh de Bruière!" said Stella breathlessly.

"The very same. He saw the blaze of lights at Ilsham and asked the fisherman its meaning. What he said, when told of its meaning, is not recorded, nor does anyone know exactly what happened after that, but de Bruière was a hot-tempered man, and next day the body of de Pomeroy was found in the river Dart with a dagger sticking in it. It was very regrettable, no doubt, but I've every sympathy with the fellow, haven't you?"

Stella nodded vehemently. "And then Lady Hester married him?" she asked eagerly.

The doctor chuckled. "You'd have done that, would you? So would

any girl of spirit. But Lady Hester seems to have been poor spirit
well as feather-pated. She fell into a decline, and not having me at ha
to get her out of it, presently died."

"And what did de Bruière do?"

"Like most of these hot-tempered gentlemen, who act first and think afterwards, he wished he had not been so hasty. He wished it so often and so much that presently he began to suffer from that uncomfortable condition of mind known as remorse. But being a sensible man he did not, like his lady, fall into a decline, but set to work to do something practical in expiation of his sin. The countryside, he knew, was full of ignorant poor folk with no one to teach them, or help them when they were ill or in trouble; full too of thieves and swindlers, and hot-tempered persons like himself who were far too ready with their daggers on a dark night. The more he thought about it the more he saw that what they needed was the presence among them of holy men who would teach the ignorant, nurse the sick, comfort the sorrowful and put the fear of hell fire into sinners like himself. He was a wealthy man, and had brought back further wealth from the Crusades. He decided to build and endow a monastery.

"He chose his spot well, this level space of green fields in the centre of this lovely bay, and presently the countryside was humming with activity. Masons were summoned from far and near, carpenters, carvers in wood and stone. The axes rang in the woods as the Spanish chestnut-trees were felled for the great timber roofs, and in the quarries the quarrymen made a great clamour hewing the stone for the walls. Along the narrow miry lanes the sledge wagons with their teams of straining horses went back and forth. It was all finished at last; the Abbey Church, the great barn, the cells for the monks, the cloister and library and kitchens, the school and infirmary; and in the spring of 1196 the first Abbot, Adam, with six White Canons of the Norbertine Order, took possession, the body of Lady Hester was buried in the Abbey precincts, and de Bruière himself took the vows and became a monk.

"This is the vow he had to take before the Abbot, 'I do give myself to the Church of Torre, and do promise conversion of my manners and improvement of my life, and Poverty, Chastity, and Perfect Obedience to you, Father, and to your successors, whom the Convent of this Church shall elect according to the rules of the Order.' Evidently de Bruière's manners were converted and his life improved, for one does not hear of his committing any more murders.

"For three hundred and forty-three years the White Canons were to this countryside all that de Bruière had hoped they would be. They taught the children, nursed the sick, converted the sinners, and praised God night and day in the Abbey Church, until that scoundrel Henry acking, and the Abbey, as well as Berry Pomeroy Castle, nds of his favourite of the moment, Thomas Seymour. Thomas Ridgeway, who made a manor house of it. to the Careys, and the Careys have it still. But it has eased to be a stronghold of the Catholic faith. All through the years when Catholics were persecuted there was a secret Chapel under the roof, over what used to be the Abbot's quarters, and they worshipped there at peril of their lives. Now, thank God, Englishmen are free to worship as their consciences bid them, and have been for these last twenty-six years, and the guest hall of the Abbey is now the Catholic Church for all the neighbourhood. One day, perhaps, you'll see it. Here we are. Will you stay in the gig or come inside with me and let the housekeeper give you a drink of milk?"

"I'll stay in the gig with Daniel," said Stella.

They had driven right round behind the great house, and behind the old monks' barn, and had halted outside the arched gateway that led to the servants' quarters, and he saw her looking up at the grey pile with awe. He guessed that she had the country child's fear of the mansions of the great and he did not press her to come inside. He gave her the reins and told her to let them go loose that Aesculapius might crop the grass, and to keep a firm hold of Daniel lest he get up to mischief, then he took up his bag and left them.

Daniel was no trouble. The motion of the gig had made him sleepy, and he lay on the seat beside Stella, his head pressed against her, and went happily to sleep. Aesculapius was no trouble either, for the Torre Abbey grass was good grass. Stella sat still, looking up at the grey walls against the blue sky. She could not see the sea now but she could hear it, and over the steep roofs the gulls were wheeling. The doctor had completely comforted her and into the spirit, emptied of its grieving, tranquillity came flooding. She imagined the doctor, somewhere inside the grey walls, comforting the sick man with his understanding and his story-telling just as he had comforted her, and as the White Canons had comforted the sick and sorrowful in this place during more than three hundred years. She could picture them in their white habits moving about the cloisters and the gardens and the fields; she would not have been in the least surprised if one had appeared and walked by her as she sat in the gig; indeed she fancied that she did see one and she murmured his name to herself. "Johan."

She repeated their vow to herself. "I promise conversion of my manners and amendment of my life." That was the vow that Johan would have taken. She decided that her manners were none too good; they should be converted.

The doctor was back before she had time to feel lonely, bringing for her a little apple pasty that the cook had given him, hot out of the oven. She had not realised how hungry she was until she saw it, and her little white teeth were buried in it before anyone had time to say Jack Robinson. Then she remembered, finished her mouthful very carefully and said, "Thank you, Sir. Did you have one?"

"I had a drink of cider, which was more to my liking," said the doctor, as he pushed Daniel off the seat and swung up beside her and took the reins.

"We're making cider at home today," Stella informed him. "May I give a piece of my pasty to Daniel?"

"Certainly. Your pasty and your dog."

Stella gave Daniel a large bit, to comfort him for being banished beneath the rug again, and they moved off at a brisk pace.

"I hope the poor man was feeling better when you left him?" she asked, looking longingly at the piece of pasty to which she had not yet re-addressed herself.

"Much eased by a good grumble, a good yarn and the promise of a bottle of physic," the doctor assured her.

"Were Sir George and his lady well?" she asked.

"So far as I know. Why aren't you getting on with that pasty?"

"I'm converting my manners," said Stella.

"Do you call it good manners to insult a good apple pasty by eating it cold when it was meant to be eaten hot?" asked the doctor with twinkling eyes. "Why, it's as bad as keeping the king waiting."

Stella plunged her teeth joyously into the pasty again, and to the doctor's relief was a mere merry elf until they had climbed the hill above Paignton and stopped to rest Aesculapius and look once more at the view that was the loveliest in the world. The sun was just touching St. Michael's Chapel on its hill and again it seemed to draw Stella in some special way, as though it belonged to her. "Did de Bruière build it?" she asked.

"What, Stella?"

"The Chapel."

"A sailor who had been saved from shipwreck by the monks built it as a votive chapel—that means as a thank offering. But it belonged to the Abbey. St. Michael is the patron saint of churches and chapels built on high ground, because he is 'the Archangel who loves peaks and airy stations.' To this day no foreign ship with a Catholic crew anchors in Torbay without sending a party ashore to pray in that Chapel."

"Has it got a story too?"

"A good story."

"As good as the de Bruière story?"

"Quite as good. A story of a hermit and two young lovers. But the lady had more spirit than Lady Hester. No going into declines for the valiant Rosalind."

"Tell me the story!" begged Stella eagerly.

But the doctor laughed and shook his head. "We'll keep it for another day," he said. "It's too good a story to spoil with a hasty telling, and you and I must get home in double quick time if we're not going to get into hot water with Mother Sprigg."

He touched Aesculapius with his whip and turning their backs on the sea they began the slow climb up into the hills that were their home.

III

Dr. Crane drove Stella round to the front of the farm, arriving at the gate with a great flourish, as though she were a fine lady. Then he helped her down, pushed Daniel after her and took off his hat. "Good-bye, my honey. And next time, mind you, it's to be all work and no play. And if you are one moment late I'll take a stick to your other hand. My compliments to your excellent foster-parents."

He replaced his hat and drove off, Stella waving until he had rounded the corner by the orchard and was out of sight. "Foster-parents." He had said it so easily; but then he had always known that they were not her real father and mother. But this was her real home. She went slowly up the little flight of stone steps that led to the iron gate in the garden wall, savouring the loveliness of coming home. A stone-paved path led between yew trees, clipped to the shapes of peacocks, to the green-painted front door set deep within the old stone porch, with the parlour window to one side of it and the kitchen window to the other. The flower garden was bright with Michaelmas daisies and late roses, and the sun was distilling the scent from the lavender and rosemary bushes that grew among them. The stone wall enclosed the flower garden on the south, the house enclosed it to the north, to the east and west two yew hedges had archways in them leading through into the kitchen garden and the orchard. Stella guessed that everyone would be busy in the orchard with the cider pressing and turning to her left she ran along the smaller paved path that led from the central one through the archway to the orchard.

It was a splendid orchard, stretching the length of house and stables, forming the whole of the western boundary of Weekaborough Farm. It was perfectly situated, sheltered from too much wind in this green dip in the hills yet high enough to be above the fogs. And it was correctly planted, apple trees of the same sort planted in the same row, and at the correct times the ground about the trees was dressed with sea-sand manure. The chickens and ducks lived here, for there was a pond for the ducks at the south-west corner of the orchard, and their white, buff and russet shapes were seen bobbing and lurching about contentedly beneath the trees.

The northern end of the orchard was devoted to the cider apple trees, and here was the shed that housed the cider press, but the southern end, into which the archway in the yew hedge led, was planted with the eating apple and cooking apple trees, the Bramley Seedlings, Jonathans and Blenheim Oranges, with a few cherries and damsons growing among them. The trees had borne splendidly this year and they stood proudly in the orchard grass as though they knew it.

Stella knew them so well that sometimes in bed at night she would call her favourites by their names, for she had named most of them, and seen them standing before her, each with its individual loveliness of shape and colour. In the centre of the goodly company stood the king of them all, the Duke of Marlborough, a huge Blenheim Orange beneath whose branches they stood when they came wassailing the apple trees on Christmas Eve. She ran through the orchard, Daniel at her heels, scattering chickens right and left as she went, calling softly to the trees as she passed them. "Polly Permain, you look well today. Bob Bramley, you've a gold topknot on you. John Jonathan, are you well?" But when she came to the old Duke she stopped, laying her hand upon the hollow trunk with the round knothole that was the tits' front door, looking up into the grey lichened branches above her head. The Duke had fairy powers, she thought. Mistletoe grew upon him, which was a sure sign. And all the birds loved him, and that was a sure sign too. The nuthatches were always running up and down him like mice, and sometimes in winter there was a soft mist of colour in his bare branches, made by the wings of the small birds, the chaffinches and tits, robins and finches. The Weekaborough thrush always sung his evening *Nunc dimittis* on the topmost branch of the Duke, the yaffingale visited him constantly, and when you looked from the kitchen window on misty winter mornings you could see the white owl sitting enthroned in state upon his lowest branch.

"Duke!" she whispered. "Bring Zachary here again. Please, Duke!" In answer a shower of golden leaves fell upon her head and shoulders and she ran on laughing, Daniel barking and leaping beside her, and came to the wooden shed at the far end of the orchard where they were all grouped about the cider press; Father and Mother Sprigg, Old Sol, Madge, Hodge and Jack Crocker the ploughboy. Hodge gave her a loving welcome but the others were too engrossed to do more than nod and smile. Shem, the little dun-coloured Devon horse, was going round, straining gallantly at the bar, and from between the two grinding stones the juice gushed out into the trough.

They were all happy and excited, for Father Sprigg got a good price for his cider these days. It was always in demand for sea voyages, and with the fleet so often putting into Torbay he could have sold twice as much as he made. His orchard of one and a half acres, supplemented by the cider trees in Pizzle Meadow, could produce forty hogsheads in a good year, and such was the thirst of the navy that he was getting now as much as three guineas a hogshead. Father Sprigg made three kinds of cider, the rough fermented cider that Devon men demanded, but which gave men of other counties the colic, sweet cider for those same weak-bellied foreigners, made by checking the fermentation, and by other arts, and the best cider of all, strong and luscious, made by boiling the cider and reducing two hogsheads to one. In delivering cider to the navy you had to be very careful to find out if a ship was manned by Devon men or if it wasn't, for there was a terrible row if rough cider was given to a crew of foreigners and a worse if sweet cider was given to the Devon men.

"Had your nummet, love?" asked Mother Sprigg, as she and Stella stood hand in hand, watching Madge and the men at work.

"I had an apple pasty at Torre Abbey," said Stella.

"At Torre Abbey! My gracious goodness! Only a pasty? Come in, love, and I'll give you a drink of milk and some bread and honey."

They sat at the kitchen table, and Stella ate and drank daintily, remembering about the conversion of her manners, and telling Mother Sprigg, when her mouth was not full, about the adventures of the day. Mother Sprigg smiled, and clacked her tongue in astonishment, but she felt almost as uneasy as she did when she found that Stella had acquired some new knowledge far beyond her comprehension. Visiting the houses of the great! That seemed like another barrier building up between herself and her beloved child. Yet the worst pang came at the end of the little meal, when Stella said gently, "Please, Mother, may I have my little coral, and the locket and the handkerchief that belonged to—to——" She stopped, looking pleadingly at Mother Sprigg, not liking to give the word Mother to the woman in the brave green gown in the presence of this other woman to whom last night she had said, "*You* are my Mother."

Mother Sprigg flushed but she replied steadily, "To your real Mother. Yes, love, they're yours by rights. Come up to my room and I'll give 'em to you now."

They went upstairs hand in hand and Mother Sprigg took a small wooden box with sea shells stuck upon the lid out of one of her drawers, from underneath a pile of snowy befrilled nightgowns. "There you are, love," she said. "The box belonged to my Mother, Eliza, whom I would have liked to name you after. I'll give you that too."

Stella took the box, kissed Mother Sprigg, went away to her own room and closed the door. Mother Sprigg, with an aching throat, went back to the kitchen and the blessed comforting work that was never done; and thanked God for it.

Stella sat on her bed, the box on her lap, and opened it. Inside was the handkerchief, that Mother Sprigg had carefully washed and ironed. It was quite plain, except for a monogram embroidered in one corner. Folded inside it was the coral, and the plain gold locket on a gold chain. The locket opened easily and inside, as Mother Sprigg had said, was a curl of dark hair protected beneath glass, and a scrap of yellow paper with something written on it in the language which Mother Sprigg said no one could make head or tail of. But she could not have shown it to Dr. Crane, for he would have known. . . . It was Greek. . . . Stella had not advanced far enough in her lessons to make head or tail of it either, but she knew the look of the words from the doctor's books. Her heart beat fast. Dr. Crane would know what was written here. He would tell her. She fastened the locket round her neck, under her dress, and put the handkerchief and coral back in the box and the box in her little chest. Then without giving herself time to think or feel, leaving all that for bedtime, she ran downstairs again to help Mother Sprigg make the bread. . . . Never, never, if she could help it, should Mother Sprigg know of the something in her that cried out in longing for her real Mother as it never cried out for Mother Sprigg. . . . As they rolled and shaped the dough together she was her merriest elfin self. Funny little scrap, thought Mother Sprigg. Did she feel anything at all?

## IV

That night Father Sprigg did an unprecedented thing, and jumped a few chapters of the Book. "Seeing the harvest's so good this year, especially the apple harvest, and us like to make a good thing out of the cider, we'll pass in thanksgiving to the thirty-third chapter," he informed his astonished household. Then he cleared his throat, wetted his forefinger and turned the pages.

" 'Blessed of the Lord be His land, for the precious things of heaven, for the dew, and for the deep that coucheth beneath.

'And for the precious fruits brought forth by the sun, and for the precious things put forth by the moon,

'And for the chief things of the ancient mountains, and for the precious things of the lasting hills,

'And for the precious things of the earth and fulness thereof, and for the good will of Him that dwelt in the bush. . . .

'Thy shoes shall be iron and brass; and as thy days so shall thy strength be. . . .

'The eternal God is thy refuge, and underneath are the everlasting arms.' "

The brightness fell all around Stella, streaming from a small round sun in the air, that was that one word "precious"; and this time she looked up at once and met Old Sol's eyes and smiled. If she had any dread at the thought of bedtime, and facing thoughts about her Mother, they were banished. The whole universe, the living and the dead, those who dwelt in the lighted places and those in the dark outside, became to her no longer separate entities but one small thing, that round small thing up there in the air, no bigger than a hazel nut but bright as a diamond; and it was held securely in the hand of God, who for its very preciousness would not let it fall.

## CHAPTER VII

### I

After he had said good-bye to Stella Zachary had found a bed for himself behind a haystack, as he had told her that he would, but it had been Father Sprigg's haystack at the bottom of Bowerly Hill, just the other side of the lane from the Weekaborough flower garden. When he had left her he had started to go north up the lane to the village, and then he had changed his mind and turned back. He had a sentimental longing to spend the night as close to Stella as he could. The two weeks since he had deserted, like the wretched weeks on board that had preceded them, had been weeks without kindness and without a home, and the friendliness and compassion of the little girl had seemed wonderful to him. And she had not seemed like a stranger either; she had seemed like someone whom he had known always.

He had always felt alone. His grandmother, though she had loved him so much, had followed the fashion of the time and for the good of his soul had permitted no real intimacy between the respectful obedience of his youth and the autocracy of her years and experience. Few young people had come to her house, and the older men and women who had been so kind to him had been distantly kind; they had believed with Lady O'Connell that youth should be seen and not heard. Though he had scarcely realised his loneliness there had always been an inexplicable hunger in him. Now that he had been with Stella it was no longer inexplicable. Everyone needed someone in the world who was like their other hand. You can't either hold much or do much with one hand only. It is with both hands that a man lifts the garnered gold of the wheatsheaf and the brimming bowl of milk, with both hands that he builds his house, with both hands, clasped together, that he prays. That had come to him with a flash of insight when Stella had laid her hand upon his knee, and he had turned it over and laid his palm against hers. You cannot gather the harvest of work alone, or make a home alone, or pray always alone, and he had known it when Stella's hand lay against his. Yet he had tossed her hand away again, as though he had been tossing a bird to freedom. She was only a little girl, and he could not take her captive yet. He had his man's way to make in the world before he could come back to the farm from which her father had driven him away.

Curled up upon the further side of the haystack, hidden from the eyes of the farm, he considered his position. During the last fortnight he had gradually sunk into the condition of being too dulled by weariness to consider anything. He had spent the whole time tramping from farm to farm, asking for work but never getting it. Sometimes he had been driven away like a stray dog with a stone whistling past his ear, sometimes he had been given a hunk of bread and a drink of milk, or rags to bind up his feet when his shoes wore out, but always he had been turned away. Most of the farms had had their full complement of labour, and in any case he was obviously without the strength for hard work. And then, too, since the mutiny they had all been so afraid of being caught harbouring mutineers. So he had just gone mechanically on, blundering round and round the idea that he would find a home at some farm as a moth blunders round a candle flame, and so he might have gone on until he dropped dead or the press gang got him, had he not blundered into Stella and had a sense of direction restored to him again.

He did not think it odd that an unknown little girl should in so short a space of time have become to him the reason for existence; like Stella herself he was still young enough not to find anything odd; he did not waste consideration upon that, only upon the problem of his next move. He was not going to find work at a farm, that was obvious. Where then? Where, in all this lovely country of hills and valleys, was there a roof that would consent to shelter him and walls that would accept and not rebuff? A thatched roof and ivy-covered walls set in a musical valley beneath a purple hill. He started violently. He had been half asleep and in the half sleep he had seen it again, the house he had imagined at the head of the stream in the valley behind Torquay. Well, when morning came he'd go there, and see if his dream had any existence in material reality. It was a crazy idea, but it was the only alternative he could think of to his present blundering. He wriggled close into the haystack, shut his eyes and fell asleep.

The same dawn that woke Stella, bringing her back from the far place, woke him, bringing him back from the same place. Lying awake the night before, suffering with him and for him, she must have identified herself with him so completely that she had taken him with her, for as far as he knew he had never been there before. He could not remember where he had been but he knew he had been somewhere, for he awoke saturated with the peace of the place, glowing with the reassurance that if he'd not beached his boat this time he'd sailed close enough to the shore to see the lie of the land and smell the fragrance of it. Yet within five minutes of waking he had forgotten all about it, and was wholly occupied with the problems of the day. The first thing to do was to climb this hill, at whose foot he had been sleeping, and find out where he was. If he could see the sea then he would know in what direction he must travel to reach that valley.

Bowerly Hill had been well-named, for it was indeed a comely hill. Its green turf sloped gently, and the wind-twisted old yew tree at the summit had a personality of its own. Bowerly Hill was the Weekaborough sheepfold, and something of the gentleness and patience of the sheep seemed to cling about it, culminating strangely in the compelling strength of the tree above. Zachary, going up through the grey light, felt his sore feet soothed by the softness of the dew-drenched grass, and his loneliness was eased by the companionship of the sheep. He looked at the woolly sleeping forms with a queer sort of hunger; he would ask nothing better, he thought, than to be their shepherd. Presently he passed a young one that had awakened and was cropping the turf, and he stopped and held out his hand. To his delighted surprise it came quite near to him, jerking an agitated tail, before it suddenly took fright and swerved away. He went on, and found that his feet were now following a path to the summit. Did Stella ever come this way, he wondered, climbing to the yew tree? Quite certainly she did, for the personality of that yew tree would be certain to fascinate a child. He kept closely to the path, thinking how quickly her small feet would run up it, imagining that he saw her going on just ahead of him, her green skirts swaying as she ran, imagining that he heard her singing.

The old yew tree was not tall but it spread its branches widely and its darkness was triumphantly jewelled with tiny red berries. Beneath it a small company of sheep were sleeping among the grey stones that were lying upon the hill-top. They awoke and scattered when he came among them but presently, when he sat down among the tree roots and stayed there motionless, waiting for the full light of the dawn, they came back again, gathering about him as though he were indeed their shepherd. He thrilled to their trust. Knowing nothing about it he felt sure it was not usual for sheep to be so friendly with a stranger. Was there some special beneficence about this tree? Was this space of earth beneath its arms blessed in some way? He felt that it was. One day, if he was ever able to win his way back again, he would find out. Meanwhile it was enough to sit here resting himself in his awareness of the sheep and of the tree, thinking of their mystic significance, remembering a poem his tutor had once read to him, written by St. John of the Cross, that told of the young shepherd who climbed up into the tree above his sheep and died there gladly for love's sake.

The greyness all about him began to thin and shine softly, transfused with light, and then looking round he saw the body of each sheep faintly outlined with silver, while overhead in the yew tree a network of delicate silver spiders' webs suddenly shone out like frosted spray over the old gnarled branches. To the east the sky was washed with silver light that seemed pulsing upward from a bar of molten metal that was the sea. Zachary had watched many wonderful dawns this last fortnight, beginning with the one at the harbour, and all of them had been utterly different, each with its own voice and its own tale to tell, but this one was so piercingly lovely that he could not continue to watch it. He shut his eyes, and when he opened them again for a moment the silver had turned to gold and the gulls were flying inland. Slowly and mightily their bright squadrons soared up out of the eastern light, filling the whole sky, flying so low over the shining yew tree that the beat of their wings overhead was tumultuously loud. It seemed to pull Zachary to his feet, or else the yew tree lifted him. He stretched himself to his full height and raising his arms grasped the branches upon either side, his feet held firmly in the twisting roots. Gently yet strongly the tree held him, and he could have shouted aloud in gladness. Perhaps he did shout; he didn't know. The whole air seemed crashing with music and ablaze with light.

A little later, not knowing how he had come to let go of the yew tree, or the yew tree to let go of him, he limped forward over the grass, wiping his forehead on his tattered sleeve, slightly shaken, and the world was conventionally coloured now, like a child's picture book, and he could take his bearings easily and see which way he should go to reach the sea. He took one look at Weekaborough Farm down below him, and knew it to be the home that he longed for, and one last look at the beneficent yew tree and the friendly sheep, and then went eastward down the hill. It was no good to linger. The more quickly he went the more quickly he would be back.

## II

He struck across country as a dog would have done, climbing over gates and walls, loping across meadows and fording streams, travelling slowly because of his lameness but without pause or hesitation, guiding himself by the sun and by instinct, determined to approach the house, if it existed, from the head of the valley, not from Torquay where he was still afraid to show himself.

He went so slowly that it was nearly mid-day before he reached the hamlet of Barton, and paused to drink from the stream that came through a hole in an orchard wall into a trough set to catch it, and then cascaded away down the side of the steep track that led between the cottages to the wooded valley below. "Is this the Fleete?" he asked an aged man propped against the door-jamb of a cottage. "Ay," said the old man.

Zachary sat down on a stone beside the trough to rest a little. It was queer how easily he had found his stream, how he had known at once that it was the Fleete. It seemed that in adversity he had developed an extra sense, one that he had not known he possessed in the days of ease. It had begun with his mental vision of the ivy-covered house, and his awareness of the dawn that had been the first of the dawns to have a voice for him. And there had been the time in the chapel when all the stones were shouting at him. . . . But from that memory his mind instantly shied away; he could not, would not, face the implications of it. . . . And there had been his instant recognition of the importance of Stella, and then this morning when he stretched up his arms to the beneficent yew tree and the tree had held him and he could have shouted for gladness. It was as though he was learning to reach out beyond the appearances of sun or cloud or stone or tree, beyond those things that he had been accustomed to think of as reality, and to make contact with another reality much more real than they. The adversity had been like a pickaxe battering holes in a wall, and this new sense was bringing with it a new sensitiveness about living, so that he was finding it increasingly easy to judge character, to know what people were thinking, to see beauty in everything about him, even to find the way and foretell the weather. He supposed this was all a normal part of human growth and that it happened to everyone; but that did not make it seem any the less wonderful now that it was happening to him.

He got up again and went on, following the path downhill between slopes thickly wooded with birch and oak, the young Fleete leaping and singing beside him. The trees thinned and the valley seemed blocked by a small conical hill, that shouldered itself up into the sky against the sun so steeply that it was wrapped in shadow as in a purple cloak. The Fleete swerved to the right, taking the curve of the hill, passed through a rocky gorge and then swept round again to the other side of the hill, into a small and lovely amphitheatre set high in the widening valley, looking down over the wooded slopes and the white houses of Torquay half hidden in the trees below. The roar of water sounded in Zachary's ears but it was not a waterfall that he found at the other side but a watermill built close in under the purple hill. He followed the path round to the space of green turf in front of it and stood looking.

The old mill was built of stone below, wood above, had a thatched roof and was overgrown with moss and ivy. To the right was the miller's thatched cottage, to the left was the turning wooden wheel with the water pouring over it and the pond below set among green ferns. The little garden about the cottage was bright with flowers but a mass of weeds, the windows of the mill were grimy, the paint was peeling off the doors and empty bottles bobbed about in the pond; yet there was no suggestion of poverty in the feel of the place but rather a light-hearted carelessness. The lower of the two mill doors, set one above the other in the ivy-covered wall, was open, and from inside came the clicking of the hopper and a man's deep bass voice singing powerfully, the two threads of sound adding themselves to the deep organ tones of the turning wheel and the rush of the falling water to make a loud cheerful symphony of sound that delighted Zachary.

A mill! It was his house all right, but it took him completely by surprise to find it was a mill. He knew nothing about mills but his musician's sense thrilled to the music that was bursting all about him. He went forward to the open door and looked inside and was fascinated even further. It was like the inside of a dim cave, with a succession of wooden galleries linked by a flight of wooden stairs. The air was pervaded by a rich nutty sort of smell and the flour drifted in a fine dust gilded by the sunbeams slanting through the narrow windows. Peering through the gloom Zachary could see the turning stones and the corn running down through the hopper in a shower of gold. On this day of golden sunlight it was all brown and gold, warm and rich, and the dimly seen figures of the huge man and the only slightly less huge boy moving about in the shadows looked less like a miller and his grinder than Vulcan and his satellite fashioning a sword for Siegfried out of the flowing gold.

But it was not the music of Wagner that was being roared forth by the bearded giant, but the old song "Drops of Brandy" that Zachary knew only too well from hearing the sailors singing it at grogtime. But he could not hate it today for the gay old country-dance tune went weaving in and out of the music of the wheel, the water and the hopper, so happily and infectiously that in a moment or two he was singing himself. He had had a fine soprano voice as a boy and he would be a fine tenor in a few years time; at present it was difficult to say what he was, but he had a perfect ear and the sounds he made were clear and true.

"And Johnny shall have a new bonnet
And Johnny shall go to the fair,
And Johnny shall have a new ribbon
To tie up his bonny brown hair.
And why should I not love Johnny
And why should not Johnny love me,
And why should I not love Johnny
As well as another bodie?"

The hopper clicked to a standstill, the golden stream thinned to a few drops and the miller strode over to the door. "Hey, there, lad! An' who may 'ee be, chirping like a cricket on my doorstep without a with-your-leave or by your leave? What do ee want, eh?"

Zachary found that he knew how to behave with this jovial bearded giant of a man. He did not ask humbly for work as he had done at the farms, deprecating, ashamed of his poverty and his rags, he stepped forward in front of the door, feet apart, hands in pockets, head thrown back, dark eyes sparkling. "Well, Sir, it's plain you need another lad about the place," he said gaily, grinning first at the miller and then at the great lout of a boy peering over the miller's shoulder. "One's not enough, it seems." And one of his eyebrows shot up cheekily as he darted a quick glance first at the wild patch of garden and then at the dirty windows of the mill and the doors with the paint peeling off them.

"Worked at a mill afore, eh?" demanded the miller in a voice like the last trump. "Know the work, do ee?"

"Not me!' said Zachary cheerfully. "I've worked on the land, in a sign-painter's establishment and a scrivener's office." He paused for a moment, and in extenuation of the cheerful lie there rose before his mind's eye the exquisite small garden of the Bath square where he had lived, the sunny library where he had learned to read and write and the studio of a distinguished artist where he had once been allowed to play about a bit with canvas and paint. "I can weed your garden, paint your doors, sing tenor to your bass, and learn the work of the mill in a jiffy." He paused dramatically, his eyes going from the far from intellectual face of the miller to the bovine countenance of the loutish boy. "And I can make out your bills for you in a fair hand, and reckon up the price of fifteen bushels of wheat at whatever it is a bushel, and see you're not cheated."

"Who says I'm cheated?" roared the miller in a sudden explosion of fury.

"An unlettered man is always cheated," replied Zachary equably. "A shilling a week, a bed and my food?"

"A shilling a week?" roared the miller. "Dammee! A shilling a week, vittles and bed, for a shameless young dolt still smelling of the gaol?"

Zachary did not contradict the suggestion of gaol; he thought it was a useful red herring.

"A shilling a week and my keep," he said, not cheekily this time, but with quiet determination. Then, his charming smile flashing out over his thin face, he began to sing softly under his breath.

> "Greensleeves was all my joy,
> Greensleeves was my delight;
> Greensleeves was my heart of gold,
> And who but Lady Greensleeves."

"Come on in," said the miller, "an' have a bite of dinner."

III

The deepening dusk of an evening a couple of days later found Zachary lying on a damp and dirty pallet in an attic room of the miller's cottage. Apart from the pallet and a broken chair there was no furniture in the room, for it had not been used until he came. The floorboards were mouldering away in places, the cob walls were patched with damp and the thatched roof was visible through the holes in the ceiling. The miller's wife had died years ago and he and his son lived here alone, no woman ever coming near them to tidy up. The whole house was dirty and this room in particular was a horrible little cobwebbed hole, smelling strongly of mice, its one redeeming feature being the small square of broken window which looked out upon the purple hill that had already become to Zachary his best friend at the Fleete mill. It reminded him of Bowerly Hill above Weekaborough Farm, and in so doing seemed likely to keep him sane. It even had a tree on top of it, not a yew, but an oak, and winding up the slope a path that he could just see from his window. Lying rigidly upon his back on the dirty pallet, covered by a tattered dirty blanket, Zachary stared out of one eye (the other was at present unusable) at the hill, and at the couple of stars that were twinkling above its shoulder, and tried to steady the turmoil of his thoughts against the strength and peace of hill and sky.

For he had to face the fact that life in the Fleete mill was not going to be much more agreeable than life in the cockpit of the ship that he had left. As far as the outward picture of it went his queer vision of the mill had been correct, but the peace and beauty were only in the outward seeming. The miller, Jacob Bronescombe, captivated by his gift of song and his skill as an accountant and secretary, was his friend, but the miller's son Sam was not; and Sam's physical strength was to Zachary as that of an ox to a rabbit's, and his cunning in devising methods of torture very acute. Zachary had already had a couple of fights with Sam behind the mill and had received such punishment at his hands that his face looked like an over-ripe plum and he ached all over; though the fights compared to Sam's other cruelties had been light afflictions. Sam was jealous. This newcomer who could sing all the popular songs, talk like a book, add two and five together and know what they came to, write a fair hand and swill out the kitchen with the skill of a woman, would cut him out with his father, of that he was sure. Sam was not exactly half-witted but he was not very bright at anything except inflicting pain, and he knew it. There was not room in his mind for many ideas; up till now there had only been one, his dog-like adoration of his father; now there was added to it another, hatred of Zachary and determination so to ill-treat him that he would withdraw from the Fleete mill at an early date.

Should he go? Zachary pondered this question as he lay staring out of his one usable eye at those stars twinkling above the strong shoulder of the purple hill. He knew that though the easy-going, not over-bright miller liked him and already found him uncommonly useful he was not going to interfere between him and his son. He was going to leave the two boys to fight it out alone; Zachary had asked to come here and must abide the consequences. Moreover, Jacob had a poor opinion of any lad who could not give a good account of himself in a fight. He himself was a famous wrestler, his name known all over a county famed throughout England for its mighty fighters, and Sam was already following very satisfactorily in his footsteps. A man who could not use his fists was no man at all in his opinion. Zachary must learn or get out.

Those were the two alternatives that faced Zachary. His courage was at a low ebb tonight and the first alternative seemed beyond him. In the navy he'd had about enough of brutality, bruises and dirt. How could he stay here and endure more of it? He was becoming more and more terrified of pain. He wanted cleanliness, peace, kindness and security. He stirred restlessly, groaning a little as his bruises hurt him, even sobbing weakly in the desolation and uncertainty of his mind. He sobbed himself into a stupor, then dozed a bit, only to wake again still sobbing. The moon was rising now and he could dimly see the path twisting up the hill. He looked at it, choking back his sobs in anger at his own childishness, and the effort to regain control seemed to clear his sight a little, so that the path shone out more and more clearly, and suddenly he fancied he saw Stella dancing up it, as he knew she must dance up that other hill, a gay little figure, brave and happy though she was all alone there on the hillside. She looked like a fairy's child, green-gowned, light as thistledown, but there was nothing fairylike about the warm glow of happy courage that came slowly flooding through him as he watched her; her gift to him was an entirely human fortitude, an outflowing of her own gay courage, dancing all alone there under the moon. When he looked again, she was gone; he had only imagined her in a half-dream. But the fortitude remained.

No, he wasn't going to give up, and he knew now how he was going to tackle this problem. He remembered himself in the rigging, lashed there against his will and enduring hell. And he remembered himself in just the same position in the yew-tree; only there he had held out his arms willingly and the tree had upheld him with its strength. Whatever was coming to him at this confounded mill he would give himself willingly to it and endure it to the natural end. He would not force the pace this time. He would not quit.

But as the night wore on, and he lay sleepless and feverish from his bruises, he realised that if the natural end was not to be the breaking of every bone in his body within the next few days he must use his wits. As the hours passed by he thought hard and when the dawn came he had decided what to do. He got up, almost too battered to move, stumbled down the stairs and washed himself at the pump beside the cottage door. Then he went indoors, got the fire going, laid the table for breakfast and by the time the miller and Sam came down had bacon sizzling in the pan. Jacob smacked his lips appreciatively, but Sam glowered, and got in a kick on the shin that made Zachary gasp and all but drop the frying pan.

"Give 'im back as good as he gives ee, lad!" said Jacob irritably.

"I've a better plan than that, Sir," said Zachary, limping to the table with the bacon. "I can't give him back as good as he gives—at present—and you know that—but I've a plan."

"Eh?" said the miller, drawing in his chair.

Over the meal Zachary expounded his plan. Let them both teach him how to wrestle; give him lessons in the noble art. Meanwhile let Sam leave him alone. Then at the next public wrestling match—it was in another month, they'd told him—let Sam and himself fight it out together, man to man, decently and according to the rules. And if Sam got the better of him in the fight, then he'd leave the mill. How was that? Meanwhile, let Sam leave him alone to get on with his work in peace.

Sam's eyes brightened. In another month, in another year, or two days, it would be all the same; in a fight to the finish in the ring he'd batter this puling scarecrow to a mush. But the miller, of the like conviction, looked dubious.

"He'll likely kill ee, lad," he said.

"At the end of a month, if after all your teaching I can't defend myself, then let him kill me," said Zachary. "Meanwhile, let him leave me alone. Is that a bargain?"

And the miller and Sam both said, "Ay, it's a bargain, lad."

# CHAPTER VIII

I

Dr. Crane and Aesculapius were jogging wearily homewards on a Saturday afternoon in October, a typical Devon day, warm, muted and still, veiled in grey cloud but a veil so thin that only in the far distance were colour and outline misted; near at hand the grey was luminous and the green grass burned like fire. The country sounds made a strangely hushed music, as though a mute had been placed upon a violin. Nothing moved except occasionally a yellow leaf, floating slowly down in the still air. Fragrances were especially potent on these days. One late rose would smell as sweetly as a whole bushful in June, smoke seemed incense, and the stray violets that in Devon come into bloom in the shelter of grey walls whatever the season, would give out such a scent that one would look about expecting to see a whole bank carpeted with them; and see nothing at all. These exquisite grey days were often succeeded by a gale, and so had a feeling of fragility and poignancy, and usually the doctor savoured the beauty of them to the last drop, aware of the turmoil that was probably to come, but today he was too tired to be conscious of much except the blessed quiet, and the warmth.

He had been summoned to a village far out of his beat to help another doctor with a difficult confinement. He had been there all night and most of today, and had helped to save two lives. He was glad of that, but not so glad as he would be when he had had a hot bath, a meal and a sleep; then he would be glad indeed for the young wife whom he had saved was much beloved. As a doctor he had seen much of love and always fought like a tiger to save it from the rending of pain and death.

"Love is the divinity who creates peace among men, and calm upon the sea, the windless silence of storms, repose and sleep in sadness. Love sings to all things which live and are, soothing the troubled minds of gods and men." It seemed fitting to speak those words of Agathon upon this calm and peaceful day; just as it had seemed to him fitting that they should have been written on the scrap of paper in Stella's locket. For to his mind they fitted the child Stella. She had, if he was not mistaken, a great gift of love; not troubling passion, but love in the sense of the old word charity, a thing most peaceful, deep and still. And written as they were in Greek, in a fine scholarly hand, they proved to him what he had already guessed, that Stella was the child of cultured parents. He would give a good deal, he thought, to know who they were, and how the young mother had come to be involved in the tragedy of the *Amphion*.

The rest of the glorious passage went on singing itself in his mind. "Yes, love, who showers benignity upon the world, and before whose presence all harsh passions flee and perish; the author of all soft affections; the destroyer of all ungentle thoughts; merciful, mild; the object of the admiration of the wise, and the delight of gods; possessed by the fortunate and desired by the unhappy, therefore unhappy because they possess him not; the father of grace, and delicacy, and gentleness, and delight, and persuasion, and desire; the cherisher of all that is good, the abolisher of all evil; our most excellent pilot, defence, saviour and guardian in labour and fear, in desire and in reason, the ornament and governor of all things human and divine; the best, the loveliest . . ."

Where was he? Bemused with fatigue, and with the hypnotic splendour of the words, he had taken a wrong turning; or rather Aesculapius, unchecked, had taken a wrong turning. Instead of heading for home they were heading for a small hamlet close to Torre Abbey. The doctor pulled Aesculapius to a standstill in some indignation.

"It was my belief, after all our years together, that you could be trusted to take me straight home when a job of work was completed," he growled. "What's the matter with you? About turn."

But Aesculapius refused to turn. He jerked his head free and moved forward again. Once more the doctor reined him in and once more he moved forward.

"Have it your own way," conceded the doctor. "But if I'm not wanted at the village when we get there, if this is some wild goose chase you're leading me, there'll be no bran mash for you this night."

He spoke with vexation and sighed wearily, yet he did not force Aesculapius. He knew the sure instinct of a wise old horse, far more highly developed than that of a man; even of a doctor or priest whose professional antennæ are kept perpetually quivering and outstretched by the pull of so much need.

The narrow lane down which Aesculapius had brought him branched into a wider one and he found himself part of what was for this country neighbourhood quite a stream of traffic; a couple of gigs, a wagon piled full of country folk, a dozen yokels on foot and innumerable dogs. "What's toward?" he demanded of one of the gigs.

"Wrestlin' match, Sir."

"Wrestling?" said the doctor, and his weariness suddenly forgotten he settled his hat more firmly on his head and permitted Aesculapius to carry him forward at a brisk pace. The wrestling of the Devon men was rather a brutal sport, entailing physical damage of which professionally it was his duty to disapprove, yet as a Devonian born and bred he could not but take a pride in the traditional skill and courage of his countrymen. And, in these days of war, it was good training.

When he reached the village green the match had already been in progress for some time and the crowd of men and boys, and women and girls too, was compact about the four sides of the roped-off hollow square of grass that was the ring. But his gig was a high one and pulled up behind the thinnest part of the crowd made an excellent grandstand. Aesculapius, having reached the end of his instinctive journey, stood like a rock.

II

The roped-off ring was about twenty yards in diameter and within it, watching the wrestling, were the three triers, or conductors of the lists, men of great experience in the art, intent upon the keeping of the rules and the honour of a great occasion. They decided all disputes immediately and without appeal. One of them, the doctor knew, would be in possession of the purse of perhaps six or eight pounds subscribed by persons of property in the neighbourhood, which would be presented to the winner at the close of the match. The wrestling began usually in the early afternoon and went on sometimes until dusk, the excitement increasing when the lanterns were lit and the crowd leaned over the ropes lynx-eyed to see fair play.

The rules were simple, but they had to be kept, and roars of fury greeted any slightest infringement of them. The wrestlers might take hold anywhere above the waistband but not below it. They might kick below the knee until blood streamed and bones were broken, but they must not kick above it. . . . The men from Dartmoor were especially feared, for they kicked like the devil, and when kicked themselves their endurance passed belief. . . . At the outset of the match every man who twice in succession threw another man upon his back, belly or side became a standard for the purse. When the number of these men had been reduced to eight they each received a crown. Then these eight fought it out until the bitter end, until only one remained. To be one of the eight was accounted a great honour. To be the winner was to be held in greater honour in the neighbourhood than the king himself.

The doctor settled himself comfortably, with pleasurable anticipation. It was a perfect day for the great game; no sun to dazzle the fighters, no cold wind to nip the spectators, and everywhere that lovely deepening of colour that was the day's special gift. No matching an English crowd for good-humoured, sensible gaiety, thought the doctor, glancing at the rosy country faces, and the bright gowns and cloaks. Many of the gigs and wagons had bunches of flowers tied to them, or rosettes of coloured ribbon. As far as the doctor could see there was not a single anxious shadow upon any face. They were at war, and might be invaded by the enemy next week, but with the happy if exasperating capacity of the English for refusing to contemplate disaster until the final moment, they were not sparing a thought for that. And however the wrestling went today there would be no rancour or hysteria. There would be no questioning the decisions of the triers and no bitterness in defeat. And no kicking of a man when he was down, either. The injured and defeated would be so tenderly cared for that they would collect almost as much glory as the final eight.

And by gad, thought the doctor, running his eye over the wrestlers, here was a fine bunch of young men for you! Where else in the world would you see such broad shoulders, such strength and muscle? And that in time of war, when so many men were in the services. And where a fellow lacked physical strength he made up for it by agility and skill, like that dark-haired boy there, slim as a hazelwand yet wiry, with more strength in his arms than you'd expect, and using his feet so cleverly that he'd not been thrown yet; though he was scarcely the type for this sport and was not likely, the doctor thought, to stay the course for long. Fine young fellow, though.

Gradually the doctor's interest and attention became focused upon him, to the exclusion of others. Who was he? Not a country yokel. He had a thoroughbred air that touched the doctor so deeply that more and more his consciousness was centred painfully upon the boy; almost in his own body he could feel the labouring of his lungs beneath the aching ribs; feel the thrill of fear that came with the consciousness of ebbing strength, and the courage that mounted with such desperate effort to subdue it. Dammee, but he liked the fellow's face with its startling contrasts; the sensitiveness of it with the delicate lips and flaring nostrils like those of a startled horse, and then the broad thinker's forehead, the obstinate jaw and sombre eyes beneath thick dark eyebrows. He was down! No, he was not. He'd saved himself by that clever footwork. Down? Not he. He'd thrown his man, thrown him flat on his back with as neat a twist of his wiry arms as a man could wish to see. He was one of the honoured eight now, and he'd won the honour with as fine a display of skill and courage as any the doctor could recollect. He found himself cheering like a youngster, the last of his fatigue forgotten in delight.

There was a pause now. The eight received their crowns, put on their coats and rested themselves, surrounded by admiring friends. But the dark boy appeared to have no friends. He waited alone. The doctor noticed that the ragged coat that he slung round his shoulders was several sizes too large and looked as though it had been bought for the price of a drink from some old clothes pedlar, but that he possessed what few of the others had, and that was a fine cambric handkerchief, not a man's handkerchief but a woman's, small and white. But he did not use it, he took it out of his pocket, looked at it for a moment, folded it carefully and put it away again, as though it possessed great value for him. Suddenly the doctor remembered Stella's young vagabond Zachary, the boy from the moon, and the handkerchief she had given him. He had promised himself to look out for Zachary, and at first he had done so, but had forgotten him again as the weeks passed and no boy in the least like Stella's description came his way. Was this the fellow?

His scrutiny was now so intense that Zachary felt it and looked his way. Their eyes met and the doctor smiled, and there was in his smile such extraordinary tenderness that he might have been a father smiling at his son. Zachary's face, that had been white with exhaustion, flushed scarlet. His lips parted, and his eyes clung to the doctor's as the eyes of his patients so often did, when it seemed that in him lay their only hope. As with his patients, so with Zachary, the doctor tried to infuse his own confidence and courage into the steadiness of his answering look. Then abruptly Zachary looked away, closed his lips, relaxed his tensed muscles and waited quietly, the hand that had replaced the handkerchief still in his pocket, holding it. The doctor too relaxed and waited until the wrestling started again; and it seemed to him that all that the boy was feeling of fear and exhaustion he felt too.

He understood the fear when he saw Zachary confronting that great lout of a fellow Sam Bronescombe. In the moment or two before they closed with each other Zachary stood quite still, while Sam moved from side to side with the prowling movement of a wild beast, but in the intensity of the one and the restlessness of the other the doctor was aware of the same deadly purpose; these two had come here to fight each other and they meant their fight to decide more than their relative strength and skill. The doctor stood up, and he felt as anxious as at the crisis of a pneumonia case. Sam Bronescombe! All Zachary's intelligence and skill would not avail him against that brutal young lout with his ox-like strength and the Dartmoor toughness in his legs. The doctor tried to add his shouts of encouragement to those of the rest of the spectators, but only a croak would issue from his aching throat.

Zachary kept going longer than the doctor would have thought possible, though the blood ran down his shins and nearly all the breath in his thin body must have been squeezed out of him by Sam's brawny arms. But he lost his footing at last and with a savage twist Sam whirled him round and flung him brutally upon his back. He lay still where he had been flung, looking like some long-legged dead bird upon the grass, a heron or a stork who had been shot upon the wing and fallen untidily, but his stillness had scarcely become ominous before the doctor had jumped from his gig and was beside him.

"Get back, you fools!" he said angrily to the crowd that had collected, and knelt to examine the boy with hands that for the first time in his doctor's career were not entirely steady. Something of his own anxiety communicated itself to the onlookers; they were quite silent as he made his brief examination and they echoed his quick sigh of relief with quite a gale of gusty good fellowship.

"No more than stunned, as far as I can see at present," said the doctor, standing up. Then his eyes, falling upon Sam, where he stood in the attitude of a conquering and most self-satisfied hero, blazed with a fury so sudden and alarming that Sam positively fell back a pace. "But no thanks to you, you young brute! You fought fair but you flung to kill. If you win the purse, my lad, I wish you no joy of it."

He stooped and lifted Zachary in his long immensely strong arms as though he were a feather weight, hardly knowing what he meant to do with him; just to get him out of this. He looked grotesque enough, with his bow legs and bowed shoulders, holding the gawky boy, yet no one laughed and a tall thin man with a cold colourless face, severely dressed in black, who stood watching, was suddenly poignantly reminded of something; some scene that he had seen somewhere, some scene in a tragedy. What was it? He snapped his fingers. He had it. King Lear, with his dead child in his arms. Instantly he stepped forward, roused to helpful action as only the memory of bereavement could rouse him.

"The cottage where I lodge is exactly behind you, Sir," he said to Dr. Crane in his beautiful, incisive voice.

The doctor followed him, still conscious of nothing at all except the boy in his arms. Aesculapius followed too, bumping the gig over the rough grass, and conscious of certain human affairs now brought to a happy conclusion by his own personal intervention he thrust his head over the low fence of the cottage garden and chewed contentedly at a succulent bush within.

III

Zachary, coming painfully back to consciousness to find himself flat on a table in a book-lined study that smelled deliciously of hot coffee, with the doctor attending with conscientious thoroughness to the condition of his legs, was dimly aware of being in the presence of two of the most singular-looking elderly gentlemen he had ever set eyes on. Then, the doctor's ministrations being quite extraordinarily painful, he shut his eyes again, gritted his teeth, groped with his hands for the edges of the table and took no further notice of them for the moment. Yet through the singing in his ears and the buzzing in his head he heard a very astonishing question and answer pass between them.

"Your son, Sir?" enquired the beautifully modulated voice, with its slightly foreign inflection.

"Never set eyes on him till today," growled the deep-toned rich voice with its west-country burr. "But after today I should say, most probably —my son."

Zachary was unable to puzzle this out; he had all he could do at the moment holding on to the edges of the table and keeping still. Yet he felt there was some vague comfort in the last remark; and in the rest of the talk that flowed over his head, though it did not concern him, there was comfort too; the comfort of familiarity.

"You've the first edition, so I notice," said the deep voice. "I recognise that binding. Were you personally acquainted with the Doctor?"

"I had the honour of meeting him once or twice in London," said the voice that was like music. "A profound scholar. Without doubt your greatest man of letters in this generation—and that a generation which has produced Swift, Goldsmith, Addison and Pope. Now that you have applied those bandages Cordelia should be more comfortable. I should suggest transferring your child to the settle. The coffee pot is boiling."

"Cordelia!" ejaculated the deep voice indignantly. "The boy may have a girlishly delicate appearance, but, dammee, he fights like a man!"

"Nothing personal was intended, Sir," said the other voice courteously. "The spectacle of you with the boy in your arms reminded me of that poignant scene. You remember?" And he quoted with a strange depth of feeling that silenced the doctor, "'. . . she lives. If it be so, it is a chance which does redeem all sorrows that ever I have felt'."

Shakespeare! How long since he had heard Shakespeare quoted, Zachary wondered? There was healing in the sound of the words, and in the feel of those strong arms lifting him, and the feel of the cushioned settle. And then he was gulping hot coffee and was in partial possession of his wits again. Yet he was still highly bewildered. Who was he now? Anthony? Zachary? Cordelia? Was he to begin life all over again for the third time? But he did not want to be Cordelia, who had nothing to do with Stella. Zachary had. Therefore he must remain Zachary.

"I'm Zachary," he said.

The doctor nodded reassuringly, pulling up a chair beside the settle. "I know. Zachary Moon. My name is Crane. I'm a crusty bachelor doctor, living alone. Is there any reason, Zachary, why you should not come home with me and pay me a visit?"

"I don't think so, Sir," said Zachary. He was silent a moment, puzzling it out, trying to remember if he belonged anywhere now, and if so, where. "No. I don't think I belong anywhere. I was at the mill, working for Jacob Bronescombe. He liked me, but Sam didn't. I told Sam that if he threw me today I'd clear out."

"Then you've cleared out," said the doctor. "Good. Now keep still and sort out your addled wits while I take a stroll round his bookshelves with our host. Then we'll drive home."

Zachary couldn't take it in and did not try. He merely knew it was all right. He lay for a little with his eyes shut. Then he opened them and gazed in astonishment at the two men facing each other at the other side of the room, deep in talk, precious volumes in their hands, two infatuated scholars who seemed not to have met before but whose mutual love of learning had now apparently made them friends. They were so entirely different, the one broad-shouldered, heavy, short, bow-legged and hunch-backed, the other tall, graceful and thin, that the contrast between them would have been ludicrous had not each man possessed his own tempered and impressive quality. Both these men had obviously suffered much, and suffered it in such manner that to the outward eye one was now rock and the other steel. No one, now, would be likely to get the better of either of these men; no one would be likely to dare to try.

Yet Zachary felt no fear of the doctor with his great strength, growling voice and almost grotesque deformity, only reverence and a quite astonishing affection. He would not forget, as long as he lived, the moment in the ring when he had looked round and met the doctor's eyes. The tenderness in the man's brown weatherbeaten face had been like spring water gushing out of a rock, and like water it had refreshed Zachary. Why should a stranger look at him like that, as though he mattered? He did not know; but the mere fact that in this harsh world a stranger could feel for a stranger an almost divine compassion was an earnest to him that the world might not after all be quite as harsh as he had thought it was. He had been sickeningly afraid, hopeless and discouraged before. Afterwards, though knowing quite well what the outcome of the fight with Sam would be, he had felt strong and serene.

The other man, at first sight, lacked the doctor's compassion. His appearance reminded Zachary of certain aristocratic emigrés whom he had known in Bath, and for this reason, half Frenchman that he was himself, his heart warmed to him, even though in the man's colourless coldness there was nothing to attract warmth. He looked a prematurely aged man. His thin hair, receding at the temples, immaculately brushed and tied with a black ribbon, was white. His thin, tight-lipped, fine-featured face was the colour of parchment and stamped with a reserve so icy, a control so hard, that it was difficult to think of it relaxing or softening into any human weakness or tenderness. The only softness about him was the grace of his tall spare figure and the beauty of his voice. He was severely dressed in black, with a meticulously folded plain white stock. His dress was that of a savant, but the set of his head and shoulders was almost military. His hands were well-shaped and looked surprisingly youthful and strong in contrast with his face. Zachary had the feeling that he had seen him before, but in his dazed condition he could not remember where.

Yet at the moment of departure this ice-man surprised Zachary so much that he could scarcely collect himself to say good-bye politely. While the doctor carried his bag out to his gig it was he who came to Zachary, helped him to his feet and steadied him with an arm about him. The feel of the arm was surprising in the first place; it was strong and there was a goodwill in the feel of it that almost equalled the doctor's. Zachary looked up gratefully, responding to kindliness as a flower to the sun, and met the glance of a pair of unusually bright grey eyes. Then the man smiled, and it was as though light broke from his face. If the breaking out of the doctor's hidden compassion was like spring water gushing out of a rock the breaking out of this man's inner light made one think of a rapier flashed in the sun. Zachary blinked. When he dared to look again the rapier was back in the sheath and the man's face was as before, set hard in its icy reserve. He felt shaken. It was his first experience of that transfiguration which can take place when something, someone, touches the spring which releases a great man's hidden quality. It did not occur to Zachary, either then or later, that it might have been something in himself that had touched the spring. He did not know yet that in constant evocation and response, and in them only, lie the elements of spiritual growth.

They were half-way down the garden path and the doctor, stowing his gear in the gig, was not attending to them. "Zachary," said the man, "you and I have seen each other before, I think. Do you remember? In the chapel of St. Michael. I hope very much that we shall meet again one day."

Zachary nodded, speechless. Aesculapius, regarding them benevolently between his blinkers, looked extremely smug.

# CHAPTER IX

## I

THE doctor was no pamperer of the young, far from it, but he put Zachary to bed and kept him there for a few days. Zachary had no objection. If he moved his legs hurt, his head ached, and he felt more tired than he had known one could feel, so he lay still and slept, rousing only when Tom Pearse woke him up by jabbing a horny thumb into his painful ribs and thrusting a tray with something to eat or drink beneath his nose, or when the doctor came to attend to his legs. Yet in spite of his sleepiness he found himself becoming aware of his surroundings, with no sense of unfamiliarity or vagueness but with that comforting sense of reality, almost of recognition, which comes when what is about us is what we want and can accept as part of ourselves. No more, now, of that exhausting never-ending struggle to hold off from himself the pressure of alien horrors. There was nothing about him now, either spiritual or material, from whose contact he need shrink, and every strained nerve in his body seemed separately to relax, to leave off jumping and twanging, to sit down quietly and take a rest.

His room was a small one over the porch. The truckle bed was narrow and hard, there was the minimum of furniture and no pictures on the whitewashed walls, but it was all scrupulously clean, and the coarse white sheets smelt of the rosemary bushes upon which they had been spread to dry. The blue and white check curtains swung at the open window and through it came the country sounds, the wind in the trees, the patter of rain, the church clock striking, the clip-clop of horses' hoofs, the crowing of cocks and the voices of little children. There were good clean smells in the house; baking bread, the doctor's antiseptics and tobacco, Tom Pearse's furniture polish and yellow soap.

Tom Pearse himself might have been a jarring note, for only half a glance out of one eye would have convinced any observer that he was a seaman, had been one and would continue one until his last hour, however many years he might continue for love of the doctor to perambulate upon dry land. He was a true bluejacket, a fine and rather rare type in these days of the press gang, "every hair a rope yarn, every tooth a marline spike, every finger a fish-hook and his blood right good Stockhollum tar." He had round bright blue eyes set in a crumpled clean-shaven face with a purplish pock-marked nose and a large smiling toothless mouth, permanently half-moon shape with good humour. He still dressed as a seaman in long loose blue trousers flapping comfortably round his feet, a short round blue jacket with brass buttons and a canary waistcoat. He wore his grey hair in a pigtail and walked with a rolling gait. Yet seaman though he was Zachary accepted him as being not of the past but of the present, for the good humour in which he was steeped like a cherry in sugar was of this life, not of that; it might have been met with upon other happier ships but it had not existed upon his. So he liked Tom Pearse and his liking was reciprocated. Tom, in his sea days, had been gunner, he had looked after the "younkers," kept their clothes in order, and catered for them. He was a born mother, and without jealousy. It was a delight to have "a young gennelman" to care for again.

Zachary woke up one evening rather suddenly just at twilight, with no pain in his head and a very clear mind. He lay for a little, thinking. The doctor was out, he knew, and Tom was working in the garden, just below his window. He sat up slowly, moved his still painful legs cautiously from under the covers and sat on the side of the bed; a comical figure in the doctor's befrilled nightshirt.

"Tom!" he shouted, "what did you do with my clothes?"

"Clothes?" yelled Tom, and spat contemptuously. "Did ye call them rags ye come in clothes? I wouldn't have demeaned the kitchen floor by washing it over with 'em. They're burnt."

"Well, I want to get up. What shall I put on?"

There was a pause in the rhythmical thud of Tom's spade and Zachary could picture him scratching his ear in some bewilderment. Then he came stumping indoors and up the stairs to his own little room in the attic. Presently he reappeared with his painted black canvas kit bag slung over his shoulders. "It ain't no manner of use riggin' ye up in the doctor's clothes, with him so short in the leg and broad in the shoulder as he be, an' ye a ganglin' scarecrow of a lad all leg an' no beam. But here's me best shore-going-slops wot I 'ad in the navy afore I put on weight. 'Tisn't every lad as I could abide to see struttin' around in me shore slops, but ye're a good lad an' I'll be proud to lend 'em to ye."

He opened his kitbag and a most astonishing assortment of brilliant garments tumbled out. The men in Zachary's ship had been poor pressed men, dressed in just anything that had come to hand in the purser's slop chest, and Zachary had had no idea what a variety of garments could be collected by a dressy old seaman of long service and artistic taste, who had preferred to spend his money when ashore in a foreign port on dress rather than grog or women. White duck trousers, striped blue and white trousers, a red shirt, a white shirt, a spotted shirt, a spotted waistcoat, a striped waistcoat and one of scarlet keyseymere. Jackets of blue and yellow. Stockings of good white silk and black shoes with big silver buckles. A low tarpaulin hat with a black ribbon dangling from it, bearing the proud word *Agamemnon*, a painted straw hat with ribbons falling rakishly over the left eye, a beaver hat, a tam-o'-shanter and a fur cap. And three large handkerchiefs, red, yellow and green, for twisting round the head as a turban, and two of fine black silk for wearing round the neck. Zachary gasped.

"Admiral Nelson liked us smart," said Tom with tender reminiscences, laying them on the bed. "There, now, lad. Take your pick."

But Zachary in his weakened state felt incapable of making a selection and Tom arrayed him as a mother her child in a white shirt, with collar open at the neck in the Byronic manner, a black silk handkerchief knotted round the throat, white duck trousers, scarlet waistcoat, blue coat, white silk stockings and buckled shoes. Those glories hung rather loosely on Zachary, but a belt round the waist kept them tethered, and when Tom had polished the shoes, and applied the doctor's hairbrushes to Zachary's rough head until it ached worse than ever, he was highly satisfied with the result of fifteen minutes' hard labour.

"Ye've no looks to mention but ye look a gennelman," he conceded. "An' I'll lay the supper in the dinin' parlour."

Zachary went rather shakily downstairs to the doctor's study and sat there waiting in the chair facing the windows. He had seen this room only once before, on the night of his arrival, but had scarcely noticed it then. Now he sat taking it all in, the books, the engravings of the doctor's heroes, the neatness, cleanliness and peace, and wondering painfully if he had really heard the doctor say a few nights ago, "After today—my son." Well, he'd soon know.

He heard the gig drive up, Tom go out to take Aesculapius to his stable, and then the doctor's firm footfall in the hall. With his heart beating like a sledgehammer he stood up and bowed. The doctor's hand came down kindly on his shoulder. "Hey, lad! And what made you get up?"

"I was able, Sir," said Zachary.

"Good. Now I'll go and change and have a wash and then we'll eat. I missed dinner altogether and I'm hungry as a hunter. After the meal we'll talk. By gad, look at you in Tom's shore slops!"

Tom had been determined that the occasion should do justice to his slops. He had put four lighted candles on the round mahogany table in the panelled dining parlour, and two on the mantel piece, and cooked an unusually appetising meal. The doctor came down in his best blue coat, a fresh flower in his buttonhole and his eyeglass in his eye, and opened a bottle of Madeira and another of port. During the meal he kept the talk flowing upon politics and the arts, and Zachary did his best to keep his end up, though the Madeira went instantly to his head and the port to his legs, and the sight of the candlelight reflected in the beautiful panelling, the gleam of silver and the luxury of a white napkin, brought back his Bath home so vividly and reduced him to such a state of nostalgia that he could hardly keep his hands from shaking. But he kept his shoulders braced and his voice steady and was thankful to see that the doctor did not seem to be observing him as he talked and ate.

There was not a thing about him that the doctor did not observe; his good and easy manners, his considerable intelligence, his eager yet humble mind that was already sufficiently well-informed to know that it knew nothing, his distress and his determined mastery of it. He felt the same sort of delight that he had felt when the little Stella stood upon his doorstep and demanded to be told about Trygaeus. There was quality here; good malleable stuff ready for the punching into shape that it was his delight to give. And in the case of Zachary he was conscious that there was something more, a hunger crying out to his hunger. It seemed too much to hope that this boy was fatherless; though in that cottage after the wrestling he had felt for the moment convinced of it. Of all the denials with which in his youth his physical deformity had confronted him the hardest of all to endure had been the denial of marriage and fatherhood. He could remember as though it were yesterday the sickening frustration and despair with which he had seen first one woman and then another turn with shrinking from his proferred love; and in those days the very sight of children had been a torment. He was annoyed to see that he had spilt his wine. Zachary, he noticed, had not done so. The boy had controlled emotion better than he had; and that though it was obvious he had a weak head for his drink.

They went back to the study, where Tom had lit the candles and kindled a fire of applewood and pinecones in the basket grate, and pulled up the chairs to the fragrant blaze. Zachary tried to take the cushionless chair but the doctor motioned him to the comfortable one. "I'm used to this one," he said, as he filled his pipe. And tamping down his tobacco he smiled a little, remembering the ridiculous austerities that he had practised so desperately in his youth. "I keep under my body and bring it into subjection." The hard chairs, the straw mattress, the plain food, the water instead of wine, the struggle to turn towards the things of the intellect a nature almost wholly attracted by the things of the body. Well, he'd won the fight. There was no sensual hunger that he had not conquered now except the hunger for a child; and that was not a wholly sensual hunger, somewhere about it there was the creativeness of the artist and the selfless love of God. What was this boy's particular demon, he wondered? Not the sensual demon, that was clear from the natural austerity that showed itself already in his face. Something else. Something that tore with equal savagery at the stuff of his soul and nearly broke his heart.

The doctor lit his pipe and puffed at it, watching the boy. Zachary, now that the momentary inebriation caused by one small glass of Madeira and a thimbleful of port, had subsided, was feeling the better for a good meal and the warmth of the fire. But he did not sit relaxed in his comfortable chair, he sat stiffly, his hands clasped between his knees, nerving himself to say something. Then he said it.

"Thank you, Sir, for your goodness. I am quite well now. I must not encroach any longer upon your hospitality."

"Where were you thinking of going, boy?" asked the doctor. "Have you a home?"

"No, Sir. But I am perfectly capable of finding employment for myself. I found it before."

There was a touch of defiance in the tone that made the doctor smile, though he liked it. "Yes, you did. At the mill. But I doubt if that was exactly suitable employment for a fellow of your type. I have a suggestion to make, Zachary. There is a spare room in this bachelor establishment. I like the company of boys. So does Tom. Stay here until we find some employment more suited to you than working a hopper. And even then, if you have no home of your own, you might like to look upon this house as not such a bad imitation. Got any parents living?" He put the query casually, blowing smoke rings, but never in his life had he waited more anxiously for an answer to a question, and when Zachary shook his head he could have shouted in his joy at the early demise of a probably most excellent couple. "Well then, you might look on me as a father for as long as you have any use for the commodity."

So he *had* heard aright in the cottage. Zachary flushed scarlet to the roots of his hair. His throat swelled and choked him as completely as a quinsy. He clasped and unclasped his hands and could not look at the doctor. Yet he must look at him. He must say something. He turned his head somehow, their eyes met and the doctor knew what was Zachary's particular demon. Hundreds of times as a doctor had he seen that particular look in the eyes, when a man or woman was suddenly released from fear, but never so nakedly revealed as now.

"No need to thank me, boy," he said easily. "If your need was great, so was mine, and I've no doubt we'll shake down together very comfortably. You can tell me what you like about yourself when you like, or not at all, just as it pleases you. You'll find me a crusty old bachelor to live with, I'm afraid, but at least I'll always respect your reserve."

"I'd like to tell you everything now, Sir," said Zachary. "I would rather there was nothing that you did not know."

"Very well then," said the doctor, and he leaned back in his chair, stuck his feet on the fender and opened to Zachary, as to so many before him in this room, the comforting depth of his comprehending silence.

Stumblingly at first, then with growing confidence as he sensed with what absolute justice the doctor was taking his halting sentences and building them up into the complete picture that would be his judgement, Zachary told his story. He told the bare facts, neither exaggerating the cruelty of others nor his own suffering, making no excuses for himself, trying to match the doctor's justice with his own. "I——deserted," he said, and only the agonising little pause between the two words told the doctor that he knew now, if he had not known then, that that had been a battle that his demon had won.

There were only two parts of the story where the doctor's intuition was aware of something that had not been told. Some experience had come to the boy in the chapel, and again on Bowerley Hill, which his inexperience was incapable of describing. Perhaps he would be wise never to attempt to describe them; these experiences of adolescence, these first tentative apprehensions of eternal values, seemed only ridiculous when put into words; yet in the shaping of his destiny nothing that ever happened to a man had a greater importance.

There was a third reservation, but this time only a partial one; Zachary was not able to tell the doctor exactly what Stella meant to him. For one thing, she seemed too precious to be talked about, and for another he scarcely understood himself what had happened between him and Stella. Yet the doctor understood well enough, and understanding felt for Zachary a deep respect; for a boy or young man who could so fall in love with a little girl was a man whose love would never be time's fool. It had not been so with himself, he remembered grimly; his first love had been for a lady of mature charms and had been wholly of the senses. He remembered how Stella had grieved for Zachary; was probably still grieving for him. The boy must have set his impress upon her very deeply, perhaps so deeply that little girl though she was no other image would ever wholly efface it. "Let me not to the marriage of true minds admit impediment." He'd do his best, but in the confusion of times such as these, cruel times of danger and war, the slow growths of love were apt to be torn up by the roots before they could come to flower. . . . The story was done and he sighed a little, the anxiety of the deep love of fatherhood already heavy upon him.

Zachary's anxiety, as he waited for the doctor to speak, was of a different sort. The old man's silence had told him exactly what the doctor thought of his act of desertion. What would he do if told he must go back to the navy? His mind baulked. As in the chapel, his soul seemed full again of that defiant shouting, "I can't do it, I tell you. It is not possible. Flesh and blood cannot endure it. I tell you flesh and blood cannot endure it." Had he shouted aloud? He gripped his hands together and the sweat ran down his temples.

"Is there anything that you would especially like to do, Zachary?" asked the doctor gently.

Zachary relaxed a little; apparently he had not shouted aloud. "Yes, Sir. I'd like to be a shepherd at Weekaborough Farm."

The doctor was startled. This intelligent boy a farm labourer? Well, perhaps he knew best what was good for him just at this juncture. Out there on the hill with the sheep he'd find quiet and healing; and that he must undoubtedly have before he could once more come to grips with his demon.

"But I understand, Zachary, that your services have already been somewhat violently rejected by Farmer Sprigg?"

Zachary grinned. His relief that the doctor made not the slightest suggestion of his returning to the navy was so overwhelming that he felt quite light-headed. "Yes, Sir. But I was dressed like a scarecrow then."

"And now, in Tom Pearse's shore slops, you look like a moulting macaw."

"Perhaps, Sir—" suggested Zachary tentatively.

"Very well, lad. Tomorrow we'll drive to town and fit you out in a manner likely to impress Farmer Sprigg, and then you can try your luck again. And now as your medical adviser, I suggest bed—though as your father I'd prefer to keep you here till midnight."

Zachary got up, looked at the doctor, tried to find words, failed to achieve anything except, "Good-night, Sir," bowed and left the room. Dr. Crane sat silently for some while, the boy's eyes and his face still vividly before him. He smiled as he pulled at his pipe, profoundly contented. Capricious fortune took it into her head sometimes to lay upon a wound a salve of such value that a man became positively glad of the wound. . . . Had he been able to choose his son, he thought, he would have had him in no wise different; and not every father whose son was bone of his bone and flesh of his flesh could say the same. . . . But no, he did not believe in capricious fortune but in a carefully woven pattern where every tightly stretched warp thread of pain laid the foundation for a woof thread of joy.

II

For some while now there had been a bit of disagreeableness going on at Weekaborough Farm, and a few days later it came to a climax. It concerned the musical obstinacy of Jack Crocker, the ploughboy, one of whose duties it was to sing counter-tenor to Sol's bass in the beautiful chant which animated the Weekaborough oxen when they pulled the plough. Jack could not sing the chant correctly, and what was worse, he would not try. It was not that he lacked music in his soul; he could whistle "Drops of Brandy" as true as a blackbird, and when he sang "Spanish Ladies" to the pigs the noise in Pizzle Meadow was almost deafening. But that strange old musical ploughing chant was somehow inimical to him. He said it gave him the belly-ache. Jack was of the earth, earthy, and the strange stirrings in his inner man that took place when Sol laid his hands upon the plough, lifted his seamed old face to the sky and began to sing, gave him no pleasure. He located them, incorrectly, as in his belly, and his spirit rising in revolt within him he either refused to sing at all or out of deliberate malice sang flat. He was a tiresome boy altogether, urban as well as carnal-minded, and had frequently expressed a desire to go to Plymouth and work in his uncle's butcher's shop. Told by the perpetually exasperated Father Sprigg to blast his eyes and go there, he nevertheless stayed where he was. He liked the pigs, he said; and he was indeed very handy with the pigs, also carnal-minded creatures, and partly for that reason was kept on. But chiefly he was kept on because the Sprigg family, like all Devonians, were deeply enrutted folk. They liked to go on as they always had gone on. Any change, they felt, was bound to be for the worse.

Sol, unlike Father Sprigg, bore with Jack's delinquencies with infinite patience and good humour except just in this one matter of the chant; and in this one instance he beat even Father Sprigg in the power of his wrath and his profanity in expression of the same. Indeed at ploughing times Father and Mother Sprigg, Madge and Stella, got very anxious, for it could not be good for such an old man to get so very angry.

"It'll settle itself one of these fine days," Mother Sprigg would say comfortably; and upon a beautiful morning in the middle of October it settled itself once and for all.

There had been a week of wind and rain following the grey still day of the wrestling match, and then a good drying wind, and now the half-acre field on the slope of Tafferty Hill was in exactly the right condition to be harrowed for the sowing of the autumn crop of winter oats. The beautiful oxen, Moses and Abraham, were harnessed to the equally beautiful plough, the zewl, made twenty years ago by the Gentian Hill carpenter, a man famed for miles round for the splendour of his craftsmanship, and the little party of two oxen, one old man and one young boy set out for Tafferty Hill; watched with some misgiving by Mother Sprigg and Madge, for there was that in Jack's wickedly gleaming black eyes and Sol's grimly set old mouth that seemed to presage trouble. But Stella, though she also noticed Jack's eyes and Sol's mouth, had a heart within her like a singing bird. She had been kept at home for more than a week by the wet weather and a streaming cold, and now it was a beautiful morning and her cold was gone. The behaviour of her heart kept her perpetually a-jig upon her toes as she helped Mother Sprigg make the beds, her eyes were sparkling and her dimples peeping, and suddenly abandoning all attempt at decorum she flung Father Sprigg's goose-feather pillow into the centre of the bedroom floor and turned a somersault upon it.

"For gracious sakes!" ejaculated Mother Sprigg.

Zachary meanwhile was coming up the hill from the village most suitably attired in breeches, leather gaiters and rough frieze coat, with his hair cut short and one of Tom's less spectacular shirts open at the neck. He whistled as he walked but he did not feel quite as confident as he sounded. He had said to himself that he would go away from Weekaborough, and then come back, and he had done, was doing, just that; yet he knew in his heart that the small journey he had taken was not sufficient to have earned him any sort of permanent return. This was no more than that far glimpse of the Delectable Mountains that Christian had seen before he went down in to the valley to fight with Apollyon.

He reached the top of the hill, and the great Danmonian fence that was the boundary of Father Sprigg's land upon the north. He went through the gate and stood looking down upon the Weekaborough valley, and away to the moors upon the west and the sea upon the east, as Stella and Sol had done. The season was more advanced now and there was a cool nip in the west wind that was driving the white clouds like flocks across the sky, with their shadows racing beneath them over the fields. Yet the beauty was as great as before and Zachary, taking great gulps of the life-giving wind, feeling it reach right through his clothes and caress his skin with its coolness, gave a sudden shout of triumph. Oh God, the freedom of it! To be able to shout when you wanted to shout, to feel health pouring back into a strengthening body and climb the hills on feet that were healed and swift. And if this joy were only fleeting, what of it? He would live in the moment, as the gulls did, and shout as they did for joy of the sun and the wind.

There was a flock of them wheeling just down the hill to his left, their wings flashing in the sun and the wind catching their strong voices so that their crying soared now loud, now soft, above the chanting that mingled with the faint bell-like jungling of harness. This music was so attuned to the spirit of the hour that Zachary was conscious of it at first only as part of the natural music of earth itself; of the music of the wind and the swaying branches, the stirring grasses and the rustling leaves. Then it swelled and drew nearer, and he was conscious of it as something supernatural, something that awed him to complete silence and stillness, even as the chanting of the mass had done, and the ringing of the Sanctus bell, in the days of his young boyhood that seemed now such centuries ago.

He listened spellbound for a moment, until a sudden false note, sticking into his musician's spirit like a stiletto, followed by a howl of imprecation upon the other side of the hedge, brought him suddenly to earth. He ran down the lane to a gate upon the left, leaped upon it and found himself looking down upon such a comical scene that he swung his legs over the top of the gate and sat there laughing, unseen by the protagonists in the comedy down below.

A field of red earth was being harrowed but the team of beautiful sun-coloured oxen had come to a standstill while the ploughman, an ancient with a bent old body like a brittle tree, and a brown seamed face with a stubble of grey beard upon it, like a lichen upon apple tree bark, belaboured the hind quarters of a small boy whom he held wedged between his twisted old legs as in a vice. Fury had lent the ancient an almost youthful energy, for his blows flailed down with surprising strength and he swore so loudly meanwhile that his voice rose easily above the howls of the youngster. Zachary made no attempt to go to the rescue of the victim; the horrible false falsetto note had been quite deliberately inserted. The young wretch deserved all he was getting and he was even sorry when with a twist the scoundrel wrenched himself free, dived between the old man's legs and raced off down the hill. The old man staggered, recovered himself, wiped his forehead on his forearm, then turned and laid his hands once more upon the plough. The oxen moved forward again, turning downhill, the white cloud of gulls rose and followed, and the old man's voice, very frail, yet so sure and sensitive in pitch and tone, rose lonely and serene in the immemorial chant that his fathers had sung before him century after century over these same green hills.

Zachary listened, awed and silent again; it was still lovely but it lacked the tenor notes. He tried them softly under his breath, at first tentatively, then more surely, remembering the rhythm of the chanting of the mass. The plough with its wheeling gulls reached the bottom of the hill, turned and came up again, and as it neared the steepest part of the slope Zachary was sure of himself and the music. Singing, he pulled off his coat, jumped off the gate and walked to meet the team, still singing he swung in beside Sol and bent his weight to the plough, still singing they moved together up the hill, swung and turned, the gulls turning with them. Sol, after one glance at the boy beside him, accepted him as he accepted everything, calmly and without astonishment, and rested himself in this blessed comradeship of a tuneful kindred spirit. As for Zachary, wave after wave of exultation beat through him as he gave himself for the first time to this blessed action of the following of the plough. The tread of the oxen, their deep and quiet breathing, the ring of the harness, the creak of the plough, the wind, the cry of the gulls, his own voice singing, Sol's deep bass accompaniment, the rhythmic swing and turn at the start of each ascent and descent, the swath of rose-red earth curling back from the coulter like foam from a ship's prow, it seemed to him all one action, one glorious paean of adoration rising from the altar of earth to the throne of heaven.

Sol fitted no words to his music; if there had ever been words he had never known them, and neither had his father; his chanting was a succession of vowel sounds flowing so smoothly and effortlessly that though there were no words they nevertheless gave the impression of ordered language. But Zachary quite unconsciously found himself singing actual words. "Et introibo ad altare Dei; ad Deum, qui laetificat juventutem meam. And I will go unto the altar of God: to God who giveth joy to my youth." He was unaware that he was singing words from the mass, unaware that this chant of the plough had centuries ago found its way from the chanting of the monks in the great Abbey at Torre to the fields of the countryside about it. The Holy Bread upon the altar of the Abbey, the Holy Bread springing from the furrowed sod of the fields, had both seemed equally a sacrament to the men of these days. "Spera in Deo, quoniam adhuc confitebor illi: salutare vultus mei, et Deus meus. Hope in God: for I will still give praise to him; the salvation of my countenance and my God." The plough swung round again. Zachary had lost all sense of place or time. Though the stars in the sky were dimmed by the bright sunlight, yet they were singing. His muddy vesture of decay seemed no longer to enclose him, and the harmony within his soul soared up to meet their music like a lark.

"Gloria Patri, et Filio, et Spiritui Sancto. Sicut erat in principio, et nunc, et semper, et in saecula saeculorum. Amen."

The plough had stopped. The patient oxen stood with heads drooped wearily. Old Sol was chuckling delightedly, rubbing his hands up and down his thighs, enjoying the dumbfounded astonishment of a tall stout man leaning over the gate. Zachary, utterly stunned by the sudden descent to earth, rubbed his hand across his eyes, then blinked confusedly at a picture he had seen before, and memorised with loving care; a little figure in a red cloak standing behind a gate, a pointed chin propped on top of it, a row of small finger-tips to either side; and down below a furry countenance thrust engagingly through the lower bars. . . . Stella and Hodge. . . . So he had seen them when he said good-bye in the moonlight, so he saw them again now in the bright sun, and so he would see them in memory when he was parted from them, until the end of life. He gave a cry of delight and strode towards them, and like a flash Stella had scrambled to the top of the gate, fallen down upon the other side, jumped up again and flung herself into his outstretched arms. He picked her up, not kissing her, not even wanting to, loving the feel of her in his arms, warm and thin and palpitating like a little bird, loving her laughter, laughing with her, with no desire to do anything any more except to stand in the sun and laugh with Stella. Sol was still chuckling, and Hodge, who by some extraordinary deflating process had flattened himself sufficiently to get through the bars, was leaping about them and laughing too.

Only Father Sprigg, still upon the wrong side of the gate, exploded abruptly into one of the most impressive rages that even Sol, in all the long years of their acquaintance, had ever seen.

"What the devil!" demanded Father Sprigg, becoming at last coherent after most desperate and heroic efforts to control his language in front of Stella, and wrenching the gate open so violently that he nearly had it off its hinges. "And who may you be—you—you—ugh!—you—twily young scoundrel! You dare touch my girl—you—foreigner! Hodge, come here! Stella! I'll take a stick to you, laughing in that brazen fashion! Hodge! Sol, you maundering old dotard, I'll give you the sack for this—letting a foreigner get his dirty hands on my plough!" He advanced upon Zachary, his big nobbly stick raised, once more roaring like a bull.

"Stand up to 'im, lad!" whispered Sol.

Zachary pushed aside Stella and Hodge, who had planted themselves protectively in front of him, came up courageously to Father Sprigg and bowed to him. The nobbly stick dropped, and so did the farmer's jaw. In this presentable and courteous young stranger he did not recognise the ragged boy whom he had once already got rid of from his farm.

"I ask your pardon, Sir," said Zachary humbly. "I am staying in the village with Dr. Crane. I am his—sort of—relative. I passed this way and your ploughman was having trouble with his boy who ran away. I stayed and helped him."

"Sings counter-tenor like he'd been born to the plough, Sir," exulted Sol. "Abraham an' Moses, ee got un goin' at sich a pace that if ee hadn't 'appened along, geowering an' maundering, we'd 'ave 'ad the work 'alf done by this time. Let un bide, Sir, an' 'im an' me, we'll 'ave the 'ole field ploughed by nummet time."

"Let him bide, Father!" pleaded Stella. "It wasn't his fault about me. I just jumped on him, like I do on you. He's my friend, you see. Hodge's too."

Father Sprigg looked at Hodge. That worthy was standing beside Zachary with slowly rotating tail, his tawny eyes very bright, his head cocked slightly to the left with his right ear slightly raised and the left, torn ear drooping. A drooping left ear was always a sign of serene relaxation in Hodge; a sort of "all's well" signal.

"An' for why are you so set on ploughing my field?" demanded Father Sprigg of Zachary.

"I want to work at Weekaborough Farm, Sir," said Zachary, still humbly but looking Father Sprigg straight in the eye. "Dr. Crane thought you might be so good as to give me employment. I think, Sir, you could teach me to be a good shepherd as well as a good ploughman."

"I'm already suited. I've the boy Jack Crocker," snapped Father Sprigg.

"Bolted to Plymouth, by the look of 'im," growled Old Sol. "An' bolted or no I'll not endure the screechin' o' that boy no longer, Master. Two notes flat the 'ole while. A cat on the thatch is sweet 'armony compared to it. If ee stays I go, Master, an' so I tell ee straight."

Father Sprigg was still looking hard at Zachary. An amused smile flickered in the boy's eyes and touched his lips with an extraordinary sweetness. All unknown to himself an answering smile came into the farmer's eyes. They both knew Sol was lying. He'd not remove his old feet from the beloved soil of Weekaborough while he had the strength to drag them one after the other. "He needs a bit of help, Sir," murmured Zachary.

"I've never had no foreigner working on my farm," growled Father Sprigg obstinately. By foreigner he meant a man who was not a west country man; and by his speech he knew Zachary hailed from Sussex, or Wiltshire, or the Hebrides, or some such outlandish place that he'd never set eyes on and that seemed to him as remote as Russia or the West Indies. "There ain't no foreigner ever worked at Weekaborough."

Zachary took a deep breath. "When a homeless man sees a bit of earth that seems to him lovelier than any bit of earth he ever saw, do you blame him if he tries to stay there?" he asked. "You can become a native by love as well as by birth. Give me a trial, Sir. I'll serve the land well."

Stella, who all this time had stood scarcely daring to breathe, saw the obstinacy of Father Sprigg's mouth relax a little. Zachary had unconsciously touched the right note. Had he promised to serve the farmer well it would have meant less to Father Sprigg than his offer of service to the land. For a moment or two Father Sprigg looked out over the valley at his feet, this great valley held between Bowerly Hill and Tafferty Hill, between the moors and the sea. Then he looked back at Zachary.

"I'll speak to the doctor about ye," he said gruffly.

# CHAPTER X

## I

ZACHARY went to work with a will, delighted to find himself not totally unequal to the labour of a full grown man about a farm. It gave him courage and confidence again, as the doctor had hoped it would. He broadened and strengthened and put on weight, and after only a short time of trial and error Father Sprigg and Sol really found him uncommonly useful, and that quite apart from his gift of music, which made new creatures of Old Sol and the oxen. He was amazinly good with animals, especially sheep, and Father Sprigg suspected that when the summer came he would find that the bees liked him. He had all the makings of a good bee man, with his patience and reverent love for all small creatures.

It was this reverence of his that set the minds of Father and Mother Sprigg instantly at rest about Zachary and Stella. That he loved the little girl and found her the delight of his life it was plain to see, and she followed him about like his gleeful shadow, yet the daily companionship bred no carelessness in him; he treated her always as though someone had just that moment put into his hands some treasure that could be sullied by a breath or smashed by a hasty movement. Yet though they did not worry, Father and Mother Sprigg marvelled a little at the companionship between the two. They had only just come together yet they seemed now not properly themselves when they were apart. Zachary, coming into the farm kitchen and not finding Stella there, would for a moment or two look like a lost dog. Stella, if Zachary were late, would drift round in a bewildered way, exactly like a small shadow who had lost its substance. Yet when the one who was awaited came they would have no exuberant greeting for each other; they would just relax and be themselves again, a divided thing made whole. There was something here that went deeper than the normal affection of two young things for each other and puzzled Father and Mother Sprigg.

It did not puzzle Dr. Crane, aware that he was in the presence of Shakespeare's marriage of true minds, yet he observed this rare thing with interest, never to his knowledge having met it before. Shakespeare was right, it had nothing to do with the body, and undoubtedly it was true in the sense of being a thing that would not pass. As to the why of it, that was beyond him. A man might as well ponder the "why" of the dawn and the spring. The element of eternity in these things stood as a witness to something. Better leave it at that. He did so, meanwhile perceiving with delight how the various contrasts in the dispositions of these two locked one into the other, built firmly upon the foundation of their unities. Stella's fearlessness and Zachary's fear, her love of adventure and his of security, her serenity and his anxiety, she with her externe's sensitiveness to the suffering of others and he with the interne's power of suffering unduly in his own mind and body. And both of them with their gift, perhaps quite natural in two whose vocation it seemed to be to shadow forth the timelessness of love, of apprehending and making contact with that which exists behind the appearance of things. And both of them, too, with the artist's love of beauty and the scholar's love of learning that are a part of that gift.

Dr. Crane refused to teach them together; he did not want Stella's mind strained by trying to catch up with Zachary, or his kept back by trying to keep her company on her level. He still taught Stella on two mornings a week, when Zachary was working at the farm, and Zachary's education was carried on ruthlessly in the evenings. No fatigue on the part of either of them was allowed to interfere with it; though for both of them physical fatigue was apt to vanish with the opening of a book. They were utterly happy together. Neither of them had known that the relationship of father and son could be so good as this.

But on Fridays, when Father and Mother Sprigg drove to market and Zachary's work at the farm finished early, he and Stella both had dinner with the doctor and for an hour before the meal he would read aloud to them, delighting in the contrasts and affinities of their minds and the happiness of their comradeship in the world of books. Then when dinner was over Zachary would take Stella home and before the daylight faded they would ramble round the farm together, Hodge and Daniel at their heels, and what they said to each other then the doctor did not know, for they did not tell him, and he did not ask.

II

Friday, November 23rd, 1804, a still and beautiful blue day, was the last of these Fridays, but the doctor did not read to them that day. When Zachary and Stella arrived they found the gig at the door, the doctor struggling enthusiastically into his greatcoat, and Tome Pearse in a similar state holding the head of an equally excited Aesculapius.

"Fleet's in!" cried Tom to Zachary. "The Brest fleet. Admiral Cornwallis. Reddleman brought the news. What about dinner, Sir?"

"Dinner be damned!" said the doctor, slapping his beaver hat on the side of his head. "We'll be off down to the shore while the light's good. Up with you, Zachary and Stella. You come along too, Tom. You can hold on behind."

He lifted the excited Stella off her jigging toes and swung her up, climbing up after her. Zachary stood where he was, his head bent, kicking at a stone. The very mention of the Brest fleet had made him turn suddenly cold. His old ship had been, was, part of it. . . . The eyes of the ship would be on him.

"Coming, Zachary?" asked the doctor.

Zachary looked up and smiled. "Could I stay at home, Sir? You know, today you were to have read to us from Hippolytus. May I stay and read to myself?"

The doctor began to quote from Hippolytus.

"'Could I take me to some cavern for mine hiding,
In the hill tops where the sun scarce hath trod;
Or a cloud make the home of mine abiding,
As a bird among the bird droves of God.'

By all means, boy. Stay in the cavern if you like."

He spoke kindly but Zachary saw something almost like contempt in his eyes; or what might have been contempt, had the doctor been a man capable of feeling such a thing. And on Stella's little face was a look of comical dismay. A wonderful junketing like this and Zachary not to come too! Without a word he swung himself up beside her, smiling down at her suddenly dimpling face, rosy with delight now inside the scarlet hood. Tom Pearse leaped up like a monkey behind and they were off, Aesculapius going like the wind.

"I wish it was Admiral Nelson, not Admiral Cornwallis," said Stella. "I wish Admiral Nelson would come to Torquay."

"He's been, my honey," said the doctor. "But you were too little a maid to take much interest in Admirals at that time. That was three years ago, when the Earl of St. Vincent was a guest at Torre Abbey and the little Admiral came from Plymouth to visit him. There were grand doings at that time. A most elegant ball and supper and masquerade at the Abbey, and your humble servant, being an old *Agamemnon* man, actually invited."

He smiled in delight at the memory and launched into reminiscences as they bowled along. He told them of the tumultuous welcome which had greeted Admiral Nelson when he arrived to hoist his flag on the *San Josef* at Plymouth. As he passed through the fleet the yards were manned, bands played, guns roared and the cheering rolled like thunder. When he drove through the streets in an open carriage with Captain Harvey, in full uniform, with blazing stars and gold medals on his breast the crowds in the streets nearly went wild with delight. When the carriage stopped sailors ran to grasp his one hand, and men and women knelt on the cobbles of the streets crying, "God bless your honour!"

"Why do they love him so much?" wondered Stella.

A low growl came from Tom Pearse behind them, a growl comprised of deep hatred of unnamed persons and even deeper appreciation of Admiral Nelson. "Cares if ye live or die!" he rumbled. "Men are men to Admiral Nelson, not cannon fodder. 'My poor fellows,' he calls 'em. Did ye hear what Nelson said of the men who mutinied at Spithead, and were hung from the yard-arm or flogged for asking to have their wages paid and to be given food that wasn't more maggots than meat? Said they were right! Took their part, an' he an Admiral! 'We're a neglected set, we sailors,' he said. It's a wonder the bloody government didn't hang him for it. There's never a man who's once sailed with Lord Nelson who wouldn't give the poor soul of him to sail with him again, even to hell, knowing he'd be damned when he got there."

"That'll do, Tom," chuckled the doctor, and began to tell them about Nelson's flagship, the great *San Josef*. He told them about the battle of Cape St. Vincent, fought with such valour against the combined fleets of France and Spain, by a small company of men who only a short while ago had been through the bitterness of the mutiny, and how Nelson and Collingwood had covered themselves with glory by the fury with which they faced and fought the two noble battleships of the Spanish fleet, the *Salvador del Mundi* and the *San Josef*. Nelson had brought the two Spanish ships into Plymouth, the *San Josef* with her sails in ribbons and her masts all blown away. Later he had cruised in her around the Devon coast with his fleet, and the Devon men and women had crowded down to the shore to see the sight. Stella could dimly remember that. She could remember sitting on Father Sprigg's shoulder on the cliffs at Livermead and watching the white sails passing by, and of how the names of the great ships, spoken by the men and women about her, sounded like music.

What was the matter with him, Zachary wondered, that he could not thrill to the music of great names, and the splendour of great deeds? Why was it that for him the horror of war completely overlaid the glory? It was not so for other men. To them it was all worth while, because of the glory. And what *was* glory? What did they mean by this glory that was something more than the love of country? He had the love of country, but it was not enough. He had not this other love, that seemed for most men to be interwoven with the first. He did not know what it was.

They had reached the low stone wall where the doctor and Stella had paused before to look at Torbay spread out below them, and they stopped here again. The ships of the Brest fleet were at anchor in the bay, their gilded carving and bright paintwork gleaming in the sun, their sails hanging loose to dry, their reflections mirrored in the calm sea as though they were swans resting quietly upon the water. The scene was so still, so peaceful, that it was like a painted picture. It seemed impossible at this moment, to imagine those ships in action, fire blazing from their gun-ports and the great hulls rocking to the concussion and reverberating din. For Zachary, the thought of the fighting that he had not yet seen and so much dreaded, robbed the scene of all its beauty.

They drove slowly down the hill, the doctor and Tom trying to pick out the different ships; there was the Admiral's flagship with St. George's banner flying from her foregallant masthead, and there was the *Goliath*, and there the *Impetueux*, and there the *Venerable*. Driving through the lanes at the bottom of the hill they could no longer see the ships, but at Livermead they saw them again from a different angle.

"They'll be off when the wind shifts," said Tom Pearse. He regarded the blue sky, where a few silver mackerel clouds were floating in the blue, and sniffed knowingly. "Maybe tomorrow. There's a change comin'. Saint Michael, see how clear he stands. He's whistlin' up a wind for 'em."

They followed the direction of his glance. The chapel of St. Michael upon its rock, was extraordinarily clear against the sky. The blue and silver and gold of this perfect day seemed to have sunk into the rock and to have coloured it. Stella, half-shutting her eyes, could almost imagine a great angelic figure standing there, wings spread, sword in hand, whistling up a wind to carry the fleet away to fight the French.

"Let's climb up to the chapel!" she cried impulsively.

"It's long past dinner time, Stella," said Zachary.

The doctor looked at Zachary's set face and this time he administered no flick of the whip. He was not going to force the boy a second time. Once was enough. Besides, his own rheumatic legs and Tom Pearse's were not as good at scaling heights as they had been. "We'll keep the chapel for another day, my honey," he said to Stella. "But I'll tell you the story of the chapel as we drive home. Then when you do go, you will know whom to expect to meet there."

Stella was instantly enthralled, her momentary disappointment forgotten. To meet there? She had felt before that she and the chapel belonged to each other in some special way, but she had not known she was to meet people inside. What people?

"Angels?" she demanded.

"Sit still and listen," said the doctor, turning the gig and heading Aesculapius for home. And Zachary and Stella listened with all their ears, as children will when their instinct tells them that some story has a special significance for them, but Tom Pearse turned his head towards the sea and never heard a word; he was intent not to miss one single last glimpse of those great ships upon the quiet sea.

III

It was not a quiet sea, but a storm, with which the doctor began his story, and it had raged five centuries ago. The monks of Torre, saying compline within the Abbey church that night, could scarcely make their voices audible above the roar of the wind and the crashing of the great waves on the shore. In the middle of compline the west door opened suddenly, letting in a gust of wind that made the candles gutter in their sconces, and the abbot, turning round, saw the wild figure of one of their goatherds standing in the doorway.

"A ship in distress, Father!" he cried. "A large ship driving towards the rocks."

The monks did not finish compline. Living so near the shore they were used to doing what they could for sailors in trouble. They lit the storm lanterns they kept in the church for this very purpose, seized a coil of rope and fought their way through the wind and rain, down to the shore where the waves were thundering in like mad horses. They could dimly see the great ship driving in upon the rocks, but the storm was so fearful that there was little they could do. With all their heroic effort they saved the life of only one man; and he was half dead when they pulled him to shore. They nursed him back to life in the Abbey infirmary and then he told them that in the hour of his danger he had vowed, should his life be spared, to devote it to God. When he recovered he kept his vow. Helped by the monks he built a chapel upon the rocky summit of the hill close to the Abbey, and here, looking out over the sea where his ship had been wrecked and his friends drowned, he lived the life of a hermit until he died, saying the offices ordained by Holy Church and praying unceasingly for the living and the dead. And always, when a storm raged, his voice could be heard praying aloud in anguish for the safety of those at sea.

Three hundred years later a young boy of the neighbourhood was in trouble. One day he climbed to the chapel and knelt and prayed there. He had been told the story of the hermit, and when his prayer was finished he stayed on in the chapel thinking about the story and wondering if it was true. And then he must have slept a little and dreamed a dream, for it seemed to him that it was night in the chapel, with two lamps burning in the recesses in the north wall, and looking towards the east he saw a rough stone altar there and an old white-haired man kneeling in prayer before it; and he heard the words of the old man's prayer and he prayed for all those enduring storm, darkness and fear, whether in the mind or in the body. And then the old man raised his head and looked at the boy, and their eyes met, and the old man smiled. . . . And then it seemed that the old man came to him and that they talked a little. . . . And then it was once more daylight in the chapel, and there was no one there but the boy alone, and he could not remember what it was that he and the old man had said to each other.

He spoke to no one of this dream or vision, excepting only to a young girl called Rosalind whom he loved, and to her he spoke of it one evening when they sat together outside the chapel. He was saying good-bye to her there, for he was setting out upon a long journey in search of wisdom, a journey that would take him across the sea. But he promised he would return, and she promised to visit the chapel on every anniversary of his departure. They would never forget each other, they said. Then he went away.

Three years passed and he had not returned. Rosalind kept her promise. She did not forget her lover and on each anniversary of his departure she visited the chapel. On the third anniversary she still kept her word, though the night was cold, dark and stormy. Climbing up to the chapel she was surprised to see a light inside, and when she came to the door she saw two lamps burning in the alcoves in the north wall, and an old white-haired man kneeling at prayer. He got up when he saw her, and smiled, and came to her. He told her that her lover was on board a ship that was even now out in the bay, driven by the rising storm, and that his safety depended upon her courage. He said, "Since these strong walls were raised no storm has swept along this coast like this which comes tonight." Together they went down to the shore and there in the fury of the storm that followed Rosalind stood steadfast, refusing to be driven away by wind or rain. It was she who first saw the great ship driving towards the rocks, as long before the monks of Torre had seen another ship, and she who dragged from the water the body of her lover, brought almost to her feet by a great wave. She and the old man carried him to the nearest house, where he was skilfully cared for and brought back to life again. By the morning the storm had ceased and Rosalind, looking at the door, saw the old man lingering there. She left her lover and went to say goodbye to him, and he told her that as long as the chapel stood it would always hold help and comfort for those who prayed there. Then he blessed her and left her and neither she nor her lover ever saw him again. But they did not forget him, and the chapel was a holy place to them both until they died.

The doctor told the legend of the old hermit as well as he could, because he loved it, as he loved all the legends of this country, and when he had finished Stella had eager questions to ask. Where did Rosalind live when she was a little girl? What was her lover's name? Where had he been across the sea? Where did they live when they got married? What did they do? The doctor said he did not know, and he refused to concoct imaginative answers. Perhaps one day Stella would find out for herself. Zachary had smiled at parts of the story, told so simply to please Stella, but he did not smile as he put his one question, and the doctor answered it with equal seriousness.

"Did the fellow find the wisdom he was looking for?"

"Yes. He found it."

IV

The next day, Saturday November the 24th, the wind changed and freshened as Tom Pearse had foretold. Clouds had come up before the wind and it was quite dark when the doctor got back from his rounds, and he and Zachary sat down rather late to their evening meal. The Admiral had signalled an immediate departure just before five o'clock, Tom Pearse told them as he handed the vegetables. They did not ask how he knew this. He always knew everything. News travelled among the country people with quite miraculous rapidity, and if it was anything to do with the fleet Tom Pearse seemed to be able to smell it in the mind of a man a mile off.

"It'll be a job to work out of the bay in this darkness, Sir," he said to the doctor. "Dirty weather on the way too. Better to have waited till morning."

The doctor looked at the opaque blackness outside the window, and in the little pause they could hear the moan of the rising wind.

"Admiral Cornwallis knows his job," he said slowly.

Tom Pearse sniffed dubiously and poured out the claret.

The doctor and Zachary were sitting reading in front of the study fire when they heard the low boom of a gun. The doctor lifted his head and waited. Ship in distress. Tom Pearse's head came round the door. "Puttin' in Aesculapius, Sir," he said briefly. The doctor grunted, read steadily to the end of the paragraph, then closed his book and reached for his doctor's bag. "Coming, Zachary?" he asked. Zachary nodded and got up.

Bundled up in thick coats the three of them packed into the gig and drove off into the windy darkness. Scuds of rain came now and then upon the wind, lashing their faces. The darkness hindered their pace not at all, for Aesculapius knew every inch of these roads. Yet he slowed down as they neared Smokyhouse, where the door stood open showing the glow of firelight, and a man's bulky figure blocked against it. He hailed them and the doctor stopped. "Take me along with ee, doctor?" shouted George Spratt. "Make haste then, George," the doctor called back. George swung himself up behind, breathing beer down their necks, and they were off again, swaying perilously down the steep hill, the roar of the sea sounding always louder in their ears.

"The *Venerable*, Captain Hunter, on the rocks on Paignton Ledge," growled George. "Allus the one ship lost in every great storm. Torbay claims her."

Zachary pondered this idea of George Spratt's, remembering the doctor's story of the day before. Was there some sort of demon in Torbay, living down there in the submerged forest that yielded the antlers of deer to the fishermen's nets, that now and again must claim a victim?

"Know any details, George?" asked the doctor.

George knew all about it of course. While the *Venerable*'s anchor was being secured one of the seamen had fallen from it. A boat was ordered away but one of the falls being let go too soon it was swamped, a midshipman and two sailors being drowned. . . . Zachary felt cold, thinking of that wretched midshipman. . . . A second boat was lowered and the first sailor saved. Meanwhile all the ships were tacking, but the *Venerable* having lost way was unable to gain her position and to avoid collision was forced close to the shore. The heavy swell had caught her and now she was on the rocks on Paignton Ledge. It was George's opinion that the guns would not avail her much, for the rest of the fleet was probably out of hearing.

Paignton village was deserted, for everyone had gone down to the shore. They put up Aesculapius and the gig at the inn, where one lame ostler had been left in charge, and fought their way down to the beach through the wind and rain. The flares and hurricane lamps lit up a scene that seemed to Zachary like some scene in hell. The crowd upon the beach might have been a multitude of lost souls, figures and faces now hidden in darkness, now leaping suddenly into view lit by crimson light. The waves breaking on the beach leaped savagely, the flung white spray turned to flecks of fire now and then by the flares, and the scream of the wind rising above the boom of the guns was a dreadful thing to hear.

They could dimly make out the doomed ship on the rocks. The sea had made a complete breach in her and the waves were pouring through. At sight of her, and at thought of men aboard her, all his old hatred of the sea swept over Zachary, sickening him. Then the nausea passed and rage took its place. Why was no one doing anything? Were they all to stand here and watch those men drown? He must have shouted aloud in his fury for he felt the doctor take his arm and shake it, shouting something unintelligible. Then he saw that there were some boats tossing about the *Venerable*, and that a handful of courageous fishermen were trying to get more boats off the beach. Evidently the guns had been heard by at least two of the other ships, they had sent their boats, and the order had now been given to abandon ship. The *Venerable* was almost on her beam ends now and looked as though she might break in two at any moment. Yet her guns still fired, and would do as long as any of her seamen remained on board.

Then began one of the most splendid efforts to save life that Torbay had ever witnessed. The fight continued all through that stormy pitch-black night. One after the other, the small pitching boats passed under the *Venerable*'s stern, and her officers, keeping the saving of their own lives till the last, helped their men in. Lines were flung and made fast on the shore, and other men tried to haul themselves along to safety, but the surf was so tremendous that most of those making the attempt were either drowned or dashed to pieces upon the rocks. There was less loss of life from the boats, for few of these attempted to get to shore but rowed out to sea to the ships that had sent them, but some were capsized, and no one could survive in that terrible sea. At five in the morning Captain Hunter at last consented to leave his ship. In single file, the junior officer leading, the officers and ten seamen who had declared they would die with their officers and refused to leave without them, scrambled into the last two boats, while a few officers, for whom there was no room in the boats, succeeded in climbing to safety along the bowsprit. Only one man was left behind, a drunken marine who refused to get into the last boat. He alone went down with the *Venerable*.

Throughout that night Zachary worked as hard and as courageously as any man upon the beach. Soon after the doctor had shaken him by the arm he found himself in one of the boats, taking an oar behind George Spratt. Theirs was one of the few boats that got out to the *Venerable* and back with a boatload of sailors without capsizing. Later he was in the sea, up to the waist in ice-cold water, Tom Pearse beside him, struggling to save the exhausted men clinging to the lines. Later still he was inside the inn at the harbour, labouring with the doctor to bring back life to half-drowned bodies. And all through the night it was his rage that kept him going, rage lit now and then by some sort of light, a triumph of some kind. He reasoned nothing out through the turmoil of the night; just found himself possessed alternately by the rage and triumph.

It was still dark when at last there was no more for them to do; and the rescuers carried the rescued back to their homes with them, for hot drinks, hot baths and bed. The doctor captured two young officers and drove them home in the gig. Zachary, George Spratt and Tom Pearse followed on foot. They were too weary for much speech, but Tom said to Zachary, "You did a man's work this night, Sir," and George growled agreement. Zachary nodded. He knew he had. His rage had gone now, but the triumph remained, and though his teeth were chattering it warmed him through.

## CHAPTER XI

### I

STELLA did not know when she woke up the next morning what had happened during the night. They none of them knew at the farm yet, though the grown-ups had heard the boom of the guns and guessed the neighbours would have some tale to tell at church today. Stella jumped out of bed and ran to look at the day; the wind was dropping and the rain clouds were passing away, and soon it would be blue and clear after the storm. She sang as she dressed, for she liked Sunday. It was an exciting day. Breakfast was exciting, with fried ham instead of just porridge. Father Sprigg in his militia uniform, in which he drilled recruits before church, was exciting, and so were Mother Sprigg and herself in their best clothes. And church was exciting, with all the singing and the parson's voice booming so loudly.

After an early breakfast, and with the work upon the farm finished for the morning, there was the business of getting Father Sprigg into his uniform, a gorgeous affair of scarlet and white and gold that seemed to grow ever tighter as the weeks went past. They all helped, Old Sol cleaning his glossy black top-boots and Madge his jingling accoutrements, Stella brushing his hat and Mother Sprigg easing him into his coat and soothing his ruffled feelings. For getting into his uniform always upset Father Sprigg. Good patriot though he was this business of spending time on drill, when there was work to do about the farm, acerbated his temper. He wished he could settle it with Bony in single combat, once and for all, and have done with the business.

"Single combat, like David and Goliath," said Stella today, as he gave explosive vent to these views. "Only Bony is a little man, and it seems it is the little man who wins."

Father Sprigg, purple in the face as his befrogged coat came into position, regarded his precious child with an unfavourable eye, and Mother Sprigg hastened to pour oil upon the troubled waters. "David beat Goliath, Stella, not because of his smaller stature but because the Lord fought upon his side. Therefore your Father, fighting Bony, would win."

"Then does the Lord always fight upon the side of the English?" asked Stella.

The four adults present gazed at her in shocked astonishment. This questioning of an established religious principle upon the Lord's day seemed to them to smack of blasphemy.

"To hear ee talk a body'd think ee were a foreigner!" gasped Madge.

"Perhaps I am," said Stella.

"That's enough of your nonsense, child," said Mother Sprigg with sudden severity. "Come along upstairs at once and get your Sunday clothes on. Make haste to your drill, Father. We'll not be long after you."

Leaving Madge, Sol and Hodge to look after the farm and cook the dinner Mother Sprigg and Stella set off on foot for church, dressed in their best. Madge and Sol would go to evening church, carrying a lantern and the Weekaborough Prayer Book, which neither of them could read but which looked well. Stella carried it this morning, taking both hands to it, for it was very heavy with its thick black covers and strong brass clasps. It was an heirloom, like the Book, and the Spriggs had used it for generations. Stella loved carrying it, for if she had been feeling cross before it made her feel good-tempered again.

Mother Sprigg and Stella looked delightful in their best, Mother Sprigg in her dove-coloured merino, with a grey cloak and bonnet to match, and Stella all in softest green, with cherry-coloured ribbons to her bonnet and a little white frill inside. She had white mittens and a small round brown muff hanging on a cord round her neck. She was very loving to Mother Sprigg all the way to the village because she knew she had hurt her, as she always hurt her by any suggestion of a difference between them. She ought not to have said that about being a foreigner. She had not meant to say it; the remark had just slipped out. And perhaps she ought not to have wondered, either, if God always fought for the English. Of course the English were always right; if they were not they would not be English. . . . She decided that she must try not to wonder about things quite so much. It only led to trouble.

As they went down the hill to the village the church bells began to ring and Stella gave a sigh of pleasure. The Gentian Hill bells were old and clear-toned, and the Gentian Hill bell-ringers rang them with consummate art. On one of them was engraved, "Jesu merce, Ladye help," and upon another, "Draw neare unto God," and Stella always fancied that she heard these words pealing through the bell-music. As they came to the village the ferocious bellow of Father Sprigg drilling his men in the open space before the Church House Inn mingled with the sound of the bells.

Everyone came early to church these days, so as to watch the drilling, and they were very proud of their husbands and sons and brothers and grandsons, standing there in two irregular lines, shouldering the pikes that between drills were kept inside the church. They should of course have had muskets but they had not been issued yet; and probably when the French landed, they would still not have been issued. But that was not worrying the men of Gentian Hill. It was their belief that one Englishman with one pike was the equal of six Frenchmen with six muskets any day. Father Sprigg was occasionally not so sure, and it was this uncertainty, as well as the irregularity of the two lines confronting him, which he could never get dressed correctly however hard he tried, that caused him to bellow so ferociously as he drilled his squad.

They were a mixed lot, apart from the stiffening of a few militia men, labourers, farmers, shepherds and thatchers, young and old and middle-aged, of all sizes and shapes, but all with the placid good-humour of the Devon men, and all with the same obstinate refusal to be hurried no matter what the urgency. Let Father Sprigg shout as he might, they obeyed his orders in their own time and at their own pace.

"They wouldn't hurry, not if they heard the French had landed this morning!" said a voice behind Stella. "Come away, Greensleeves! You don't want to watch this play-acting, do you?"

It was Zachary, white-faced and hollow-eyed and suffering severely from reaction. He had slept heavily after the potent hot drinks Dr. Crane had administered to them all the night before, and it had been torment to be dragged out of his dreams at ten in the morning by the doctor's determined hand. But the doctor saw no reason why his household should miss church because they had attended a shipwreck the night before. His guests he left to sleep on, but not Zachary and Tom Pearse. They must do their duty.

"Come, Stella," he begged. Talk of the wreck was bubbling up excitedly among the crowd of villagers gathering in their Sunday best, and he did not want Stella to listen to it. She did not like to slip away unnoticed by Mother Sprigg, deep in conversation with the woman next her, but she always went with Zachary when he wanted her. And she knew he would not stay and watch the drilling. He always seemed to shrink away from anything at all that had to do with the war.

They went in under the lychgate into the churchyard and passed the church porch, the bells pealing over their heads, and Zachary averted his eyes from the proclamation pinned there upon the notice board. Not that that did him any good, for certain phrases of it seemed seared into his memory. "Address to all ranks and descriptions of Englishmen. . . . Friends and countrymen, the French are now assembling the largest force that ever was prepared to invade this kingdom. . . . They have spared neither rich nor poor, old nor young. . . . No man's service is compelled, but you are invited voluntarily to come forward in defence of everything that is dear to you. . . . Your king and country. . . . Victory will never belong to those who are slothful and unprepared." It was really a very long proclamation and in the middle of the night Zachary would find to his astonishment that he knew it all.

"Did you see the wreck, Zachary?" asked Stella.

"Yes, Stella. The doctor and Tom and I went down to Paignton. Wasn't it good that all those men were saved?"

Stella, who had been very much afraid that perhaps they had not all been saved, gave a quick sigh of relief and towed him round to the north side of the church where there was no one but themselves and where the sound of the drilling came to them only very faintly. Here the graves were very old and moss-grown, and three of the five splendid old yew trees that grew in the churchyard spread their branches widely. Stella had a great affection for these yews with their bright red berries hanging like lamps in the darkness, and also for two among the graves that lay side by side and seemed even older than the rest. The gentians for which this churchyard was famous grew about them, and upon each of them one could still see the faint carved outline of something that might have been a fleur-de-lys, or perhaps a half-opened gentian.

"Hundreds of years ago, when Englishmen went to war, they carried bows made of the wood of the churchyard yew," she said. "The doctor told me. They carried yew tree bows at Agincourt."

Zachary, who had been looking unseeingly at the two old graves half buried in the grass at his feet, lifted his head suddenly like an angry colt. "It was not for making bows that the monks planted five yew trees in every churchyard," he said bitterly. "It was to remind people of the five wounds of Our Lord. To use the wood for war was a desecration."

Stella's small face looked troubled. Her mind was still pursuing the train of thought that had started when Father Sprigg was struggling into his uniform. "It was wicked to take the wood if the English were fighting a wrong war," she said, "but not if it was a right one, like this. Father thinks the English never fought a wrong war, but I think they were wicked to go to France and try to take away their homes from the French. But now the French are trying to take away our homes from us, it's a good war we're fighting." She sighed with relief, having got it straight. "Do you hate the French, Zachary? Lord Nelson does."

"No," said Zachary sombrely. "My mother was French. Lord Nelson's mother wasn't."

"Nor do I," said Stella. "But most people do."

"It's not the mark of a good patriot to hate the enemy," said Zachary. "It's the mark of a patriot to love his country."

"Do you love England?" asked Stella.

"Yes."

"Would you enlist and fight for her, like the proclamation says on the door, if you were grown-up?"

She asked the question in all simplicity. He had never told her he had been in the navy and deserted. Only the doctor knew that. His face went tight, as though he had the toothache, and he evaded the question, by lightly asking her one. "Would you, Greensleeves? If you were a man and grown-up?"

She nodded seriously, then suddenly dimpled, becoming a child again. "And I'd make myself a bow out of the yew tree on Bowerly Hill. The arrows would fly fast from it because that tree was once an angel who turned himself into a yew. . . . At least that's what I used to think when I was little."

"Why did you think that?" demanded Zachary eagerly.

"Because the branches spread out like wings, and because when you climb up into the tree you feel winged yourself."

Zachary laughed. "Yes, that's true. There's the one-minute bell going and you've got Mother Sprigg's Prayer Book."

The doctor had joined Mother Sprigg and they were both waiting in the porch. Here the families divided, the Weekaborough pew being upon the left hand side of the church and the doctor's on the right. "Voluntarily to come forward in defence of everything that is dear to you," shouted the notice board to Zachary as he passed.

II

The church of Gentian Hill was old and lovely, with beautiful perpendicular windows and a fine stone rood screen. The eighteenth century three-decker pulpit and the box pews cluttered the floor space but the pillars leaped free of them, soaring up to support the barrel roof of Spanish chestnut. The gallery was at the west end of the church and the band was already tuning up as the doctor and Zachary knelt down on their straw-filled hassocks and covered their faces with their hats. Zachary as a Catholic had no right at all to be in Weekaborough Church but where the doctor and Stella went he went too, if he possibly could, quite prepared to do a bit extra in purgatory to atone for it later. And though the amazing noise perpetrated by the Gentian Hill band in the gallery did not compare favourably with the chanting of the mass to which he was accustomed, and was besides an offence to a musician's ear, Devon folk being anything but musical, yet he managed to enjoy this service. If it was an unholy din it was hearty and greatly enjoyed. There was not a man, woman or child who did not sing at the top of its voice; unless otherwise engaged in the gallery blowing or sawing away at bugle, trombone, clarinet, trumpet, flute, fiddle or bass viol. The service seemed to Zachary to be a part of this country life that he was getting to know so well, this self-satisfied, hard-working and full-blooded life of an independent and contented people. It did not seem to him to have much to do with religion; there had been more true worship, he thought, in the ploughing of the half-acre field; but it was a great social occasion, as delightful as the Christmas wassailing and the pagan harvests home of which the doctor had told him.

The Gentian Hill parson matched the service. No one could have called Parson Ash a spiritual looking man. He was short and fat, with a round, pink and exceedingly shrewd face, twinkling black boot-button eyes and a rollicking laugh and smile. He rode to hounds with a verve astonishing in a man nearer seventy than sixty, and was a good shot. He was a bachelor, and as the younger son of an aristocratic family, who had put him into the church because they did not know what else to do with him, was well off. He was hospitable, kept an excellent table and a good cellar. He could carry his drink well and tell a good story. He performed his duty, as he saw it, excellently, never forgetting a christening, wedding or funeral and getting through the ceremony in record time. He saw to it that his church was clean, his churchyard tidy, his clerk and band punctual. He himself was always well-dressed in well-brushed clerical black with white bands, an old-fashioned white cauliflower wig and a jaunty black shovel hat. He did not personally visit the sick, for fear of infection, nor the bereaved because grief depressed him, but he sent them soup and port wine by the hand of his housekeeper, and if he caught little boys thieving he beat them good and hard. The village was proud of him and liked him. He minded his own business, let them mind theirs, and never preached a long sermon.

In fact he never really preached a sermon at all, he read it out of a useful little book containing a couple of short homilies for each Sunday in the year, with Christmas thrown in extra, and read it so fast that no one could hear a word. Not that anyone wanted to. The sermon gave them the chance of a nap after the musical exertions that had preceded it. Parson Ash had no objection to his congregation going to sleep; he'd have done the same in their place; in fact he always obligingly woke up his clerk Job Stanberry himself, leaning over the edge of the pulpit and slapping him on his bald nodding head with the book of sermons. The sound of Parson's book coming down on Job's head was the signal for everyone else to wake up too, and get going on the last hymn.

Sometimes Zachary wondered what Stella and the doctor thought of this, to him, curious church service. . . . Stella, having been brought up with it, did not think anything about it. The noisy jolly business was just Sunday Church, connected in her mind with her best clothes and the Sunday beef. It had not yet occurred to her that God was to be found in Gentian Hill Church in any special way; God was everywhere and if to her in one place more than another, then on Bowerly Hill, and in those moments when the brightness fell from the air. The doctor's sentiments were what Stella's would be in twenty years' time. In the grace of pillars and arches, soaring clear of the ugly box pews, in the words of psalms and collects, so ancient and so lovely, he seemed to himself to lay his hand upon an enduring golden thread of devotion passing through the beads of the years. It might be obscured by pagan or indifferent years but would not be snapped while there lived one single man or woman who remembered God.

The last hymn before the sermon ended with a crash, the blowers and sawers of bugle, trombone, clarinet, trumpet, flute, fiddle and bass viol expending their last ounce of breath and strength upon the final deafening chord, and everyone sank back exhausted, yet smiling with a sense of duty done. Job Stanberry the clerk folded his arms and closed his eyes and Parson Ash in the pulpit cleared his throat, adjusted his spectacles and with his book held close to his nose began to read rapidly. Dr. Crane was thankful to doze off but Zachary, in spite of only a few hours' sleep, was wakeful, his hitherto muddled mind suddenly most miraculously clear. He lifted his straw-filled hassock to the seat and sat on it, and thus elevated he could look over the top of the Crane pew to the Weekaborough pew across the aisle. He could just see the top of Father Sprigg's bald head, and Mother Sprigg's grey bonnet, but nothing at all of Stella. But he could picture her sitting there between them, her small feet side by side on the hassock, her mittened hands folded inside her muff, her pointed elfin face very serious inside the white-frilled green bonnet. What was she thinking about? The yew tree on Bowerly Hill, perhaps, its darkness lit by the small red lamps of its berries, as his rage last night had been lit by those queer gleams of triumph.

That rage had been the first real rage of his gentle life, and he realised now that it had been against malignant power that he had flung it, the evil thing that pursued men so ruthlessly through their mortal days, striking at them with whatever weapon came to hand, with pestilence, famine or storm, sparing "neither rich nor poor, old nor young." Last night he had fought that malignancy in the person of the storm, in defence of those men broken on the rocks and drowned in the sea, but now it was personified for him by that vast army assembled across the Channel, sons of the men of the Terror who had murdered his father and mother. He had said that he did not hate the French, and he did not, for their blood was in his veins and he was not capable of hatred, but at this moment the rage that was still in him was spending itself against the power of that army even as it had dashed itself against the power of the storm last night; and this time it was not a ship's crew of men unknown to him who were in danger but Stella.

"In defence of everything that is dear to you. . . ." It was there that the triumph lay, in the fact of love. That company of men on the beach last night, of whom he had been one, had loved their human kind enough to risk their lives to save them; even as the monks of Torre had done in that first shipwreck, and the girl in the doctor's story. And he loved Stella enough to go back to the hell he had left to try to keep her safe. It would probably not be of the slightest use. He was not such a fool as to think that the return of one midshipman to his duty was going to hold back that vast army. Over and over again the dark power submerged the small lit lamps of love. Yet in a flash of vision he saw them, as each was submerged, lighting another, and knew that while one still shone total darkness, the ultimate triumph of malignancy, would not descend.

"Voluntarily to come forward." He knew now how one managed it. Enduringly unwillingly on board that vile ship he had been broken. Acceptance at the mill had somehow brought him to the doctor. What had Hamlet said? "The readiness is all." He hoisted himself off the hassock, which was most uncomfortable, settled himself in the corner of the pew and went to sleep.

III

The two young officers whom the doctor had brought back from the wreck slept until the aroma of three o'clock Sunday dinner penetrated their slumbers, when they arose starving, donned the uniforms that Tom Pearse had dried and pressed for them, and descended precipitately to the dining parlour. They were in the resilient state of very young and very healthy men whose spirits leap only the higher for having been somewhat dashed. And they found themselves very much alive after having been very nearly dead, and confronting in the dining parlour the most varied and appetising meal they had seen for weeks. The doctor and Zachary had slept again after church and felt much refreshed. Only Tom Pearse, labouring all day over the drying and the ironing of clothes and the cooking of the dinner, had had no repose. But then he needed none. He was tough. And so altogether it was something of a festive occasion.

Tom had made a rabbit pie and roasted a round of beef. He had borrowed a succulent ham off the Parson's housekeeper and pigs' trotters in brawn from the Church House Inn. He knew of course that in the houses of the aristocracy men of quality never sat down to a dinner of less than fourteen meat dishes, or a supper of less than seven, but on this occasion four was all he could manage at such short notice; but he had cooked innumerable vegetables, made a superb syllabub and polished the dishful of rosy apples from the Weekaborough orchard. He had also brought up port and claret from the cellar, and burgling the key of the doctor's medicine cupboard from his pocket while he slept had laid hands upon the smuggled French brandy, which he had always suspected to be just where it was; between the camomile and the castor oil and labelled "Linseed Tea." He had lighted all the candles he could find and waited himself at table with a face so red and beaming that it quite outshone them all.

Conversation was not fluent at first; they were all too busy eating; but over the apples and wine it flourished exceedingly. Tom Pearse, who should have withdrawn at this point in the proceedings, remained where he was, all ears behind the doctor's chair, throwing in an eager word now and again. The two young men were both keen seamen, one of them the son of a Post Captain and the grandson of an Admiral, and were delighted to find the doctor and Tom of their fraternity, and talk of naval affairs was eager and informed.

Only Zachary was silent, but the doctor noticed that there was no strain about his silence; he sat listening to the talk as though he liked it, sitting easily and gracefully, his long fingers slowly and lovingly peeling one of the apples from Stella's beloved Duke of Marlborough. His dark eyes shone in the candlelight and suddenly he smiled delightedly. It was when the talk had turned to Admiral Nelson, and one of the young men had spoken of the Admiral's belief in his "radiant orb." No one knew exactly what he meant by it, but it seemed that in some hour of dereliction and despair in his youth some sort of star had seemed to rise in his darkness, beckoning him on to glory in the service of his country. That was the sort of thing that appealed to Zachary, and several times after that he looked up and smiled at the young men with an easy comradeship that delighted the doctor. It had grieved him that during the past weeks his son had seemed to shrink from contact with men of his own rank; almost as though he felt himself branded in some way. The painful shrinking had vanished now, and that fugitive air of distinction that was always his had deepened for the moment into the peaceful yet challenging distinction of men whose ease has been won by the discipline of strife. There was something about him tonight that could not be silenced by his silence and it caught the attention of the two young men; especially one of them, the Post-Captain's son, Rupert Hounslow. They turned to him more and more frequently, as though charmed by his smile, anxious to make him talk to them. At last Rupert, not more than five years his senior, spoke to him directly.

"You did a good job of work last night. I saw you when I was helping to get one of our poor fellows into your boat. You handled your oar as we do in the navy."

"Yes, Sir," said Zachary quietly.

"Are you in the service?"

The doctor's fingers tensed so suddenly on the delicate stem of his wine glass that it snapped. Mercifully the glass was empty. In the twinkling of an eye Tom had replaced it with another and filled it to the brim. Through the slight confusion of the moment he heard Zachary's voice replying with equal steadiness, "I used to be in the navy."

"Invalided out?"

"No, Sir. I deserted."

In the pause that followed the two men flushed with embarrassment but the doctor drained his glass as though he drank a toast, and Tom cleared his throat with a loud rasping crescendo as triumphant as a trumpet blast. Zachary let the peel from his apple, unbroken from start to finish, fall delicately upon his plate, wiped his fingers upon his napkin, squared his shoulders and met Rupert Hounslow's eyes unflinchingly. "I would like to go back, Sir. I can take whatever punishment is just and right. But I do not know what I should do to get back. What should I do, Sir?"

Rupert leant forward, his arms on the table, intent upon the boy. The doctor, looking at his sensible freckled face, liked him. He and Zachary talked now as though they were alone together.

"Was it a bad ship?"

"No, Sir," lied Zachary.

"Then why did you desert?"

A pulse twitched in Zachary's cheek. "I hated the sea."

"What's your name? Dr. Crane told me, I think, but I've forgotten. Was it Moon?"

"No, Sir. Anthony Louis Mary O'Connell."

Zachary gave it in full, with a childish simplicity, almost as Stella would have done with her emphasis upon the importance of names. The doctor, listening intently, knew that by his steady recitation he was deliberately wringing the neck of Zachary Moon; at what cost only he himself knew.

"I know a Captain O'Connell by reputation. An Irish Catholic. He bears the name of Mary too. Any relation?"

"Yes, Sir. He is my cousin."

"Were you on his ship?"

"Yes, Sir."

"Then you lied when you said it was not a bad ship."

"Could you help me to get back to it, Sir?" was Zachary's only reply to this.

"No, I couldn't. But I'll help you get another ship. I've got to get another ship myself. I must catch the next coach to London. Will you come with me?"

Zachary looked at the doctor. His face was set like a mask now and his eyes that had been bright were suddenly opaque and dull.

"Yes, Anthony," said the doctor. "The mail coach, Mr. Hounslow, leaves the Crown and Anchor at Torquay at ten o'clock on Tuesday morning. That's the day after tomorrow. You should be in London in twenty-four hours. If you have finished your wine, gentlemen, we will adjourn to the study."

## CHAPTER XII

### I

ZACHARY had been brought up to believe that those who do right are happy. He found next morning that this is not necessarily the case. In church, his decision made, a sort of peace had descended upon him, and had carried him through the evening. When they had gone to bed that night, after a discussion on ways and means with the two officers in the study, Dr. Crane had come with Zachary to his room. He had said practically nothing but his immense pride and delight in his son had been so heart-warming that Zachary had gone to bed almost happy and had slept well. But on Monday morning he awoke in the small hours to a cold desperate misery, worse than anything he had known yet, and rolling over and burrowing his head in the pillow he cursed himself for a damned fool. He was going back to the life of the sea that he hated, to war and wounds and death, from which he shrank with such loathing and horror, and most of all he was cutting himself off perhaps for ever from a life that he loved, from a father whom he loved, and from Stella who was the other half of himself. And he was doing it himself, by his own act. This lunacy had not been forced upon him, he had deliberately chosen it. He could not now remember the various steps, the chain of reasoning, that had brought him to this crowning disaster, he only knew he was the biggest fool God ever made. Yet throughout that abysmal hour he did not once consider turning back. He had taken one of those steps from which, for a gentleman, there is no turning back. . . . Tom Pearse banged on his door and he rolled out of bed to wash himself in a basin of cold water, get dressed, have his early and solitary breakfast and start off in the half-dark for his last day's work at Weekaborough Farm.

Lifting the latch of the kitchen door, clumping in in his heavy boots into the warm fire-lit friendliness of the beloved old room, he hoped for the first time that Stella would not be there this morning; in fairness he must tell Father and Mother Sprigg at once that he was leaving them, but it would be easier for Stella if he could tell her alone. Luck favoured him. They were all there finishing their breakfast, except Stella, who had run out to have a word with Daniel and the stable cats.

"Mornin', lad," said Father Sprigg jovially but thickly, one cheek being much distended by a huge mouthful of bread and jam.

"Mornin', Zachary," chorused Mother Sprigg, Madge and Sol. They were all fond of him and their welcome this morning seemed even warmer than usual. Hodge came and leant his head against his knee and Zachary steadied himself by a hand on the dog's warm head. Bluntly he told them what he was going to do tomorrow. There was a moment of stunned astonishment and then Father Sprigg brought his great hand down with a crash on the table.

"Good for you, lad!" he roared triumphantly, good patriot that he was. "Going for a sailor, is it? That's the style, lad! That's the style! Poor old Bony, it's like to be his death blow."

Madge clapped her hands, her round cheeks flushing a deeper crimson as she tasted already all the delightful emotions of the woman who sends a man whom she does not really care about as much as she thinks she does to a war of whose horrors she is completely ignorant. But Mother Sprigg, that born mother, was grave, seeing the misery in the boy's eyes. And as for Sol, his old face went grey and his mouth shook. He knew suddenly that he would not plough again. When the time came for the spring sowing there would be no strong young man swinging along beside him, no clear voice singing that chant that alone gave him strength to follow the plough. For the first time the shadow of death fell upon him and he bowed his head upon his chest. Zachary went to him and stood behind him, gripping his shoulder. "I'll be back for the spring sowing, Sol. I'll be back by the spring."

But Old Sol shook his head. Then he fumbled in his pockets and took out his bull-roarer. "Take it, lad," he muttered hoarsely. "I've had it man an' boy, an' my father afore me I b'lieve, but I'd like ee to have it. It'll likely cheer ee up in foreign parts."

Zachary hated the bull-roarer almost as much as Stella did; its uncanny din always made the hair rise on the back of his neck and caused him to look uneasily over his shoulder; but he could not refuse the old man's gift. "Thank you, Sol," he said, and pocketed the thing with the gloomiest foreboding.

"Who's to tell Stella?" asked Mother Sprigg. "It had best be me."

"I'll tell her," said Zachary, with such decision that Mother Sprigg had to yield. "I'll be on Bowerly Hill at noon. I've a load of sea sand to cart to the clover field. Please, Mother Sprigg, will you let her bring my nummet to me there?"

"Ay, lad," said Mother Sprigg gently.

"After that, you'd best get home," said Father Sprigg. "There'll be plenty to see to. I'll miss you on the farm, lad." He looked up. "And remember, boy, when you're away, that whenever you come back Weekaborough Farm will have a right good welcome for you. Remember that."

Zachary turned on his heel precipitately, his boots making a great clatter on the flagstones, and left the room, banging the door.

"Seems as though he don't want to fight Bony after all," said Madge wonderingly.

"Hold your vlother, girl," said Mother Sprigg with most unusual irritation.

II

The clover field, on the far slope of Bowerly Hill, had borne such fine crops that it had exhausted itself, and Father Sprigg had decreed a thorough manuring. Zachary had spent a blissful day on the shore with Father Sprigg and Stella, filling the panniers of the pack horses, Shem and Ham, with the fine sea sand formed of the fragments of broken shells, and carting it back to the farm.

Now, mixed with dung, it stood in a heap in the yard ready to be loaded into the panniers again and carted to Bowerly Hill. Using Shem, the dun-coloured pack horse, Zachary worked like a fury all the morning, thankful for the hard labour, thankful to Father Sprigg and Sol for their understanding that left him to do it alone, thankful to Mother Sprigg for keeping Stella busy indoors. But hard though he tried to drug himself with work the familiar sights and sounds and sensations refused to be banished from his consciousness, they came pressing upon him as though trying to burn themselves into his memory. The sheep white against the green grass. The pricked ears and alert head of beautiful little Shem, toiling uphill so gallantly with his loaded panniers. The cattle with their coats of clear dark red, their fine horns and deer-like faces. The spring of the turf beneath his feet. The feel of Hodge's rough head against his hand. For a little he fought against his awareness of these things, then he yielded. He might be glad, presently, to remember it all again.

The work was finished at last and he sat beneath the yew tree to wait for Stella. It was a grey day, but fine and clear and warm. He sat with his hands hanging between his knees, his head bent, Hodge at his feet, hearing the crying of the gulls and the wind in the branches above him.

But he made no attempt to recover the ecstasy of the day when he had climbed into the branches, and they had held him, and the gulls had come beating up out of the gold. It would have been no use. Nothing of that sort can ever be recaptured.

There was a grey moss-covered stone half buried in the earth at his feet, one of the many that lay here around the yew tree, and he looked at it dully, unconsciously kicking it with one of his boots. A cushion of moss, loosened by the heavy rains, slipped, and he thought he saw something carved upon the stone. There were faint marks upon the stone, almost obliterated by time and weather, something that might have been a fleur-de-lys such as was carved upon the wall in St. Michael's Chapel, and upon the two old graves in the churchyard. He was too wretched to be particularly interested, but the thought of the chapel reminded him of the legend of the hermit, and Rosalind and her lover, and he suddenly thought of a plan that might keep Stella from forgetting him. He might be away for years and she was only a little girl; how could he possibly expect that she would not forget? He had no right to bind her with any promises but he could ask her to remember him in the same way that Rosalind's lover had asked her; the sort of way that would appeal to a little girl. (Had Rosalind been a little girl?) And as time went on, if he did not soon return, she might remember that Rosalind and that boy had been lovers, and had married in the end.

Hodge, lying at his feet, lifted his head, sniffed, then bounded up and leaped off down the hill. Looking round Zachary saw Stella running up the path, in and out between the grazing sheep, quickly and lightly as a fairy, as he had always imagined her, swinging his nummet tied up in a scarlet spotted handkerchief. He got up and stood waiting for her, staring so that he would never forget the picture that she made. She wore her scarlet cloak over her green gown and little white apron, but the hood had fallen back from her tumbled dark curls. She stopped to pat Hodge, then looked up and saw him and laughed, running on again with Hodge leaping beside her, her face rosy with the running uphill. The quiet grey sky, the green grass and the gay little figure dancing in and out between the sheep. It was not possible that he could ever forget.

She was too excited by the unusual adventure of bringing him his nummet to notice his strained stillness. They sat down together beneath the yew tree, on two of the grey stones, the sheep about them, and she untied the scarlet handkerchief. Zachary stared at the sight of his nummet. Mother Sprigg was not a demonstrative woman but she could always express her feelings through the medium of food, and she had packed up a nummet fit for the gods. . . . A slice of pork pie. Apple pasty. Saffron cake. Devonshire splits with clotted cream and damson jam inside. . . . Zachary knew that he must dispose of it all, though it choke him. Luckily Stella and Hodge, sitting one on each side, were quite prepared to help.

"I've got something I must tell you, Stella," he said when the nummet was finished.

"Nice?" asked Stella, shaking the crumbs out of the scarlet handkerchief.

"No."

She looked at him, folded the handkerchief neatly, put it away in her hanging pocket and clasped her hands quietly on her lap. The flush had gone and her pointed elfin face, with sweet mouth and sombre eyes, had a very adult gravity. No, she was hardly a little girl. . . . Not like other little girls. . . . She had some strange inheritance of wisdom that set her apart from other children of her age. Because of the wisdom it did not seem difficult, once he had begun, to tell her who he was, what he had done, what he was going to do. It had never seemed to him strange that she had never asked him any of the usual childish questions about himself, except just his name at that first meeting, and it did not seem to him strange that when he had finished the story she did not make any outcry but accepted his going, as she had accepted his coming, without either astonishment or curiosity. That was like her. She had the courage that accepts instantly, without recoil, and the reverence in love that towards man is without possessiveness and towards God without rebellion. For a moment or two her stillness, her silence, so at one with the quiet and peace of the day, were like balm. Then he began to grow a little scared, and looked at her. She looked like an old woman; or a changeling who had never at any time been a child. In his panic he put his hand on her shoulder and shook it.

"Stella!"

She seemed to find it difficult to turn, to look at him, as though the blood in her veins had turned to ice, yet when she did speak it was childishly enough. "Zachary, I wanted you to be here for Christmas. There's the wassailing and the carols and the mummers and everything. Zachary——" She caught her lower lip between her teeth and was silent again. He put his hands round hers, still lying clasped on her lap, and held them tightly, as though making a vow.

"Stella, if I'm not at home this Christmas I'll be home for lots of other Christmases, I promise."

"Promise?"

"I promise. And when I'm away you'll write me a letter sometimes, Stella, won't you? I'll write to you."

Stella nodded, the candles lighting up again in her eyes at the thought of letters building themselves up like a bridge over the awful chasm that had suddenly yawned between her and Zachary.

"And there's another thing you can do," he went on, "you can go to the Chapel of St. Michael, like Rosalind did, and remember there that I'm coming back again."

Stella actually smiled. "I'll go, like Rosalind. . . . But that man was away for years, Zachary."

"And I'll only be away till I've licked Bony," he said, and laughed, and jumping up swung her to her feet. "I'll race you down the hill, Stella."

They did not run very fast. The race was a mere device to get them from the top of the hill to the garden gate, where they must say good-bye. At the gate he picked her up and kissed her, holding her tightly, but only for a moment. Then he put her down, watched her until she reached the shelter of the porch, and then tramped quickly away down the lane, round the corner by the orchard and up the hill towards the village without once looking back, fixing his mind upon a mental picture, resolutely conjured up, of Stella in the arms of comforting Mother Sprigg.

But Stella had not gone to Mother Sprigg. She had stayed in the porch, sitting on the seat in the deep shadow. Even as a small child it had never been her habit to run crying to Mother Sprigg with her cuts and bruises. She had always had the feeling that one's hurts are private things; and the deeper the hurt the more private. And this parting from Zachary was the worst thing that had ever happened to her; indeed the only really bad thing that had ever happened to her in all her happy life. She did not know how she was going to bear it. She stayed for a long time in the porch, sitting very upright on the seat, crying silently. Presently she pulled out her Mother's locket, that she always wore beneath her dress, and looked at it. She supposed her Mother had had to bear a great many things. Grown-up people did. But she did not suppose that she had cried. She went on holding the locket until she had got the better of her tears, and then she went indoors and up to her room to wash her face.

III

The turmoil of packing over, and the two young men tactfully gone to bed early, Dr. Crane and Zachary sat for the last time talking in front of the study fire. The doctor had a few things that he wanted to say and he said them, though with small hope that they would penetrate the wretchedness of the boy beside him.

"You've done the right thing, Zachary, though as far as you can see it's not done you any good. Not much glory about it, as far as you can see. You feel damnable. That's of no consequence—feelings don't matter. It's action that matters, and from fine action some sort of glory always breaks in the end; though God knows how long you may have to wait for it."

"What *is* glory?" growled Zachary suddenly.

"I can't explain. You'll know one day. But there's one thing which out of my doctor's experience both in war and peace I think I can explain, and that's how to deal with fear." Zachary started, and the doctor thanked God he had captured his attention. "To begin with, don't fight it, accept it without shame, just as you would accept any other limitation you happen to be born with, a cast in the eye, or a lame foot. Willing acceptance is half the battle, as you've probably discovered before this. Be willing to be afraid, don't be afraid of your fear. As a doctor I can tell you that every man has within him a store of strength, both physical and spiritual, of which he is utterly unaware until the moment of crisis. You will not tap it until the moment of crisis, but you can be quite certain that when that moment comes it will not fail you. It's not easy to believe this, but you must do it. And there's another thing which you must do; learn how to live with alien horrors and not let your nerves crack beneath the pressure of them." Again Zachary started, remembering his relief when he came to this house and realised that the fight to hold off that pressure was over at last. "Again, don't fight; if you fight you'll crack. You can't fight foul language, foul smells, sweat and dirt and all the rest of it, the only thing you can do is to live amongst it both with acceptance and withdrawal. That sounds paradoxical but it's perfectly possible. You're not befouled by another man's obscenities and brutalities, though you may feel you are, but only by your own, and if you have strangled your own then the door of escape is open for you and you can go through it to the fortress when you wish. There is a fortress, you know."

Zachary knew. The stones of the Chapel had cried it out, and later, through that extra sense that adversity had developed in him, his mind had grasped the existence of that something behind. Yet what is the use of knowing a thing, he thought bitterly, when you are unable personally to experience the truth of it? Your knowledge is about as useful in the darkness as a lantern with no light in it.

"You can experience the reality of what you believe in only one way, by putting it to the test," said the doctor, interpreting his silence aright. "There is nothing at all that will light up the flame in your lantern except the wind of your going. Nothing else at all."

They were silent, and then Zachary said slowly, "I've said good-bye to Stella." He felt he wanted the doctor to know how he felt about Stella, yet it seemed unexplainable.

"She'll not forget you," said the doctor, as though no explanation were necessary.

"She's only a little girl," said Zachary, moving restlessly in his chair. "I can't expect——"

"A very unusual little girl," said the doctor, "of whom unusual things may be expected. She is not the child of Father and Mother Sprigg."

Zachary suddenly sat straight up in his chair, tense and eager. "Not the child of the Spriggs! Does she know that?"

"Yes, she knows."

"Why, Sir, she never told me!"

"I imagine that loyalty to Mother Sprigg would have kept her from telling you. Mother Sprigg is possessive and likes it to be thought that Stella is really her child. Stella, with her intuition, would sense that. But I think it is right that you should know. You'll keep your mouth shut."

"Yes, Sir."

Dr. Crane, thankful to give Zachary something to think about apart from his own misery, told all that he knew of Stella, and Zachary listened eagerly. "That explains her," he said. "I could not understand where she got it from—her wisdom—not like a child's."

"Father and Mother Sprigg have plenty of wisdom."

"Not that sort. Unearthly. As though she were a fairy's child."

"She's human all right." The doctor laughed, went to his desk and came back with a folded scrap of paper. "This was written inside Stella's mother's locket. I copied it out in the Greek in which it was written. Your Greek is equal to the strain, I think. And you know 'The Banquet'."

Zachary took the scrap of paper and translated slowly. "Love is the divinity who creates peace among men, and calm upon the sea, the windless silence of storms, repose and sleep in sadness. Love sings to all things which love and are, soothing the troubled minds of gods and men."

Zachary had read the words often and they had had little meaning for him, yet now in his extremity it seemed as though they had actually been written for him. For a sudden brief moment he was in that core of quiet that exists at the heart of every storm; the fortress. He folded the paper again.

"You can keep it," said the doctor. "And now we'd better go to bed."

IV

All was bustle next morning at the Crown and Anchor, in whose yard the mail coach waited. Torquay had no church, and no resident doctor, but such was the thirst of both natives and visiting seamen that it had five little inns, and the Crown and Anchor was the most flourishing of them. It looked out over the harbour and had a bakery to one side of it, so that passengers could supply themselves with buns and pies, as well as bottles of ale and porter, before setting out on the hazardous two-days' journey to London.

When the doctor, Tom Pearse and Zachary in the doctor's gig, followed by the two young officers in another hired from the Church House Inn, arrived at the yard, all was bustle and confusion. Samuel Rowe the postmaster, who presided over the tiny room in a cottage at the Strand which was known as the Torquay Post Office, was delivering the mail with great volubility. He was a great character; he had been postmaster since 1796 and would continue in his office until 1846, his daughter Grace carrying round the letters for five pounds a year. Passengers, most of them young men in uniform entangled in weeping wives, were struggling to take their places, chickens were squawking, dogs barking, small boys darting hither and thither, cats getting under foot, the guard was blowing his horn to round up stragglers and the driver shouting to the landlord. A mixed crowd of sailors, ostlers, serving maids, the baker and his boy, ancient gaffers tottering on sticks, babies in go-carts and all the rest of the human flotsam and jetsam that collects where anything is going on, were milling round in a state of pleasurable excitement.

The mail coach provided Torquay's only contact with the great world, apart from the comings and goings of the ships in the harbour. The stay-at-homes, watching the departure, could vicariously taste the excitement of travel, could journey to London along the grand new turnpike roads that were so much talked of, seeing the sights along the way; other counties and villages of England that were almost as strange to them as foreign lands. And the coach's arrival was even more exciting than its departure, especially in these days of war when it brought news of king and court and parliament, of battles and great deeds. Not a few, watching the departure this morning, could remember the day only three years ago when the coach had dashed in decorated with laurels, the guard blowing his horn, and one of the travellers had stood upon the coach's roof, after it had rocked to a standstill in the inn yard, the *Extraordinary Gazette* in his hand, and had read aloud to them the news of the peace of Amiens. All the bells had pealed, the bells of Saint Mary Church, of Torre and Paignton, and the guns of the frigates in the bay had boomed out the news. There had been thanksgiving services in the churches and bonfires lit upon the hills, and they had all gone mad with joy. But it had not lasted. Only two years later the coach had arrived with the news that war had broken out again. There was no trusting Bony. He did not want peace until he had conquered the world. And now, today, the times were as anxious as ever and almost every traveller upon the coach was a young man in uniform.

"Good-bye, my son."

Dr. Crane's large hand descended upon Zachary's shoulder and stayed there a moment or two, gripping hard, as though he were trying to give the boy some of his own immense vitality. His eyes, at this moment of his pride, were blazing. Zachary, bracing his shoulders beneath the painful grip, steeled himself to meet the doctor's eyes, though the love in them turned him breathless with pain now that he must leave it.

"Good-bye, Sir." He turned and held out his hand to Tom Pearse. "Good-bye, Tom." He turned his back on both of them and looked up at the coach without seeing it. They were to travel outside, he remembered. But he saw Rupert Hounslow's freckled face, smiling down at him, and his outstretched hand. He grasped the hand and was swung up. He smelt the straw and the horses, heard the crack of the whip and the coach wheels grinding over the cobbles. Looking down he saw the doctor's face once more and wondered why it should look so glad. The guard was blowing his horn again and the water in the harbour dazzled his eyes. There were still flowers in the gardens of the Strand and smoke curled up from the cottage chimneys. The coach rocked over the bridge that crossed the Fleete and the sea was behind them, and at first sight it looked as though there were no way out from this enchanted valley. But there was a ribbon of a road winding between the round green hills and the coach found it and followed it. The sound of the horn died away in the distance and presently the Strand was quiet again, with no sound except the crying of the gulls and the lapping of the water against the harbour wall.

# *BOOK II*

# THE SEA

# CHAPTER I

I

It was Sunday, October 20th, 1805. Mass had been said in the old guest hall of Torre Abbey. This was now the Catholic Church of the neighbourhood, and the little group of worshippers, some of whom drove many miles over abominable roads, through every kind of weather, to their Sunday mass, were gathering now in the entrance hall, where beyond the great doors their carriages were waiting in the autumn sunshine. They were a small community, a few of them from great houses in the neighbourhood, others gentlefolk living in retirement at Torquay, attracted there by the proximity of the Abbey, with a sprinkling of a few émigrés and naval officers on leave; all of them almost like courtiers in their devotion to Sir George and Lady Carey, in whose house they worshipped, and whose hospitality was at times for the poorest among the émigrés a bulwark against the hunger of which they would sooner die than speak. For they were all aristocrats; as they moved there was the rustle of silks, the clink of shoes against stone, a breath of perfume, the music of gentle voices speaking gently; want was a vulgar thing that was not mentioned in polite society.

What they were mentioning now, as they stood in the entrance hall, were the affairs of the day. They were gloomy enough. Napoleon had been crowned Emperor in Notre Dame. Austria had been ruinously defeated, and amongst all the nations of Europe it seemed that only England really stood firm against the enemy; and even she had her half-hearted politicians, her bungling administrators who sickened the hearts of the willing and the brave. Thanks to the vigilance of Nelson and Cornwallis the threatened invasion of England had not yet been attempted, but the fleets of France and Spain still remained intact, and the danger was not over. Nelson had been on the long chase to the West Indies and back, but he had not caught them. Now he was eating his heart out in the Mediterranean, but he could not bring them to battle. As this war dragged on and on hardships were increasing. At times there was something almost like famine in the towns, with riots among the hungry people. The activities of the press gangs ever becoming more brutal, and intermingled with patriotism there was a good deal of bitterness and discontent. There seemed no end to it all and hearts were heavy. . . . Though just at the moment, among this group of men and women, there was the rekindling of hope that comes when an aesthetic experience of great power and beauty has just laid its spell of peace upon the mind. Not hope of anything in particular. Just hope.

The Sunday mass at Torre Abbey was in these days always memorable. The Abbé de Colbert, the chaplain of Torre Abbey and the spiritual director of all who worshipped there, made of it always a poignant and deep experience for those to whom he ministered. Each of the familiar prayers, spoken in his extraordinarily beautiful voice, soared up like music and fell again as light; there was a new quietness in their minds and new faith in their souls, and the intensity of his own devotion lit theirs. When the Abbé celebrated it seemed as though dullness and dryness had never been. . . . Which some of them thought odd, for the Abbé when not engaged in his priestly duties seemed to them a dry old stick; so austere as to be scarcely human; not a likeable man at all. . . . But the more discerning were not surprised. To them there was always something stimulating about the Abbé even at his most uncompromising; a suggestion of banked fires that kept them always on the watch for the glint of gold.

But whether they liked or disliked the Abbé they always paid him the tribute of intense awareness that is given only to quality of a high order. Engrossed in conversation though they were, as they gathered in the hall, they heard his light footfall behind them; conversation died to a murmur and they turned instinctively towards him. He smiled frostily as he came among them, bowed to Sir George and bent to kiss the hand of Lady Carey as he courteously but firmly refused her invitation to dinner. . . . His manners were those of the Versailles of twenty years ago, highly stylised and encased in ice, and somewhat shattering. . . . He was, as always, immaculately and simply dressed in black, but in frock coat and white stock, not in the soutane and white bands of the priest. He said that he thought such a costume would attract too much attention in such an obstinately Protestant country as England, and if there was one thing which he disliked more than another, it was to be the focus of attention. In a sudden moment of expansion he had once said bitterly to Sir George that he wished he was a hermit in a cell; only so would he enjoy that complete seclusion from the human race which was the goal of his ambition. To this remark Sir George had replied frigidly (for he disliked those who disliked the human race, being somewhat partial to it himself) that the Abbé surely had the next best thing to it. His nearby lodgings, a small bedroom and study in a cottage looking out upon a village green, were surely as quiet a retreat as any man could wish for. The Abbé had replied that a village green was not as quiet as it sounded. It could be at times an uncommonly noisy place, especially when a wrestling match was in progress; not always an ideal spot for a man engaged in literary pursuits.

For the Abbé in these days of his exile employed himself in the writing of books so erudite that only men who were his equals in scholarship could understand a word of them; and of these there were perhaps some dozen in England and the same number upon the Continent. When he was not looking after his flock, or writing books, he was going for long swift walks by himself, and when he was not doing any of these things he was at prayer.

His history was known to his fellow émigrés in bare outline, but no more, for he never spoke of his past life. He had been the third son of the Comte de Colbert, and his childhood in his parents' chateau must have been happy enough, and presumably his young manhood too, for he had been sent into a crack regiment, and held the rank of Colonel at the age of twenty-five and had spent much time in attendance at the gayest court in the world. He had been gay himself, gifted with every grace of mind and person, but his gaiety had been a thing of excess; there had been no young men at the court so wildly extravagant in all they did as the young Colonel. He had not always been in France, for he had seen foreign service with his regiment, and had distinguished himself in it, but wherever he was his abounding vitality had made him immensely popular; he had been a flame at which others warmed themselves. And in the day of retribution his courage had still been as a flame. He had not joined any of the first waves of émigrés who, led by the Comte d'Artois, had escaped from France after the fall of the Bastille. He had served the King while this was possible, then he had gone home to do what he could to protect his parents. It was said of him that when the mob came to burn the chateau and murder its occupants he had fought like a tiger until he had been wounded. The village curé, it was said, had rescued him and hidden him. When he came back to life again it was to find himself Comte de Colbert, for he was the only one of his family left alive. Then he became a fugitive, and it was at this time that he was joined in his wanderings by a woman whom he loved; who she was and whether he was married to her, the Torre Abbey community did not know. Somehow they had escaped together and reached England, a child had been born to them and they had been happy. Then the woman and the child had died and the Comte had gone to Ireland. Nothing was known of the years he had spent in Ireland except that while there he had become a priest. Two years ago he had come to Torquay, the cold, hard, yet immensely impressive man known to the Catholic community as the Abbé de Colbert.

That was all any of them had been able to discover about him, and none of this information had been supplied by himself but had been pieced together for the most part by an energetic émigré, one of those busy ladies who can know no happiness until clairvoyant research into the lives of their friends has left those friends with scarcely a cranny in which to hide. . . . Though it was felt by all that in the case of the Abbé she had not been so successful as usual. There were some big gaps in the narrative, and no doubt these gaps contained occurrences which had played their part in transforming the gay young soldier of Versailles into this enigmatic and prematurely aged priest. . . . For the busy lady had calculated that the Abbé could not possibly be as old as he looked. He was, she declared, only in his late forties.

He looked sixty as he moved about the hall, paying his devoirs to first one group and then another, almost with the impartiality of royalty, saying not more than a few words to any of them, excepting only to Mrs. Loraine, a very old lady whose beauty and dignity had always attracted him. She was a widow whose two sons had both died fighting in India. She lived alone in a little house near Torre Church, and he liked her because she never spoke of her sorrows; nor of her rheumatism nor her straitened means, which caused her to come to mass in all weathers, not in a carriage, but very slowly and painfully upon her feet, leaning upon an ebony stick. He had actually been to call upon her once and she had asked him to go again, but he had not gone. Understanding him she had not resented this. She smiled at him with affection now, as he bent over her hand, but was careful to say nothing to detain him. A moment or two later he managed to escape. His vanishing tricks were well known to his flock. He could disappear with the ease of a shadow when the sun goes in.

II

He strode away through the park with the swiftness and ease of a young man; and the relief of the solitary who has recaptured his solitude again. Though he was fasting he scarcely felt tired. During the last fifteen years or so he had passed through one of those furnaces of suffering and hardship that break the body of a man of weak constitution, but temper the body of a strong one to whipcord and steel. The Abbé's constitution had always been remarkable, and he was now whipcord and steel. He regretted it. He was thinking this morning, that if he was to live to ninety like his grandfather then he was still only half way through. And since Thérèse had died the time had seemed long. That was the way of it in loneliness. When they had been together the years had flown, and even the bad things they had endured had not seemed to last so long because they had been together. And now one solitary and uneventful week seemed a century. He supposed he ought to try and be more companionable, but he had lost the trick of it; and that after being one of the most gregarious young men in all France. Because the things that he had seen men do to each other had made him shrink from the human race, and because over there in Ireland, after she had died, the time of solitude in the monastery by the mere had restored his reason, he had come to think that only celled was he safe. The world was a madhouse, he had thought, and as most of the men and women in it were what you would expect in such a place it was best to have as little contact with them as possible. But during the last year, as in quietness his mental balance had slowly steadied, he had felt ashamed of his shrinking; it was a sin in a priest; and just lately, at rare intervals, he had felt what was almost a longing to go out from himself once more and search among the criminals and fools for the few who were neither.

They existed here and there, the wise and gentle, the brave and gay; and the incurious. Among the little community he had just left were many excellent men and women, he knew, but their curiosity, searching his wounds like a surgeon's probe, was a thing that he could not yet endure. King Lear and his child had been incurious, they had neither asked him his name nor told him theirs, they had just come and gone like the visitants of a dream, leaving him with the memory of the old man's wisdom and scholarship and the look of astonished gratitude that had flooded the boy's sensitive face in response to his act of common courtesy. That evocation and response had touched him more than he had realised at the time; he was not sure that it was not the boy's look which had awakened in him this strange new wish for companionship. Several times lately he had wished not that these two had been curious but that he had. . . . He had been a fool not to ask their names.

He looked up and saw St. Michael's Chapel, with its grey walls almost silver in the frosty sunshine. He had not been able to stay as long as he had wished in the Abbey Chapel after mass; courtesy had demanded that he go to the hall and speak to the dispersing congregation; he decided he would climb up to St. Michael's Chapel and continue his thanksgiving there. It was the place that he loved above all others in this district. It was, for him, steeped in the sense of sanctuary; peace after storm, thanksgiving for danger past, prayer for those still out in the wind and the weather; and he could always be certain of solitude there. The bovine English Protestants looked upon it as a Popish relic and let it alone, and the few Catholics in the neighbourhood were mostly too well stricken in years to attempt the steep climb up the rocks, or else they were also too bovine, the bovinity being in their case the result of nationality and over-eating rather than of religion. Apart from the Catholic crews of visiting foreign ships, who came but seldom, he could only once recollect having seen anyone praying there, and that was the King's son.

He climbed up quickly and easily and entering the Chapel looked eagerly about him. Absurd, he thought, to love the place so much that he had to look each time to see if all was well with it. Bare and empty as it was, while it stood it could not suffer change. No one could take away the rough rock floor and vaulted roof, the piscina and the two empty niches in the north wall, with the flower carved on the stone between them. It varied only with the weather, with the colour of the shadows and the quality of the light; blue today, bright and brittle as spun glass. He knelt near the piscina, facing the place where once the altar had been, and through the unglazed east window the sun streamed in on him, so that he scarcely felt the cold.

"Laudate Dominum, omnes gentes: laudate eum omnes populi. Quoniam confirmata est super nos misericordia ejus: et veritas Domini manet in aeternum."

Words. They were so small, so light, they waited so humbly about a man, ready for his use, yet they could deliver him from mortal weariness more swiftly than any other form of music. . . . Music. . . . The wings of Perseus that for mortality had no existence apart from the body yet were not of it. Wings upon aching feet. Prayer upon the lips. Heaven and earth. Eternal life in the bread and wine. Words had already lifted him into the silence and he worshipped there for he did not know how long. Then coming back again, without knowing it, he spoke aloud, "Sit nomen Domini benedictum: ex hoc nunc, et usque in saeculum."

III

Some sound disturbed him, a small rustle like that of a mouse. He looked round, expecting a mouse, and saw a small girl in a green cloak and bonnet sitting sedately on a hummock of rock, her hands folded inside a round brown muff, regarding him very seriously out of a pair of starry grey eyes. Meeting his glance she smiled with the utmost friendliness, and the smile went through him with a stab of pain. He got up almost shakily, one hand against the wall, and stared bleakly at her with a face grown so suddenly haggard that any other child would have been scared stiff. But not Stella. Apart from her natural fearlessness there had never been anyone yet who had been unkind to her. Having met with and given nothing but love all her life love was what she expected to receive and give.

"Don't your knees ache?" she asked sympathetically.

"Slightly," said the Abbé stiffly. He had recovered himself, but he still stood where he was, one hand against the wall. He had not the slightest idea how to talk to children. He knew nothing about them. His own child had been so small a creature when death had come. . . . Death. . . . Thérèse. . . . He felt dizzy again for a moment. Would he never get over it?

He perceived that the child had moved slightly. One small mittened hand came out of the muff and was laid upon the rock in invitation. She smiled and cocked her head on one side like a robin. Women! They knew how to beguile a man almost before they were out of the cradle. But no, upon a second glance he saw that there was no coquetry about her; merely motherliness. He crossed the Chapel and sat down beside her on the low rock with some difficulty, his long legs stretched out ridiculously before him. So they sat, side by side, wrapped in their cloaks, looking at each other, the winter sunlight falling on their faces.

"Do you suffer from lumbago?" asked Stella. "Sir," she added suddenly as an afterthought. She had been trained to say "Sir" and "Madam" to her elders, but she often forgot, not out of disrespect, but because the deep interest she took in everybody gave her a sense of nearness to them that was inimicable to formality. For the same reason she often forgot her curtsy too.

"I thank you, no," said the Abbé. "I just found it difficult to sit down because I am so much taller than you are."

Stella smiled, glad that he did not have lumbago. "Father Sprigg has it," she said. "It's most painful. Mother Sprigg warms salt in the oven and applies it to where the pain is, and then he feels better."

"Are Father and Mother Sprigg your parents?" asked the Abbé. He had quite forgotten that he did not know how to talk to children. This lovely child had done more than entirely put him at his ease; though her smile had given him the wild stab of pain, and though he ached with it still, yet the fact of her was to him a gift of joy and wonder. It was so many years since he had had this sense of reverent acceptance of a treasure, that he had forgotten the feel of it. But now he could remember other times. The day when as a small boy he had first gone to midnight mass and the curé had given him a lighted candle. The day when he had looked up and seen Thérèse coming towards him, her hands cupped about the gift she brought. The sight of the white swan flying over the mere in Ireland. The day when the old curé, looking back at him from the tumbril, had smiled. All little things, yet gifts that had had power to save. And she was a little thing, this child, an elfin creature. While he questioned gently, and she answered quietly and politely, he saw her small, brown, heart-shaped face, the determined upper lip and straight little nose, the laughter in the curves of the lips, as a man sees who will never forget. Even so had he seen the candle flame, the cupped hands of Thérèse, the reflection of the swan's wings in the mere, the gladness in the smile of his friend, and known that he had reached a milestone in his life.

"Father and Mother Sprigg are my father and mother," Stella answered. This statement did not seem to her a lie. They had saved her. They loved her. To say that they were not her father and mother would have seemed to be, as the doctor had guessed, disloyalty.

"You live in Torquay, child?"

"No, Sir. I live at Weekaborough Farm, near Gentian Hill."

"You are here alone?"

"Dr. Crane brought me to the bottom of the hill. He's gone to see a patient and then he'll come back and fetch me. Those were lovely words you were saying when I came in. Like Zachary used to say sometimes."

"You like words?"

She nodded.

"So do I," he said. "They are like wings, are they not."

"They fly up," she said, "and then they fall down again like light."

"Yes, I know. And this Zachary whose words you liked, is he your brother?"

He saw how the laughter left her lips and her eyes darkened. "No. He's gone away to sea, and I come here to remember that he will come back. Like Rosalind."

The Abbé knew something of the legend of the place. "Once a year, like Rosalind?" he asked.

"Yes. This is the first time I've come. Zachary went away on November the twenty-seventh, so I really ought to have waited till November again, but I have come earlier because . . ." She stopped and looked a little troubled.

"Could you tell me why?" asked the Abbé gently. Yes, she could tell him. She never found it hard to tell people things; if she could find the words. She had only hesitated because Mother Sprigg had said strangers did not always want to be bothered with all one's affairs. But this man seemed to want to be bothered.

"Last night I dreamed about the country where one goes. You know the country, Sir?"

"Yes," said the Abbé.

"Zachary was there, but I could not find him. He was afraid. I know he was there, and I know he was afraid, but yet I could not find him."

"That was natural," said the Abbé. "Fear is a lonely thing. Even those who love us best cannot get close to us when we are afraid."

"When I woke up I wondered why he was afraid," said Stella. "I thought perhaps there was a storm——"

"And so you came here to remember Zachary in this place especially set apart for prayer for those at sea."

"Yes. The doctor came to listen to Old Sol's bronchitis—it's noisy—Sol's our ploughman—and I asked him to bring me here. Mother Sprigg was not pleased. It meant I could not go with her to church. But this is church, isn't it?"

"Certainly it is. Have you already prayed to le bon Dieu for your friend, my child?"

"Yes. I was here quite five minutes before you knew that I was. It was me getting up and sitting down that made you turn round."

"And this Zachary who is not your brother, he is a child of neighbours, perhaps?"

"No. He has no father or mother. But the doctor looks after him."

Lear and Cordelia? The Abbé opened his mouth to enquire eagerly as to the appearance of the doctor and Zachary, then it suddenly struck him that for a man who resented curiosity as deeply as he did, he was asking an appalling number of questions. He had noticed before that the one idea of adults, when conversing with children, seemed to be to ask them questions. Extremely vulgar and ill bred. Though in his case his vulgarity had been caused by the intense interest he felt in this little girl. No, interest was hardly the word; it was more than interest. But there must be no more of this ill-mannered questioning. She had most courteously and sweetly satisfied his curiosity. Now he must satisfy hers, if she had any.

"When I was a little boy," he said, "perhaps a little younger than you are now, I had a very happy Christmas. All my Christmases were happy, but this one, I remember, was especially good. My father and mother, my brothers and I, lived in a big old house on the edge of a pine forest, and inside the forest was a small village with a little church, and every Christmas Eve we walked through the forest to a service there at midnight. This particular Christmas Eve was the first time I had been allowed to go with the others; until then my mother had thought me too small to go. It had snowed, I remember, and my father carried me on his back. I remember what fun I thought it to ride on my father's back, and how wonderful it was in the forest, with the lanterns my brothers carried sending their warm light over the snow, and the stars shining above us through the branches of the pine trees, and the church bells ringing.

"Nearly all the village people had gathered in the church when we arrived, but they had left seats for us near the crib and the Christmas tree. All through the service I stared at the little crib, with the lights burning about it, and at the Christmas tree with its lighted candles, and I was full of wonder and delight. When the service was over the old priest, because I was the youngest there, and because this was my first attendance at midnight mass, took a lighted candle from the tree and gave it to me.

"I lighted a candle for every soul in this parish, Madame," he said to my mother. "One hundred and fifteen souls aflame with the love of God; or if they are not the more shame to them." Then he looked at me. "Carry the candle home, my son, and do not let it go out."

"I was too young to understand his meaning, but I understood that the candle must not go out, and going home I would not let my father carry me, even though I was tired and my legs ached, because I thought there would be more wind up there than down below. I walked behind him all the way, so that his broad back should keep the wind off my candle, and because the snow was deep I trod in his footsteps, like the page in the footsteps of Good King Wenceslas."

"And the candle did not go out?" asked Stella eagerly.

"No, not then." He paused and added slowly, truth compelling him. "Not until later."

"But it was lighted again?"

The man saw once more the white swan flying over the mere, and the flash of its wings in the sun. "Yes, it was lighted again."

"Tell me more about when you were a little boy," commanded Stella eagerly. "Sir," she added.

He laughed, looking down at her eager face, suddenly remembering many happy incidents of childhood, forgotten until now, that he would like to tell her. His Torre Abbey friends would have been astonished had they heard his laugh; they thought he never laughed. But a growing sensation of hunger reminded him that the doctor had perhaps a considerable round to make before he could go home to dinner.

"And your friend the doctor," he asked, "is he fetching you here or waiting for you below?"

"He'll wait below," said Stella. "He doesn't like climbing up here. He has the rheumatics."

The Abbé crossed to one of the windows and looked out. Down at the foot of the rock he could see a gig. The horse was a grey gelding, and the elderly gentleman sitting on the high seat wore a many-caped great-coat and a curly-brimmed top-hat poised at a singular angle. Even at this distance, slightly aided by imagination, the Abbé thought he could make out the flash of an eyeglass and a large and broken nose, and most joyfully did he recognise the person and equipage of the King.

He turned back to Stella. "We must keep the other stories for another day, for the good doctor is waiting." Then he asked just one more question. "Will you tell me your name, my child?"

She had got up and stood facing him, her hands inside the muff. "Stella Sprigg." He smiled at the Stella for it pleased him, then unconsciously made a little gesture with his hand, as though repudiating the Sprigg.

"Please, Sir, what is your name?"

"Charles Sebastian Michel de Colbert," he said, his eyes twinkling as hers grew round with astonishment and dismay. "But most people call me the Abbé, and others just mon Père."

"Mon Père," said Stella gravely and sweetly.

She had him completely overturned again, as by that first smile. Hardly knowing what he did he held out his hand to her to lead her from the chapel, as he had held it out to many a great lady at Versailles. Stella, though entirely ignorant of court manners, did not hesitate for a moment. She curtsyed low, and rising from her curtsy, took one small hand from her muff and laid it delicately upon his wrist.

## CHAPTER II

### I

He thought of her ceaselessly, and was astonished at himself. He, who had never cared for children, to have been so enchanted by a farmer's child of the name of Sprigg. It was ridiculous. Enchanted, that was the word. Moonstruck. As though she had really been some fairy creature, some white witch who had cast a spell over him, he strove resolutely against the ever-present thought of her. But it was no use. The small green-clad creature stood before him at his desk as he wrote, leaning against his shoulder to see what he had written, sat upon his knee while he was reading (and once or twice he actually caught himself reading aloud because she so loved the beauty of words) and kept him awake at night with the haunting of her smile.

And yet he was not really companioned because his loneliness had quite suddenly become a burden. Eating his solitary breakfast a fortnight or so later he wondered if loneliness pressed upon other elderly people as it was now beginning to press upon him. Quite possibly. Contented with his cloistered state he had not hitherto considered the loneliness of others. That was shameful, and he a priest in charge of souls. Personal sanctity, for which he had striven with such desperation ever since his sojourn in the Irish monastery, was not enough. He had been regarding it as an end in itself instead of as that which determines the quality of what a man can do for his fellow men. Mrs. Loraine, for instance, widowed as he was widowed, her children dead even as his child was dead, was loneliness to her not a treasure but a grief? Folding his napkin he decided to accept the invitation that she had given him so many months ago and pay her a morning call.

Wrapped in his cloak he stepped out into the bright sunshine. The weather upon this seventh of November was still what it had been when he met Stella, cold and frosty, but cloudless and most lovely, and he enjoyed his short walk to Torre. Mrs. Loraine's attractive little white house, separated from the lane in front of it by a wooden palisade, and with a pebbled path leading up through a small flower-garden to the front door, was opposite the lychgate of Torre Church, and close to the holy well of St. Elfride, where the water bubbled up clear and cold from great depths and in all the centuries had never been known to fail. It was a very lovely spot with a clear view down to the sea through a break in the trees. There was a right of way through the churchyard; there were nearly always children playing there and sheep grazing among the tombstones. The bells of Torre had a very sweet tone as Zachary had already discovered, and in the spring the fields were enamelled with buttercups; and Mrs. Loraine had told him that she knew where to find patches of precious gentian.

The Abbé walked up the pebbled path and lifted the brass knocker on the front door. It was a small door painted deep blue, with corinthian columns either side and a fanlight over it. The knocker was highly polished and the stone step before the door as snow white as the muslin curtains draped in the windows. Beyond one of the windows there was a conservatory with a scented climbing geranium inside it growing against the wall. The small house in its small garden had an air of distinction. Once seen it was not forgotten.

The door was opened by a stout elderly maidservant in mob cap and apron, a dour-looking creature, but the Abbé knew that she had served her mistress with devotion for many years, and doubtless would do till the end of their lives. Like many another mistress and maid they were a typical example of one of the best of human combinations, two people living together who do not allow their mutual respect and affection to be cheapened by striving after too great an intimacy. The Abbé was no believer in too much intimacy. Even when two human creatures felt themselves to be each the complement of the other he still did not believe in it. He and Thérèse had always respected each other's privacy of mind and body. Human beings, precariously making their souls, could not press in too closely upon each other without damage, he thought. The instinct for fusion was one of those immortal longings whose complete satisfaction was not for this life.

He followed the maid into Mrs. Loraine's parlour and found himself bowing with extreme formality, then straightening and meeting the amused glance of her cool blue eyes he knew there was no danger here. His hostess was one of those women who even in an overcrowded room can create a sense of spaciousness. Whatever the tragedies of her life she was unresentful. She had never made demands upon life, filling the atmosphere about her with hot clamour; wherever she was it would seem cool and quiet.

"Pray be seated, Monsieur."

She spoke in exquisite French and as he sat in the Chippendale chair she indicated there was a gleam of amusement in his eyes too. Unworldly though she was she had her little vanities. One was her proficiency as a linguist. Another was the perfection of taste which distinguished the appointment of her room and the adornment of her person. A third—shared by her maid Araminta—was the fairy lightness of the heart-shaped queen-cakes served to her morning callers with their glass of wine.

"I have called to pay you the compliments of the season, Madame."

"What an unexpected honour, Monsieur. And you are indeed prompt with your good wishes. We are more than a month from Christmas yet."

He did not resent the touch of irony. He answered humbly, "I have been too long a recluse. I have been most remiss in leaving my friends to know of my regard through intuition only."

She smiled at him. "It is a pleasure, Monsieur, when one's intuition is proved to be not at fault."

For a moment or two they enjoyed the delicate innuendo and elegant repartee of the art of conversation in which they had been trained, meanwhile watching without appearing to do so the gradual unfolding of this hour placed like a flower in their hands. For such was unconsciously the attitude of each of them towards each new phase of each new day; it was not unimportant; it had some new discovery hidden within it for the finding. It was the attitude of the trained mind collecting the evidence; in their case for the Christian thesis that all things, somehow, work together for good.

Mrs. Loraine, the Abbé believed, was nearer eighty than seventy, but she held herself upright in her high-backed chair, disdaining to lean back, her mittened hands quietly folded in her lap, her small feet in their heelless slippers resting upon a tapestry footstool. Her abundant white hair was piled high on her head and she wore a lace cap with black velvet strings tied beneath her pointed chin. A white lace fichu crossed the bosom of her voluminous grey silk dress, that spread itself over her many petticoats with the hoop-like effect of a past age. She was of the opinion that she had come to the time of life when a woman should dress in the style that suited her regardless of fashion, and she needed the solidity of many petticoats, for there was nothing of her. Were hands to hold her, the Abbé thought, she would feel like a starved bird; there would be nothing but brittle bones beneath the plumage. But only physically was Mrs. Loraine an old woman. Her blue eyes, her smiling mouth and her fresh clear voice were young. Her memory was perfect and her judgments quick and decisive.

Her fresh and dainty room with its spinet, Chippendale furniture, muslin curtains, miniatures, books and china was perhaps a little overcrowded, but the shelves and cabinets held nothing that was not beautiful. Exploring one of them only would have kept a careful little girl happy for a whole day, thought the Abbé. He was sure that Stella was careful. She had the deft movements of those who do not drop, bump or trip.

The wine was brought in, and the little heart-shaped cakes. He ate one, wishing he could see Stella eat one. He was sure she ate as a bird eats, with decisive enjoyment, finishing it all and leaving no crumbs. So many children fidgeted and gobbled. She would do neither.

There was a beautiful cedarwood workbox, inlaid with ivory, on the table beside Mrs. Loraine. He thought it was India work probably sent her by one of her dead sons. The lid was lifted and he could see that inside there were carved lids that lifted up from different compartments, ivory spools wound with coloured silks, an emery cushion shaped like a strawberry, a silver thimble and a pair of scissors fashioned in the shape of a bird. . . . Was it a swan? . . . Stella had perhaps reached the age when little girls had to sew samplers.

He realised suddenly that for the last five minutes he had not been attending to a word his hostess was saying, and started guiltily.

"Your thoughts wander, Monsieur?" There was a hint of severity in Mrs. Loraine's tone, for she had never expected to be confronted in her own parlour by anything remotely resembling bad manners from the courteous Abbé.

"Forgive me, Madame. I was thinking how a child would delight in that workbox of yours."

"Yes," said Mrs. Loraine. "There is much in this room that would delight a child. It is a grief to me that I know very few children. I am a little shy of them, I think, and hesitate to ask them here."

She spoke gently but he noticed a stiffening of her lips as she finished speaking and he accused himself. He believed that her grandchildren had also died in India. Fool! What was the matter with him today? But having gone so disastrously far his instinct told him it would be best to go yet further, even to the taking a step towards that intimacy with another that he so dreaded.

"I, too, am shy of them. My own child died so young."

She looked up quickly, her cheeks flushed with her pleasure that he should thus confide in her. If he had hurt her he had healed that hurt again. She must be even lonelier than he had guessed. Well, if he was in for it now it was his own doing, not hers. He steeled himself to endure her questioning.

But no, he had judged her aright, when he first entered the room. She asked him no questions. She had shown him, by that look, that he could say what he liked, when he would, and that was all she wanted of him.

In his gratitude that he need not speak of Thérèse and the child he began to tell her instead about his meeting with Stella in the chapel, and of how he had gone with her down to the foot of the hill and renewed acquaintance with Dr. Crane. He told her of his first meeting with the doctor, and of the boy Zachary, and she was eagerly interested.

"You must see this child again," she said. "And bring her to see me. It is not right that we should allow our reserve to cut us off from young society. We need it, especially at Christmas. You should pay Stella a visit and take her a Christmas gift."

The Abbé was horrified. "Madame! The farmer and his wife, her parents—I do not know them. I could not possibly intrude myself——"

"But this Dr. Crane, did he not express a wish for a closer acquaintance with you?"

"He did me the honour of hoping that we should meet again but he gave me no definite invitation."

"Then you must take the initiative and wait upon him yourself; and then perhaps he will take you to see Stella." She looked about her, then lifted the workbox to her lap, her mittened hands winding spools and lifting mysterious lids as she tidied it. "I'll just set this to rights and then you shall take it as a gift to the child."

"Madame!" cried the Abbé in horror, "I could not possibly do such a thing! I can see it is a great treasure. Madame, I could not deprive you——"

"You will do as I tell you, Monsieur," the old lady interrupted him suavely. "The little maid doubtless sews her sampler, and doubtless finds it a burden, as I did at her age. A pretty box will ease the burden. There are many trinkets here that will amuse her; see this little pair of scissors shaped like a swan."

"I had noticed them, Madame."

"Yes. I thought that you had. Your eye had a very acquisitive gleam, Monsieur, when it rested upon this box. I thought to myself at the time—it cannot be for himself that he wants it."

"Madame, I protest—" In his mingled delight and distress he was suddenly excessively French, his hands speaking for him, his eyebrows shooting halfway up his forehead, his eyes alight as the eyes of an Englishman's are never alight. She laughed delightedly. Was this the man whom the Torre Abbey community spoke of sometimes as a dry old stick? But she had never described him so; she had been one of those who had always been aware of the banked fires.

"Believe me, Monsieur, I am delighted that Stella should have the box. It is right, you know, that we should practise the virtue of detachment from worldly things, especially as we grow older. You have often said as much in your excellent sermons. Will you be so good as to ring the bell? Araminta shall pack up the box that it may be easy for you to carry." He walked to the bell, his eyes on the scissors, and she laughed again. "If you wish, Monsieur, you may hold the scissors until Araminta comes. They are a good bit of workmanship. Italian, I think. I have had them all my life."

He sat down again, smiling, the scissors in the palm of his left hand. The curve of the swan's neck was very lovely. His face grew grave again. It was strange, he thought; Stella and a swan had been linked together in his thoughts before today.

Araminta entered and was told what she had to do. "It is for a child, Araminta," said Mrs. Loraine. "A Christmas gift. So put silver paper first with a coloured ribbon. Then stout paper and string."

Araminta's expression was invariably so profoundly disapproving of mankind and all its works that it was not possible for her to deepen the profundity, but she sighed heavily, exhaling the air with a slight hissing sound. If Mrs. Loraine, with Paradise just round the corner, was sitting light to material possessions, trying out her wings like a lark, Araminta was sitting more and more heavily, like a broody hen; it was almost with a swirl of feathers that she snatched the box to her, covering it with her apron, and tramped to the door with an indignation so heavy that it shook the room. Mrs. Loraine remained undisturbed. She had found that a spirit of detachment from Araminta's moods, as well as from possessions, was necessary to the preservation of her serenity in old age, and she had set about practising it some fifteen years ago. She laid one hand upon the little console table beside her, to still its agitation, and the other upon the Abbé's arm to still his.

"You have given me great pleasure, Monsieur, by this visit. You will call again, and bring the child, her parents permitting?"

"I will indeed, Madame."

She rose with the help of her stick, and stood with head bent humbly for his blessing. Seeing himself as he gave it as a wriggling worm at her feet he pronounced the words rather less perfectly than usual, but with happiness, for he was glad that he also had something to give. He bowed and left her, and Araminta helped him into his cloak in the hall, and handed him the parcel, with movements so correct and yet so expressive of outrage, that Mrs. Siddons herself could not have given a better performance.

II

He had some business to transact in Torquay, and striding along over Ladybird Walk, the box under his arm, unknown to himself he hummed a tune. Any of his Torre Abbey friends, hearing him, would have been surprised, too, to see him pause at the Fleet bridge, look about him, and then sit down on the parapet with apparently no purpose in view except to bask in the sun and watch the gulls wheeling about the boats in the harbour. They were accustomed to think of the Abbé as one of those men who pass rapidly from point to point, from task to task, so intent on redeeming the time because the days are evil that they have no leisure to pause and enquire if perhaps the bad days have a few good points about them after all.

The Abbé, blinking at the bright wings of the gulls, feeling the sun upon his cheek, was as astonished at himself as they would have been. Work upon his latest book awaited him at home, yet he had no inclination to go and do it; instead he took off his hat and closing his eyes against the bright dazzle of wings and water, lifted his face to the sun. It was warm, beneficent. Had it always been so, through the past desolate years? Had the wind always had this invigorating tang, the sea murmured with this music about the hulls of ships? He had no sense of sin, sitting there upon the wall and wasting his time; instead he had a sudden sense of guilt because he had not done it before. It occurred to him that because all that he had possessed and loved, wife and child, home and country, had been taken from him, he had made a virtue of necessity and deliberately courted dereliction, as he had striven for personal sanctity, as though it were an end in itself. The ingratitude of it! And all the while the patient sun had waited, and the hungry hearts of friends. The patient sun? He smiled, remembering St. Francis of Assisi, a man who had never permitted his poverty to include the loss of creatures. "Our brother the Sun . . . O Lord, he signifies to us, Thee." With what infinite silent patience did His glorious Majesty wait to have his warmth and light noticed by the ingrates he kept in being.

III

The quiet, the peace, were suddenly shattered by an astonishing turmoil. Jumping up, the Abbé saw the mail coach approaching, hours before its time, the horses all in a lather, the men on the roof waving their hats, the postilion blowing his horn, a crowd of excited men and women, children and dogs, running along beside it, cheering, shouting and barking, all making for the yard of the Crown and Anchor. The Abbé dropped hastily over the low parapet to the field below to avoid being trampled underfoot, then followed behind. The harbour came suddenly to life. Men came running up from the ship-building yard, women leaned out of the windows of the houses along the harbour wall, questions were shouted and answers yelled back. The Abbé, striding fast towards the Crown and Anchor but disdaining to run, could make out nothing except the one word "Victory!" This endless, dragging, heartbreaking war had at last produced a victory. When? How? The coach had passed on, but men and women who had come hurrying after it from the houses up the valley were about him now, running to the inn. "At sea. Off Cape

Trafalgar." The Abbé no longer disdained to run, and reached the inn yard as breathless as any.

But the shouting and cheering had died when he got there. A man was standing on the coach roof reading aloud from the paper that he held, and the packed crowd stood in shocked silence about the coach and the steaming horses. "Admiral Nelson killed in action." They were so stunned by the blow that they could hardly rejoice in the news of a great victory, or the knowledge that for the time being, at any rate, the dread of invasion had been taken from them. Men took off their hats and women wept. The Abbé, removing his hat and crossing himself, found that Frenchman though he was his years in England had not left him immune from the spell that Nelson had cast over his countrymen. He was as shocked and grieved as any man there. What was it about this particular man that apart from his courage and ability as a naval commander had so captured the imagination of his generation? A compassionate man in a brutal age, a man of simplicity and singleness of purpose in an age of bewildering complications? But there was more to it even than that, the Abbé thought. He was perhaps a man in love with glory: one of those who could strike it out of the stuff of life, like flame from stone, and kindle the glow of it for others as well as himself.

For the benefit of those who were still arriving the man on the coach was reading the announcement of the victory all over again, and the Abbé listened carefully. On Sunday, October 20th, the enemy ships had left Cadiz and the English fleet had prepared for battle. On October 21st the enemy fleet had been sighted at dawn; the battle had not been over until sunset. Eighteen of the enemy's ships had been accounted for. Enemy casualties had been reckoned at over five thousand, with twenty thousand prisoners. The English casualties had been one thousand six hundred and ninety. After the battle a storm had raged, delaying the sending of news to England. Despatches had not reached London until November 5th.

There were many other details, but the Abbé's mind fixed suddenly upon the date, Sunday, October 20th, the day of preparation for battle. That had been the day when he had met Stella in the chapel; the day she had been so certain the boy Zachary would be afraid. Where had the boy been upon that day? He remembered that after he had taken Stella down to the doctor's gig, and talked a little to the doctor and watched them drive away, he had returned to the chapel and prayed earnestly for those in peril at sea. He had had no special premonition of great events, either that day or the next; he had simply been uniting himself with the child Stella, who had had more prescience than he. Where had Zachary been on October 20 and 21st? Thoughtfully, hat in hand, he left the inn yard. As soon as he could he must go to Gentian Hill and find out.

# CHAPTER III

I

RUPERT HOUNSLOW was as efficient as he was kind hearted, and as persevering as he was both. Skilfully aided by distinguished influence in the background he got Zachary back into the Navy with the maximum of speed. There had to be unpleasantness, of course; a good deal of it. Zachary's cousin had to be informed that he was still alive, and being on leave in London at the time had insisted upon an interview that was sore and painful in every possible sense of the word. But the distinguished influence saw to it that Zachary did not return to his cousin's ship; he served a gruelling probationary period upon a ship of the Channel Fleet, and then, taking the place of a midshipman who had fallen sick, was transferred to a frigate sailing to join the Mediterranean Command. Foreign service, Rupert Hounslow had thought, would be good for him; broaden his mind. It did much more than that. When he entered upon it he was a badly scared boy; when he returned from it he was a self-reliant man.

The probationary period had been almost as bad as the months on his cousin's ship; but not quite, for this ship was a good ship; a rough-and-ready justice prevailed upon it and brutality was not, as upon his cousin's ship, the order of the day from the Captain downwards. But Zachary found that he hated the life as much as ever, was as seasick as ever, and as borne down as before by cold and exposure, exhaustion and sleeplessness, and decided that he was obviously not cut out for a sailor. The knowledge that he was doing his duty gave him no pleasure whatever. He hated his duty, and decided that he was not cut out for a hero either. So far as he knew he was not cut out for anything in particular; unless it was to be a shepherd upon Bowerly Hill. But he dare not think too much of Bowerly Hill, or of Stella and the doctor, because then the homesickness was worse than the seasickness and he became even more incapacitated for the work that he had to do.

He tried to do it well and willingly, since he had to do it, and achieved an outward show of zeal and cheerfulness that he found to his astonishment was as useful to him as a suit of armour. Upon his first ship his only weapon had been his obstinacy, which had deceived no one as to the true state of his craven mind; he had been like a tortoise on its back, immovable but vulnerable and inviting prodding. Now he was the right way up, and no one had any idea how vulnerable he really was.

Beneath this shell he went secretly exploring for the fortress that he knew of, trying as the first step to learn that trick of detachment that, he thought, is like diving, not so simple as it looks. He tried to practise it in all sorts of small ways. The doctor had given him a few books to bring away with him, and lying in his hammock at night he would try and shut out the din and stench of the lower cockpit and read. He did not take in very much but every now and then some lovely phrase would shine up at him from the page, as though it were a pinprick in a dark curtain, letting in the light. When vile things happened outside himself he managed now always to find something to pay attention to besides the vileness; the flash of fine anger in one man's eyes when another was flogged at the gangway; the sudden gleam of moonlight through a rent torn in the clouds by the frenzy of a storm; good things that only came into being because of the evil. But detachment from the physical wretchedness of his own body, from mental and nervous misery, that was a harder thing to learn; not much use to try, he thought sometimes; when the evil tears at your own flesh, that's another kettle of fish altogether. Yet even here one was not quite helpless; the mere effort to concentrate upon something other than one's own wretchedness was, even if it failed, in itself something of an escape.

His shell of cheerfulness was something more than a protection, it was an attraction too. To his further astonishment, he found that a few among his messmates seemed to like him. They were not, as before, all his enemies. No, it was not quite as bad as it had been before; though bad enough.

The probationary period came to an end and he was transferred to the frigate. A voyage in stormy weather from the English Channel through the Bay of Biscay to Sardinia, in the month of December, in a strange ship in the company of men whom he did not know yet, did not at first seem an improvement in his lot. Rather the contrary. He thought that this time he would really die of seasickness, complicated by some sort of fever that he had picked up. He hoped he would. It was no comfort to be told that Lord Nelson, to whom they were carrying despatches and under whose command they would find themselves when they reached their journey's end, had never succeeded in conquering seasickness either. He cared nothing for Lord Nelson. Nor did he expect to reach his journey's end; nor wish to. The Christmas of 1804 came and went, but he could not even think of Stella and the doctor, and the wassailing and mumming at Weekaborough. He could only think of how he was to keep upon his feet. That had been all that mattered; just not to be defeated in this effort to keep upon his feet.

Eight bells. The pipes of the boatswain's mates penetrated the snaky nightmares of an upset inside, and even while struggling in the grasp of a boa constrictor, which was coiling itself tighter and tighter round his middle, he knew that the morning watch was his, rolled out of his hammock and clutched the stanchion beside him. He had learned now to catch hold of the stanchion first thing, lest he fall headlong. Clutching it, he became slowly aware of some curious facts. He was dizzy and trembling as usual, and his head was aching, but he was not retching. . . . And the ship was steady. . . . In the dim light of the swing lantern he reached with one hand for his coat and trousers and dragged them on. Dressing, while clinging to the stanchion, had been a great problem in the past weeks, but he managed it more easily today. Another midshipman, possessed of a cast-iron interior and a kind heart, who also had the morning watch, brought a basin of cold water and he soused his head in it, banishing the last of the snakes.

"Storm blown itself out and we're anchored, by God!" whispered the other midshipman, a ginger-haired urchin just turned fifteen, Jonathan Cobb. Then he gripped Zachary firmly by the elbow and towed him towards the ladder. He liked Zachary. He himself was tough, stocky and profane, impervious both to education and good manners, so his liking was at first sight surprising, but he had a queer motherly streak in him, which caused him to cherish the ship's cat and the seasick. Also he liked pluck and considered that Zachary had it, throwing up the way he did, in a fever half the time, yet never asking to go to the sick bay.

"Where are we, Cobb?" croaked Zachary, stumbling up the ladder.

"Sardinia," said Cobb.

They reached the top of the first ladder and were confronted by a glimmering grey shape. It was Snow, the ship's cat, a creature who had been born white, but was caressed so often by Cobb, who washed only under compulsion, that you would not have known it. "Hi, Snow! Good old Snow!" He scooped the cat up under one arm and pushed Zachary up the next ladder. They reached the deck and the icy air almost knocked the breath out of them; but the stars, that had been hidden for nights on end, were shining again and the whole world was bathed in moonlight.

Clinging to the rail, Zachary looked about him and caught his breath with something more than the cold. The fleet was riding at anchor off the coast of Sardinia; the long, lovely shape of the island lay before him. The sea was peaceful and still, lit by strange lights. The weight of glory in the sky was almost terrifying. The great ships resting upon the gleaming sea, their poop lanterns shining softly, were dwarfed almost to nothing by the splendour above; yet each had its own dreamlike and perfect beauty. The light was as bright as day, yet unearthly. There was no sound, and the silence, the stillness, were like the hush in the auditorium before the curtain rises on some great drama, and for the first time since he had been at sea a brief thrill went through Zachary. There was a leap of joy in him, like a flame lighting up in a dark lantern. At that moment he believed it was worth it. This moment of supreme beauty was worth all the wretchedness of the journey. It was always worth it. "For our light affliction, which is but for a moment, worketh for us a far more exceeding and eternal weight of glory." It was the central truth of existence, and all men knew it, though they might not know that they knew it. They followed each man his own star through so much pain because they knew it, and at journey's end all the innumerable lights would glow into one.

Cobb was pulling at his sleeve. "Look! There's the Admiral's flagship. You can see the Nelson chequer painted on her hull."

Zachary sighed, rubbed his knuckles in his eyes and stared at the *Victory* lying there at anchor under the stars, with one bright star in particular seeming to burn like a lantern just above her masthead, and another kind of thrill went through him. He had never seen Lord Nelson, had never even wanted to, yet it meant something to him now that he was serving under him, for he had remembered Nelson's "radiant orb," about which they had talked in the doctor's dining parlour. This man was consciously following glory, was in love with it, and so were they all because they followed him. Whatever was before them now the end of it was going to be something memorable, something symbolic and worth while.

Cobb was pulling at his sleeve again. "Come on, you moonstruck fool. Come on!"

The ship was coming to life, the everyday normal life of the morning watch, and Zachary came back to normal with it. There was a racket in the galley, where the cook was lighting his fire. The watch were tumbling up with buckets, scrubbers, brooms, holystones and sand to clean ship. Cobb and Zachary went each to his station, Cobb still gripping the cat. The pumps were rigged, the wheel and look-outs relieved. A few hours later, when the boatswain piped to breakfast, the sun was rising in a clear sky, but it was starting to blow again, a bitter wind from the north-west. Yet the surge of cheerfulness, the sense that something was about to happen, had come to every man on board, not only to Zachary. Men whistled as they worked that day, and at dinner time, after the grog had been served, the strains of "Drops of Brandy" could be heard echoing from every ship in the fleet.

"And Johnny shall have a new bonnet,
And Johnny shall go to the fair,
And Johnny shall have a blue ribbon
To tie up his bonny brown hair."

The clouds had covered the sky again by mid-afternoon and a heavy gale was blowing, yet no one seemed to care. The sense of expectation grew and mounted and reached its culmination when two look-out frigates came flying in to the roadstead like birds, and a signal raced to the masthead of the *Victory*. "The enemy is at sea."

II

The end of this particular adventure was not yet, but for Zachary the ten months that led up to the end were entirely different from the months that had preceded that starry morning. He was as sensitive as ever, he hated being at sea as much as ever, his fear was still a demon that had to be ceaselessly dealt with, yet there seemed a light upon these days, lit by the born leader of men upon the flagship.

A few hours after the signal they were off upon that chase of four thousand miles, all round the Mediterranean and then to the West Indies and back, that was to be one of those failures that live in history more thrillingly than many victories. It was a gallant and crazy endeavour, made by ships that had been so long at sea that they were scarcely seaworthy any longer, and from the moment when the *Victory*, with a light at her stern, had led the Fleet in wind and darkness through the narrow dangerous passage between the Biscian and Sardinian rocks, to the blue summer day when they returned from the Indies to the Mediterranean again without having caught the enemy, no meanness tarnished it at all.

A midshipman who had had a classical education, even though he might be extremely seasick, could not fail to be thrilled by the Mediterranean. Nelson manoeuvred his ships through the straits of Messina in terrible weather with great skill, and Zachary looked with awe upon Scylla and Charybdis and the fires of Stromboli. He saw Tunis, Malta and Crete, and in an interval between storms, in a calm sunrise, saw the coast of Greece with rose-coloured rocks reflected in a mother-of-pearl sea. Then back again, the enemy having escaped them, the length of the Mediterranean, past the coast of Spain with its white houses built among the orange groves, and good-bye to old and lovely Europe and away to the West Indies.

The crossing of the Atlantic was not as quick as it might have been because the battered old *Superb*, only able to limp along, kept them back. But courtesy forbade that she should be left behind and she did her best to make up for lost time by sailing when the other ships stopped, her studding-sail booms lashed to the yards. It was fair weather and Zachary became downright happy. He could bear to think of home now, and wrote long letters to Stella and the doctor (though heaven only knew when they would get them) describing the chase down the Mediterranean and back, with the glimpses of ancient glory seen through the spray and the rain. And he tried to capture upon paper the special flavour of the blue and lovely days he was living through as he wrote. Most of the men on board, impatient to catch the enemy, found the slow days intolerably hard to get through, but for Zachary, in no hurry at all to make acquaintance with battle and death, they were halcyon days. He managed to forget the purpose of them in the magic of each as it came, and soaked up the beauty and sunshine into himself to his infinite strengthening and refreshment.

The routine of each ship went like clockwork, the days were leisurely, and for the first time Zachary knew that life lived upon the sea could be as gracious and friendly as life upon the land. The gentle rhythmic dip and rise of the painted hulls in the blue water, and the sound of the wind in the rigging, seemed to become a part of the rhythm of his beating pulses, just as the rhythm of the ploughing had done at Weekaborough, and the wind in the trees. He looked up at the towering sails over his head as he had looked up into the branches of the yew tree on Bowery Hill, and a race to the masthead, which once had turned him sick with terror, was now almost enjoyable; like climbing into the yew tree and being held there safely. The ship was home and his hammock in the cockpit was his own particular corner of it, and he would lie there reading happily until he slept, oblivious at last of the noises around him. The night watches held no more terrors. They were still and lovely, with stars that were new to him blazing in the sky and gold and silver fish streaking through the phosphorescent water. He made no intimate friends apart from Cobb and the cat, but his carefully cultivated efficiency and cheerfulness, his natural gentleness, brought him liking and respect. They had leisure now for the social graces, and he enjoyed these. The midshipmen were invited in turn to dine in state with the Captain and sat at a table set with silver and glass and fine china, with the stern windows open on the calm sea. There was plenty of good talk and good wine, and afterwards perhaps a stately pacing upon the quarter deck and discussion upon affairs of state. These idyllic days might be the briefest of interludes but Zachary vowed that he would never forget them. He knew now that every kind of life and situation holds somewhere within it for the finding its own kernel of quiet, each small possession of mortal peace a symbol of the eternal fortress and a door to it. He would be able to hold on now through the months of storm, remembering the days of peace at the heart of them to which the way was sure.

The whole of the West Indies meant less to Zachary than his one glimpse of the coast of Greece, but he did blink approvingly at those islands looking like chunks of jewels lying on the sea, and rolled the music of their names on his tongue with appreciation. . . . Trinidad. Martinique. Dominica. . . . "They sound like archangels, Cobb," he said. But Cobb only swore. He was spoiling for a fight, and they had just missed the enemy for the second time.

Round again, homeward bound once more for Europe, and the old *Superb* still labouring after, all sail set to catch the enemy before they reached Cadiz. They were short of food now, the ships were in worse case than ever, the enemy had five days start and they did not catch them. The *Victory* and the *Superb* sailed for England, leaving the rest of the Fleet to watch for the enemy to come out again. It was the end of the great chase, but not of this particular adventure. Nelson would quickly be back again. The enemy would have to face the music sometime.

Through those baking midsummer days they watched Cadiz as a cat a mousehole. Those days were, for Zachary, no longer tranquil, in spite of the blue sea and the warm sun and the scent of the orange groves drifting to them from the coast of Spain. They were all keyed up to an almost intolerable sense of expectation, a small fleet waiting for battle with a much larger one, and irritable at the iron discipline imposed by Collingwood in Nelson's absence. Cobb was bad-tempered with excitement, Zachary with dread. Even Snow the cat was off colour. For Zachary the battle had begun already, as he fought not to be afraid of his fear. He could no longer concentrate successfully on the books he tried to read, but as before single sentences stayed with him and steadied him, especially those sentences that were written in Greek in Stella's locket. "Love sings to all things which live and are, soothing the troubled minds of gods and men." Love of God, love of country, love of glory, love of a little girl, love of the stars at midnight, it lifted you out of yourself and away from your fear.

Nelson was in England for only twenty-five days, but the weeks of his absence seemed as many years to the waiting fleet. And then, one evening at the end of October, the *Victory* quietly slipped in amongst them again. With Cadiz and the enemy so close there could be no salutes or hoisting of colours, yet Zachary felt that the little man over there upon his quarter-deck must surely feel the surge of affection and relief that went through the whole fleet; it was something almost tangible in the silence of the still, warm, orange-scented dusk.

The atmosphere subtly changed. The days of waiting were now tingling with activity as Nelson moved his squadrons here and there like chessmen, trying to tempt the enemy out and at the same time to prevent them escaping into the Mediterranean. Cruising with his frigate squadron close to Cadiz, actually able to see those great ships within the harbour, Zachary's dread mysteriously lessened. It was said that they were outnumbered and outgunned. What of it? If they were victorious the greater the glory, and if not, the greater the glory too. If he was right, and glory was simply the symbolic thing that blazed out at the other end of supreme effort sustained with supreme fortitude, then it was unimportant whether you were victorious or not; indeed you were victorious if the fortitude remained unconquered. And as for the fortitude itself, it came with the effort, as Dr. Crane had said.

October 5th, and exciting news passed through the English Fleet; the enemy in Cadiz were getting their troops on board, and the Spanish squadron at Cartagena had their topsails up. October 9th, and the Cadiz Fleet had bent their topgallant sails. October 10th, pouring rain and the frustration of further waiting. October 18th, fine weather again with an easterly wind; perfect weather for the enemy to put to sea. October 19th, and the combined fleets of France and Spain had begun to come out; they could see them in the distance. October 20th, and the news had raced from masthead to masthead, "The enemy's fleet is at sea." But daylight of that Sunday morning found the world shrouded in sea mist and they could not see them; they could only see at intervals the towering cliffs of Cape Trafalgar.

There was something menacing about those cliffs, seen through the rents in the mist, and Zachary kept the dawn watch in the company of his demon. He had imagined that he had fought Apollyon before, but he had been mistaken. Until now the dark wings had merely brushed him in passing and he had beaten them off as one beats off the wings of a swooping bat, but now the evil thing was as close to him as though it had made itself a part of him. Like the mist it was around him, in him and choking him. It was too close for him to see its obscene face or feel its foul breath; so close that there seemed nothing to struggle against. Yet he struggled. Motionless, his face set, he fought a queer battle that was nothing at all except the fight to keep his body still and his face set. That was all. Everything that precept and experience had seemed to teach him through all the months that lay behind him went from him as though it had never been. He did not recall Stella or home, for his memory seemed frozen by his fear. He merely kept his watch.

The boatswain's pipe sounded, his watch was over and he had other duties to do. As he had fought to keep still he fought now to remember what they were. He remembered and throughout the morning he did them stonily and speechlessly but well. His will still functioned and his body in obedience to his will. During the morning the mist lifted, the wind shifted, and voices about him proclaimed that it would be today. It made no difference to him when they said that, for the demon could come no closer. Yet as the morning wore on something did make a difference to him; something akin to the growing sunlight that warmed his frozen body touched his frozen memory and he remembered Stella. No more than that. Just Stella.

The afternoon passed and he was able to wonder at the functioning of his will and the obedience of his body; and wondered too if that which he had learned and forgotten was that which steeled his will. The evening came and the voices said it would be tomorrow. It made no difference to him that they said that. Tomorrow or the next day, it made no odds. Whenever it was he believed now that he could stand the test. As a sailor knows that the worst of a gale is over, even though the wind still rages, so though the demon was still with him he knew that the worst of his fight was done.

It was a queer night lit by strange lights and eerie with the boom of guns. The English ships signalled the whereabouts of the enemy to each other with blue lights and gunfire, and at midnight Zachary's frigate could see the orange glow of lamps from the stern cabin windows of thirty-three men of war; and they were not English ships. And overhead, above the blue lights and the orange lights, the stars shone fitfully through the clouds.

October 21st and just before dawn the English Fleet altered course. They had drawn the enemy fleet well away from Cadiz and now they turned to the north-east, ready to attack. There was a slight mist, and a heavy swell that made Zachary feel seasick again, until he came on deck and saw, only a few miles away, the great ships whose lights they had seen at midnight, and in the beauty and terror of the sight forgot himself completely.

After that he had no time to remember anything. The signal "Prepare for battle" was flashed through the Fleet, the drums beat to quarters and each man ran to his duty. The ship's company had tied silk handkerchiefs round their heads, to protect their ears from the roar of the guns, and stripped to their waists. They worked quickly and quietly, carrying wooden bulk-heads, canvas screens, furniture and crockery to the hold, dousing the sails with buckets of water and sanding the decks, making the guns ready, preparing the cockpit for the wounded, setting buckets of water, tourniquets and swabs where they would be needed, and all within the six minutes allotted for the task.

By seven o'clock the English ships were sailing in two columns, Nelson and the *Victory* leading the northern column, Collingwood and the *Royal Sovereign* leading the southern, towards the five-mile-long curve of the enemy ships. They sailed steadily, with all sail set, and by eleven o'clock there was only three miles between them. The sea was smooth now, the sky clear of cloud, both sky and sea gloriously blue, and the sun blazed down upon a scene so lovely and so brilliant that it took Zachary's breath away. The English ships had most of them been painted with the Nelson chequer, black bands between the yellow of the gundecks, and black ports, and their poops were bright with gilding. The French and Spanish ships were painted scarlet, black and yellow; the great *Santissima Trinidad* could be clearly seen in all her glory of vermilion and white, with a white figurehead. Above the bright colours towered the forests of masts and the swelling sails.

As the English men-of-war rolled gently on their bands began to play. The sailors seemed excited, happy and fearless, sharpening cutlasses, polishing guns and singing to the music of the bands. Some of them danced a hornpipe and others called out instructions as to the dispersal of their property if they were killed. "Bill, you can 'ave me trousers. Tom, you can 'ave me best 'andkercher." But not as though death were anything very imminent. A signal flew to the masthead of the *Victory*, "England expects that every man will do his duty" and as the message passed down the lines it was greeted with a tremendous roar of cheering. Could this be war, wondered Zachary, this sunshine, brilliance, music and cheering? He was standing behind the First Lieutenant, whose messenger he would be throughout the battle, with his heart beating like a sledge hammer. But not with fear. Only with awe at the intolerable beauty of it all.

Then another signal flew from the *Victory's* mast-head, the signal for close action, and in a very few minutes the enemy had opened fire. The two English columns sailed on stoically enduring it, holding their own fire, for perhaps twenty minutes, until the two spear-heads, the *Victory* and the *Royal Sovereign*, had broken the enemy column, and one by one the great ships behind them sailed into the fight, sweeping out fanwise each to attack her prey.

The strategy of the battle, the perfect carrying through of a brilliantly conceived plan, was as lost upon Zachary as upon any other seaman taking part in it. For them, after the fury broke, it was merely hell. For months Zachary had been dreading this ordeal and he found it worse than anything he had conceived of even in his most lurid imaginings. Afterwards he wondered how it was possible for men to keep sane in the midst of such an infernal uproar. He had yet to discover under what appalling conditions men can keep sane; provided it does not go on too long.

The cannons along both sides of the two gun-decks were all thundering and flashing fire, the heavy carriages banging and leaping at each recoil, and above those the upper battery of cannonades roared at each shot. The hissing and screaming of the round shot seemed to tear one's head open, and every now and then there was an ear-splitting crash as the shots struck home. It was an appalling uproar but perhaps it was merciful; the men were so dazed by it that the terrible sights they saw did not strike home quite as they would have done without it. The evil smelling black smoke from the burning powder poured everywhere so that it was hard to breathe for the stench of it. It was difficult to see much in the murk; and that too was merciful; but now and then the filthy black clouds would part and there would be some strange and terrible sight framed in black smoke as in a picture frame. Once Zachary saw the picture of two great ships locked in a death grip, drifting before the wind, and did not know that they were the *Victory* and the *Redoubtable*, and that down in the dimly lit red glare of the *Victory's* cockpit Nelson at the moment lay dying. And another time he saw the vermilion and blue of an enemy hull looming right above their frigate like a great cliff; for a brief moment he could see the torn smoke-blackened sails and the sharpshooters taking aim in the rigging; then the guns blazed again, the ship rocked and shuddered and the smoke once more blotted out the picture.

The fight continued, becoming harder for those who were left as the ranks were thinned on the ships. Yet each man continued able to do what he had to do, and Zachary was no exception. He obeyed his orders instantly and accurately and seemed to have the strength of ten men in the fulfilling of them. He had known a few thrills of bitter fear during the first terrible twenty minutes of slow advance, but once the fight had begun there had been no more of that. Hour after hour it went on, the work and discipline of the wounded ships functioning all the while with order and purpose. Men toiled at the guns, in the magazines, in the rigging, carrying the wounded, flinging the dead and dying overboard, running messages, repairing under-water timbers. Hour after hour upon each ship the master-at-arms went upon his ceaseless rounds, noting how all was going, hour after hour the officers maintained their ceaseless vigilance, keeping the machinery of the fight turning over. Hour after hour, admirals and captains, cocked hats on their heads, stars and orders shining on their breasts, paced their quarter-decks until they died, and hour after hour, down in the stifling cockpits, the surgeons and their mates, sleeves rolled to their elbows, endured the worst horror of it all.

It was extraordinary to have it over, for the thing had seemed eternal. Yet at sunset it was over. By sunset the last of the battle noises had died into silence, the stricken ships were being prepared for the night, and the wretchedness of exhaustion and reaction had each man in its grip. But they had won a great victory. Zachary, sitting on a coil of rope with his arms on his knees and his aching head in his arms, told himself that over and over again, but could not seem to take it in. They had won a glorious victory. The fleets of France and Spain were defeated. England was safe now from invasion. . . . Stella was safe. . . . The frigate, though badly battered, was still seaworthy. He himself had suffered no more damage than a slight flesh wound in his right arm and a splitting headache. And he had stood the test. That strength had been there. All that the doctor had told him had been perfectly true. He had every cause to rejoice. But he couldn't, for Cobb was dead. Cobb was dead, and the cat.

He lifted his head from his arms and picked up something that lay on the deck beside him. It was a pitiful mess of blood and dirty white fur, stiff and cold. Somehow it had seemed the last drop of misery, when he had come stumbling up the slippery ladder from that terrible red cockpit, where they had summoned him to say goodbye to Cobb, to fall headlong over something at the top and find it poor Snow. What had she done, poor Snow? The ship's goat was dead too; he had seen it blown to bits with his own eyes. He'd liked that goat. . . . But the animals at Weekaborough were safe, the yard cats that Stella was so fond of, and Hodge and Daniel and Seraphine, the oxen and horses and his precious sheep. . . . But with Snow lying across his knees he couldn't seem to visualise them very clearly; not even Hodge.

"Bloody young fool!" said the irritated voice of the senior midshipman, passing by. "Aren't there enough good men dead but you must blub like a cissy over the cat? Here, blow your nose, for God's sake!"

Zachary had not known he was blubbing, but he found now that his nose was in the most disgusting state. He held out a hand for the flung handkerchief and blew it. . . . But it was not really the cat, it was Cobb, who had died hard. . . . Suddenly the body across his knees was a horrible thing. He picked it up, carried it to the rail and flung it overboard. It made a very small splash, not like the resounding splashes the men's bodies made when they hit the water.

He straightened and looked about him, and wretched though he was the artist in him could not fail to be gripped by what he saw. The smoke of the battle, no longer shot through with flame but delicately tinted by the colours of the sunset, was rolling away towards the land, leaving the scene strangely bright and clear. The sky was ultramarine on the horizon, dark blue overhead, with a few stars pricking through, the sea below deep green. There was no wind, but a heavy Atlantic swell upon which the brilliantly painted captured enemy ships, and the more sombre black and yellow English ships, rose and fell, many of them with trailing rigging, sails full of shot holes, shattered masts and gaping wounds in their sides. Some of them lay with a sharp list. Of the two great ships who with their Admirals had led the fleet to victory Collingwood's *Royal Sovereign* looked like a wounded stag, and Nelson's *Victory* had her mizzen-topmast shot away and her sails riddled. Upon the swell there rose and fell bits of wreckage with men clinging to them, and boats were putting off from the ships to save what lives they could. Far away in the distance, like white birds on the horizon, Zachary could just see the sails of the enemy ships that had escaped and were flying for Cadiz. The darkness deepened and the ship's lanterns shone out across the water. The *Royal Sovereign* had her full complement of lights, but something seemed wrong with the *Victory*. Zachary stared and blinked, then found the senior midshipman once more beside him, and caught his arm.

"The *Victory*!" he said.

"What's wrong with the *Victory*?" asked the other crossly.

"Hardly any lanterns. They've not lit the Admiral's lights."

The elder boy stared. Communication between the ships was difficult. Their frigate knew nothing about the fight except that they had won it.

"No Admiral's lights," he said stupidly.

"No," said Zachary.

They continued to stare stupidly, their faces grey in the waning light. All through the fleet men were staring stupidly at the *Victory*. Triumph changed to incredulous pain as the darkness and silence deepened. Victory? They had no joy in her any longer, for she had come to them veiled in darkness, like the ship that bore her name. Nelson was dead.

## CHAPTER IV

### I

A FEW days after the news of Trafalgar reached Torquay the Abbé, that man of an iron constitution, was seized with an attack of the grippe. He paid no attention to it, illness in himself being a thing which he considered beneath his attention, but he did not go out to Gentian Hill, for he was sneezing most explosively and coughing in a manner to match the sneezes, and he did not wish others to be similarly afflicted. Moreover he seemed to have insufficient control over his legs for much walking. The weather too had suddenly turned most inclement, cold and wet. He sat in his sitting-room working at his latest book, holding his aching back stiff as a ramrod, forcing his aching head to intellectual labour with a certain amount of difficulty but standing no nonsense from it, shivering but disdaining to wear a cloak indoors. Ready to his left hand as he wrote was a tall pile of neatly folded fine linen handkerchiefs, a pile which diminished in height as the day went by, each handkerchief when used being transferred by him with fastidious distaste to a clothes basket which stood upon the floor to his right. Under the table at his feet lay Rover, his landlady's dog, to help in the disposal of the next meal which should be brought to him. Rover always lent most kindly assistance at meal-times, for the Abbé was not a man of large appetite, yet did not like to hurt his landlady's feelings by appearing unappreciative of her cooking. Since November 10th, Rover had had practically all the Abbé's meals and had put on weight considerably. The two of them continued in this manner for a week, until one morning after a bad night the Abbé found himself with a sharp pain in his chest, extreme difficulty in breathing and a most irritating inability to get out of bed. He was outraged and rang the bell.

His landlady, Mrs. Jewell, her hands folded at her ample waist, surveyed him with a knowing eye. "What you need, Sir, is a good blooding," she said. "I've said so time and again this last week, but no attention would you pay to what I said. Now you're the worse for it. I'll send Jewell for Parker."

"You will do nothing of the kind," said the Abbé. Parker was a very hail-fellow-well-met barber-apothecary whose coarse jokes did much to enliven the sick beds of the Jewell family but were not at all to the taste of the Abbé. "If it is your opinion that a physician is needed you will send for Dr. Crane of Gentian Hill, but for no one else," and he shut his eyes.

"Dr. Crane!" ejaculated Mrs. Jewell. "If poor Jewell is to go trampin' all the way out to Gentian Hill in this weather then I'll have the two of you in your beds, an' me with but the one pair of hands."

She rustled indignantly from the room, returning a few minutes later, followed by Rover, with some hot milk which she helped him to drink. But she maintained an outraged silence and then went away again. The Abbé did not know whether she meant to send for Dr. Crane or not. He hoped she would. He felt now that he would very much like to see the doctor.

Thumps and snorts beneath the bed told him that Rover had gone to earth there, in hopes that the next meal would be somewhat more exciting than the last. Rover was an ancient black retriever. The Abbé had had a dog rather like him in his boyhood at the Chateau. What had the creature's name been? Jules Tête-Noire. He had had the smallpox as a small boy and Jules Tête-Noire had spent almost the entire period of his illness thumping and snorting beneath the bed. During the long nights his young master had been much comforted by his presence, and the Abbé was comforted now by the presence of Rover. Soothed by the hot milk he presently dropped into a restless feverish sleep and in his sleep the past was with him again.

II

The window was set wide to the early morning sunshine and the scent of the pine forest drifted through it. Tête-Noire was beneath the bed, and his mother, young and beautiful, was standing beside him. She laid her hand on his shoulder and he opened his eyes to look at her. Yet when he did look she was no longer young; her face was white and ravaged, though she spoke calmly enough. "They are here, Charles," she said.

He had lain down dressed the night before and he was up in a flash and racing down the beautiful stone staircase to the hall below, where his father and his brothers, inarticulate with fury, were dragging the heavy furniture across the hall and putting it against the stout oak door. . . . None of their servants were to be seen; they must have run away. . . . The Comtesse sat down on the stairs. "I do not think it is any good doing that," she said tonelessly to her husband and sons. "If we resist they will certainly kill us, but if we do not resist they may have pity."

But her men did not even hear her. She had not supposed that they would. Every primitive instinct had been roused in them by the mob they had seen through the windows, surging through their garden, trampling their flowers underfoot, hacking at their yew hedges and rose trees, men armed with any weapon they had been able to lay their hands on, pikes, axes, hay-forks, flaming torches, cudgels, anything, a mob gone mad with hate and no longer human. The Comte and his sons in their rage were hardly human either. Their only idea of defending their own was the furious jungle method of tooth and claw. Having barricaded the door and primed their muskets they went each to a window of the hall.

It was no use talking to them. The Comtesse straightened herself, lifted the rosary from about her neck and began to tell her beads. Her face was calm and her eyes quiet.

They fired through the windows until the chateau was on fire, the door battered in and the mob upon them, and then they drew their swords. Four skilful swordsmen, wrought up to the highest pitch of fury and ecstasy in defence of all they love can hold a mob at bay for quite a long time. Charles found a fierce mad joy in it, that was not diminished when he saw his eldest brother die; he only fought more wildly. He was fighting with one man when another wounded him in the thigh with a pike. Then a flung stone struck him on the head. A whirling darkness seemed all about him then, lit with flashes of flame. Against the darkness he saw one last picture; his mother kneeling on the flagstones of the hall holding her eldest son's body in her arms, her face still calm and her lips moving. It was a strangely quiet picture. Then there was only the darkness.

It seemed to possess him for a long time, a scorching darkness that was hot upon his body as the flames of the burning chateau had been hot, and shouted in his ears as the mob had done. It had a horrible smell too; the nauseating smell of unwashed bodies and filthy clothes that is the very breath of poverty. He tried to get away from it, twisting this way and that, but it would not let him go; it had bound chains upon him and they bit into his flesh. Sometimes he shouted back at it, and when he did that he thought that his mother came to him and gave him a drink and then he was quiet. It seemed to go on like this for an eternity, and then slowly and intermittently the quality of the darkness changed. Sometimes it became cool and very quiet and instead of the smell of poverty there came the scent of the pines. His mother came more often and he was conscious that she had grown young. He had grown young too. He was a small boy again and he had come through the snowy forest to his first midnight mass. He was kneeling staring at the crib and the Christmas tree with its lighted candles and all about him there echoed the lovely chanting of the mass. He wriggled his cold toes in their snowboots, and sniffed the scent of the fir tree mixed with the smell of the incense and the candle grease, and he was happy. He blinked at the candles and wished he could have one. If he could have one, he thought, he would carry it home very carefully through the forest and he would not let it blow out.

But he could not carry it home because he could not walk. He was lying flat on his back, and when he tried to move his head hurt him. He was not a boy either. Nor happy. He was a man, and sick, and pressed upon by a load of intolerable wretchedness that was not only of the body. But the scent of the pines was with him, it came borne on a cool breeze through some open window. And there were candles, two of them; he was lying blinking up at them, and at the shape of a cross outlined starkly against a pale shimmer of light. And they were chanting the mass. No, not chanting it, saying it. And two voices only, an old man's voice and a woman's voice answering. He supposed it was his mother. He shut his eyes and listened and darkness flowed back again, but this time a darkness entirely purged of terror.

He opened his eyes and though the candles had been put out the light was brighter, and outside in the forest there was birdsong. It was summer, he remembered. His mother was coming towards him slowly, with head bent, carrying something very carefully in her hands, as though it were an exceedingly precious gift, something that could be easily smashed, like youth or joy. He spoke her name gently, a pet name that he had for her. She stopped then and looked up and she was not his mother, she was a slim woman wearing a peasant girl's simple grey dress, with dark hair cut short like a boy's. She put what she was carrying on a stool, and it was only a cup of milk after all, and came and stood looking down at him. Perhaps a couple of years ago she had been young and beautiful but she was neither of these things now, and rage rose again in the heart of the man looking up at her because of the things that happened to women in France in these days. Then she smiled, and her face was transfigured. There were stars in her eyes when she smiled, and a light upon her face, and her mouth took on the curves of happiness that the contours of her worn face had lost. She was so young when she smiled that she looked like a little girl. Charles loved her then, at once and for ever.

"What did you call me?" she asked.

"Something I call my mother. I thought you were she."

Her smile died and the light in her face went out like a blown candle, but the compassion that took its place was so deep that it seemed to reach out to him and hold him, and because of it his grief did not quite overwhelm him then, nor destroy him in the days that followed.

They were strange days of angry misery and hopelessness, with a queer attempt at happiness trying to struggle up through the anger, in which the bewildering kaleidoscope of impressions that tumbled about him gradually fell into shape. He was lying on a hard bed behind the altar of the little church in the pine woods, he discovered, suffering from burns and concussion, and a wound in the leg that was not healing as satisfactorily as it should. They had carried him here from the chateau, the Curé told him; the church had seemed the best place to hide him, safer than the presbytery. The old man was vague about the "they" who had performed this act of mercy, though his burnt and still bandaged hands and arms suggested that he might have had something to do with it, but the woman in the peasant's dress, whose name was Thérèse, answered his questions more fully when they were alone together.

III

The Curé had been away from the village, visiting a dying woman at an outlying farm, when the mob had come to the chateau. They were a part of that multitude that was now surging across France, an army of starving peasants, men come up from the gaols and slums of the towns like rats from sewers, suffering and maddened men who had forgotten pity but still knew the meaning of justice and had taken it into their hands. Thérèse spoke of these men with a sort of agonised compassion, but Charles, the new Comte de Colbert, could feel for them nothing but a loathing that at times shook and exhausted him as though it were a fever. The Curé, returning home with a companion from the farm, had seen the smoke from the burning chateau, and had run there. The mob had looted what they could from the chateau and then the flames had driven them away. They did not drive the Curé away; he got in through a window and found the bodies of his friends. Finding Charles still alive he had dragged him out first. He would have gone back if he could and brought out the dead too, but by the time he got Charles out that was no longer possible.

"He did it alone?" asked Charles, lying with his face turned away from Thérèse while she replied quietly and truthfully to his questions.

"The villagers were afraid to go with him to the chateau, but a few men, your servants I think, who had run away to the village, followed behind him and hid in the forest, and it was they who carried you here."

She got up and left him. She had an unerring instinct for knowing when he wanted to be let alone.

Later, looking from his own stalwart frame to the bent body of the little old Curé, he said with a lift of his scorched eyebrows and a grim attempt at a smile, "You are a stronger man than I thought, mon Père."

"I'd never have got you through the window, my son, without the help of Thérèse," confessed the old man. "She's a tough young woman."

*"Thérèse?"* ejaculated Charles.

"She had come with me from the farm," said the Curé placidly. "I had told her she was not to follow me inside the chateau, but when I had dragged you to the window there she was just climbing through."

He went ambling off to the vestry to make his bed. He slept in the vestry so as to be able to look after Charles at night. Thérèse slept at the presbytery with the Curé's housekeeper. Who was this dear and brave woman? Charles, loving her, taking from her the happiness that she seemed able to bring him whenever she came near him, like a gift in her two hands, a gift so strange in the midst of so much wretchedness, yet knew nothing at all about her. She was easy and friendly with him, a compassionate and most skilful nurse, yet there was that in her reticence that forbade questioning, and a dignity that might have been chilling had she not been so vital and loving a creature. And the Curé, whenever questioned, ambled off to do something or other, and Charles as yet was unable to get up and follow him.

Yet the day came when he was able. Limping, he followed the old man into the vestry.

"Mon Père, who is Thérèse?" he demanded, holding on to the table, his voice hard and his face hard because he loved her so much, and his legs were trembling beneath him.

"My son," said the Curé mildly, "do not address me in my own vestry as though at the pistol's point."

"I must know, mon Père. You do not understand. I must know."

The old man looked at him keenly and saw how it was with him. "Sit down," he said abruptly. Charles sat down and they faced each other across the table. The old man's gaze held the younger man's steadily for a moment or two, as though he were trying to prepare him for yet another disaster, and then he looked down at his knotted old hands clasped upon the table, and began to speak quietly, as if to himself, as though Charles were not there in front of him.

"I will tell you about Thérèse. Perhaps I should have told you before. Do you remember that Carmelite convent at Hauteville by the bridge? You may never have noticed it. A gloomy looking little place with high walls round it. My sister was Prioress there. Some weeks ago the Terror reached Hauteville. I will not speak of what happened, either in the town or the convent. Yet always in these times of judgment there is a remnant that is saved; one here, two there; to me it is one of the signs that God still lives. You were saved from the burning chateau. My sister and one novice, a young woman called Marie Thérèse, were saved from the Carmel. For a few days they stayed hidden in some hovel in the town, then, dressed as peasants, they set out to come to me. That was all my poor sister could think of, that she must get to her brother. They walked by night and hid by day and begged their food as they could. They reached Pierre Guérin's farmhouse at the edge of the parish and there my sister was taken very ill. They sent for me and it was a great joy to us both, a joy that we took as a gift from the good God and as a mark of His providence, that I could be with her when she died. There remained the problem of the novice Marie Thérèse. They would not keep her at the farm, and so I decided to bring her back with me, to be cared for by my good housekeeper, until we decided what to do. Coming here, we saw the smoke from the chateau, and you know what happened then."

There was a long pause, and the Curé, waiting for the younger man to speak, still did not look up.

"A novice," said Charles at last. "She is still only a novice."

She had seemed to bring him the gift of joy on the first morning and he was still hanging on to it. The Curé went on speaking again, his quiet voice giving no hint that he knew he was taking away the very last handhold this man had left.

"The novitiate at Carmel is a long one and she is nearly at the end of it. It is a strict order, as you know, and it is seldom that any woman joins it who is not convinced of her vocation. Thérèse has only one longing now, to get back to Carmel. She comes of a distinguished family and bears a great name, but is almost as alone in the world as you are. Her only living relations now are a family of cousins with a chateau near Toulon. We both think that she should try and get to them, for down there in the south they say the Terror has not struck. Her cousins would help her to find some other Carmel where she could finish her novitiate. How she is to accomplish that journey we do not know. We are not thinking of that just now. Our duty now, hers and mine, is towards yourself. When you have your strength again the way will open for Thérèse. For the moment the road runs quite straight before the three of us. When we get to the cross-roads we shall know it and receive the guidance of God."

Charles had nothing to say. He understood her now; the dignity and reserve that stiffened her compassionate friendliness no longer puzzled him. As a sick body to be nursed and an unhappy soul to be comforted he meant a great deal to her, but as a man nothing at all.

"Take your trouble to God before the altar, my son," said the Curé. "You will be alone. I am going back to the Presbytery."

Still without looking at him he went away. But Charles did not go round into the church and kneel before the altar in prayer to God. He went to the back of it, where his bed was, flung himself face downwards on it, and cursed instead. Once the Curé had lit for him in this place the light of the love of God, and he had carried it back safely through the forest. But since then it had gone out.

## IV

Someone betrayed them. Charles, for the Curé's sake, was careful to keep hidden during the day, but as he got better and able to walk again he would sometimes go out into the forest after dark. During the sleepless nights his wretchedness would sometimes get more than he could bear and he could not keep still. It helped then to wander about in the forest for a while. He must have been seen there.

One warm autumn night he wandered further than usual. He wondered as he walked, whether it would be best not to go back but simply to walk on and meet whatever doom might come. Nothing could be worse, he thought, than the life he was leading now. Living so near his home gave his grief no chance to begin to heal. The day by day companionship with Thérèse drove him nearly crazy with love and desire. Then he knew that he could not do that. His longing to get away was simply the coward's craving to escape from a particular bit of suffering without enduring it right through to its appointed end, and that was a thing that a man could not do. They were not yet at the cross-roads of which the Curé had spoken. He sat down under one of the pine trees, his back against its trunk, and sat staring into the darkness. There was a certain comfort in it. When a man's mind and spirit are full of darkness the sunshine can seem an insult.

He stayed there longer than he knew, and he must have wandered further than he knew, for he lost his way going back, and when he reached the church it was full daylight and he was limping and exhausted. He had expected to find the Curé saying his mass but there was no one before the altar except Thérèse, kneeling upon the lowest step, straight, still and absorbed. The sight of her praying always filled him with rage, for she knelt as though locked into prayer. He had seen that locked look before, in craftsmen and artists doing their chosen work and mothers caring for their children; it spoke of a consecration of personality beyond the reach of change. He flung himself down on a bench, and in his miserable anger he did not care if he disturbed her. He wanted to do more than disturb her, he wanted to go to her and seize her by the shoulders, drag her from her knees into his arms and hold her there until he had battered down her will to his. He groaned under his breath, grinding his heel angrily on the stone flags. She had not heard the protesting creaks of the bench but she heard his light groan, hardly more than a sigh. She got up instantly and came to him.

"Where have you been? Why do you wander about at night like this and exhaust yourself? Now, when you need your strength, you have not got it."

She spoke quickly, urgently, almost with a hint of anger, this woman whom he had believed could never be anything but serene and poised. He looked at her and got up, suddenly strong, revitalised by the instinctive knowledge that they had got to the cross-roads after all. The inaction was over. It would be to do now and not only to bear, and that would not be so hard.

"Where is the Curé?" he asked her sharply.

"They have taken him. They came here to take you, but he told them you had left him long ago. Then they took him, in punishment for having sheltered you."

"Why in the name of God did he not swear that he had never set eyes on me?"

"He was prepared to tell a lie for you, he who probably had never told a lie in his life before, but you could scarcely expect him to make it of the type that would save his own skin also."

In anguish for the beloved man they were suddenly both angry, flashing out at each other in their pain. Thérèse recovered first. She put her hand on his shoulder, for he looked ready to dash wildly after the Curé.

"There is nothing you can do. They came nearly an hour ago. They had been rounding up prisoners all over the countryside. They had them standing in carts with their hands bound. It is too late now. There is nothing you can do now."

"No," he said. "They will take him to prison and perhaps he'll die there like other priests who have helped and hidden worthless men like me." He looked at her. "Did they see you?"

"Yes. We were together here in the church when they came. He was filling the lamp and I was sweeping the floor. He told another lie—for me this time. He said I was his servant, and they believed him." She looked pitifully at Charles. "And I let them believe him. That was all I could do for him—let him save us both. He was happy that he had done it. He looked back at me from the cart, Charles, and he looked full of fun like a small boy going to a party."

It was the first time that she had called him Charles. And the hand that had been on his shoulder was now held in his and she did not pull it away. In spite of her steady composure he knew that she did most desperately want his help.

"Shall I take you to Toulon?" he asked gently.

Suddenly her control broke and she began to laugh and cry together, but the laughter was uppermost. "How in the world do you propose that we should reach Toulon?" she asked, wiping her eyes on the back of her free hand as a child would have done. "Walk there?"

"Yes," he said.

"And what chance have we of arriving?"

"One chance in a thousand. Yet there is that chance. We shall find those who will help us, and when a country is in a state of chaos a couple of refugees more or less are scarcely noticed. Shall we try it, Thérèse?"

She looked at him and he saw that fringed by their wet lashes her eyes were dancing. He knew then what sort of a little girl she had been; gay and loving danger. He had been gay too, he remembered, hundreds of years ago, and he still loved danger.

"Do you trust me?" he asked.

"You need not have asked that," she said.

He was an exceptionally resolute and quick-witted man and she was a disciplined woman, trained to endurance and obedience. Where others would have been lost, they, by reason of what they were, backed by what Charles called incredible good luck and Thérèse called the providence of God, survived the sufferings of that time and reached Toulon.

## V

The journey had a poignant start. Late one night they came to a town and made their way to a little bakery kept by an old servant of the de Colbert family. They had meant to avoid the towns as much as possible but they were not yet used to the struggle of their vagabond existence, Charles was not yet strong, and they were both so worn out that they decided to risk the loyalty of the old servant. She did not betray them. She and her son fed them, gave them their own beds, washed their clothes for them while they slept and gave them food and a little money to take with them on their journey. But they seemed in a great hurry to get them out of the house in the morning. They woke them before dawn, called them to coffee almost before they had had time to dress, and hurried them out into the street while the light was still grey, giving them very particular instructions as to which turnings they were to take.

Yet early in those streets though they were they found plenty of people about, most of them of the type whom Charles called savagely the sewer rats and Thérèse pityingly those poor mad wolves, all hurrying one way with that ravening look in the eyes and that cruel sharpening of the features that takes away all humanity from a face and is the most hateful thing that one can look on in this world. They caught scraps of talk and knew why their kindly hostess had been so anxious to get them out of the town. The guillotine had been set up in the market square and men and women would die this morning. Charles glanced at Thérèse, then took her hand and held it hard. Yet he had misunderstood her. It was not fear, nor horror at the thought of sudden death, that had blanched her face, but the look on the faces that passed by.

He saw a deserted alley and pulled her down it, though that was not the quick way out of the town that he had been told to follow. They took another turn, and another, and did not quite know where they were. Then they found themselves in a narrow passage between two houses and at the other end of it they could see a lane and hear carts rumbling over its cobbles. They were market carts, Charles thought, bringing fresh provisions in from the country, and would show them which direction they ought to take. He hurried Thérèse down the passage and there at the end of it they saw the carts go by. But they were not market carts, they were three tumbrils full of prisoners coming out through the gates of the prison at the end of the short lane, and driving down it to the thoroughfare beyond where the wolves were waiting for them. The shock was so great that they stood stock still in the shadows of the passage, holding hands like two children. There were both men and women in the tumbrils, standing with their hands tied behind their backs, young and old, priests and nuns among them. A few faces were blanched with anger, a few with fear, but most of them were proudly composed. Charles felt a throb of pride. His breed died well.

The last cart passed them. An old priest stood at the back of it, speaking cheerfully to a frightened woman beside him. He looked round as the tumbril passed the passage, looked straight at them, and he was the Curé. The peace in his face made him look much younger than when they had seen him last. Then he saw them and smiled, and his face was so transfigured that for one extraordinary moment it seemed as though the grey street was full of sunshine. He looked like a boy in love. Thérèse gripped Charles's arm with both hands, yet needlessly, for though at sight of that old man giving his life for him his whole being was one aching desire to run after the tumbril, climb in and go with the Curé to his death, he did not even stir. He knew what he had to do; accept the sacrifice and look after Thérèse. And for that one moment he even managed to accept it gladly. He looked at the Curé, as Thérèse was doing, and smiled. Their smiling faces was the last thing the Curé saw before the tumbril reached the end of the lane and drove out into the mob beyond.

The noise they made was detestable. Charles flung one arm round Thérèse and held her tightly against him, her left ear against his shoulder, his right hand pressed against her right ear. He had forgotten now that he had vowed that throughout this journey he would never touch her, never kiss her or put his arm round her. He felt only the desire of great love to pull the beloved right inside his own being, wrap himself body and soul about her to protect her from all harm.

Presently it was quiet again and he lifted Thérèse's face in his hands in dread of what he would see there. It shocked him to see it almost as happy as the Curé's had been. For a moment he felt chilled, almost repelled. His arms dropped to his sides and there was reproach as well as misery in his eyes. Did she not realise that the good old man had given his life for a young man of no worth whatever, a man whose life from the beginning had been distinguished by nothing but carelessness, self-indulgence, and a hard and cruel pride? Did she not know what he was? Was it not a terrible thing to her that the innocent should die for the guilty and the old for the young? Apparently not. She looked up into the agonized face above her and smiled. But she said nothing. He was in no fit state to hear anything that she might have to say. She took his hand and led him back down the passage, and it was she who found the way out of the town.

VI

But in the weeks to come, when they walked together through the fields in the sunshine, sheltered in barns and behind haystacks from storms of rain, or sat in the woods at evening building their camp fire and cooking in it the eggs and vegetables they had begged or bought (and sometimes stolen) during the day, she said a good deal. She tried to make him see the Curé's death as she saw it, not as a revolting execution, but as a death died joyously for another, just such a death as he would have chosen if he could. It had been a gift to him from the good God, and it had been a gift to them too, not a hideous mischance, that they should have seen him going to it. If they had not seen what they had they might never have known what had happened to him; now they knew that he was safe in Paradise.

But Paradise was no more than a word to Charles. Try as she would she could not make real to him those realities that were so gloriously real to her. What was real to him in these days was remorse for all that he had done and been, and his love for her and the misery it caused him. For the more she struggled to make the Catholic faith mean much to him, the more he realised how much it meant to her and how it claimed her whole allegiance. But through the days and nights he did carry one comfort with him, and that was his memory of the look on the Curé's face, that look of a boy in love. In the meaning of that, whatever it was, there did seem some hope, both for himself and for the world.

Their journey continued and they found themselves just two among many refugees, all flying south from the Terror. It was said that the English held Toulon and that there was safety there. Safety for so many, wondered Thérèse and Charles? For a few perhaps, but what of the rest? This thing that was happening now had happened so often before and would happen so often again in the history of the world. The evil, like a volcano, broke through the crust of things, and the foul lava flooded the earth, while over the roads of the world the refugees fled from the known to the unknown horror, from darkness into darkness again, with always the unconquerable hope in their souls that in the night ahead there would be some star.

"That is why men go on living," said Thérèse. "They go on believing that somehow, somewhere, there will be something for them."

And it was her faith that they believed rightly. Charles had no such faith. But he had Thérèse, and his memory of the Curé's face.

They did not go straight to Toulon, but turned aside to find the chateau where Thérèse's cousins lived. They found it empty and deserted.

"They must have been afraid," said Thérèse with a touch of scorn. "Perhaps they went to Toulon. We'll follow them there." They reached Toulon in Christmas week, together with many other refugees, and heard the ominous news that the English had evacuated the town. With some money that Charles had kept all this while in a bag hanging round his neck he managed to rent an attic for Thérèse in a filthy tavern near the harbour. She got one night's peaceful sleep there, while he lay in the passage outside her door so that no one could reach her without trampling on him. But the next day the Terror also reached Toulon. Nothing that Charles had seen in Paris had equalled the horror that broke now in that Christmas week of 1793. It finished Charles and Thérèse. They were more exhausted than they knew, and Thérèse had been more shaken than she knew by the sight of her cousin's empty chateau. Suddenly, unexpectedly, her courage and control broke. At night in the tiny attic room high above the dreadful street, and lit by the flames of the burning town, she broke down and wept uncontrollably. She lay in Charles's arms that night, and sobbed herself into peace. It seemed no sin to them then. It seemed to be all there was.

In the morning there began that stampede for the boats in which so many lives were lost. That was the only way of escape now, by boat to Leghorn where was the English fleet. Charles and Thérèse joined in the fight for life that began at dawn and continued for so many terrible hours, and which Napoleon Bonaparte, who witnessed it, could never forget. Thérèse was past caring what happened so long as she and Charles could die together, but Charles would not give up fighting for her while he lived, and to him it seemed that death by drowning from a capsized boat, or even death trampled underfoot by the crowd on the quay, was to be chosen for her rather than the Terror. And once embarked on this last hazard all his old resolution and quick-wittedness returned to him.

Somehow he got them into a boat, and it was chiefly owing to his skill and courage, and the last ounce of his strength, that the boat finally reached Leghorn. The scenes there were as terrible as at Toulon, and Nelson on board the *Agamemnon* in the Leghorn roads was haunted by them for the rest of his life. But Charles and Thérèse had good luck, or, as Thérèse insisted, the mercy of God was still with them. Charles collapsed as the boat reached the quay, and the man who helped Thérèse lift him ashore was an Englishman to whom he had once been of service in Paris. This friend possessed a retentive memory and commanded an English ship, and he took them to England.

## CHAPTER V

### I

In London the French colony made them welcome, for they bore great names and had endured much suffering, and even in their desperate plight there was a royalty about them both that made it seem natural to care for them with reverence. Charles, tough as whipcord, recovered completely, but Thérèse was never again the strong woman that she had been. Yet she revived enough to lead a normal life again and to marry Charles. To her now there was no doubt that she must do that. She knew she would do him irreparable harm if she were to leave him now. What it cost her to make that choice she was careful that no one should know; least of all Charles. If she could not love him quite as he loved her, yet in gratitude she would do him honour. Resolutely she vowed that she would be happy, without regrets and with no backward glance. She was not Sister Thérèse now, by her own decision and choice she was the Comtesse de Colbert, and she would play her part in the world that she had wanted to renounce as well and as happily as she could.

And so to her husband's delight she accepted the pretty clothes that their friends gave her, and wore them with an air. She went to the opera and the play with Charles, took care of her beauty and re-learned the forgotten art of brilliant conversation. She had been a fine musician and an exquisite needlewoman and she polished up these accomplishments and taught music and embroidery. Charles, a fine linguist, taught languages. They managed to make a living and a small home, two rooms in Orchard Street, and a child was born to them there.

She came prematurely and nearly cost her mother her life, yet when once the fear and pain were past she made her parents' happiness a thing as nearly perfect as happiness can be in this world. She was a lovely little thing, but almost from the beginning strangely mature. She seldom cried, never grabbed or screamed if defrauded of what she wanted, and though she was always happy she was quietly and attentively happy with the small things near at hand. Her mother, gazing into the deep eyes of her small daughter, could understand the unchildish wisdom. She was the child of grief as well as love; they could not expect her to be quite as other children. Her father boasted that he saw in her signs of remarkable intelligence as well as remarkable beauty. That was to be expected, he thought, for upon either side she had a fine inheritance. They called her Marie Thérèse.

They could not afford a nurse for their baby and so in those days they went out very little and spent their evenings reading together. To please his wife Charles had become a practising Catholic, though not a very devout one, and now to please her he read the Christian apologists, while she to please him studied Greek and let him put her through a course of his beloved classics. Each was strangely captured by the books beloved of the other. St. Augustine's glowing love of God, the startling beauty of the sentences in which he daringly confessed it, helped Charles to understand Thérèse's certainty. Thérèse, making acquaintance with the wisdom of the Greeks, could almost understand how this to Charles had seemed enough, and how he had halted here.

One night, arguing over Christian and pagan conceptions of love, each had written down sentences they liked on scraps of paper and passed them across to each other. Charles had written, "Love is the divinity who creates peace among men and calm upon the sea, the windless silence of storms, repose and sleep in sadness. Love sings to all things which live and are, soothing the troubled minds of gods and men." Thérèse smiled as he handed it to her, thinking how well the words fitted the turmoil of much of their life together, and she folded the bit of paper and slipped it inside the locket that he had given her on their wedding day. She had written, "Blessed is the man who loves Thee, O God, and his friend in Thee and his enemy for Thee. For he alone loses no one who is dear to him, if all are dear in God, who is never lost." Charles, remembering how nearly she had died when the child was born, did not smile, but he too folded the paper and put it away in his pocket-book.

## II

Thérèse was never well after the birth of the child, the two little rooms in Orchard Street were noisy and airless, and she got less well as time went on. Charles, through the same good friend who had brought them to England on his ship, was offered a post as secretary and tutor in a country house in Ireland. He accepted the offer gladly, for he thought Thérèse would get well there. Yet when the time came to leave, both Thérèse and little Marie were ill of some fever and could not travel. They decided that he must go without them, for he had been told that he must take up his work upon a certain date and he must not fail his patron. The wife of their friend would look after Thérèse and the child meanwhile, and as soon as they were well again, and he had found lodgings for them in Ireland, he would come back and fetch them.

Charles found his work to his liking and his employers kind. They let him have a small cottage on the estate and he joyfully made it ready for Thérèse and Marie. He had just got leave to go back to England and fetch them when a letter arrived from Thérèse. She and Marie had quite recovered and there was no need for him to come and fetch them. The frigate *Amphion*, commanded by their friend's nephew, was sailing from Plymouth to Ireland with troops on board, and several officers' wives were sailing too. She and Marie had permission to go with them and were leaving for Plymouth immediately. There was to be a farewell party on board and she had re-trimmed the green gown that he liked so much. By the time he got this letter she and Marie would be on the sea. It was lovely September weather. They would have a good voyage, she was sure. There would be "calm upon the sea and the windless silence of storms," and soon they would be together again.

But Charles when he got this letter felt no elation, only a most unreasonable fear that shadowed the days and nights until the day when there could be no more shadows because the darkness was complete.

Years later the Abbé could not remember very much about the man who had gone back to Plymouth and tramped the streets day after day, asking crazy questions of every man he met who had had anything at all to do with the tragedy of the *Amphion*. There had been friends with him, he believed, trying to help him, but he had not taken much notice of them until one of them found a man who described a dark-haired woman in a green gown whom he had helped to lift drowned from the water, with her dead child clasped in her arms. This evidence, combined with the fact that if Thérèse and Marie were not among the few who had been saved then they must be numbered among the three hundred dead, convinced him at last. They took him to see the long lines of the graves, but they could not tell him which held the bodies of his wife and child. The explosion had caused such fear and distress in the town, they told him, that there had been much confusion. . . . So it was only for this that he had saved Thérèse; to die among scenes as terrible as any at Toulon or Leghorn and to lie in a nameless grave. . . . This was the end of their great and happy love. There was a war on, he remembered, and in a world at war love was apt to be short lived. He was merely one of many.

III

He went back to Ireland and he imagined that he was doing his work quite well, until his patron told him that it was not so and advised a change and rest. Not far away there was a monastery beside a mere, and he went there, and the monks nursed him through the physical and mental collapse that descended upon him once the compulsion of work that had kept him going was removed. Tough as he was he recovered physical strength very soon, but mental and nervous health were not so easily recovered. The monks let him alone. He read for hours in the library, worked hard and furiously in the garden, tramped for miles about the quiet countryside, and he thought that he got no better. Yet unknown to himself the wisdom of the books he read, his contact in the garden with earth and sun and wind, the quiet mere where among the rustling reeds the birds found sanctuary, were all good medicine. He was only dimly aware of the stillness and peace, yet he drank of them.

He still could not think of Thérèse and the child without coming near to madness, but more and more often he thought of the Curé and remembered that look on his face of a boy in love. The memory of that look became one with the pleasure that he was just beginning to take once more in scholarship, one with the warmth of the sun and the reflection of the birds' wings in the mere. That was natural, he supposed, for they were a part of love. To love is wisdom, warmth and light. In that look he had felt once that there was hope, both for himself and for the world. However dark the age there were always men who loved enough to give their lives for others. Wisdom never quite died upon the earth. There had never yet been a day without, somewhere, birds' wings flashing in the sun and water lapping on a quiet shore. Eternity was a fact. Intellectually he had always known it, coldly and without conviction, but now the dry bones of fact seemed slowly to clothe themselves with flesh. Love was not just an emotion to be experienced or an abstraction to be argued about, but the actual stuff of eternal life, and the Curé had known it, as in love with God and man he went to the physical death that was without power to extinguish it in him. And Charles found one day that he knew it too, not as a man awake at midnight knows that the sun exists, but as the same man knows it when the sun has risen and he is steeped in its warmth and light.

A little later he found that he could think of Thérèse and the child. One night he lay sleepless, thinking of them, with aching longing but no longer with madness. With the first light he got up and went down to the mere. It lay grey and still beneath the grey sky, the wind rustling in the reeds. The sky brightened and the ripples at his feet gleamed with silver. The strange, eerie cries of the marsh birds, waking in the reeds, came to him very faintly. A moorhen darted out from her lair, patterning the water in her wake with arrows of quicksilver, and a string of wild duck went beating up into the sky, their green necks iridescent in the growing light. The sun rose and the light was so dazzling that Charles shut his eyes that were weak and aching from sleeplessness. But he felt the warmth on his face and heard through the rustling of the reeds the beating of great wings. It was the swans, who often at this hour flew from this mere to a more distant one that was their day-time feeding ground. He opened his eyes again and saw them sweeping up into the sky. They passed many together, in arrow formation that echoed the arrows of quicksilver with which the moorhen had patterned the water. Then one passed quite alone, flying low over the mere. The sun caught her pure and lovely plumage, edging it with gold, and her reflection in the water seemed to linger there even after she had passed upon her way, flying it seemed straight into the heart of the sun. Charles did not know why the passing of the swan touched him so deeply. It seemed to work some sort of liberation in him. He thought of Thérèse again, and this time the thought of her, and the thought of God, "eternal, immortal, invisible, the only wise God," were inseparable in his mind. He bowed his head in his hands and for the first and last time in his adult life he wept.

## IV

When he came to himself again it was to see old Father Joseph crawling along towards him beside the mere with his strange sideways, crab-like crawl. Father Joseph was eighty-six years old and never spoke unless he had to. He was exceedingly infirm and was always much engrossed in getting his body to the appointed places at the appointed time, and in trying not to be a nuisance to his brethren when he got there. He had the cell next to the one which had been given to Charles, and though they had little intercourse with each other Charles had been from the beginning very much aware of Father Joseph. The old man's great domed forehead and deep eyes spoke of the fine intellect that was still his, and the marks of his holiness were stamped upon his face as a king's seal is stamped upon wax. Sometimes during a bad night he would suddenly think of that holy face, remember that Father Joseph was in the cell next to him, and be calmed. And in chapel the next morning most probably the old man would come and kneel next to him, lowering himself to his knees with extreme caution and loudly cracking joints, and not disdaining the younger man's help when it was necessary to get up again. Sometimes he and Charles were together in the library and then he would smile at him, and sometimes even croak out a word or two, but only about the weather, so that Charles had come to feel quite safe with him, knowing that the old man would make no attempt to violate his secret anguish or to offer him advice; that was the last thing he wanted.

He was astonished now to see Father Joseph beside the mere; though it was close to the monastery he had not known he had the strength to get even so short a distance. He went to meet him and found him, as he expected, short of breath. They sat down together on a boulder beside the mere, the water lapping at their feet, the peace enfolding them, and said nothing at all while Father Joseph got the better of his breathlessness. When he had done it he straightened his sagging shoulders, placed his hands one over each knee and cleared his throat. This meant that he felt he had to say something and collected his strength to that end. Charles turned courteously, expecting the usual croaked comment upon the beauty of the day. Instead the old man said quietly, without looking at him, "You have wept, my son."

That was all. Charles could do what he liked now, confide in him or not, just as he pleased. He had loved the younger man on sight, as a father his son, and for months he had been upholding him with his prayers. Now the time had come to let him know it. Upon waking this morning and looking from the window of his cell he had seen Charles going down to the mere and had known that the time had come. He had performed the slow, difficult task of dressing himself with humility and patience, and tackled the path to the mere with courage and determination, and here he was. Charles could use him or not, just as he pleased. But he hoped that he might be of use, and Charles knew that he hoped that. It was not possible to disappoint so old and holy a man; even such a man might the Curé have been, had he lived. There was not much that he managed to say that first morning, before they had to go back to the monastery, but the next day and the next, when they sat together in the library, or on a bench in the sun in the garden, he said more, until at last Father Joseph knew it all.

Charles began the story with that day in his boyhood when the Curé had lighted the candle for him; and he ended it with the white swan flying over the mere, her feathers edged with flaming gold, her reflection seeming to linger on the water after she had flown away into the sun. Father Joseph saw the connection. "The flame of the love of God is lit again in your heart, my son," he said. "You doubtless know St. Augustine as well as I do. 'Blessed is the man who loves Thee, O God, for he alone loses no one who is dear to him, for all are dear in God, Who is never lost.' "

Charles caught his breath. Those were the words that Thérèse had written on the scrap of paper that was even now in his pocket-book, though through all these months he had not been able to bring himself to look at them. Now that he had heard them uttered by another he thought that he would be able.

The next day, as they sat in the garden, Father Joseph asked him what he meant to do with himself now that he was nearly recovered and must leave the monastery, and received in reply the poignant gesture of the hands with which a Frenchman can express his hopelessness with no word spoken.

"Your wife turned from the religious life for your sake," said Father Joseph slowly. "Has it not occurred to you that you might take upon yourself the vows she did not make? Give yourself to God in her place?"

Charles was speechless, the expression upon his face one of almost comic astonishment and dismay. How could he, the man of the world, a man who had been so great a sinner, who had won so hardly to his faith, and held it now so precariously, become a monk?

"I have no vocation for the cloister, Father," he said at last.

"No, I do not think that you have," said the old man. "But I think it possible that God might have a use for you as priest and scholar. You have no plans for yourself. Well, that is of no consequence, as God most certainly has. You have merely to wait and pray until they are revealed to you. There is the bell. We must go in."

And in the end it seemed to Charles the only thing to do. It seemed to him a terrible thing, almost an insult to God, that he should take this step merely because it seemed the only thing to do; but old Father Joseph seemed quite satisfied, his argument being that if there seemed nothing else to do then this was the thing to do. The lack of ardour and devotion in himself that so distressed Charles didn't distress Father Joseph; the fact of Charles's distress told him that they would come into being one day, when this man was less exhausted and frozen by adversity and grief. Not long after Charles's ordination as priest the old man died, and it was Charles who gave him his viaticum upon a morning of early spring, warm and fragrant, pulsing with newborn life and the ecstatic clamour of the birds.

## V

But for the man who was now the Abbé de Colbert there was no warmth, no melting of his ice-bound winter. He went back to London and worked there as a priest, but he who had once been so accomplished a courtier found it hard now to make contact with other human beings. These English men and women in this comfortable England, had known no Terror. Those of his compatriots who had known it had not known bereavement quite like his. His experience and his suffering seemed to have put him at a vast distance from them all, and his tortured nerves so shrank from further pain that he was afraid to try and bridge the gap. He shrank more and more in upon himself and at last it was chiefly as scholar and writer that he earned his bread and served his Church and God.

At times he was almost happy, feeling that his life of stern self-discipline brought him very near to Thérèse and the life of discipline she would have lived at Carmel, aware when he administered the sacraments that as priest the Curé lived again in him. And he had his faith, real and living now at last, since the passing of the white swan. But at other times he was near to despair. "Blessed is the man who loves Thee, O God." But dared he say that he loved God, when he could make so little contact with his fellow man? He loved no one at all upon this earth, at times it seemed to him that the candle the Curé had lit for him in his boyhood was out again and would never be re-lit, and he would echo the words of Job, "Oh that I were as in months past, as in the days when God preserved me; when His candle shined upon my head, and when by His light I walked through darkness."

While he was in one of these moods of despair he was asked if he would go to Torquay and take care of the small community of Catholics who worshipped at Torre Abbey; there were only a few of them and he would have ample time for scholarship; and in a mood of despair he went. He was doing no good in London. In the country he might do better, he thought. It might be that the peace and beauty of it would ease away the iron that was clasped about his heart.

### VI

It was clasped so hard that breathing was difficult and painful. Struggling against the weakness and oppression he had a sudden sense of warmth, companionship and growing light. "He will deliver his soul from going into the pit, and his life shall see the light. To do all these things worketh God oftentimes with man. To bring back his soul from the pit, to be enlightened with the light of the living." He thought he was lying on the hard bed hidden behind the altar in the little church in the pine woods, and Thérèse was coming towards him carrying some precious gift very carefully in her hands. "Thérèse!" he murmured.

"Could you not even light a fire?" said a deep voice angrily. "Dammee, the room's like a vault!"

"I've not had the time yet, Sir," said another voice indignantly. "With poor Jewell off to Gentian Hill in all this weather to fetch you, who was to bring the wood in? I've but the one pair of hands."

It was the righteous wrath that was so warming, the hand holding the wrist that gave him the sense of companionship. He opened his eyes and in a gleam of sudden sunshine saw the weatherbeaten ugly old face of Dr. Crane bending over him, the eyes alight with that heartening anger, the high broad forehead creased with concern. He smiled politely and the doctor's indignation was immediately turned upon himself. "The criminal folly of not calling me in before! Do you think that the grippe is a thing to be trifled with at your age? What a vast amount of trouble men of your temperament do cause in the world!"

"If he'd listened to me he'd have had the barber in and been blooded long before this," said Mrs. Jewell.

"Blooded be damned! My good woman, are you or I to get that wood and light that fire?"

She left the room and Dr. Crane made his examination. "You are a very sick man," he said bluntly. "But if you wish to live I give you my word that I can pull you through. If you don't no doctor on earth can do anything for you."

For so long Charles de Colbert had thought of death as the best gift that life could bring, and for a moment a thrill of relief went through him; he had only to stop fighting now, only to let go. But had he? Through his bewildering weakness he was very much aware of the man beside him. The doctor had brought the cold tang of the winter's day with him into the room, and that together with the smell of strong tobacco, of leather riding boots and the chrysanthemum in his button-hole, was clean and invigorating. Dr. Crane had pulled up a chair beside the bed, had sat down and was waiting. He was aware of the courage of this man, his love of a good fight, his patience and friendliness. Above all of his friendliness. He thought confusedly that it would be extremely discourteous of him to disappoint this man. He was finding speech increasingly difficult, but politeness was second nature to him. "My good Sir, I will try my best to do credit to your skill," he murmured.

"Good," said the doctor.

Both men kept their word and fought a hard battle for a week; both at times thought it was a losing battle, but both held on. At the end of the week the Abbé's iron constitution abruptly asserted itself, the fight was over, and in a few days' time the patient was recovering with astonishing rapidity.

"Well, you're through," said the doctor with satisfaction one morning. "But I do not trust your convalescence either to yourself or Mrs. Jewell. A more incompetent couple, where illness is concerned, I have yet to meet. As soon as you are fit to be moved you will come to me at Gentian Hill and spend Christmas with me."

"Though deeply grateful for the invitation, Sir, I fear I am unable to accept it," said the Abbé suavely. "I am the chaplain of the Torre Abbey community and have my duties to attend to."

"I have seen Sir George upon the subject," said the doctor. "I have told him that you will be unfit for your duties until after Christmas. I understand that he knows of a priest, who will be pleased to stay at the Abbey over Christmas and take your place there. I will of course drive you to the Abbey to attend mass whenever you wish, but only as a member of the congregation."

There was a flash of anger in the Abbé's eyes. He was not accustomed to be dictated to. He glared frostily at the doctor and the doctor glared back. In the matter of the health of his patients, as indeed in most other matters, he was accustomed to dictate. Then abruptly on both sides the anger died. There had come into being between them a mutual respect and liking that their mutual obstinacy would never be able to cloud for long.

"Thank you, I shall be glad to come," said the Abbé quietly. He looked at the man sitting beside him, his heavy shoulders and large head outlined against the window. It seemed to him that the doctor had spent an abnormal amount of time with him during his illness. He seemed to have been aware of him sitting there, a figure of power, very often and for very long periods. . . . There had been one whole night, for instance. . . . He had seemed almost kinglike in his strength; though by morning the heavy shoulders had been sagging a good deal. "I am afraid your other patients have been neglected of late," he said.

"All of them in the condition when a little neglect could do 'em nothing but good," said the doctor. "Indignant with me some of them may be, but there are times when indignation can be a very powerful stimulant. I've known patients whom I deliberately neglected get up in their indignation and be the better for it."

"Do your patients ever leave you?" enquired the Abbé dryly.

"Frequently."

"Not those who have ever been sufficiently ill for you to have fought for their lives as you did for mine."

The doctor smiled. "No, not those."

"I wondered at times why you fought so hard," said the Abbé.

"Doctors are fighting men. I would not admit that I need any further incentive to put up a good fight than the presence of the enemy death. Had I needed it there was in your case the fact of my friendship for you. You put up a good fight yourself. Why? You do not strike me as a man whose past experience has made him much in love with life."

"The same reason. My friendship for you." He paused. "There were two more reasons, I think, though the reason of friendship was the one that was clearest to me. We Christians may not dismiss ourselves from life, failures though we may be. Perhaps least of all when we are failures." He stirred restlessly. "I cannot leave this life until I have again made contact with my fellowmen."

The doctor nodded. "Did you ever make it?"

"I thought that I did. I was exceedingly gregarious as a young man."

"Only with your own kind," said the doctor, stating a fact, not asking a question. "Not with the dirty, the ignorant, the wicked, the thieves, murderers and harlots; who so often turn out upon intimate acquaintance to be the best of us all." A look of horror and distaste spread itself like a mask over the Abbé's proud and fastidious features. "You've a long way to go. But for the sake of your immortal soul I'm glad I saved your life." He grinned disarmingly at his outraged patient. "To each man his own devil," he said cheerfully.

## CHAPTER VI

### I

The Abbé arrived at Gentian Hill a week before Christmas in a condition of silent frost that would have chilled less warm hearted men than the doctor and Tom Pearse. It was a long while since he had stayed as a guest in another man's house, and he was so inhibited by shyness that his courtesy almost, though not quite, forsook him. He was profoundly irritated too by the idiocy of intellect, weakness of body and depression of spirit left behind by his illness. Altogether he was very miserable and wished he had not come. The doctor and Tom Pearse, aware of his wish, remained unaffected by it. They had him here for his physical good, not necessarily for his pleasure, and though they hoped the one would result from the other they were both of them single-minded men who attended to first things first. Tom Pearse cooked him nourishing and most delicious meals, kept the wood fires replenished and then let him alone. The doctor supplied him with plenty of light literature and let him alone. Finding himself let alone the Abbé's taut nerves relaxed a little. Courtesy dictated that he should eat the meals and sit by the fires, though both of them were of the type that his austerity would have instantly condemned had he been his own master, and read the books, an insult to his intelligence though he considered them to be. The result was a general relaxation of his whole condition, moral and spiritual as well as nervous, which horrified him extremely until he forgot about it in his awakening interest in the life about him.

The Devon climate had performed one of its wonted conjuring tricks, and the long spell of cold wet weather had been followed by days as warm and balmy as those of spring. The birds sang and the jasmine that grew on the doctor's house was in full flower. The Abbé took short strolls about the village, and found to his pleasure that the heightened awareness of the blessedness of sun and wind that had come to him on the day he had visited Mrs. Loraine was with him still. Rosy-cheeked children passed him in the village street and he smiled at them in a terrified sort of way and received shy smiles and bobs of curtseys in return. He went to the church and though he mourned over the fungus growth of Protestantism that had overspread the Catholic structure, he rejoiced in its beauty, and did not find it impossible to pray there. He admired the fine old yew trees in the churchyard and it delighted him to find what he thought were fleurs-de-lis carved upon two of the old graves. Men, women and children came and went seeking the doctor's help, and though the Abbé saw little of them he realised with reverence and admiration how great is the power of a man whose goodwill is not bounded by creed or class.

One evening Parson Ash came in, as he often did, to smoke a pipe and drink a glass of brandy with the doctor, and the two priests, one on each side of the study fire with the amused doctor between them, gazed at each other in astonishment, then tried politely to establish some sort of contact across the gulf that separated them. But they could not do it. The good points of each were not apparent to the other, and presently the doctor with twinkling eye refilled the Parson's glass and turned the talk to ferrets, while the Abbé courteously excused himself and went to bed.

He was happy and at ease after the first few days, and on other evenings he and the doctor talked long over the study fire. They spoke sometimes of Stella and Zachary. Stella had not been to the doctor's since the arrival of the Abbé, she was deep in Christmas preparations at the farm, but the fact of her nearness was to the Abbé an added warmth in the glow of these days. He had not forgotten her during the days and nights of his illness, she had lived most vividly in his dreams, and Mrs. Loraine's box had come with him to Gentian Hill. The doctor thought it would be a hard Christmas for Stella, for the ships returning from Trafalgar had brought a letter from Zachary telling them that he was safe but that his frigate was remaining in the Mediterranean. And Stella had hoped he would be back for Christmas.

"It is disappointing for you as well as for Stella," said the Abbé.

"Best for the boy," said the doctor. "The painful process of being turned from the boy to man by adversity is sometimes more quickly completed if there are no interruptions."

He talked a good deal, with pride and delight, of his adopted son, but not very much of Stella, for he did not suppose the Abbé was the type of man to be interested in little girls.

But on Christmas Eve, the weather being still fine and his patient having gained strength amazingly, he suggested a visit to Weekaborough Farm.

"All well-to-do Devon farmhouses keep open house on Christmas

Eve," he said. "There is the ceremony of the wassailing of the apple trees, and then the yule-log and the Christmas bread. If you are not too tired to come I think you would be interested. Here in the heart of the country the fairy world is still very much with us, you know. Perhaps, deep down, pagan traditions have a firmer hold on the people than the Christian faith. At this moment in England, I am afraid that if you want real Christian fervour you must turn to the followers of John Wesley rather than to the Established Church."

"So I have observed," said the Abbé dryly.

The doctor smiled. "Yet interwoven with the bright colours of the fairy lore you will find threads of gold that are the remnant of the old Catholic faith. There are the mummers. And there is the chant of the plough. It will be an irreparable loss to England when that is no more heard over the Devon hills. Would you like to come with me?"

He had expected a cold but courteous refusal. To his astonishment the Abbé said almost genially, "I would like to come. I am not averse to fairies and I have a Christmas present for Stella."

In the clear golden afternoon they set off in the gig, Tom Pearse behind.

"It's early yet," said the doctor. "We'll drive up to the top of Beacon Hill that you may see the view from there."

The lane that lead to the Beacons was the same lane that led to Weekaborough Farm, and as they drove past the Abbé exclaimed in delight at the beauty of the old house. "I have always thought our old French chateaux—those that are left—the most beautiful homes in the world. Yet I am not sure that the English farmhouses and manors are not their equal," he said. "That one is almost worthy to house the fairy child Stella."

Aesculapius's brisk trot became a walk when they came to the steep lane that wound up to the top of Beacon Hill, and the doctor and Tom Pearse got out and toiled along beside him. They stopped at last beside a gate leading to a field, and hitched Aesculapius to the gatepost. Then the three men walked a little further up the green slope until they reached the summit of the hill and found themselves beside the Beacons. There were two of them, one of furze and one of turf, and near them was the watchman's wooden hut. At the first sight of the enemy out at sea the furze would be lit to give a good blaze, then the turf, which would burn less brightly, but would last longer. And then, leaping from hill-top to hill-top the news would spread all over the countryside.

"You there, Isaac?" called the doctor, looking in through the doorway of the little hut. But the old man inside, whose turn it was to keep watch today, was fast asleep. "No matter," chuckled the doctor. "Since November the twenty-first we have scarcely needed the watchers on the hill-tops. Thank God."

"And Admiral Nelson, God rest his soul," chimed in Tom Pearse, belligerently.

The Abbé absently crossed himself, but he was scarcely paying attention. He was gripped by this spectacle of England spread out beneath him. Only a very small portion of her, one aspect of a country of many aspects, but for him now at this passing moment, England. They were upon the summit of a ridge of hill; not really much of a hill but so much higher than the round green hillocks below that it seemed to have lifted them very high into the sky. The Abbé looked west over the rolling country of woods and pastures and orchards to where the sun was just setting behind the purple ridges of the moors, and east to the calm sea. The colours of the winter woods, of the fields and tilled earth, were delicate and lovely in the sparkling light, here and there wood smoke coiled up from the scattered farms and cottages, and sheep and cattle upon the distant slopes looked like toys set down there for a child to play with. A few late gulls were flying home to the sea and the rooks were cawing in the tall elms. There was no hint of wildness here, no exaggeration, no harshness of contrast or of outline. It was hard at this moment to realise that beyond the narrow strip of sea was France where he had endured so much. And all the while here the sheep had been quietly cropping the turf and the wood smoke curling lazily up into the still blue air.

"It must seem a little smug to you," said the doctor. "Too tidy. Too prosperous. A little self-satisfied perhaps. And the people of England, to refugees from Europe, must seem the same."

The Abbé smiled. "Perhaps—yes. Yet if you seem to us sometimes like children playing a game on your small safe island, you are kindly, hospitable children. Though most of you will never understand the broken adults who stumble to you from across the seas you will never shut your doors in our faces. And you have a strength, a sort of reluctant toughness that is hard to get at, but is there. I believe that if the storm had broken here you would all have become adult in a night. Now and again you see a hint of the toughness in the landscape. Look at that tree there, and those old grey stones."

Just below them was Bowerly Hill. The old tree looked stark and black in the surrounding softness, and the heavy stones, contrasted with the moving bodies of the grazing sheep, seemed to press into the grass with immovable strength.

"We will go back that way," said the doctor, "while Tom takes the gig down along the lane."

They walked down the green slope and came to the yew tree. The

Abbé said nothing, but he stood for a moment attentive to the spell of this place, his face absorbed as though he listened to the far off call of a hunting horn, or the roll of a drum. The doctor smiled; to him it was always the roll of the drum.

"Our yews grow to a great age," he said. "Though I think this one is not more than a couple of centuries old. And they have always been sacred to us. To the Druids first and then to the Christians."

"Always this fleur-de-lis," said the Abbé, stooping. "In the Chapel of St. Michael, on the graves in the churchyard, and here on this stone."

"You've a quick eye," said the doctor. "I noticed this one for the first time only the other day. But is it a fleur-de-lis? I thought of it as an unfolding gentian. . . . You are listening again. Do you hear it?"

"Yes," said the Abbé.

II

Stella and Hodge meanwhile were sitting beside Old Sol in the chimney corner in the Weekaborough kitchen, Stella stitching at her sampler. Sol never left the chimney corner now, except to go to his bed. In the recent cold wet weather he had succumbed abruptly and completely to his infirmities; old age had felled him, as a gale fells a twisted old tree. He could neither get up nor sit down without help, and Father Sprigg carried him upstairs to bed like a child in his arms. Dr. Crane said he'd be no good again; he guessed him to be well over eighty years old. Father and Mother Sprigg had received this news philosophically, had engaged a new ploughman, and now looked after Sol as they would have looked after a faithful old dog who had grown old in their service. They were kind, they were sorry he was no good any more, but it was all in the course of nature, and they were not breaking their hearts about it. Neither was Sol. It was warm in his chimney corner, he could still enjoy his food, and he had seen death so often that he took it entirely for granted. It was just a thing that happened, like the sowing and the reaping, the falling of the leaves and the snow, and there it was.

But Stella could not feel this way about it. Nobody had told her that Sol was going to die, yet she knew sooner or later he would do so, and she was outraged and distressed, just as she was outraged by those last chapters in the gospels. When she was sewing her sampler, preparing her lessons or stoning raisins for cakes or puddings, she would bring her stool to the chimney corner and sit beside Sol while she worked. And sometimes she would talk to him and tell him stories. She doubted if he paid much attention to what she said, but she knew that he liked to have her there; she would look up and see him with his old face softened with tenderness for her, and his eyes bright with amusement. She was dimly aware that it was her distress which amused him; he regarded it much as he had regarded the rare tantrums of her childhood; it was just an expression of extreme youth that she would presently grow out of. Yet she could not imagine herself ever becoming philosophic about the things that happened to other people. Her own small buffetings she accepted willingly enough, subconsciously aware of her deep reserves of strength that would always be equal to the demands made upon her endurance, but other people's buffetings sent her into a humbling rage at her own powerlessness. Here was Old Sol becoming daily more knotted up by his rheumatism, and there was nothing at all she could do to unknot him. And presently he would die and go right away from them all, and if he did not like it there she would not be able to sit beside him and make it nicer for him. Having Sol away would in some ways be worse than having Zachary away, because she knew that Zachary would come back one day, but Sol would never come back. It was his own pain that flayed the hide off Zachary, it was the pain of others that did it to Stella, but both of them now had felt on the raw the burning touch of things as they are, and were growing up fast.

"Things be as they be," said Sol suddenly and cheerfully. Every now and then he made these cryptic remarks, gazing into the fire, or at Stella with his bright amused eyes. She did not understand him, and he had no words to explain what he knew. It was only by the tranquillity with which he wore the burning garment of things as they are that he could reveal his innate knowledge that the hands that had put it upon him were the hands of love. "And it be Christmas Eve, see."

She understood the last remark. She had been rebellious all day, because of Old Sol, and because Zachary had not come home. But that was wrong. Christmas was no time for moods. Christmas was like a star fallen down upon the earth, a miraculous thing. If you were paying proper attention to it you were so astonished that you couldn't pay attention to anything else. She looked up and laughed, and then looked round the room at the Christmas preparations. Sol looked too, chuckling as he noticed the old familiar setting for the miracle. It struck him now, as he looked upon it for the last time, as extremely comic. Its comicality had not occurred to him in other years, so much a part of it had he been. Now, withdrawn from it all as he turned to leave it, he saw how funny it was that a falling star should be welcomed with all this food and greenery.

The great cave-like kitchen looked magnificent, Stella thought, and well it might, for she and Mother Sprigg had been labouring at it for days. Fir and holly decorated the dresser and all the odd crannies and shelves, and the grandfather clock had a branch of yew from the tree on Bowerly Hill. Mistletoe that had been cut from the Duke of Marlborough hung from the central beam. The great table, pulled back against the dresser, was loaded with food. Arranged in rows at the back were rabbit pies, mutton pies, pigs' trotters in brawn, a round of cold beef and a huge frilled ham sprinkled with brown sugar. In front were apple pies, mince pies, syllabubs, Devonshire splits, saffron cake and mounded dishes of Devonshire cream and candied fruits. The great wassailing bowl stood ready with its ladle, and the holly-trimmed platter was waiting for the Christmas bread. There was ale and cider, and Mother Sprigg's homemade damson wine, elderberry wine and sloe gin. Throughout Christmas Eve, Christmas Day and Boxing Day the front door of Weekaborough would stand wide in welcome to all who might come, be he angel, prince or peasant. Father Sprigg's dislike of vagabonds evaporated at Christmas. The dirtiest scoundrel was welcomed, warmed and fed.

But the happy traffic had not started yet, and Stella and Sol were alone in the kitchen. The fire burned low, waiting for the new yule-log to replenish it. The apples for the wassailing bowl were roasting in the ashes and the Christmas bread was baking in the bread oven in the wall, and delicious warm smells were creeping out into the kitchen. It was so still and quiet that the ticking of the grandfather clock sounded very loud. One could hear the rustling of the settling ashes, the scamper of a mouse in the corner and the click of Stella's needle against her dented little brass thimble. She was getting on faster with her sampler now, because she was turning it into a gift for Zachary. She had done quite a lot of the border of stiff little apple trees and strange birds that went all round the edge, and in the middle she was going to embroider a frigate in full sail, with dolphins and seagulls sporting round it. When it was done she would frame it and Zachary should have it for a picture to hang on the wall. But she was aware that she had set herself a very difficult task. She would get on better, she thought, if she had a really nice workbox, with skeins of bright colours in it, and a real silver thimble.

III

"Stella! Stella! Tom Pearse has just driven into the yard and the doctor and some friend of his are coming down the hill."

It was Mother Sprigg, calling down the stairs. The quiet hour was over and Christmas was beginning. Stella and Sol looked at each other and their eyes were bright. Then Stella rolled up her work, put it away in the cupboard under the window-seat and shook out the folds of the new frock that Mother Sprigg had made her for Christmas. It was soft grey wool, patterned with small red roses, and she had a new white apron to wear with it. Then Mother Sprigg bustled in, rosy and smiling, and smelling faintly of the lavender that she always kept between the folds of her best winter dress of dark crimson wool, followed by Father Sprigg creaking loudly in his Sunday suit. Then Madge came in from the yard, followed by Tom Pearse, and the doctor's loud rat-tat sounded at the open front door.

"I'll go," cried Stella, and with Hodge at her heels ran out to the hall to bid him welcome. "God bless you, Sirs," she said, as Mother Sprigg had taught her to say to all who came at Christmas, "and send you a happy Yuletide and a prosperous new year." Then holding out her flowered skirts on either side she curtsyed; not the usual quick bob of a country child, but the full-blown curtsy of a great lady. (Where in the world had she learned to curtsy like that? wondered the doctor.)

"You remember Monsieur de Colbert, Stella?" he asked her.

But she had evidently not forgotten. Her thin brown face was alight with pleasure as she rose from her curtsy and she looked up at the Abbé as though looking to see if he was just as she remembered him, Apparently he was, for she smiled and held out her hand. "Welcome to Weekaborough, mon Père. Mind the step."

He took her hand and held it, looking down at her, but he did not say a word. The doctor, divesting himself of his greatcoat, looked at the couple curiously. Why should the child's smile have made the man look for one moment as though mortally stricken, and then in the next moment, as he smiled back, almost as radiant as the child herself? There was a curious likeness in the steadiness with which each looked at the other. The rosy evening light shining through the open kitchen door softened the hard outlines of the Abbé's face and took the angularity from his tall figure. He had been visited by one of those strange moments of metamorphosis from which none of us are safe, when for an instant, brief as a flash of lightning, some strong emotion, helped perhaps by a trick of the light, clothes us with an outward seeming that was ours twenty years ago, or will be ours in twenty years' time, and the startled beholder knows what we looked like when we were young, or what we will look like when we come to die.

He had great beauty once, thought the startled doctor. Beauty, elegance and fire.

Stella too. It was not a child who stood there, it was a woman in a grey dress, moving through the shadows with head bent, carrying some precious gift very carefully in her two hands.

"Stella!" he cried almost sharply, and she looked up and laughed, a merry girl who had just been given a Christmas present, a brown paper parcel that contained she knew not what. Yet even when met by the glow and warmth of the kitchen, and Father and Mother Sprigg's greetings, the doctor remained shaken. That young man had had so striking a beauty, and the attitude of the woman had been one of sorrow, and he was powerless to halt either the passing of the one or the coming of the other.

With the arrival of fresh neighbours he was abruptly himself again. Stella and the Abbé, he saw, were sitting in one of the window-seats, happy in each other's company. He put the shock they had given him out of his mind, and let the country festival he loved take possession of him.

The two on the window-seat were oblivious of the laughter and talk around the fireplace. Stella was unpacking her parcel very slowly, her cheeks flushed and her lips parted, finding the moments of anticipation so delightful that she must linger over them.

"Shall I cut the string?" asked the Abbé, producing his pocket-knife.

"No, Sir!" ejaculated Stella in horror, for she had been trained not to be wasteful. "It's a very good piece of string."

Her nimble fingers managed the knots and folded the string and brown paper carefully, and then she gave a sigh of delight at the sight of the silver paper and the scarlet ribbon. She took off the ribbon and smoothed it lovingly. "Is it mine too?" she asked.

"Of course! Of course!" said the impatient Abbé.

She tied it round her waist, and then she began taking off the silver paper. She knew that excitement was making her much too slow, but she could not help it. She did not get many presents and she was almost too happy to breathe.

The paper fell away and the box of carved cedarwood and inlaid ivory lay on her lap. She had not known that such beautiful things existed. It was a box for a princess. It was the sort of box in which the Lady Hester would have kept her jewels when she lived at Ilsham Castle. No, it was even lovelier than that. She remembered how she had thought once that words could be made into caskets to hold visions. This was as unearthly as one of those caskets. She looked up at the Abbé, her face transfigured. "Has it got dreams inside it?"

"Look and see," he said.

She lifted the lid a little way and looked inside. She gave a small cry of ecstasy and lifted it right up. "A workbox!" She forgot the Abbé. She forgot everybody and everything. She lifted the enchanting little covers and saw the reels of coloured silks inside. She took out the emery cushion like a strawberry, held it cupped in her hands and said that Curlylocks had strawberries and cream when she sewed. She took out the silver thimble and found it fitted exactly, and murmured something about Lady Hester having one just like that. She lifted the scissors and said at once, "It is a white swan flying over the water." She unearthed treasures that the Abbé had not known were there; a velvet pin-cushion like a scarlet toadstool, a needle-book made of a scrap of gold brocade, lace bobbins with beads hanging on the ends, some faded scraps of silk and satin, a child's necklace of blue glass beads and a tiny pair of paste buckles. She lifted each treasure and held it, murmuring to herself before she put it back again, and the Abbé gathered from her murmuring that each was the starting point of a fresh dream in her mind.

As the child was now oblivious of everything in the world except her box, so he was oblivious of everything except the child. He found himself learning every detail of her off by heart. The shape of her head with its short boyish curls, the curve of her neck, the outline of her thin brown cheek with the long dark lashes lying on it as she looked down at her box, the short upper lip and the determined chin. Her eyes he knew already, star-bright and of an unusually dark grey, and her smile that had such power to shake him. And yet it did not seem so much that he was learning the child as remembering her. She seemed so much a part of him that he longed to establish some physical contact with her, to touch the twisting curl in the nape of her neck, to put his arm round her and feel her heart beat against his hand. It was entirely ridiculous. It was like falling in love all over again.

"Well, my dear heart, did you ever see anything so lovely!" Mother Sprigg was standing in front of them, staring dumbfounded at the box. Stella looked up at her. "Monsieur de Colbert has given it to me."

"Given you that lovely workbox? A little poppet like you? Well, I never! It's a box for a fine lady. Well!" Mother Sprigg hardly knew which of her emotions was uppermost, delight that her precious child should have such a lovely gift or sadness that she herself had not been the giver of it. And who was this fine gentleman, anyway, that he should give her child such a gift? He had risen and was standing politely before her.

"I hope the child has thanked you nicely, Sir," she said, and there was a tiny edge of sharpness to her voice. "Stella, have you thanked the gentleman for his gift?"

Stella had been putting the box away in the window-seat cupboard, where she kept her special treasures. Now she turned round, her face suddenly scarlet with distress. "No, Mother, I—didn't."

"Well, of all the ungrateful girls!"

And now her voice was so sharp that the tears came suddenly to Stella's eyes. Not knowing what she did she slipped her hand into the Abbé's, half for protection, half to show him how sorry she was that she had not said thank you. He gripped her hand tightly; bone of his bone she seemed.

"Madam, she was not ungrateful," he said. "Never have thanks been more charmingly expressed."

His stilted way of speaking annoyed Mother Sprigg. She disliked him intensely. A foreigner. And it hurt her to see those two standing there as though siding against her. She looked from one face to the other and it was an added aggravation to note that both of them had dark grey eyes. "Get your cloak, Stella," she said shortly. "It's time we went to the wassailing."

IV

The merry company trooped out to the orchard led by Father Sprigg carrying the wassailing bowl filled with cider and apples, followed by Madge carrying a tray of glasses. It was getting dark now and Amos the new shepherd and Dick the new boy, and two of the guests, carried lighted lanterns. Stella, with her usual understanding, had attached herself like a limpet to Mother Sprigg, and the Abbé stood with the doctor delighting in the beauty of the scene.

They had grouped themselves in a circle about the old Duke of Marlborough, and they stood for a moment quietly. In the sudden silence they could hear an owl hooting, and a church clock miles away tolling the hour, and a strange long surging sigh that was the full tide tugging at Paignton beach, but that in the eerie twilight sounded like the sighing of the earth itself. The rough grass was already silvered with a heavy dew and the motionless branches of the apple trees made intricate patterns in silver and ebony against the deep bottle-green sky. The lantern light sent a warm glow over the rosy weather-beaten country faces, suddenly so intent and quieted. What were they all thinking of, wondered the Abbé. Father Sprigg's rugged bearded face, as he stood holding the great bowl where the hot roasted apples sizzled in the cider, sending up a fragrance almost like incense, was as absorbed as that of a priest officiating at some sacred mystery. They were all looking at the apple tree and he was no longer a tree but an old wise pagan god of fertility who stood as the guardian of this farm, seeing to it that the crops should not fail nor the well run dry, nor the ewes cast their lambs nor the trees fail to bear their fruit in due season. Someone began to sing and voice after voice took up the song. The words, beginning "Health to the good apple tree!" were just rhyming doggerel, but the chant to which they were set sounded to the Abbé far older than the words. Wassail was a Saxon word. As old as that? He could believe it.

The song ended, and each man and woman took a glass, dipped it into the bowl and drank a toast to the god. Then Father Sprigg carried the bowl to the apple tree and poured out all that was left as a solemn libation over the twisted roots. Then it was over and laughter and merriment broke out again.

They trooped back to the kitchen, dim and quiet now with Old Sol sitting beside the dying fire. No one spoke while Father Sprigg and Amos brought in the yule-log from the yard and laid it on the hearth. It was a branch of quick-burning ash that had been carefully dried so that it should catch alight quickly. Father Sprigg piled small branches of apple wood around it, and Stella plied the bellows with all her strength, and in a moment the flames were roaring up the chimney. Mother Sprigg meanwhile had gone to the bread oven, lifted out the Christmas bread, hot and spicy with a golden top, and laid it upon the holly-decked platter on the table. From a jar on a shelf she took a mildewed grey morsel, the last crust of last year's bread, and threw it on the flames. The hitherto quiet company cheered lustily. Fire and bread had not failed through the year that had passed, and the burning of the last crust in the flames of the new yule-log had assured fire and bread for the year to come.

Then Mother Sprigg and Madge lit all the candles and everyone became very merry, eating and drinking, laughing and talking with amazing heartiness, and the doctor perceived that the entertainment would soon be no longer to the Abbé's taste. "We'll slip away," he said. "Stella, come with us to the garden gate."

Stella was glad to slip away too. She loved the wassailing and the kindling of the yule-log, but not the noisy hour that came after. It seemed to spoil those quiet moments when the libation had been poured out and the flames had leaped up. Wrapped in her cloak she walked sedately down the garden path between the two elderly gentlemen. The moon had risen now and the stars were bright. There was no breath of wind.

"Stella," said the Abbé, "the workbox belonged to a very old lady, a friend of mine who lives at Torre. She gave it to me for you. Will you come with me one day to visit her?"

"Thank you, Sir, I will come whenever you wish," she said. Then she curtsyed to him. "Good night, Sir. A happy Christmas." She turned to the doctor and curtsyed again. "Good night, Sir. A happy Christmas. Good night, Tom. A happy Christmas."

She stood at the top of the steps and watched them climb into the waiting gig. She had suddenly become very remote. Her small lifted face looked white in the moonlight and though she was smiling her smile was not that of a child. Her cloak fell in straight folds to the ground. Behind her the warm light streamed from the open parlour door, but it did not seem to have anything to do with her. She belonged to the shadows of the garden, to the stillness and the strange shapes of the clipped yew trees. The Abbé, parting from her with difficulty, remembered those old fairy stories of sea nymphs and wood sprites who left their own world to be the foster children of human peasant folk, and how they brought great joy with them, but sometimes sorrow too.

"She lives in a world that is not her own," he said to the doctor as they drove away.

The doctor looked at him sharply, slightly startled. "If she does, she is completely contented in it," he said.

"They are always contented," said the Abbé, "for they have the freedom of more worlds than one."

They drove home in silence. The doctor's thoughts were with Zachary, the Abbé was thinking of Thérèse.

## CHAPTER VII

### I

STELLA at the kitchen door was confronted by Mother Sprigg. "Go to bed, child," she said. "Take a cup of milk and a roasted apple and get to bed, or you'll be fit for nothing in the morning. Sol's gone already."

But Stella, unseen by Mother Sprigg, helped herself to a good deal more than a cup of milk and an apple. Taking a large willow pattern plate from the dresser she dodged around the table, between the merry guests, piling it with pigeon pie and rabbit pie, ham and beef and cake. This she deposited on the floor of the dark passage leading to the yard and was back again to fetch not a cup but a bowl of milk, a roast apple and clotted cream in a pink lustre dish and a pocketful of lumps of sugar. The Abbé, had he seen her at this moment, would not have compared her to any creature not of this earth. She was sparkling with human naughtiness as she called to Hodge and shut the kitchen door behind them.

The Christmas party in the stable was not as noisy as the one in the kitchen, but it more than equalled it in enjoyment. Stella brought Daniel in from the yard and lit the stable lantern with the flint and stone that was always kept there. Seraphine and the current kittens were in the stable already, having been banished there to be out of the way of the trampling feet in the kitchen, and so were Shadrach, Meshach and Abednego the stable cats, Moses and Abraham the oxen, the mare Bess, and the two little pack horses Shem and Ham. While the dogs ate from the willow pattern plate and the cats lapped from the bowl of milk, Stella fed the oxen and horses with the sugar. She loved to feel the warm gentle nuzzling in the palm of her hand. She patted their necks and talked to them and wished them a happy Christmas. Then she sat down on a pile of hay beside the cats and Hodge and Daniel and taking her horn spoon from her pocket she ate her baked apple and clotted cream out of the pink lustre dish. Ten minutes later the plate, the bowl and the dish were so clean that Stella decided that washing upon the morrow would be superfluous. She stacked them in a neat pile and lay down on the hay. Hodge stretched himself at her feet and Daniel lay curled up against her left side. Seraphine was close in her basket with her kittens. Shadrach, Meshach and Abednego, that poor battered crew, lay close upon her right.

Stella had not outgrown her childhood's sensitiveness to colour, scent and sound. The orange glow of the lantern, the warm velvety shadows of the stable, the contented purring of the cats and the breathing of the oxen, the smell of the clean beasts and the hay, seemed to weave themselves together and make for her a cloak of warm tranquillity. Wrapped in it she lay still, reaching down inside herself for that deep peace in which her being was rooted like a tree. Awareness of that peace gave her the deepest happiness that she knew. Sometimes it came, as now, like a deep echo of outward tranquillity, like a bell ringing far under the sea in answer to some church bell on the earth, and those were the moments when it lasted, but she had known it come also in moments of trouble and stress, though it was no more then than a touch, gone in a moment yet sufficient in strength to steady one for much longer than its moment of duration. With one hand she smoothed Daniel's rough head, with the other she rubbed Shadrach behind his ears. The animals, she guessed, were at peace too. She thought they were always more aware of their roots than human beings. They did not rush about so much. They took time off to stand still. And Zachary? Was he at peace? She looked up at the square window where she had first seen him and been so frightened until Hodge had reassured her. And now the stranger at the window was so a part of herself that there was scarcely a waking moment that she did not think of him, or a dream that had not got his thin lanky figure moving through it.

She shut her eyes. She had had a long and tiring day. The purring of the cats, the breathings and munchings of the horses and cattle, were sleepy sounds. She was sinking down and down through depth upon depth of peace, the green water closing over her head, but she was not afraid because she knew that there would be something to stay her before she fell out of existence altogether. It was with no sense of shock that it stayed her, the awareness of arrival came so gradually that she found herself walking forward to the tolling of the bell without having realised that her feet had touched the ground. Though it wasn't ground, it was silver sand jewelled with bright shells. The seaweeds all about her were some of them like flowers and some like stars, and the strange creatures that floated past, weaving in and out between the trunks of the trees, were gold and silver, translucent, luminous. The light was not of the earth. It was deep green, clear, without warmth, but not chill. It was the trees that told Stella where she was, the trees and the tolling of the bell. Though their trunks had become like polished ivory, and their branches bore, not leaves, but flowers and stars that were living creatures, she knew that these trees had once grown in the air and sunlight, and that the bell had rung out over green fields and red Devon earth. She was not far from home. It was from these depths of peace where she was walking now that Torbay fishermen drew the antlers of harts in their nets. Men had hunted through this forest and the winding of their horns and the baying of their hounds had made deep music here, and the bell had tolled them to vespers at the ending of the day.

And now of the old music only the bell was left and she was the only human being in all this strange great world to answer the summons. She paused and looked back and saw the print of her lonely feet on the silver sand. Yet she did not feel alone, for she knew it was not just the movement of the water that was ringing the bell. There was no movement of the water because far up above her head, on the sea's surface, there brooded "the windless silence of storms." Some person was ringing the bell.

She walked on until a strange sight checked her. She thought she saw the skeleton of some huge animal lying there on the sea's bottom, until she looked again and saw it was the wreck of a ship, its hull crusted with barnacles and crimson seaweeds wound about its ribs. What ship was that? Was it the ship that had brought the hermit to Torre Abbey? Or the ship that had brought Rosalind's love home to her? In which of the great storms had it been lost? She remembered how the Torbay fishermen and the country people thought some demon lived down here who sucked down one ship in each storm. And perhaps it did; there were evil things about everywhere except in heaven. But it was not here this Christmas Eve. She was not afraid when she looked at the wreck, not even when she noticed some human bones lying half buried in the sand beside it; because she knew her Shakespeare.

> "Some say that ever 'gainst that season comes
> Wherein our Saviour's birth is celebrated,
> The bird of dawning singeth all night long;
> And then, they say, no spirit dare stir abroad;
> The nights are wholesome; then no planets strike,
> No fairy takes, nor witch hath power to charm,
> So hallowed and so gracious is the time."

One is safe everywhere on Christmas Eve.

She ran on and presently she saw the church, looking like a grey rock. It was so small that it looked as though it had been made for two people only. The bell swung slowly in the belfry and light shone from the door.

She reached the door, stepped in over the doorstep that was silted up with sand, passed into the church and knelt down. She knew that someone was standing behind her, just inside the door, ringing the bell, but she did not look to see who it could be, though the nearness of whoever it was made her intensely happy. At first she was too much in awe to look anywhere except at the floor upon which she was kneeling, and which was made up of a mosaic of small and beautiful shells. Then she looked up and saw that the tiny church was just like a cave. There was nothing in it at all except the beautiful sea creatures that clung to the walls and the roof. A bunch of them, like a cluster of stars, was in the centre of the roof and it was from them that the light shone. Yet there was no mistaking this place as a church. It would not have occurred to Stella to do anything here except kneel down.

The bell stopped and the person who had been ringing it came and knelt beside her and slipped his hand into hers, and it was Zachary. They did not speak to each other for they were listening intently to the mighty surging murmur that was all about them. It ebbed and flowed like waves, it broke against the walls that protected them and then receded. It was a great eager swell of sound and yet the quiet was unbroken, it was a roaring wind and yet nothing stirred. It was the voice of the sea itself.

"If I take the wings of the morning, and remain in the uttermost parts of the sea, even there shall Thy hand lead me, and Thy right hand shall hold me. . . . Whither shall I go then from Thy Spirit, or whither shall I go then from Thy presence?" Zachary and Stella looked at each other and smiled. The presence was the peace and the peace was the presence. If you could only sink down deep enough to find it there was no separation, for you could find each other there.

A trumpet sounded or the horn of a long dead huntsman. The surging voice of the sea was receding, this time without return, and Zachary's fingers were slipping from her grasp. Stella gave one bitter cry, that was lost in the sound of the trumpet that was not a trumpet at all but a cock crowing. "The cock that is the trumpet to the morn." It was the Weekaborough cock and she slowly opened her eyes.

She was back in the stable again and it was only in a dream that she had been with Zachary. Yet though it had been only a dream she found that she was kneeling upright as she had been kneeling in the church under the sea. Outside in the yard the cock was still crowing. It must be midnight! Her heart beat fast. That strange false dawn that comes about two or three in the morning, when the cocks crow and the animals stir and wake, and look about them and sleep again, for no reason of which a mere man is aware, comes early on Christmas night. Then it is at midnight that the cocks crow and the animals wake, and a legend that is alive in almost every country of the world says that they kneel and pray.

"While all things were in quiet silence, and night was in the midst of her swift course, Thine Almighty Word leaped down from heaven out of Thy royal throne." She looked about her. Hodge and Daniel and the cats were lying still, but they were all awake and their eyes in the lantern light were uncommonly bright. She could not see the oxen and the horses, but she was intensely aware of their wakefulness. All her short life, since she had been told of the Christmas night legend, she had longed to be in the stable at midnight and see if it was really true that the animals kneeled down, but Mother Sprigg had always seen to it that she should be in her bed at that time. And now here she was. The first stroke of midnight sounded very faintly floating through the still night from the church over the hill, and she covered her face with her hands. She listened to the twelve strokes of the bell and the beating of her heart seemed to keep time to their rhythm. Then the church bells began to ring and it was Christmas Day. She took her hands from her face and met the bright glance of Hodge. His mouth was open and he seemed to be laughing at her. She looked round and all the animals seemed to be laughing at her, not in ridicule, but with a kindly tolerant tenderness. Well, they seemed to be saying, you were here but you kept your face covered, and you don't know now whether we kneeled down. I had to, she said, for it was your hour and I had no right to be here.

She put out the lantern, and followed by Hodge went out into the yard, that was almost as bright as day in the moonlight. They climbed up the thatch together and in through her window. It struck Stella that she did not manage the climb as easily as usual. Was she growing up? Only children climbed roofs and trees, not grown women. She must be becoming a woman. She did not mind. Zachary must be nearly a man now and she wanted to be a woman to match him. In her room she listened anxiously but as on the night when Zachary had appeared at the stable window luck was with her, for Father and Mother Sprigg had not come to bed yet. She undressed and got into bed and curled herself up like a ball, as she did when she was supremely content. It had only been a dream about Zachary but it had been a dream that had made her happy. And why say "only a dream?" That patient long suffering man Saint Joseph had not said "only a dream." He had taken his dreams very seriously indeed, and a terrible thing it would have been for the world if he had not.

11

Christmas Day followed its accusomed happy course. There was church going in the morning. Gentian Hill church was a bower of greenery and packed with every man, woman and child in the village, all dressed in their best. Last year the threat of invasion had been still hanging over them, this year it was lifted, and though the war still raged and many husbands and sons were away, and many had died, yet there was a new lightness in all their hearts. Up in the gallery the band made a shattering, deafening row, the performers upon the wind instruments red as turkey cocks as they blew and trumpeted, the fiddlers nearly wrenching their arms out of their sockets, but try as they might they could not drown the roar of sound in the body of the church below that was the congregation singing the Christmas hymns. When Parson Ash stood up in the pulpit and opened the book that contained a homily for every Sunday in the year, with Christmas thrown in extra, no one, with the exception of Job Stanberry, the clerk, went to sleep. The homily that was thrown in extra was part of the Gentian Hill Christmas, and as such worthy of attention. Most of the congregation knew it by heart by this time; all but the last few words. "And so, beloved brethren," intoned Parson Ash, commencing the peroration, "let us join our praises to those of the angels at this holy season, and open our hearts in welcome to——" And down came the Parson's book on Job Stanberry's head as usual, so that still no one knew what the last words were. Stella on the whole was glad because she could employ herself all the way home thinking of all the glory to which it was possible to open one's heart on Christmas Day. . . . The God of love. The Holy Child. Wonderful. Counsellor. The mighty Father. The Prince of Peace. . . . It was enough to make one's heart crack and break if one thought about it too long

The Christmas dinner at Weekaborough, which was shared by several lonely neighbours and strolling vagabonds who had come through the open door and not been refused, was colossal. The kitchen was filled with steam and heat, laughter, noise and bustle. It was the only part of Christmas that Stella did not enjoy very much, and the fatigue of it left her with dark smudges under her eyes. When the men were sitting round the great fire with their pipes and glasses, and the women were stacking the dishes and carrying them to the scullery, Mother Sprigg whispered, "You can slip away, love, if you like. The parlour fire is laid and you can light it. Here's the key."

"Mother!" gasped Stella, and squeezed her hand in gratitude. She was hardly ever allowed in the parlour by herself, such was Mother Sprigg's fear that the child might break something, or tear something, or leave a smudge somewhere. It was the holy-of-holies and was kept locked, the key living in Mother Sprigg's pocket. Mother Sprigg herself went in once a week to dust and polish, and to light a fire if the room felt damp, and sometimes she let Stella help her, but when they had finished she led her firmly out and locked the door. It struck her that Mother Sprigg, too, must think she was growing up, if she was now to be trusted alone in the parlour. She took her workbox and sampler from the window-seat cupboard and slipped out into the shadowed hall, unlocked the parlour door and went in.

She lit the fire of apple logs and fir cones and the two tall candles on the mantelpiece, and sitting down in one of the two high-backed chairs beside the fire she looked about her. The parlour was a small room. Its stone floor was covered by a moss-green carpet, curtains of green velvet hung at the window, and the walls were panelled in dark oak. Whenever she was in the parlour Stella imagined herself in the secret heart of a dark mysterious wood. The treasures in the parlour increased this feeling. The two footstools that stood before the high-backed chairs had been embroidered by Mother Sprigg's mother in a cross-stitch pattern of sweet-briar, with small white roses and blood-red thorns, the kind of impenetrable briar that enclosed the Sleeping Beauty. The oval frame of the fire screen enclosed dried and pressed wild flowers under glass, anemones and wood sorrel, primroses and white violets. On the mantelpiece, between the tall silver candlesticks, stood a china shepherd and shepherdess with crooks and flower wreathed hats; only they were so beautifully dressed in panniered flowered gown, embroidered waistcoat and velvet coat, so elegant altogether, that Stella thought they were really a prince and princess, carrying the crooks just for fun. A small escritoire stood against the panelled wall, and on top of it was a goose-feather pen and one of those large sea-shells which hold for ever the murmur of the sea. A mirror so old that you could scarcely see yourself in its strange green glass hung upon another wall, and over the mantelpiece hung a small curved hunting horn, just such a horn as might have been slung over the shoulder of the prince when he slashed his way through the briars to find the Sleeping Beauty. This horn, like the mirror, was very old, and Father Sprigg did not know how it had come into the possession of his family. It had a silver band round it which, like the silver candlesticks, was always kept brightly polished.

There was nothing else in the little parlour and it needed nothing more. For the first time it struck Stella that it was a room for two people only, as the chapel under the sea had been for two people. It had two chairs, two footstools and two candlesticks. It belonged to the prince and princess on the mantelpiece. "To me and Zachary," she said. She had once asked Mother Sprigg if the room was ever used, and Mother Sprigg had said yes, when a bride and groom drove back from church they would step in for a few minutes' peace and quiet before they joined the noisy guests in the kitchen. And when a baby had been christened it would lie in state here in its cradle. And when anyone died in the house the body would lie here in its coffin, like the baby in its cradle, until the hearse came and they took it off to church. And so she had thought of this room as having no personal connection with her, but only with the babies, brides, bridegrooms and corpses who had hitherto used it. But tonight, quite suddenly, it had become her room, hers and Zachary's. She opened her workbox, put on her new silver thimble, took a needle from the brocade needle-case, cleaned it in the emery-cushion that looked like a strawberry, threaded it with a bit of crimson silk and began to sew.

She had not drawn the curtains and outside the window was the deep blue of a winter dusk seen from a candle-lit room, "Gentian blue" she said to herself. She could just see the shapes of the clipped yews and was glad because she knew them all and loved them, just as she loved the apple trees. She could not see Bowerly Hill, but she could picture the old yew tree and the fallen stones, and the sheep lying in the blue dusk as though folded in Our Lady's cloak. She pictured the Christmas shepherds up there with them. One of them, she thought, was a very holy man. She imagined him sitting on one of the fallen stones, wrapped in his cloak, looking out towards the sea. Because he was a holy man the sheep had gathered close about him. The Christmas stars were bright over his head and his shepherd's crook was in his hand.

Then she forgot about him because the room was beginning to talk, as a room does when someone settles down within it whom it feels belongs there. The small fire whispered beside her and the sea-shell murmured. The dress of the shepherdess rustled as she leaned towards the shepherd, who was singing a song to her under his breath. A phrase of music came from the horn hanging on the panelling and the candle flames leaped and laughed. All the infinitesimal sounds together made up the voice of the room. "Yes," said Stella. "Thank you. I won't forget." And she sighed with relief, for what she had heard comforted her angry grief for Sol. Her childhood was slipping away from her and she was not hearing as clearly as she used to do. She could remember the time when she had been able to hear the feet of a fly on a window-pane and the music of the stars. Tonight she had had to listen very attentively to hear what the room was saying, and perhaps after all, as time went on, she would forget what it had said. But she would remember that it had said something that was full of reassurance, something about coming back to the awareness of childhood again when one had finished being old; hearing again, seeing again, only more clearly than before. And it would be good to be a woman, it would have its compensations. She thought of the bride and groom standing here together after their wedding, and of the baby in its cradle, and she smiled as she sewed.

III

The man who sat wrapped in his cloak under the yew tree, looking out to sea, sighed and got up reluctantly, obeying the promptings of a conscience that suggested the sitting out of doors in a December dusk was not the wisest course of action for a man recently recovered from an illness. The doctor would doubtless have forbidden his walk here, had he been at home when he set out. Yet the evening was as balmy as spring and one seldom took harm from doing what one wanted to do. He had had to come back to this place of strength, sit here for a while and let it toughen his fibres, listen to the silence that wrapped itself about the music he could not hear and put his finger in the print on the stone. When he stood up to go he found that the sheep had gathered close about him. That was odd, he thought. He had borrowed a stick of the doctor's to help him up the hill and leaning upon it he moved among them like a shepherd.

He saw the warm glow of firelight and candlelight shining from the little parlour as he went down the hill. Was Stella there? He crossed the lane, went up the steps and into the garden. He moved noiselessly among the yew trees until he could see into the small green parlour. She was there, her dark head bent over her sewing, looking like a fairy-tale princess in her bower. The open workbox stood on a stool beside her, the candlelight caught the gleam of silver on a horn that hung upon the wall. He was a lover again, his soul in his eyes as he watched. For perhaps ten minutes he stood motionless, and then, as a lover might have done, he flushed. What right had he to spy on her? This was a hateful thing that he was doing. He turned abruptly away, then with a sudden exclamation drew back again into the shadows.

Who was this mounting the steps and lifting the latch of the gate, the rising moon glinting upon his silver helmet and the crimson rose stuck jauntily behind his ear? Was it the owner of the fairy horn, come to claim it in his lady's bower? The young knight strode up the garden path, and the Abbé just noticed that he had a crimson cross upon his breast before his startled attention was captured by the sight of a large green dragon wedged in the gate. His tail was caught in the bottom bar and he swore loudly as he tugged it free. Stella heard him, glanced through the window, jumped to her feet, darted from the parlour and appeared at the front door, clapping her hands delightedly. "St. George!" she cried. "St. George for Merry England! A happy Christmas!"

"A happy Christmas to ee all at Weekaborough," shouted St. George heartily in broad Devon. "How do ye fadge, maid Stella? 'Tis a bowerly woman ee be growin' then."

The Abbé, enlightened, smiled and drew back into the shadows to watch the happy scene to its conclusion. He would never forget, he thought, the picture of the moon-washed house with its beautiful tall chimneys soaring up against the first stars, the door flung wide in welcome with the light streaming out, and the bright figures of the mummers moving up in procession through the dark yews to be welcomed by the little girl in the flowered dress, dropping a curtsy to each in turn of the fairy-tale figures whom she knew so well. St. Andrew, St. Patrick, and St. David, Saladin and the King of Egypt, the Prince of Denmark with his blackened face, the Fool with his bells and motley, old Father Christmas and the valiant Slasher, and other strange creatures masked like the spirits in Comus, with a Trumpeter in a scarlet cloak bringing up the rear. This last character halted at the front door, turned and blew his trumpet. "To commemorate the Holy Wars," he cried, "and the happy festival of Christmas." Then he went in with a last swirl of his red cloak and the door was shut.

The Abbé walked slowly home, wondering what sort of a masque was being performed now in the cave of the Weekaborough kitchen. Some strange confusion of the Crusaders and the three Wise Men, the fairies and the saints, something woven of such diverse strands, reaching back to such distant centuries, that no one knew what it meant any more. But these country folk did not worry about the meaning of things. It was the penalty of too much so-called education, the Abbé thought, that one tended to feel oneself more and more a spectator of the drama of life rather than an actor in it. Those people, caught up in the pageant of the earth itself, did not analyse. They were better employed playing their full-blooded and richly satisfying parts.

"What you said was true," he said to Dr. Crane that night. "In the deep heart of this country the fairy world is still quite extraordinarily near the surface."

## *BOOK III*

# THE CHAPEL

# CHAPTER I

I

THE sunshine of a May morning filled Mrs. Loraine's parlour, where she and Stella sat sewing. Mrs. Loraine was making a scarlet flannel petticoat and Stella was working on her sampler.

"Just six months ago today, Stella, since you came to me," said Mrs. Loraine.

"Yes, M'am," said Stella, "and two years and four months since mon Père first brought me to see you."

They looked at each other and laughed. It seemed incredible that just over two years ago they had not known each other, and now they knew that they would always know each other.

"There are just seven people in the world about whom I feel that," said Stella.

"About whom you feel what, child?" asked Mrs. Loraine. She could not always follow the quick flights of Stella's mind—it was like trying to follow the dartings of a swallow—but she found the effort to do so immensely rejuvenating. She had forgotten how stimulating the society of the young can be. Stella launched out into each new day like an explorer into undiscovered country. Her own mind and soul, the world about her, were equally full of marvels to be encountered one by one with astonishment and joy. Mrs. Loraine, making her discoveries with her, found them familiar yet forgotten treasures. She had found these jewels herself once, turned them over, marvelled at them, and put them aside uncomprehended. Now finding them all over again in Stella's company she had more understanding. In her old age she had come back to the place where she had started from and had discovered that the intuition of youth and the wisdom of age were two keys that unlocked the same door.

"That I shall know them for ever and ever," said Stella, and dropping her work she ticked them off on her fingers. "Father and Mother Sprigg, Sol, Dr. Crane, mon Père, you, Ma'am, and—Zachary."

Mrs. Loraine knew all about Zachary. Stella had not actually told her much about the young sailor, now serving under Hardy on the South American station, but she had told that little in such a way that the old lady was now aware of Zachary as an actual presence in her house. She marvelled that the love of a thirteen-year-old girl for a boy whom she had not seen for more than two years could have such evocational power. Yet it was so. When Stella came into the house Zachary came in too. It would hardly have astonished Mrs. Loraine had she met him one day upon the stairs or in the garden, and she would have recognised him at once.

"How does one know that about people?" asked Stella.

Mrs. Loraine, remembering that this awareness of an eternal relationship had come like a shaft of light upon her fourteenth birthday (Stella, as always, was beforehand with hers) laid down her work also and thought about it. They were always dropping their work, these two, while they bent their heads over Stella's newest discovery.

"I think it's a case of recognition, Stella," said the old lady slowly. "I think God creates what one might call spiritual families, people who may or may not be physically related to each other, but will travel together the whole of the way. And it's a long way."

Stella nodded. One walked through a door when one died. But that was only one door. There might be others. But the strangeness on the other side of the door would not be so frightening if you had members of the family with you, some of them taking you up to the door and others there to meet you on the other side. And she saw that Mrs. Loraine was right about recognition. Zachary, mon Père and Mrs. Loraine herself had never seemed strangers to her. Her mother would not seem a stranger when she met her at the door.

They became engrossed in their work again, and while she stitched Mrs. Loraine retraced in her mind the steps that had brought Stella to her home. At their first meeting their recognition had been swift and happy, and she had noticed that in Stella's shy delight in her house, her parlour and her treasures, there was a good deal more than the curiosity of a child. There had been something of the pleasure of a home-coming. The Abbé had noticed it too. "She felt in her right setting," he had said to Mrs. Loraine later.

"Is not her own home her right setting?" Mrs. Loraine had asked.

"She loves it," he had replied. "If you remember, in the old tales the fairy-children of human foster parents always loved them, though it was not always in their power to stay with them for long."

Their meetings had become more and more frequent and two years later Stella had had her first real parting with Father and Mother Sprigg. It was not a very severe parting, for she still spent the week-ends at Weekaborough, but from Monday morning until Friday evening she lived with Mrs. Loraine, and Mother Sprigg had nearly died of a broken heart when she began to do it.

It had been Stella's own doing.

"Stella, I wish you need not go home," Mrs. Loraine had cried out one day, after the Abbé had brought her to tea and they were taking their leave. It had been a real cry of distress, for the evening stretched before her empty and lonely and the rare company of the little girl had become very precious to her.

Stella, tying her bonnet strings, had considered this. Weekaborough would always be to her the dearest place on earth, and there would never be another foster-mother like Mother Sprigg, but there was in Mrs. Loraine and her little house a quality of fastidious beauty that satisfied something in Stella that had not yet been satisfied, and there was no doubt in her mind that Mrs. Loraine needed her. Araminta was so busy looking after the house that she did not have much time to sit with her mistress, and when she did keep her company she was cross. Stella, as usual, had come directly to the point.

"Would you like me to live with you, M'am?" she had asked.

"Yes, Stella."

"Well, I could not live with you always because of Mother Sprigg, but I could live half the time with you and half with Mother Sprigg."

"We'll think about it," the Abbé had intervened, and no more had been said that night.

Mrs. Loraine had talked it over with the Abbé, and the Abbé with the doctor, and the doctor with great courage had approached Father and Mother Sprigg.

"My Stella a little maidservant?" had ejaculated Mother Sprigg. "It surprises me, doctor, that you could even think of such a thing. Her father and I have brought her up to better things and I should be obliged to you if we could now consider the matter closed."

Father Sprigg had expressed himself much more forcibly and had taken much longer over it.

The doctor, when he could make himself heard, had explained that though she would be paid a little for her services Stella would be with Mrs. Loraine in the capacity not of maidservant but adopted granddaughter. Her duties would be light; dusting, washing china and arranging flowers. And Mrs. Loraine would teach her accomplishments that could not be learned at Weekaborough. Those would include the playing of the spinet and the art of genteel conversation both in French and English.

"And what time will be left for her studies with you, doctor?" had demanded Mother Sprigg.

She had thought that she had him there, but the doctor had replied humbly that if Stella came to him for only one day in the week he would be more than happy. "I have already taught her the best lesson of all, the actual love of learning," he had said, "and one day a week will be sufficient for me to keep that love alive in her."

The thought of his Stella chattering French and playing the spinet like a lady entirely won Father Sprigg. He was too large hearted, and perhaps too unimaginative, to resent, as did Mother Sprigg, benefits to Stella that would tend to separate her from them. And Mother Sprigg finally yielded too. She was a born mother, and if her possessiveness was strong her love was stronger.

And so it had come about, and Stella these last six months had grown at a most astonishing pace in body, mind and spirit.

II

Stella finished embroidering a green dolphin with golden fins, and Mrs. Loraine finished the flannel petticoat and put her feet up on the sofa, while Stella read aloud from a little book of French fables, all written in words of as few syllables as possible for those of tender years. Well grounded by the doctor in Latin she was learning French with astonishing ease and with a correctness of pronunciation that astonished the old lady. She could not understand how a farmer's child could be so swift to learn, so naturally fastidious and sensitive as was this child. She could see now how the Abbé, encountering Stella, had not been able to lose sight of her again. Stella was something that once found one held to tightly. She was one of that rare company who are the Almighty's justification for having made the human race.

Araminta came in with a glass of wine for Mrs. Loraine, a mug of milk for Stella, two queen cakes and the announcement that the hired chaise was waiting. Mrs. Loraine did now, very occasionally, take a morning drive, and she intended this morning to visit the Cockington almshouses with a basket of comforts for one of the inmates. She had had to sell a few of her treasures to pay for these drives, but she considered them good for Stella. Sometimes, as today, the drive had a charitable purpose, and Stella received instruction in the art of alleviating the necessities of the humble poor. On other days they paid social calls and sitting mute and still upon her chair (for the young paying calls must be seen and not heard), her hands folded in her lap and her feet placed side by side upon a footstool, she learned with astonishment what subjects may be discussed with propriety in genteel circles, and how, and later (from Mrs. Loraine) why. This was the only part of the training that left her cold. She thought it foolish that one could discuss the accouchement of a lady (provided gentlemen were not present) but not that of a sheep, and wrong that a vivacious tongue should be prized above rubies however silly the things that it said. And the reasons given by Mrs. Loraine for these phenomena, that sheep were not discussed because they belonged to a lower order of creation, and that silence was bad manners because it made other people uncomfortable, brought no conviction to her mind. She thought to herself that these people had never kept lambs upon Bowerly Hill and felt themselves in the fields of Paradise, nor sat beside Sol in the chimney corner and found comfort in the things that he did not say. Though there was a part of her that liked genteel society there was another part of her that would always hunger for the good sense and comfortable silences of Weekaborough.

They took their refreshment and went upstairs to put on their bonnets, while Araminta added the completed petticoat to the packets of tea, peppermint and sugar in the basket in the hall. Rather to Mrs. Loraine's surprise Araminta had not resented the addition of Stella to the household. She liked the child, she liked to hear the spinet being played again, and above all she liked to see the cedarwood workbox once more resting on its appointed table, even though it was Stella who used it now and not Mrs. Loraine.

The chaise was hired from the Crown and Anchor and it would have been difficult to say which was the oldest, the chaise itself with its motheaten cushions, the half-blind white horse who pulled it or the deaf coachman in his mustard coloured livery with tarnished buttons who sat upon the box. The whole equipage moved so slowly that it would have been quicker to walk, but on a fine May morning it was no penance to move slowly and have time to gloat over each flower and tree beside the way. They had the hood down today, it was so fine and warm, and only a light rug across their knees, and Mrs. Loraine carried her summer parasol of grey silk with a silver fringe.

"You look beautiful, Ma'am," said Stella simply, and indeed in her grey mantle and grey velvet bonnet, and sitting very upright on her seat, Mrs. Loraine was a most regal figure. Stella herself, wearing a new green cloak and a green bonnet trimmed with daisies, and holding herself with the stately grace that she had quite unconsciously copied from her benefactress, was also a pleasing sight.

As they drove slowly away Stella looked back at the small white house with its blue front door and brass knocker, and at the garden filled with a tangle of sweet-scented wallflowers. She looked too at Torre Church, and at the holy well of St. Elfride with its stone archway. The meadows between Torre village and the beach were bright with buttercups and bordered with meadowsweet. The wind from the sea, blowing over them, brought wafts of sweet scent that made her wrinkle her nose with pleasure. This hamlet of Torre was a part of her now and she loved it. Home was no longer just Gentian Hill, Weekaborough and Bowerly Hill, it had widened to take in Torre village, the Abbey, St. Michael's Chapel, Torquay and the church under the sea that she had visited only in her dream.

"And Cockington," she said to Mrs. Loraine.

"What, dear?"

"After today I shall belong to Cockington too."

"You've been there before, dear."

"Only driving past. Not going right inside the park like we'll do today. Do you think we shall see Madam Mallock?"

"I trust not in the lanes, dear," said Mrs. Loraine dryly.

Madam Mallock, the lady of Cockington Manor, was to Stella an almost fairy-tale figure. Still young and dashing she drove about the narrow muddy lanes in a gilded coach drawn by six horses, with all the speed possible under the circumstances, and meeting her was a perilous and confusing business, for her coach filled a Devon lane from hedge to hedge and the six horses could not be reined up quickly. But Stella loved meeting her, even though the meeting meant backing the chaise, or going into a ditch and sticking there. The gilded coach and Madam Mallock inside in her silks and velvet, with jewels sparkling in her ears, brightened her thoughts and her dreams for a week afterwards.

But they met nothing today as they bumped slowly along over the ruts of Robbers' Lane. Oak trees on fire with their spring leaves arched over their heads and the steep banks on either side were covered with bluebells and pink campion. When they stopped to admire the view through a gateway they could hear the torrent of birdsong that flowed up from the earth with such passion that the sound of the waves breaking on the beach was drowned in it.

They drove on through Cockington village with its whitewashed thatched cottages and its fourteenth century forge with a large pond in front of it. A stream ran down one side of the village street and the sound of running water seemed a part of Cockington. Its very name meant a settlement near the springs. Then they turned in through the gates of Cockington park. The church and almshouses as well as the manor were within the park and visitors to them might drive through it when they pleased. Most of the famous Cockington deer had been sold by the present lord of the manor but there were still a few of them left grazing under the great trees, their dappled bodies lovely in the sunlight. The trees parted, the manor came in sight, and Stella sighed with delight. She did not know of course that it was here that Hodge's aristocratic father had lived, but she abruptly thought of Hodge as the chaise jogged along. During these days when she was with Mrs. Loraine she missed Hodge most dreadfully.

The manor was a beautiful three-storeyed house with a courtyard in front of it. To the left a gateway in the wall led into the pleasance and beyond was the church. To the right were the kennels, stables and almshouses.

"Have you been inside the church, Ma'am?" asked Stella eagerly, her imagination caught by the beautiful Norman tower rising above the trees.

"My dear, I am a Catholic," said Mrs. Loraine severely.

"Have you been inside the manor, Ma'am?"

"Mr. Roger Mallock is a clergyman of the Church of England," said Mrs. Loraine with the same severity, "and the Catholics of the neighbourhood are not invited there very often. But I did go once. It is very beautiful inside. There is a minstrel's gallery, dear, a panelled dining parlour and very beautiful ceilings of Italian work, one of them showing the goddess Flora in a bower of flowers. And I believe now, dear, there is a wallpaper in one of the rooms that was taken from some captured French vessel. It represents the landing of Captain Cook upon some outlandish island and is entirely covered with palm trees and naked savages."

"Oh!" gasped Stella ecstatically.

"I believe it to be highly immodest, dear," said Mrs. Loraine dryly. "Though doubtless quite in keeping with the goddess Flora. And the gilded coach and six."

Her sweet lips folded themselves into a straight line and Stella thought briefly how odd it was that thinking differently about God tended to make even the nicest people not very sympathetic towards each other.

The chaise drew up in front of the almshouses. There were seven of them and they were nearly two hundred years old. The Mallocks were comparative newcomers at the Court; they had only lived there for just over one hundred and fifty years. The Careys had lived there before them and a Sir George Carey had built the almshouses in his old age, when it had suddenly occurred to him that up till now he had not perhaps been as good as he might have been. "Being somewhat aged he resolved to live the residue of his days to God and himself," his historian had written of him, "and knowing how pleasing to God charity and good deeds are he purposed to do something for the poor," and he built the almshouses. They had two rooms each and were all under one roof, but each had its own separate herb garden in front enclosed within a stone wall. The inhabitants could be either men or women. The lord of the manor gave them each a shilling a week with a new freize gown and a new white shirt or shift yearly at Christmas.

The old woman whom they were visiting was Wilmotta Bogan, always called Granny Bogan. She had come down in the world—come down a good long way, it was said—and become at last a weeding woman, and for the last two years had pulled weeds in the gardens of the gentry until she got too old to stoop and Madam Mallock had taken pity on her and installed her in one of the almshouses. She had weeded sometimes for Mrs. Loraine, and Mrs. Loraine did not forget her now, even though she was not really very fond of the old woman.

"You must not mind what Granny says, dear," she whispered to Stella as they got out of the chaise. "Nor the way she looks at you. She can say surprising things. She's—odd. And as she does not care for children she may be a little short with you."

They went up the narrow path through Granny Bogan's herb garden, their full skirts sweeping the herbs and sending up gusts of fragrance into the sunshine. Mother Sprigg was something of a herbalist and Stella noticed at once that Granny Bogan must be too, for she had the nine mystic herbs growing in her garden; hellebore, rosemary, lavender, sage, comfrey, rue, wormwood, marjoram and vervain. She had other things too, verbena and mint and camomile, and some plants whose names Stella did not know, but the nine held pride of place. Each little house had a small low oak door set in the thickness of the old stone wall, with a narrow diamond-framed window of ancient green glass to each side of it and two above. Granny Bogan's door was set ajar and through the crack issued steam, an aromatic scent and a low crooning. Mrs. Loraine knocked a little timidly and then whispered to Stella, "Now we must wait until Granny is ready."

They waited for ten minutes and then the crooning ceased, light steps were heard pattering across a stone floor, and the door opened. Stella, preparing as a child does to look up into the face of a grown-up, found herself, to her delighted surprise, looking straight into the bright eyes of a little old woman no taller than herself, whom she was sure she had seen before somewhere. Yet it did not seem quite correct to call Granny Bogan old, even though she had the wrinkled parchment skin and nut-cracker nose and chin of her eighty years, for her beady black eyes were so bright and her back so straight and her tiny figure so trim that she looked more like a child than an old woman. She wore a full-skirted gown of dark brown freize, a white apron and mob-cap and a scarlet shawl crossed across her chest, and was most exquisitely neat and clean. But the impact of her personality was startling, so caustic and so sharp that the unprepared were apt to recoil when her gimlet eyes bored into them, and her cackle of derisive laughter announced without words her opinion of what she had seen. But Mrs. Loraine and Stella both stood firm, Mrs. Loraine inured by previous experience and Stella because in her different way, the way not of knowledge but of instinct, she could see almost as clearly as Granny Bogan and knew at once that this alarming old woman was not really as alarming as she looked. She had known too much in her life, undoubtedly, but the evil she had put away from her at most tremendous cost and now was free of it. Stella looked at Granny Bogan and then curtsyed to her, aware of her reverence though not understanding the reason for it.

Granny Bogan bobbed to the quality, led them in and dusted a chair for Mrs. Loraine, but the humility of her actions was not echoed in her demeanour. Standing before her visitor, her little claws of hands folded at her waist, her face alight with mockery, it was the dignified Mrs. Loraine who appeared very slightly at a disadvantage. A very pungent steam was issuing from the kettle on the fire and she sneezed.

"Bless you, Ma'am," Granny Bogan congratulated her. "That's one devil gone out."

Mrs. Loraine laughed. "Sit down, Granny," she said.

Granny Bogan sat down on the second of her two chairs and watched while Stella took out the flannel petticoat and the packets of tea, peppermint and sugar.

"Thank you, Ma'am," she said briskly, and put them away in the cupboard in the wall beside the fireplace. She sounded grateful but not obsequiously so. If the gentry liked to bestow charity upon the poor, let them. It pleased them and did no harm. But Granny Bogan liked Mrs. Loraine; she might cackle with laughter at the little hypocrisies and self-deceptions with which all but the most valiant must protect themselves from too much self-knowledge, but she was always well aware of hidden loveliness too; and there was a genuine softening of her sharp bright eyes as she sat down again and enquired after her guest's rheumatism. A discussion of that complaint followed and Stella, sitting on a three-legged stool, looked about her.

The small low-ceilinged, stone-flagged room was as clean as a new pin. A bright wood fire burned on the hearth and in the large iron kettle that hung over it from a chain some strange concoction was brewing. On a rag rug before the hearth sat a black cat who took not the slightest notice of any of them. The furniture consisted of a dresser, an old oak chest that served also as a table, the two chairs and the stool. So many bunches of herbs hung from the beams overhead that one could scarcely see the ceiling at all, and pots of scarlet geraniums stood on the sills of the two small windows.

But it was the things on the dresser that fascinated Stella. Besides the few pots and pans and some bits of bright china there were glass jars filled with strange-looking liquids, bundles of odd-looking roots, a snake skin, and several bright-coloured tins that she was quite sure contained treasures too precious to be exposed to the sight. But she was careful not to stare too hard. She had not needed Mrs. Loraine to teach her that however devouring one's curiosity it is not good manners to stare too hard at other people's possessions.

"A stolen potato carried in the pocket would cure you, Ma'am," Granny Bogan was saying.

Mrs. Loraine laughed. "I don't steal, Granny."

Granny Bogan produced a withered object from her pocket. "I took a pocketful the last time I weeded at the Court," she said. "I've still half a dozen left. Take it, Ma'am. And I'll give you a bottle of my vervain mixture. A teaspoonful in a wineglass of water night and morning."

Mrs. Loraine blushed a little but she accepted the potato and a little bottle filled from one of the jars on the dresser. "How Dr. Crane would laugh at me!" she said to Stella.

"No," said Stella. "He uses vervain himself. He says it's the holy herb of the druids. He uses hellebore too. The Greeks used it."

Granny Bogan turned to her eagerly. "You know Dr. Crane, child?"

"Yes, Ma'am," said Stella. "I live at Gentian Hill."

"He's a good man. He helped me once when I was in trouble. But for him I'd have lost my greatest treasure."

"What is that, Ma'am?" asked Stella eagerly.

But Granny Bogan, opening one of the tins on the dresser with her back turned, appeared not to have heard her. Turning round she held out a little muslin bag with some dried leaves inside. "Take it, child," she said. "You see far but there may come times when you'll need to see further yet, into the future, maybe, or into your lover's heart. Then on the night of the full moon soak a few of those leaves in the water from a fairy well and bathe your eyes, and in your sleep you'll see what you will see. But you must love with a single heart."

"Thank you, Ma'am," said Stella, taking the little bag. "Is it the herb of grace? Is it rue?"

"How did you know, child?"

"My mother at Weekaborough Farm grows it, and uses it to bathe sore eyes. But I don't think anybody at the farm ever uses it to see into the future."

"There's not many knows its real use," said Granny Bogan, "and you must use the water from a fairy well, at the full moon, and you must love your man with a single heart. There's many a lass thinks she loves a man when all the time it's herself that she's loving, herself decked out in the finery he can give her, with a ring upon her finger and a body sleek as a tabby cat's with his cherishing, and——"

Mrs. Loraine arose hastily and said she thought they ought to be going.

"Such a lass would see nothing if she bathed her eyes all night," went on Granny Bogan. "Must you be going, Ma'am? I'm thanking you kindly, I'm sure, for the comforts, and don't you be letting the potato out of your pocket. And as for you, child—come again and come alone."

"Stella cannot be running about the countryside by herself, Granny," said Mrs. Loraine decidedly. "She's just a child."

"She'll soon be a woman," said Granny Bogan. "Look at the rounded little breasts she has already, and the look about the eyes that tell you——"

Mrs. Loraine swept Stella out of the cottage and down through the herb garden in some agitation. She blamed herself severely. That Granny, who as a rule disliked the young, should have taken this embarrassing fancy to Stella was most distressing.

"She's a queer old woman, dear. Forget her," she said as the chaise drove off. "And if I were you I should throw away the packet of rue."

"Are you going to throw away the stolen potato, Ma'am?" asked Stella sweetly.

Mrs. Loraine had a sense of humour. They looked at each other and laughed. The days were not as yet entirely enlightened. Even the educated had not as yet lost their faith in fairy lore.

## CHAPTER II

### I

It was not until Midsummer Day, falling this year upon a Friday, when she was once more with Mrs. Loraine, that Stella woke up in the first light of dawn and knew that she was going again to Cockington, and going alone. It was only four o'clock and her first duty of the day was not until eight o'clock, when she took a cup of chocolate on a silver tray to Mrs. Loraine in her bedroom. She dressed quickly in her lavender print gown, put on her cloak and crept noiselessly downstairs. She felt no pricking of her conscience for she had never promised Mrs. Loraine she would not go to Cockington, and her adventurousness had accustomed her to early morning escapades. But she missed Hodge, for this was the first time upon which she had set out without him. Araminta had locked the front door and taken the key to bed with her, but she unlatched the hall window and climbed through it into the bed of canterbury bells below. The garden was delicious, scented with dew-drenched stocks and gillyflowers, and because the birds were hardly awake yet she could hear the sea.

She ran across the road to the holy well, sat down on the low parapet, dipped her hands in the water and bathed her face. The water was ice-cold and the clear drops that fell from her fingers were like diamonds. The sheep in Torre churchyard were not awake yet; she could see their huddled shapes among the gravestones and could hardly tell which were graves and which were sheep. The trees were shrouded in a grey mist but the tower of the church, and St. Michael's Chapel upon its pinnacle of rock, soared free of it and seemed to catch the flames of the coming sunshine upon their summits. Apart from the sighing of the sea the world was so silent that she could hear the drops tinkling into the water from her fingers, and the fall of a rose petal from the bush beside the well. A wild rapture went through her. She remembered how as a small child she used to fling herself into Father Sprigg's arms, or dive into the sweet hay. She wanted to do something like that now, to throw herself into this beauty of midsummer dawn and be lost in it. As she couldn't do that she got up and ran down Robbers' Lane like a mad thing, her cloak streaming behind her, her curls disordered, the wind of her going whipping her wet face. She ran until she reached Yappocombe Meadow, and then, finding she could run no more, she sat down on the stile to get her breath, looking out over the grass and thyme that stretched between the lane and the sea.

Here she saw another young creature in as rapturous a condition as herself, a hare disporting itself not a stone's throw from her. It seemed quite crazy. It pirouetted upon a hind leg, its ears flapping like flags, it cavorted from side to side, leaped four feet in the air, came down again and turned a somersault, raced round and round in circles, stopped dead, rose up again like an arrow and started the performance all over again. Stella laughed till her sides ached. She had seen hares go mad before, but not as mad as this, and not in June, only in March. What was it doing now? It had turned a final somersault and disappeared in a thicket of hawthorn.

Stella fell off the stile and raced across the meadow towards the thicket, oblivious of the dew that soaked her shoes and draggled her skirt. She reached the thicket but the hare had gone; down under the roots of a tree to where the goblins lived or into the air to join the larks that were already singing high up in the thinning haze of blue; Stella was quite willing to believe either. She could find no trace of him at all, but retracing her steps across the meadow she found something else, a fairy-ring upon the grass, traced about a grey rock, and in the centre of it, growing close to the boulder, a patch of gentian. She fell to her knees with a cry of delight. They grew in the churchyard at home, and once there had been a patch on Bowerly Hill, but it had disappeared. She had not known that they grew so close to the sea. She did not pick any, for they evidently belonged to the fairies. Standing in the ring she had three wishes and then she climbed back over the stile and ran on down the lane to Cockington.

The sun had fully risen by the time she reached the park and the world that until now had been so still and shrouded suddenly awoke to music and movement. A breeze had come in from the sea and the heavy elm and chestnut boughs swayed above the rippling dancing flowers and grasses of the park. The birds sang riotously and the sound of tumbling water from a stream that ran through the park was loud and joyful. Water and wind and birdsong was the echo in this quiet place of a great chiming symphony that was singing round the world, as the pall of the night was lifted and all things came rushing up into life again with ringing of bells and beating of wings, singing and laughter and the tramp of feet. Knee-deep in grasses and moon-daisies Stella stood and listened, swaying a little as the flowers and trees were swaying, her spirit voice singing loudly, though her lips were still, and every pulse in her body beating its hammer strokes in time to the song.

The wind died as quickly as it had arisen, the birds went about their business and the sound of the water was no more than the quiet ringing of a fairy bell. The grass was still again and the deer moved quietly from sun to shadow, heads down as they cropped the grass. There was a low chuckle behind her and Stella swung round with a thrill of fear, expecting to see she knew not what, Puck, or one of those strange green goblins with conical wooden hats like tiny haystacks perched on the back of their heads; she had seen them often as a child, and though they had never attempted to do her any harm she had always run away at the sight of them. But it was Granny Bogan, wearing the battered rust-coloured sunbonnet and the earth-coloured cloak that had been her weeding-woman's uniform, and holding a large basket. Her appearance among the clumps of valerian and meadow-sweet that bordered the stream was so sudden that Stella wondered for the moment if she was really human. The goblins had had just those gem-like sharp bright eyes.

"Washing your face in the dew, my maid?" asked Granny.

"I've washed it already at the holy well, Ma'am," said Stella, curtsying.

"St. Elfride cures boils but not pimples," said Granny. "Fairy dew is best for pimples."

"But I've not got boils or pimples," objected Stella.

"Prevention is better than cure," said Granny, "and where will you find the man to kiss a pimply face?"

Stella, for the sake of peace, plunged her hands in the grass and rubbed them over her face until her cheeks were rosy.

"That's better," said Granny. "It's roses he'll want to kiss when he comes home again, not pimples. Rosalind's roses."

"Rosalind?" asked Stella, bewildered. "But Rosalind died years ago."

"She never dies," said Granny. "There's always the young one waiting for her lover, learning patience through the slow days, and he away in the world tasting the bitterness of it, struggling with the wild beasts like David the shepherd boy. That's as it should be. He must get his sinews strong upon him for his man's love and labour. And always the holy hermit prays like Moses upon the hill-top or high in the watch-tower, and the devil take him if he lets his arms drop, for then the maid forsakes her patience and the lad his fortitude, and if they come together then it's woe betide them, for their children will be squint-eyed and knock-kneed and there'll be rats in the hayrick and mildew in the wheat."

Granny Bogan uttered this dreadful prophecy like a sort of incantation, and all the time she was darting up and down beside the stream like a dragonfly, filling her basket with valerian.

"What do you use valerian for, Granny?" asked Stella, helping her.

"Valerian?" repeated Granny. "I don't hold with these fancy names. Herbalists call it capon's tail or all-heal. You apply the leaves, my honey, to fresh wounds, and they heal in the twinkling of an eye."

They had followed the stream right up to the walls of Cockington church, where it swerved aside and disappeared into the woods beyond.

"If you want to see the treasure the doctor saved for me, honey, it's hid in the church tower," said Granny Bogan.

"The church tower!" ejaculated Stella.

"My neighbours at the almshouses do not mind their own business," said Granny. "I keep nothing there that could get me into trouble. I see from the shape of your pretty mouth, my honey, that you know how to keep it shut."

"Thank you for trusting me, Ma'am," said Stella soberly. Yet she wondered why she should be admitted to Granny Bogan's confidence in this way. As they walked up the path to the church door the old woman enlightened her.

"When I die, love, I've neither chick nor child to whom to leave my treasures," she said. "For years now I've been looking into the face of every young girl I meet, trying to find one with wisdom and the power to see further than most. You are the one, my love. You shall have the two books and the other thing also, and my blessing with them. Now, don't looked scared, child. I was a black witch once but I put that evil from me, and now I'm a white witch and can do you no harm. Ask your friend the doctor. He'll tell you."

II

They had reached the dim old church of St. George and St. Mary at the Settlement near the Springs. In the stained glass windows the apostles, James and John, Peter and Andrew, and St. Martin with his sword, looked down at them benignly, the bright colours of their robes staining the worn flagstones. The walls were plastered and covered with hatchments and coats of arms, and the Squire's pew was so large and had such towering walls that it dominated the whole church. It had a fireplace in it and beautiful padded cushions.

"Madam Mallock like to be warm and comfortable," explained Granny Bogan.

She seemed in no hurry and was quite pleased to sit down and rest while Stella explored the church. There was a gallery for the musicians and a beautiful screen carved with the Devon vine pattern. Stella counted sixteen birds among the foliage, and three of them in particular captured her interest. One was eating a grape, another was killing a caterpillar and one had its beak wide open as though it were singing very loudly. Below the singing bird was a boss of the Madonna wearing a crown, holding her Babe upon her arm and a lily in her hand. Stella was sure there was some story attached to these birds but Granny Bogan did not know what it was. Stella made up her mind to ask mon Père. He would know.

The church explored, she and Granny Bogan climbed the tower stairs. Half-way up Granny stopped and opened a low door and inside was a bare room like a cell lighted by one small window. There was a fireplace with its chimney in the thickness of the tower wall and low down in the door a hole large enough to pass food and drink through, with a cupboard niche just inside in which to place it. There was the branch of an oak tree in the cell, and sockets on either side of the door into which it could be fitted to prevent anyone coming into the room. There was a table in the room, and a three-legged stool.

"Someone must have lived here!" cried Stella.

"Some anchorite," said Granny Bogan, "or some popish priest hiding from his enemies. No one comes here now but Granny and the holy hermit."

"What holy hermit, Ma'am?" asked Stella.

"Him they call the Abbé," said Granny. "I came here once and saw him sitting in the window seat reading. He is one of your true readers—he never even heard my step on the stairs or the opening of the door. Other days I've seen him crossing the park, coming this way, and once we passed each other, he coming to the church and I leaving it. We looked the one at the other and he saw what he saw and I saw what I saw, and having seen it he took off his hat and bowed to me like a courtier and I curtsyed low as the ground. . . . We've left our evil courses, he and I."

The idea of mon Père pursuing evil courses was astonishing to Stella but in no way lessened her love for him. The worse you had been the better you could be, the doctor had told her once, for it meant you had in you the power of doing a thing thoroughly.

Granny Bogan was standing by the fireplace and putting her arm up the chimney. Stella was not at all surprised. Every farmhouse in Devon had loose stones in the chimney, with a cupboard inside where the smuggled brandy was kept. Stella did not suppose that an anchorite or a persecuted priest would have possessed French brandy, but he might have kept his breviary there, or secret papers.

Granny kept two books up the chimney, and something rolled up in a piece of linen. These she laid on the table, and unfolding the linen tenderly revealed what Stella thought at first was a very large nobbly parsnip. Then she took a hasty step backwards, for upon closer inspection it looked like a dead baby.

"Nothing to be afraid of, child," laughed Granny. "It's naught but a mandrake."

But at this Stella took yet another step backwards, for she knew all about mandrake. Madge had told her about it. It grows in Germany and above ground it has a broad green leaf and a yellow flower and looks wholesome enough, but below ground its root has a human shape and it cries aloud when men dig it from the earth. If considerately treated, washed in wine, wrapped in silk, laid in a casket, bathed every Friday and clothed in a little new white smock every new moon, it acts like a familiar spirit and foretells the future and gives counsel. But growing only in Germany it is hard to come by. Only witches possess it, and they generally for no good purpose.

"It's done no harm for a long time, child," said Granny Bogan. "Not since I gave up sticking pins in wax images and making charms and spells. When I was a black witch I lived in a cottage out at Smoky, and I had a stocking full of gold pieces that men and women had given me to do harm to those they hated. And then one night a farmer who thought I'd put the evil on his pigs—and I had too—came with his lout of a son and beat me nearly to death, and took away my stocking full of gold and my mandrake. I lay there groaning in my cottage and not a soul came near me, for they were afraid. I'd have died there had not Dr. Crane heard what had happened, and though I was nothing to him yet he came and cared for me. Every day he came, and though he had no opinion of my evil practices he was as tender with me as though he'd been my son. But I made no progress for weeping and fretting for my mandrake, that I loved like a child. So the good doctor went to the farmer and so put the fear of God into him for a thief and a murderer that he gave back the mandrake. And then the doctor put the fear of God into me too. He stood by my bed, thundering at me, threatening me with everlasting damnation, till I shook for fear and vowed I'd put the black magic away from me and be a white witch until the end of my days. And I did too, though the struggle was so fierce it nearly killed me. But it wasn't only the fear that made me turn aside from the evil, it was love of the doctor as well. He's a good man, and looking into that ugly face of his, and hearing him talk, I came to prefer the light to the darkness. When I got well again he persuaded the gentry round about to give me work as a weeding woman, for a white witch with her healing medicines makes less money than a black one with her charms and spells, and he protected me until I'd lived down the evil reputation that once I had. Now that I'm here in the almshouses he still comes to see me sometimes. He's not a man who forgets his friends."

"You still have the mandrake," said Stella.

"But it has no bath of wine and no silk shift now," said Granny Bogan, "and never since the doctor saved me have I invited the evil spirit into it for harm. I do nothing with it now, child, but ask it some wholesome question now and again, and grate a little powder off it to mix with a soothing syrup for those who need to sleep deep."

Stella remembered her Shakespeare: "Poppy and mandragore, and all the soothing syrups of the world." But still she did not like the mandrake, nor relish the thought that one day it would belong to her. She was sure that the evil spirit that Granny Bogan had once invited into it was one of Them, one of that terrifying company whom Sol used to summon with his bull-roarer. She was glad when Granny Bogan wrapped it up again and turned to the books instead.

They sat the one on the window-seat and the other on the three-legged stool and examined them. The first was a worn leather-bound book of the type in which ladies of fashion wrote their diaries, but in it Granny Bogan had written not a diary but her recipes for making healing medicines, salves and lotions from herbs. There were pages of them, all inscribed in a handwriting as spidery and pointed and beautiful as Mrs. Loraine's.

"What lovely writing," murmured Stella.

"I was a lady once," said Granny Bogan briefly, and then, turning the pages, "there's no disease in the world, my honey, for which the Lord God has not provided the cure growing in the good earth, and when you're a wedded wife with a brood of children there's no sickness they can take but you'll find the medicine for it here. You'll never lose a child, my love, if you never lose this book."

"I'll always keep it safely," Stella promised. "But, Granny, how did you learn to make all these medicines?"

Granny Bogan gave her cackle of laughter. "From a child I've loved all flowers and herbs and growing things," she said. "I learned much from the wise old gardener at my father's home, and more from our housekeeper, who was a great herbalist, but the most precious receipts I learned from the Good People themselves, those that have the charge of the nine mystic herbs and all the healing plants." Stella's eyes opened wider and wider and her mouth was slightly ajar. "You're a country girl born and bred, aren't you? Did you never see the Good People?"

"Sometimes the goblins—when I was little," murmured Stella.

"Not the others? Well, they're hard to see. I saw them when I was young and innocent; no more than shadows falling on the flowers, but I'd know it was them. I'd sit out in the herb garden with the book on my lap, my quill pen in my fingers and my inkhorn by my side, and I'd know how to use the herbs about me and I'd write down what I knew.

They've no voices that we can hear but they know how to make themselves understood when they've a mind."

Granny closed the herb book and opened the other. Its leather cover was so stained and mildewed that it looked as though it had been bound in the bark of a tree, and the thick stiff pages were the colour of autumn leaves. The centre of each page was covered with exquisite writing too, but the ink was so faded and the letters so curiously shaped that Stella could make out nothing at all except that the book was written in Latin. All round the margin of each page the writer had drawn exquisite little pictures, faintly coloured here and there, of birds, beasts and flowers.

"What is it, Granny?" asked Stella.

"I can't tell you, child," said Granny Bogan. "It would take fine eyesight, and a fine knowledge of the Latin tongue, to make it out, and I'd neither when I found it up there in the chimney cupboard two years ago. That was when I first came to the almshouses and came up here to find a safe hiding-place for my mandrake and my herb book. I guessed there'd be a hole in the chimney, and there was, with the book inside it. I knew it was a good book the moment I held it in my hands, but the mandrake bade me show it to no one for the time was not come. Take it, child. Hold it and turn the pages."

Stella took the book and held it between her hands for a moment or two. Yes, it was a good book. She felt as she did when she carried the Weekaborough prayer-book to church, quiet and good tempered. Then she turned the pages again, exclaiming in delight at the loveliness of the little pictures. There was one of a clump of gentians growing beside a mossy stone in the middle of a fairy-ring, just as they had done in the field this morning, and one of the sheep beneath a yew tree, and another of a hare turning somersaults.

"Do they always turn somersaults on Midsummer Day?" she asked Granny Bogan.

"Of course, child. Midsummer Day is a great day for the birds and beasts, the flowers and the Good People. It is their revelling time. It is the climax of warmth and growth and the whole earth leaps and sings for joy. You felt it in the park this morning. You were swaying in time to the music, knee-deep in the flowers. Now close the book, for it is yours, and get back to Torre for your breakfast. And here's my mandrake and the book of simples. They are yours too. Hide them under your cloak and take them home and keep them safe."

"No, Ma'am, no!" cried Stella, shrinking back. "They are yours still, not mine."

"I'll not live out the year," said Granny Bogan placidly. "I'll sleep easier tonight, knowing them in safe keeping."

But Stella still hesitated, frightened by the mandrake and the one of

Them who had once been invited into it. "Couldn't they stay here, Ma'am?" she pleaded.

"I'd be easier if you took them, love," Granny Bogan insisted. "But speak of them to no one, child, except, if you wish, to the doctor and the holy hermit."

Then she got up briskly, as though the matter were settled, and led the way out of the little tower room and down the stairs.

III

Stella was home in time to take Mrs. Loraine her cup of hot chocolate as usual, and all through that Midsummer Day she was outwardly her usual serene and happy self. Yet inwardly her thoughts were in a turmoil and she was longing for the evening, when Dr. Crane would fetch her and drive her back to Weekaborough.

The longed-for moment came at last and she was sitting beside him in the gig, Aesculapius carrying them along at a brisk pace, bound for home She looked up at him with delight. He had a rose in his buttonhole this Midsummer Day, his hat was cocked at a more acute angle than ever, and his smile as he looked down at her warmed her right through. At her feet was the wicker basket in which she carried her clothes and few treasures (the workbox, and the box covered with shells that Mother Sprigg had given her) backwards and forwards from Weekaborough to Torre. It had a lid, and the lid this evening did not shut.

"More treasure trove in the basket?" asked the doctor, eyeing it.

"Yes," said Stella. "A mandrake and two books."

"God bless my soul!" ejaculated the doctor.

Stella poured it all out in a flood, and the doctor gave her story his silent attention all the way up the long steep lane from the sea to the hills.

"Nothing to be afraid of, honey," he said when she'd done. "I know Granny Bogan well and she is now a good as well as a wise woman, and she'd give you nothing that could harm you."

"But the mandrake!" cried Stella. "What *is* a mandrake?"

"The root of a pretty yellow flower called mandragore that grows in Germany."

"But Granny Bogan said that she invited an evil spirit into it."

They had reached the top of the hill and the doctor drew the gig to the side of the lane, dropped the reins and let Aesculapius crop the grass. "Let's have a look at my old friend the mandrake."

Stella dived into her basket and produced the mandrake in its linen wrapping, the book of simples wrapped in her clean night-shift and the good book in her best apron.

"There he is," said the doctor, and unwrapped the mandrake and set it on his knee like a baby.

"Don't say he!" implored Stella. "It makes it sound alive."

The doctor laughed and wrapped the root up again. Then he became grave. "Now listen, my honey. You remember your Shakespeare? 'There's nothing good or bad but thinking makes it so.' That's the root of the whole matter. The universe about you is charged with opposing forces—angels and devils, good and evil, light and darkness—you can call them what you will—and as you think of things and people you invite into them one or the other. Think evil things of a man and you've done your poor best to make a devil of him. Think there's a demon in this bit of root and you've made the thing potent for evil. And the other way on. Is that clear to your ladyship?"

"Yes," said Stella, and took the mandrake back without a trace of fear. "It shall be my doll. A good doll. I'll keep it in my room to frighten away the mice."

The doctor laughed and picked up the book of simples. Aesculapius went slowly on, snatching at mouthfuls of grass when he felt like it, but his master was too absorbed to know what he was doing. At last the doctor closed the book and handed it back. "You'll soon know more than I do about the healing powers of the earth," he said briefly.

"Granny Bogan said the Good People taught her about the herbs," said Stella. "Could they have done that? Are there really Good People, or are they something that we've made up?"

"What should you say was the opinion of Will Shakespeare on that point?"

"I should say he believed in them," said Stella slowly.

"I should say the same."

"Then are they real?"

"Why not?"

"Can't you tell me something *certain* about them?" demanded Stella a little impatiently.

"Can't you tell me?" continued the doctor. "You are nearer to childhood than I am, and it is children who are wisest in these matters."

"I used to think I saw goblins," said Stella, "and I used to run away."

"And Granny Bogan used to think the Good People told her the secrets of the herbs. And in both cases the thought had results—you ran away and Granny wrote down medicinal receipts. So there must have been something in it."

And that was all he would say upon the subject of the Good People. Dismissing them he picked up the second book. It absorbed him as much as the other had done; so much that Stella began to think they would never get home that night, and pulled at his sleeve. He turned and looked down at her, his eyes strangely abstracted, and then laid it gently on her lap.

"It's yours, my honey."

"What is it?" she asked. "Granny knew it was a good book but she could not read the writing."

"Some sort of an old tale, Stella, written about this country in which we live, but that is all I can make out. The writing is difficult and I am not much of a Latin scholar, you know. Greek was my first love. Keep the book very carefully and when the opportunity comes show it to your friend the Abbé. He's a fine Latinist."

Then he whipped up Aesculapius and they bowled home to Weekaborough at a fine pace, arriving at the garden gate in the first glow of the sunset. Carrying her basket Stella darted like a swallow up the path, through the front door set wide to welcome her, across the hall to the kitchen and into the arms of Mother Sprigg. They were all there, Father and Mother Sprigg, Sol, Madge, Hodge and Seraphine. She flew from one to the other as though she had not seen any of them for years. The firelight glowed warmly in the great kitchen and the shadows played hide-and-seek in the cave-like crannies of the walls and beneath the low beams of the ceiling. The brass pots and pans twinkled and shone and there was a delicious and all-pervading smell of rabbit pie. Soon the candles would be lit and they would have supper, and then Father Sprigg would open the Good Book and read the evening chapter and magic would fall from the air. Wherever Stella might go, whatever she might do, Weekaborough would always be home.

# CHAPTER III

## I

ZACHARY, lying in his hammock with his eyes shut and his hands behind his head, could hear the crackle of the fire, see the play of the light upon the brass pans and Stella's dark head bent appreciatively over her plate of rabbit pie. He could actually smell the pie, its fragrance rising triumphantly above the loathsome smells of the after-cockpit, and wrinkled his nose appreciatively.

"What are you grinning at, you ass?" growled a surly voice beside him.

Zachary opened his eyes and looked with amusement at the vast mound of bones and rags and ill-temper heaped untidily in the next hammock. This was Mr. Midshipman Michael Burke who had now filled the place in his life left empty by Cobb. Zachary had not the love for him that he would always have for the never-to-be-forgotten Cobb, but he had filled the aching vacuum. In this new friendship the roles of protector and protégé were reversed; it was Zachary who kept his paternal eye on Mike. In this world death has a habit of intervening before we can pay our debts, and the only thing to be done is to pay them to another. Mike bore not the least resemblance to Cobb, apart from a red head, but in assisting him to be not more of a fool than he could help Zachary felt that he served Cobb and was happy in the by-no-means-easy service.

Mike was born to trouble. Even his virtues, coupled as they were with vices that destroyed their power for peace, did not seem to do him any good. His courage, linked to a flaming temper and great insolence, only led to brawls and disturbances of every kind, and his sense of justice, a fine thing in itself, did not permit him to accept the brutal punishments of the age in a manner calculated to soothe the ruffled feelings of authority. His hatred of any sort of sham was coupled with a tongue both ready and caustic, but not with the ability to suffer fools gladly. His youth had been hard and bitter and he had no gladness. Though Zachary's boyhood had scarcely been a bed of roses either he had discovered where gladness was to be found. But the permanence of God's love and nature's beauty, of man's unconquerable quest for glory, made no appeal to Mike. He was a townsman born and bred, a roysterer and a hedonist. He loved noise. All the treasures he had collected in his seafaring life were instruments of noise. The detested bull-roarer which Sol had given to Zachary was the joy of his heart. So totally at variance were their interests that sometimes the two friends marvelled at their friendship. But they were both Irish aristocrats. They had the same code.

"At the smell of rabbit pie," said Zachary.

"Can't smell anything but the usual foul stink."

"The pie I smelt was in Devonshire."

"What a damn' fool you are," growled Mike, and composed himself to slumber.

He was a few months older than Zachary. His shambling collection of large bones was meagrely covered with flesh, and when he stood, tall, round shouldered and awkward, looked upon the point of falling apart, yet he was immensely strong and powerful and no one relished a fight with him. His bony, ugly face with its haphazard features was not without charm, for his green eyes were honest and had a child's trustfulness. It was his ineradicable trust in man that was the cause of many of his troubles. He was always expecting other people to be as fundamentally decent as he was himself, and when they were not the temptation to knock them down was not always resisted. Owing to this lack of resistance his clothes were mostly in rags, but he wore them with a clumsy elegance that was part of his breeding. Zachary had never seen him with a woman but he imagined that if put to it he could be courteous.

"We're on the Thames, Mike," murmured Zachary. "London tomorrow. Gentian Hill next week."

A snore was the only answer. Mike was asleep and Zachary was free once more to indulge in the heavenly revelry of his unleashed dreams. This riotous imagination of his was not always heavenly, it could be an instrument of the devil in the devil's hands, but tonight he could drift where he would and always the scene was good.

He could picture the summer night outside with the starlight gleaming upon the bent sails. He could see the still figures of the men on watch, the faint glow of lantern light upon their intent faces, hear the lap of the water against the ship's side and the persistent vibrant hum in the rigging. He could see upon either side of the gleaming water the dense darkness that was England, and the shore lights slipping by. They were home at last. Home. Next week he would be at Gentian Hill.

They had finished their supper at Weekaborough now and were sitting round the table with bent heads, and Father Sprigg, his spectacles perched on his nose, was reading aloud from the Good Book, "There the wicked cease from troubling, and there the weary be at rest. There the prisoners rest together; they hear not the voice of the oppressor. The small and great are there; and the servant is free from his master." As the golden words fell from the air Stella raised her head and looked at Old Sol in the chimney corner. Their eyes met and Sol smiled. So he had not gone yet to that place of rest. Zachary was glad that he would see him again.

He left them there in the old cave-like kitchen and went outside. The sheep were asleep beneath the yew tree on Bowerly Hill, and the smell of hay and clover was sweet in the air. He walked up Taffety Hill, where he had first sung the chant of the plough, went through the gate in the danmonian fence and down the hill to the village. There were lights in the windows of the cottages that were gathered about the church on its small hill, and a scent of honeysuckle met him. He went up the short flagged path to the doctor's door, lifted the latch and went in. The night had turned a little chilly and there was a small fire burning in the study grate. The doctor looked up from the book he was reading, smiled as a man smiles at his only son, and motioned with his pipe-stem to the opposite chair. They sat and talked, recalling the last time they had talked in this room. Zachary said it was well with him now. He had found the knowledge he had gone to seek. He knew what glory was, and how to accept and conquer fear. He knew how to endure horror, and how to escape from it. He had travelled hard and far and the wind of his going had lit the lantern of his faith. He had learned it all now and had come home.

"All?" asked the doctor, and the slight sarcasm in the tone did not mask its pity.

Zachary was suddenly wide-eyed in his hammock. All? No, of course not. No man on this earth could ever say that. He had not learned to master his claustrophobia. How did that chapter about the prisoners go on? "For the thing which I greatly feared is come upon me, and that which I was afraid of is come unto me." The confined space of the cock-pit was becoming narrower, closing in on him like a prison, the low ceiling was coming down on his head. He was in a cold sweat of fear, his nails digging into the palms of his hands. Then with a great effort of his will he mastered his morbid panic, his mind fixed once more upon the thought of going home. What could stop it? England was there, outside, her lights slipping by in the darkness.

He relaxed again, his momentary panic past. Nothing could stop the return to Weekaborough next week. But all the same he wished it was not necessary to spend three days with Mike in London first. Mike, in duty bound, had to pay a visit to his detested guardian at Weymouth, and in spite of his hatred of the country he was considering Zachary's suggestion that he should later visit Gentian Hill, but he had vowed that he would do neither of these things unless he could have his fling in town first and Zachary knew that he must keep his eye on him while he did it. It was an obligation of friendship that could not be avoided. He owed this service to Mike first, and through him to Cobb.

They did not know at Gentian Hill that he was at this moment between the shores of England, they thought him still in the Mediterranean, where the frigate had returned after the South American service was over. He had told them that he supposed he would be there some while, and then a storm had done such damage to the frigate that she had been ordered home to refit. He smiled, picturing the joy of his unheralded return, and then his mind slipped back over the years that had passed since Trafalgar, the hardship, weariness and boredom, the storms and fevers, the sense of hopelessness and desperation as month after month went by and still they were not sent home. Yet those grim months had been his best at sea so far because for the first time there had come to him the sense of belonging where he was. He had found out how to live this life of the sea, and his adjustments had made for him a sort of groove into which he fitted as a bird into the nest that has been rounded by the pressure of its breast. He still hated being a sailor and yet he had now mysteriously become one; he was occasionally visited by the strange idea that the sea was no longer his enemy but his friend.

The idea had come to him first one Christmas night, when he had had a very odd dream. He had gone to bed bitterly homesick. It had been a vile night, wet and cold, with the old ship rolling like a porpoise and a dying gale howling through the rigging. The whole ship's company had been homesick, seasick and bad-tempered. The stink and noise of the after-cockpit had seemed worse than usual. He had lain tossing wretchedly for an hour or so, and then feeling his nervous misery getting beyond his control had exerted all his will-power to impose stillness on his body. The physical stillness fought for and gained there had come a corresponding peace upon the turmoil of his thoughts. Scenes that were tranquil and still flowed into his memory, scenes that all of them centred round Stella with her gift of serenity.

He saw her as he had seen her first, in the warm glow of the lantern-lit stable, feeding the cats, and then looking up at him, her hand resting on Hodge's back, her straight clear glance assuring him of her fidelity. He saw her again sitting beside him on the grass in the moonlight, looking up into his face and asking him where he came from. "From the moon," he said, and she laughed and called him Zachary Moon. He turned her hand over and put his own against it, palm to palm, as though they were the two halves of a shell. He saw her again saying good-bye to him, her chin resting on the top of the gate, a row of small fingertips to either side, the furry countenance of Hodge thrust through the bars below.

And then once again he was looking in through the stable window, and wrapped in her red cloak she was lying sleepily curled up in the hay. She looked up at the window and he thought that she saw him there and smiled. Then she shut her eyes and he saw her long dark lashes lying like curling fans upon her cheeks, and the childish glow of warmth that crept into her cheeks as she slept. Then he had slept too and there had followed that strange, beautiful dream of the church under the sea. He had stood there pulling the bell and had known that the bell was his own voice calling to her to come to him. And she had come and they had knelt together in the small holy place that was their own special sanctuary in the depth of the sea. And for the first time he had heard the authentic voice of the sea, mighty, reverberating, yet down here in the quiet depths more full of reassurance than of menace, and had known at last that the sea was not his enemy. He had woken up to the sound of the ship's cock crowing, and the gale had blown itself out. He had sighed and turned over, still intolerably homesick but without bitterness, and had smiled and slept again.

And he smiled now and slept, with the ship sailing on over the smooth estuary of the Thames, and the sky lightening in the east.

## II

The next two days passed harmlessly, though for Zachary with far too much noise and a great deal of exasperation. Mike's idea of pleasure was not his and he was wildly impatient to be quit of this bedlam of London and to be on the coach again, homeward bound for Devonshire.

Yet Mike's whirlwind methods of getting about gave him a bird's-eye view of the London of this period that he never afterwards forgot. Whether hurtling over the cobbles in a rocking hackney coach, or fighting his way through the crowds, Mike's raucous voice and flailing arms never failed to make their progress so meteoric that houses, shops, palaces, hovels, coaches, men, women, cats, dogs, horses, colours, scents and noise seemed to flow past like the sights and sounds and smells of a whirling nightmare, and yet to smite eyes and ears and nose with such force that Zachary felt himself perpetually reeling from the blow. The gilded coaches, with liveried coachmen on the high draped boxes, and lovely painted ladies and be-wigged gentlemen just glimpsed inside them, made their way like bright phantoms from another world through the turgid crowd of beggars and pickpockets, clerks, business men, shoppers and sightseers that thronged the narrow streets. Pedlars cried their wares, ragged urchins screamed derision at the top-hatted, cravatted, monocled young men swaggering along the pavements as elegant as peacocks. Dogs fought near the winkle stalls, and from the open door of every eating-house came a roar of conversation and the fumes of porter and roast beef. At night the town became a roaring cavern of darkness lit by flaring smoky lights. The lanterns on the swaying coaches, the torches of the linkmen, the flambeaux lit about the doorways of the great and the fireworks of Vauxhall, could do no more than fitfully illumine the murk. Zachary hated London by night more than by day. He was thankful, when on Saturday night Mike dragged him out for a last evening's revelry, that it *was* the last. Tomorrow would be Sunday, and on Monday he'd be on his way home.

Yet from the start of the evening's entertainment he was uneasy. For a beginning, Mike insisted upon putting Zachary's bull-roarer in his pocket. "Let that damn thing alone!" Zachary implored him irritably. "Put it back where you found it, Mike. It's unlucky. It's mine, isn't it? Put it back, I tell you."

But Mike was not in an obliging mood and merely thundered down the stairs and out into the street with the bull-roarer still in his pocket. Zachary followed in a bad temper, and they walked in silence to the eating-house of Mike's choice. Devouring beefsteak and onions washed down by porter, and assailed already by the pangs of indigestion, home suddenly seemed to Zachary very far away. That world of Weekaborough, where men still ploughed to the music of an age-old chant and kept sheep upon a fairy hill, seemed to have nothing in common with this noisy bedlam where he found himself. There life was all one thing, each activity growing out of another in an orderly manner that made of them all one deeply satisfying whole. Here life was split up. You had neither grown nor cooked the food you ate, and you ate it in company with men who were strangers to you. There, every foot of earth that you trod was familiar to you, but outside this hot, noisy, crowded eating-house the dark cavern of London was full of pits of even deeper darkness into which a man might fall and never be found again. He had seen a few of them, passing by, slums so appalling that the wretched creatures who came crawling out of them when night fell scarcely seemed human beings at all.

"What's the matter with you?" Mike demanded with his mouth full. Zachary pulled himself together. He was here to keep Mike's flaming temper and abusive tongue from getting him into trouble, and up till now he had been successful. It would be too utterly idiotic if his vigilance was to desert him on the last night of all.

The door swung open to admit half a dozen noisy young revellers, officers on leave like themselves. They looked round for a moment, saw two of their kind devouring most succulent steak and bore down upon them with whoops of joy.

Up till the early hours of the morning the night was gloriously rowdy and quite harmless. Between them they had plenty of money, and the amusements of the town were many. All but Zachary had digestions of cast-iron and practically unflagging energy; should energy flag for a moment it could be instantly revived by liquid refreshment. In between the visits to Leicester Fields, Haymarket and Vauxhall Gardens they wrenched a few handles off respectable front-doors, yowled like cats, and played leap-frog over the stone posts along the pavements.

It was this last amusement that led to trouble. Leap-frogging was the prerogative of the street urchins, not of the gentry, and a row of posts stood conveniently not far from an alley leading to one of the pits of darkness that so haunted Zachary. He saw the posts, he noticed the alley, and knew misgiving even before he saw the flying figure of Mike leading his battalion into action. Some sort of underground message must have conveyed itself from the posts to the slum beyond the alley, for in five minutes a band of young roughs had come surging up out of the darkness, yelling blue murder, and the fight was on.

Battles between privileged youth and the underdogs were of common occurrence in the London streets and attracted little notice, and this one would have fought itself out to the usual conclusion of everyone becoming incapacitated by nothing worse than bleeding noses and blackened eyes, had not Mike suddenly bethought himself of the bull-roarer. Having just knocked out two opponents, and being momentarily at leisure, it struck him that the glorious din of it might do something to scare the enemy and clear the fuddled heads of his own side who were getting distinctly the worst of it at the moment. He produced the treasure from his pocket, twisted the string round his finger and swung it. Nothing for a moment, then the soft whirring, then the roaring rushing wind, louder and louder, rising gloriously above the noises of the battle. The effect upon the enemy was immediate, but not quite what Mike had intended. They were not country boys and none of them had seen or heard a bull-roarer before. They saw the small brown thing whirling at the end of its string, such an instrument of glorious noise as they had never beheld before, and they coveted with a desire that could not be denied. Casting their other opponents from them as one boy they set upon Mike.

The onslaught was too much even for Mike, he slipped and fell, and a tall ragged scarecrow of a boy leaped upon him and dragged the bull-roarer out of his hand. Just as he turned the light of a flambeau fell full upon his face, wild and dark, lean with hunger and taut with misery, the dark eyes blazing with fury. Something about his face stabbed Zachary with a sudden memory; it was himself that he saw, himself as he had been on the night when he had climbed up to the stable window at Weekaborough. And not only himself. In that face he saw all the wretched homeless vagabonds who had ever lived, who ever would live, all those who never had and never would be given the ghost of a chance. Then in a flash the boy was gone, racing off with the bull-roarer down the dark alley; and not only with the bull-roarer; he had Mike's purse too.

In a moment Mike was on his feet again, tearing after, winged with rage, Zachary after Mike, those of the warriors who were not by this time incapacitated by their wounds yelling at their heels like hounds in full cry.

At the first sound of the bull-roarer Zachary's heart had sunk like a stone. He had never been able to rid himself of his superstitious feelings about it. . . . The wind, the wind, and evil spirits riding upon the wind. . . . God help them all now, for they had left the streets and plunged headlong into one of those pits of darkness into which a man might fall and never be found again. On and on they went, down and down, deeper into the darkness and the foulness, and the first of the summoned demons leaped and fastened upon Zachary. It was his own familiar demon, the fear he thought he had conquered, twisting itself about him, sucking at him like a leech, draining his limbs of strength and his mind of resolution. Turn back. What has it to do with you? You told Mike to let that damned bull-roarer alone. Whatever happens is his fault, not yours. Go back. Get out of it while there's time.

Yet he went on, keeping Mike in sight, trying to gain on him; Mike in his dangerous rage and that dark scarecrow of a fellow whose wild face had so touched him. He was dimly conscious, as he ran, of the horror of the dark alleys through which he was passing, of the filth underfoot in which he slipped and stumbled, of the terrible underworld creatures screaming at them from dark doorways. There was no light in this dreadful place, except the occasional gleam of a guttering tallow candle stuck in a broken window, but the moon had risen and its faint light illumined the two flying figures ahead of him that he knew he must keep in sight lest they be lost eternally and he with them. It seemed to him as though the three of them were now alone in the world, for they had outdistanced the others, and the figures in the doorways had seemed no more than phantoms. He fell into a heap of refuse, picked himself up and went on. And now the fear was leaving him, burnt up by some fire that had been lit in him by the wind of his going. The blood flowed warmly through his limbs again and his mind was clear.

The end of it all came with surprising suddenness. They reached what seemed the end of an alley, blocked by a door in a wall, and the one dark boy who was yet all the vagabonds of the world flung himself against the door. He had expected it to give way but someone had apparently bolted it upon the other side. He leaped back and flung himself against it again, but uselessly. There was no more he could do. He was half-starved, and had not the strength of his pursuers, but he turned with his back to the door and faced them, his fists ready. The bull-roarer and the purse he had stowed away in the pockets of his ragged breeches, though grimly aware that the pockets had holes in them. His back was to the door and he would die before he gave them up of his own will.

"Let him alone, Mike!" yelled Zachary. "Damn you, let him alone!"

But Mike's particular demon of hellish anger had got him and would not let him go. He looked back once over his shoulder and Zachary saw his face beneath the red hair scarlet with drink and hate and rage, and the murderous look in his eyes that made him seem a stranger. It was useless. He'd kill the other fellow if he could. He leaped, but Zachary leaped quicker and was between the two of them, the dark boy knocked backwards between his own body and the door.

Mike saw a dark, lean face confronting his own, was sent staggering by the blow of a fist on his jaw, and for a moment or two did not grasp the fact that it was Zachary he was fighting and that his real opponent had vanished. When he did grasp it the realisation that it was Zachary who had robbed him of his quarry, and given him that blow on the jaw, added bitter hurt to a rage that had long ago passed beyond his control.

His blows came so thick and fast that Zachary was once more gripped by panic. "Stop it, Mike!" he gasped. "Mike! It's me, Zachary. Mike!"

But it was no good. There was nothing he could do now except fight for his life. His panic steadied and he fought. The moon had risen clear above the alley and the light was not too bad. He was not Mike's equal as a fighter but he was sober and Mike was not, and he had had the benefit of the miller's training. He was aware of a ring of spectators round himself and Mike, of yells of encouragement, of whistling and stamping, hoots and groans. He thought vaguely that he was back again on the wrestling green near Torre fighting Sam Bronescombe. Somewhere in the crowd his adopted father was watching. He must acquit himself well in this fight for the underdog against the bully or the doctor would not allow him to go home. He had quite forgotten now that he was fighting Mike, to protect whom he was staying in London.

III

And Mike was lying at his feet with his head in a pool of blood, untidily, his arms and legs flung just anyhow, as he had seen dead men lying on the deck of the *Victory* before they were flung overboard. Mike was dead. His eyes were shut and his face was a greenish-grey colour in the moonlight. Mike was dead and he had killed him. While he fought he had been deaf to what was happening about him. He had not heard the shrill whistle and the sound of pounding feet as the roughs fled before the approach of the officers of the watch. He realised now that it was very quiet. The boys who had devoured steak and onions with him and Mike had made themselves scarce. There was no one here but himself and Mike and the officers of the watch.

"I killed him," he said quietly as the handcuffs snapped round his wrists. "I killed him so that he should not kill the other fellow."

He did not look at any of them, he only looked at Mike. Even when they were taking him away down the alley he still only saw Mike and the voice in his head was talking to him. I couldn't let you kill him. You'd hate to kill a half-starved fellow who'd never had a chance. You only went for him because you were in one of your rages and didn't know what you were doing. You'd have been sick about it afterwards, if you'd killed him. I had to stop you. I had to, Mike. What else could I do?

Then he was lying on the floor of some dark and filthy conveyance, lying as he had been flung, bumping along over the cobbles. There were three other men, and a woman, with him. The woman was sobbing and one of the men was swearing, but the other two were quiet. He was still staring at Mike's face with its closed eyes. That was odd. Dead men's eyes were always open, until someone closed them, and no one had closed

Mike's eyes. His wits were beginning to return and for a full five minutes he saw not Mike's face but the huddled shapes of the sobbing woman and swearing man, and the two who were quiet. He pushed himself up from the floor by his hands and heard the clink of his chains. So they were going to prison. "For the thing which I greatly feared is come upon me, and that which I was afraid of is come unto me." He had been told about the London prisons. They were places of unspeakable filth and horror and you got flung into them for any sort of offence, debt, stealing, manslaughter, anything, and you waited for your trial for weeks or months. . . . And sometimes they forgot about you altogether. . . . And if they remembered you it was the law that you were hung for almost everything. His brain reeled. But he had saved Mike from killing that wretched boy, even though it was at the cost of killing Mike himself. But was Mike dead? He did not know. And if they forgot about him in this dark abyss into which he had fallen he would never know.

## CHAPTER IV

### I

THE moon that had shone upon Zachary's fight with Mike kept Stella awake most of that night in her little room at Weekaborough. She was not accustomed to being treated in this way by her friend the moon, but she had the feeling that it was watching something that was happening to Zachary and was trying to tell her about it. When she dropped into restless sleep she saw Zachary once again as the boy from the moon with his bundle on his back, and he was finding it so heavy that he was staggering beneath it.

She got up next morning heavy-eyed and anxious, and not even the thought that it was Sunday, her favourite day in the week, could cheer her up at all. And the news brought to them by Madge at breakfast, that Sol, who had kept to his bed for the last fortnight, was unket and poorly this morning, made her feel more miserable than ever.

Neither she nor Mother Sprigg went to church that morning for they felt too anxious about Sol. Mother Sprigg, after she had made the old man comfortable and formed her own opinion as to his condition, went downstairs to make an apple pie and get on as fast as she could with the hemming of his shroud. She had been busy with this for a week past, putting her most exquisite stitchery into it. No one at Weekaborough thought this morbid of her, merely practical. Sol himself, when told by Madge that he was to have a shroud fit for the king of England himself, had been delighted, had asked to see it and derived much pleasure from the sight.

Stella meanwhile sat by Sol's narrow bed in the tiny attic that they called "the tallet," with its one small window looking towards Bowerly Hill. It was an attractive little room, made up of odd angles and corners and hardly bigger than a cupboard. Sol's bed with its patchwork quilt, a table and the stool upon which Stella sat, almost filled it. It was bright with sunshine and very quiet and peaceful. The mice had worried Sol a little when he first took to his bed, but Stella had removed this worry by placing the mandrake on his windowsill. She had dressed it in the clothes that had once adorned her rag doll and it gave great pleasure to Sol. He was often to be heard talking to it and asking it questions, and he either heard or imagined answers which gave him great satisfaction.

He also liked being read to, and Stella this morning sat with the Weekaborough prayer-book open on her lap and read him the prayers and psalms that were at this moment being boomed forth by Parson Ash and the congregation at Gentian Hill. The feel of the prayer-book in her hands, the sounds of the words she read, suddenly made her happy again. Sol seemed dozing most of the time but her happiness seemed to reach him for he smiled as he dozed, and once or twice, when the words that she read rang out with sudden beauty, he opened his eyes and his bright glance met hers as it had used to do when Father Sprigg read the Good Book in the kitchen. This mysterious eternal beauty, speaking through music, clothing itself in colour and form and light yet never itself in its own being seen or heard, how it could lock together two people who suddenly heard or saw in some way that was alike. You could never again feel quite separate from that person. She would remember till the end of her life that she and Sol had felt the same when brightness fell from the air.

II

But away from Sol the peace and happiness left her and she was miserable again for the rest of the day. And lonely too, for her anxiety about Zachary was not a thing that she could tell to anybody. Father and Mother Sprigg, had she spoken of it, would have told her not to be fanciful.

In the evening some of Father Sprigg's cronies came in to see him, and the tobacco smoke and the conversation were so thick and loud that she and Hodge escaped out of the kitchen and across to Pizzle Meadow. The evening light lay level and golden across the grass and flowers of the meadow, and the black pigs lying among the crane's-bill and vetches seemed each to be surrounded by a sort of halo of golden dust. There was no breath of wind, no sound but the tinkling of the stream as it flowed from the Pisgies' Well beneath the hawthorn tree in the far corner through the meadow to the trough, and then disappeared underground to feed the well in the yard and the duckpond in the orchard. The meadow sloped upward to the hawthorn tree and Stella climbed with dragging feet, weary and heavy-hearted with sadness for Sol and anxiety for Zachary. Hodge moved beside her, his tail tucked between his legs, sharing her sorrow.

They felt better when they were settled beneath the hawthorn tree, for it was a place where they liked to be. The tree was very old, with fantastically twisted roots and widely spreading branches, and like the yew tree on Bowerly Hill and the apple trees in the orchard it seemed a living creature with a vigorous personality all its own. Stella thought of it as a wizard, some one rather like Granny Bogan. Like the pigs it seemed tonight to have drawn a golden dusty veil about itself, and the water that welled up from the dark places of the earth, trickled out between its roots and spread into a small round pool fringed with forget-me-nots, was full of bright flecks of gold.

Stella settled herself with her back against the trunk of the tree and her feet in the forget-me-nots, Hodge lying beside her with his chin propped on her ankles. She shut her eyes and listened to the chiming sound the water made as it overflowed the pool and fell in a cascade over some mossy stones into the stream below. For generations this well had been thought to be especially beloved by the fairies, not the goblin folk who had frightened her in her childhood but the pisgies, the Good People whom Granny Bogan believed had taught her the use of the herbs. Stella had never seen any pisgies here at the well, but she always found that when she was sitting here by herself all sense of loneliness left her. It was like that now. Her back, propped by the tree-wizard, leaned against the knee of a person. It was easy to believe that there were small and kindly presences all about her, in the well, the grass, the flowers and the golden light. She did not open her eyes because she knew from past experience that if she did she would see nothing and that the sense of companionship would immediately vanish. It was only when you relied upon faith alone that you felt the pisgies with you. If you tried to prove they were there then they were not there.

A bell was ringing somewhere, very faintly, as though far away, but clear and persistent, like a voice calling; like that bell that Zachary had rung under the sea. Though she did not open her eyes she was aware of a sudden quickening of consciousness, as though she had slept for a moment and then awakened again. She heard no bell now but only the water falling. Yet she *had* heard it, and it had been Zachary calling to her in her sleep, as he had called before. She opened her eyes and the gold dust had gone from the air and the shadows were long and blue, fantastic, like the shadows of night's fingers stretched out to grasp the world. . . . Night. . . . If she could sleep long and deeply would she dream of Zachary and know why it was that he was calling her?

She slipped her hand into her pocket and there between her fingers was the muslin bag of rue. She had put it there when she left Torre two days ago, for she always took it with her wherever she went. She remembered that Granny Bogan had said she must soak the leaves in the water of a fairy well and bathe her eyes on the night of the full moon. It would be full moon tonight and here was the pisgies' well just beside her. She took out the little muslin bag and opened it, dipped up some of the clear sparkling water into her hollowed left hand, shook some of the rue into it and bathed her eyes. When she had done it she felt a little uneasy. Was she being very superstitious? What would mon Père say to such a performance? He would tell her that she ought to go to St. Michael's Chapel and pray, as she had done before when she had been unhappy about Zachary. And so she would. She would go tomorrow when she was back at Torre. Meanwhile was it wrong to invoke the help of the fairies? She was sure it was not, for if they existed they were Good People and God had made them and given them the charge of the wells and streams and the secrets of the herbs and flowers. And the doctor had said once that in this mysterious universe, where humans in their blindness see and know less than one-thousandth part of what goes on around them, all creatures exist only that they may interpenetrate and serve each other.

Reassured she got up, curtsyed to the well as an act of courtesy towards the fairies, and ran back with Hodge to the parlour for supper and bed.

III

The next morning Stella sat in the doctor's gig, the reins in her hands, her basket at her feet. The doctor was inside the farmhouse visiting Sol but he would be out in a minute and would drive her back to Torre. She had said goodbye indoors to Father and Mother Sprigg and Madge, but Hodge sat at the top of the steps scratching himself, for something was biting him, and regarding her anxiously while he did it.

"Only a few days, Hodge, and then I'll be back again," Stella reminded him.

But it was not only the parting that was making Hodge mournful. He did not like the look of her at all. Even though it was a hot day she was shivering in her sprigged muslin gown, and her face in the shade of her chip bonnet was white with fatigue, with dark circles round the eyes. It was the face of one who had not slept, though Hodge (who had himself passed a restless night pursuing the thing that was biting him) knew for a fact that she had slept deeply all night long.

The front door clanged and Dr. Crane came down the paved path between the yew trees, drawing on his driving gloves. He patted Hodge, climbed into the gig beside Stella and took the reins. They drove at a good pace, cleaving the hot honey-scented air like swimmers the foam of some warm blue sea. It was usually such fun, this breasting of the warm air, but today the doctor, looking down at Stella, could see no happiness in her face.

"What is it, Stella?" he asked. "Is it Sol?"

Stella shook her head. "I don't mind about Sol like I did. I think he'll like it there. But Zachary doesn't like it where he is."

"He's not fond of the sea, certainly, but he'll soon be home," said the doctor.

"He wasn't at sea in the dream I had last night," said Stella. "He was in a dreadful place. It was dark because there wasn't any light, except lantern light that came through a grating high up in the wall, but I could see it was dirty and looked like a sort of dungeon. There were a lot of men there and it must have been night because some of them seemed trying to go to sleep. But they had scarcely any room to lie down, and no beds, only bits of wood on the floor to put their heads on. Some of them had hardly any clothes, and the rest were in rags, and some of them did not look like men at all." She broke off and shivered in the hot sunshine, then went on again. "Zachary was there! He wasn't asleep, because there wasn't any room for him to lie down. He was sitting leaning against the wall, just under the grating, and the wall was slimy. I could see the slime shining in the light that came through the grating, and I could see Zachary's face. It was bruised, and one eye was shut up, as though he had been fighting, but it wasn't the bruises that made it look so dreadful——"

"What was it?" asked the doctor.

"The look on his face. He was afraid. He looked like the picture of Christian in Mrs. Loraine's *Pilgrim's Progress*, when he is shut up in prison in the City of Destruction, and I saw right into his heart, and I knew what he was thinking and feeling. He thought he would never get out. He was afraid he would go mad. And he wanted you and me very badly but he knew that there was no way that he could tell us where he was. I tried to call out to him that I was there, but my voice wouldn't come out of my mouth. And I tried to run to him but my feet wouldn't move. . . . Then I woke up."

"You had a nightmare," said the doctor. "What did you have for supper? Rabbit pie?"

"Milk and bread and honey. And it wasn't a nightmare. I'd bathed my eyes with rue and the water from the pisgies' well, like Granny Bogan told me to do if I wanted to see into my lover's heart."

"So Zachary is your lover, is he?" asked the doctor lightly.

"Yes. He loves me," said Stella. "Sir, where is he?"

"At sea in his frigate. You had a nightmare."

"No. I bathed my eyes with the rue."

"All the tarrydiddle that Granny Bogan told you was just a fairy-tale, my honey."

"Fairies are true and what they tell you is true," said Stella.

"That's a matter of opinion! And now listen. If any disaster had happened to Zachary I should have been told. The authorities have my name as his adopted father. But no disaster has happened to Zachary. You had a nightmare. Too much new bread and honey is very indigestible, as I've told you before."

"It was very stale bread. It was Thursday's baking. Please, Sir, you must go to London and find Zachary."

"Why London?" asked the astonished doctor.

"In one of the sermons that Parson Ash reads it says that London is the City of Destruction."

"Stella, use your wits. Just because you have eaten too much bread and honey (stale bread can be just as indigestible as new) and looked at some frightening pictures in Mrs. Loraine's *Pilgrim's Progress*, and had a nightmare, do you think that merely to set your mind at rest I should leave my patients and go tearing off on a wild goose chase to London? Old Sol is very ill indeed. Mrs. Baxter in the village is going to have a baby. Jo Stanberry has a witlowe that will need lancing in a couple of days. And there is a little girl of three years old with scarlet fever whom I do not leave now for more than a few hours at a time."

Stella was silent for some while and then she said, "No, you can't go. Sol and Mrs. Baxter and Jo Stanberry and the little girl would all die right off, and that would not be right. But mon Père could go to London instead of to Exeter."

"Is mon Père going to Exeter?"

"Yes. Sir George said he could take a holiday."

"Has he any particular reason for wishing to go to Exeter?"

"To see a man who lives there who is going to print a book he has written."

"And what makes you think Monsieur le Comte de Colbert will change all his plans just because a little girl has had a nightmare?" asked the doctor with amusement.

"Mon Père would do anything in the world for me so long as it did not harm my immortal soul," said Stella with simple conviction.

The doctor, startled, screwed his eyeglass in more firmly and looked down at her, and he was not above a slight twinge of instantly suppressed jealousy. He wondered what degree of intimacy this astonishing friendship between the French aristocrat and the English country girl had now reached. "Is mon Père suffering from any anxiety about your soul?" he asked dryly.

"He would like me to be a different kind of Christian," said Stella. "He would like me to be the same kind as Mrs. Loraine and himself—and Zachary." Furious indignation sent the blood surging up over the doctor's face to the brim of his top-hat, but it receded when Stella said quickly, "He hasn't said that to me. It was Mrs. Loraine who said so."

Well, why not, thought the doctor suddenly. The child knows now that Zachary is her lover. Their union, when it comes, should be as complete as possible.

"Mon Père will go," said Stella again.

The doctor was not so sure. He doubted if faith in the fairies formed any part of the Abbé's intellectual equipment. Nor did he imagine that a director of souls would think that a little girl should be encouraged to take her nightmares seriously. But there was another motive that might move the Abbé, and at the thought of it his face crinkled with slightly malicious amusement.

"Stella," he said, "after you have told the Abbé about your nightmare you might give him a message from me. Ask him if he dares go to Newgate and make intimate contact with the dirty, the ignorant, the thieves and the murderers. Ask him to remember a conversation he once had with me. Tell him to each man his own devil and I wish him good luck if he takes this chance of having a tilt at his. That must sound an odd message to you, my honey. See if you can remember it correctly."

Stella repeated the message three times, until she had it right, and with the glorious stretch of the bay before them they drove down the hill to Torre. It was certainly a wonderful sparkling morning. Too sparkling. The glassy brilliance of the light presaged thunder. But the doctor was now silent and no longer amused. Again and again he looked at the taut white face of the strange elfin girl beside him. Had Granny Bogan guessed rightly and was the beloved Stella really possessed of powers beyond the normal? If so——He ceased to think of her. Zachary possessed his every thought as they drove along Robbers' Lane. . . . My son. My son. . . . His love for Stella would never grow less, yet she was moving a little away from him now, away from him and nearer to the man she called mon Père, while Zachary with every day and every night entered into firmer possession of his mind and heart. He would not have much ease now until they were sitting once more one on each side of his study fire. . . . Abruptly he pulled himself up. Ridiculous nonsense. Nothing but a child's nightmare. This thunder weather made one fanciful. . . . He smiled again as he wondered what effect the nightmare, the weather and his message would have upon mon Père.

IV

The morning continued too hot and too bright. By midday the clouds were gathering on the horizon and by the evening a storm was brewing. Mrs. Loraine went to bed early with a thunder headache, and told Stella to go too. But in her room, instead of undressing, Stella put on her bonnet and a pair of stout shoes. She hated storms and the mutter of thunder in the distance made her heart beat loud, but Mrs. Loraine had been ailing all day, and needing her, and she had not been able to go to St. Michael's Chapel. And so she must go now. To stay at home would be to fail Zachary. Rosalind had never once failed her lover, and she would not fail either.

Twice, running along the lane that led to Chapel Hill, she stumbled and nearly fell from sheer weariness. It had been a dreadful day. Her dream had haunted her ceaselessly. Mrs. Loraine, always so sweet-tempered, had not been so sweet-tempered as usual because of her headache, and Araminta had been as cross as she knew how to be, and that was very cross indeed. If that was not enough mon Pére, who always came to see them on a Monday, had on this day when she wanted him so badly elected not to come near them.

The steep climb up Chapel Hill taxed her weary small body to the utmost and half-way up she had to sit down and rest, looking out to sea, her back against a rock. The bay that had been so blue and sparkling in the morning was now the colour of lead, and though there was not a breath of wind a heavy sucking swell was giving an ugly tone to the voice of the sea as it surged in against the rocks. The menacing restlessness of the sea in thunder weather always frightened Stella. No wind, and yet that strange movement. It was uncanny. The clouds were black and heavy, edged here and there with livid light, and every moment it grew darker. It will be dark in the Chapel, thought Stella, as she started to climb again, it will be dark and frightening in the Chapel.

Yet as she came near she was astonished to see light shining out from the Chapel windows, a deep orange glow that was lovely and most reassuring. The weariness went out of her and she scrambled up the last bit of the way quite quickly and came to the Chapel door. Looking in she saw a lantern burning in one of the alcoves in the north wall, and before the place where the altar had once been a white-haired man was kneeling saying his prayers. She gave a cry of delight and he turned and saw her, then got up and held out his arms and she ran across the rocky floor and fell into them. It was mon Père. It was the first time that they had clung together like this but it seemed so natural that it did not occur to either of them to be surprised.

"You're in trouble, child?" asked the Abbé, looking down at her.

"Yes, mon Père," said Stella.

They sat down together on the outcrop of rock where they had sat the first day they had met and she poured out the whole story, and then carefully, word for word, repeated the doctor's message. The Abbé nodded.

"You'll go, mon Père?" asked Stella anxiously.

"Certainly," he said briefly.

The message was like a trumpet call, but the doctor had misjudged him, for he would have gone without it. Stella's tale of fairies and eye-lotion he dismissed as nonsense but her dream he took seriously, for he had not forgotten that she had known before when things were not well with Zachary. He knew better than the doctor the strength and mystery of the union that can sometimes exist between a man and a woman; knew because he had himself experienced it. Though never before, he thought, smiling a little, had he known it come into being when the woman was still a child.

Stella saw the smile and put her hand on his knee. "Will it be all well, mon Père?"

"Yes, Stella. However bad this storm that has caught Zachary, even if it's a shipwreck, he'll come to land safely."

"But he isn't caught in a storm, mon Père."

"The storms of nature aren't the only sort of storms, Stella." He looked round at the Chapel which had now become so dark that without the lantern they would scarcely have been able to see each other. "Though there is going to be one of the natural ones very soon I think. A bad one too."

One of those sudden gusts of wind that usher in a storm swept round the Chapel, sounding exactly like Zachary's bull-roarer summoning Them, and without a word to each other, because it was the natural thing to do in this place, they knelt down and prayed for those in peril. At least the Abbé prayed but Stella was so frightened that her dry mouth felt full of dust, her cold hand trembled in the Abbé's and no words would come into her mind.

"Afraid, Stella?" he rallied her, as they got to their feet again. "I thought you were never afraid."

"I am afraid of rats and thunderstorms and Them," said Stella, her cheeks crimsoning with shame. "I was so afraid that I could not pray for Zachary."

"Show no sign of your fear, offer it to God for Zachary, and the costly gift will be a more acceptable prayer than any repetition of mere words," said the Abbé slowly.

Stella looked up at him, her eyes suddenly bright with the pleasure of a new idea. He very often now presented her with these new ideas, and always he spoke slowly as though underlining each word, so that she stowed his ideas away very carefully for future use. With a flash of intuition she knew that this one, when put into use, was going to revolutionise the whole of life.

Going down the steep path they were glad of the Abbé's lantern, for they would scarcely have seen how to pick their way over the rocks without it. The roll of the thunder was near now and the lightning was playing over the restless sea, but still there was no rain. At Mrs. Loraine's gate the Abbé stopped. "We'll say good-bye here, Stella, shall we? I'm going down to the shore."

"Mon Père!" gasped Stella in astonishment. "Aren't you going home before the storm breaks?"

He looked down at her, smiling. "I'm not like you, Stella. I enjoy a storm. I could stand for an hour watching the lightning over the sea."

She fought with herself for a moment, then came to him and put her hand into his. "I'll come too," she said.

For a moment he was on the point of sending her to bed, where she certainly should be at this hour and in this weather, then he grasped her hand tightly and they went down the lane together, for he could not forbid her prayer. Vaguely he remembered that old legend that he had heard, that fairy tale of a girl whose courage had saved her lover from drowning. But what he remembered not vaguely but with a stabbing clarity was Thérèse's fear of thunder. Her one fear, for she had not minded rats. It was he who hated rats and vermin of every kind, and all that foulness and degradation with which for love of Stella he intended to establish intimate acquaintance within the next few days.

The seashore had lost all its familiarity and become some dreadful dead country on a stricken star. The rocks were without colour in the pallid lightning and looked like the bones of prehistoric beasts sticking up out of the sand. The wind was steadily rising, roaring in the upper air as though great winged demons were rushing over their heads, yet leaving the earth itself to a waiting stillness. Stella thought she would have feared this wind less if it had been whipping her skirts about her and tearing at her bonnet strings. The roaring above and the stillness below made one wonder what would happen when the great wings swept too low. She dared not look up at the sky because she knew she would see Them there. The sea as well as the wind was rising and the waves roared and broke at their feet, stinging their faces with white torn spray. At every reverberation of the thunder a tremor went through Stella's body and every time the lightning flashed she unconsciously gripped the Abbé's hand a little harder. Her other hand was clasping her locket which she had pulled out from under her dress. She always held it in this way when she needed courage, for she knew her mother had been brave.

Yet she stood her ground, and would have stood it for as long as the Abbé remained entranced by the wild terror of the scene, but she was delivered by a sudden ripping open of the black sky above them, a crash of nearer thunder and the descent of the rain. It came suddenly, sheets of arrows hurled before the wind, abruptly restoring the world to normality. The wind was just wind now, tearing at their clothes, driving the rain against their faces, the rocks looked normal again and scourged by the rain the waves broke less violently. Before she had time to get wet the Abbé had picked Stella up in his arms, wrapped his cloak round her and with his back turned to the storm was striding along the lanes that led back to Torre. He upbraided himself furiously that he had let them stay too long, but she laughed, all her fear gone. His arms about her were as strong as iron, stronger even than Father Sprigg's, and gave her a sense of safety, such as she had never felt before. She knew now how chickens felt when they scurried under their parent's wing in a storm, and her laughter faded into a sigh of complete content.

They reached Mrs. Loraine's house and the Abbé opened the front door and set Stella gently down in the little hall, remaining himself dripping upon the mat. Araminta appeared carrying a candle and in a state of powerful indignation. "Gracious goodness, Sir, you've never taken the child out in all this wet?"

"I make my apologies the most profound," said the Abbé humbly.

"I'm not wet, Araminta," said Stella. "Monsieur de Colbert carried me."

She took off her bonnet and stood smiling up at him. But he did not return her smile. His face looked grey in the candle-light and he stood as though turned to stone, staring at the gold locket round Stella's neck.

"What ails you, Sir?" asked Araminta sharply. "Has the lightning struck you?"

"Stella, the locket," he said harshly. "Where did you get it?"

The harshness of his tone was almost ugly and it so startled Stella that unconsciously she put up her hands to hide her treasure. "Mother Sprigg gave it to me," she whispered.

The Abbé put a hand against the wall. "Fool!" he adjured himself. Gold lockets were not a rarity. The one he had chosen for Thérèse had been a cheap one, though it had been the best he could afford, and there had probably been another dozen in the shop of the same design. He achieved a smile and bowed to the startled girl still staring up at him.

"Goodbye, Stella. I shall be in London by the end of the week."

The front door banged behind him and he was gone.

"Well I never!" said Araminta.

Stella stood quite still for a moment or two, feeling extremely odd. She felt that the Comte de Colbert had vanished for ever, as the hermit had done on the night when he and Rosalind had saved her lover from the storm. When he came back to her again it would not be as the Comte de Colbert but as someone quite different. She unclasped her hands from her locket and slipped it back inside her dress with a sigh of happiness. Zachary, she knew, was saved already.

# CHAPTER V

## I

The weather broke with the storm, which had been one of the worst within living memory, and the Abbé travelled up to London in wind and rain. He had managed to secure a seat inside the coach and sat in his corner wrapped in his cloak against the icy draughts, with the raindrops that seeped through the roof dripping rhythmically upon his hat. The coach was crowded and the company not to his taste. He was astonished at himself. His visit to Exeter had been a most necessary one and it had been arranged that he should travel there with a friend of the Careys in a private barouche, and here he was travelling to the London of painful memories in a not-too-clean public conveyance which leaked and smelt of manure, pressed upon by *hoi polloi* munching onions and bread and cursing the government in voices that smote upon the delicate tympanums of his ears in a most painful manner. And why? Because a little girl he loved had had a nightmare and a country doctor had sent him a verbal challenge which his pride did not permit him to refuse. He was off on a wild-goose chase with no cogent reasons behind it. What a fool he was. He must be suffering from that deterioration of the intellect which he had been informed befell those who lived for too long in this moist, mild climate of the West Country, among these round, green, fairy-haunted hills of Devon.

Abruptly he pulled himself up. His mood was one of mere reaction, with which by this time he should have been only too familiar. One took a decision based upon that intuition which is a truer thing than worldly common-sense, and gloried in it, and then the next day there was the inevitable swing of the pendulum and the glory faded. Yet the intuition remained what it had been; true. And in any case there was nothing he would not do for Stella.

He suddenly bethought himself of another thing, a small thing, that she had asked him to do for her. It was ten days now since she had given him the book which Granny Bogan had found in the tower of Cockington Church, and asked him to make out the story for her. He had been waiting for leisure to decipher the faint handwriting and here was this tedious coach journey providing him with it. He had the book in one of the deep pockets of his travelling cloak, with his breviary in the other. He took it out and opened it, looking with delight at the exquisite little pictures of gentians on the first page, and presently he had forgotten the irritation of *hoi polloi*, the smell of onions, the drip of rain on his hat and the icy draughts. Indeed, when the time came to say his next office, he forgot his breviary also. The book opened with the legend that he had half-remembered upon the seashore, but that was only the beginning of the story which absorbed him all the way to London.

Coffee houses and hotels, and all places over-full of the human beings whom he did not much care for, were abominated by the Abbé, but he was fortunate in renting a room in the house where he had lodged during those bitter days after he had first come back from Ireland. The same landlady was still in occupation, an honest and cleanly woman who did not bother him with too much talk. The house was tall and rickety and not in a fashionable quarter, but the Abbé liked its high chimneys and wavy brown roof patched with moss, the fanlight over the door and the old worn treads of the narrow staircase that twisted in darkness around its oak newel, up and up from the narrow entry to his room high in the attic. This room was octagonal and so small that it was almost entirely filled by the four-poster bed with its curtains of crimson rep. The panelling was painted apple green with a press for clothes cleverly hidden behind it. A table and chair were in the window and on the small Adam mantelpiece was one brass candlestick.

Down below in the cobbled street there was a miniature market, with stalls for flowers and vegetables, and between two gables across the way one could catch a glimpse of the branches of green trees with the slender spire of a church rising beyond them. This was one of the corners of London from which the country scents and sounds had not yet receded. Standing at his open window he remembered how in the spring birdsong had chimed through the ringing of bells, and how on winter evenings one could hear the horns of the huntsmen coming home. He remembered the autumn smell of wet earth and bonfire smoke from hidden gardens, and the scent of the chrysanthemums on the flower stalls. Well, if he had to endure the filth of London for a while he was glad that he would have this quiet retreat swinging like a green nest high up in the clean air. . . . And it did swing, he remembered, when the wind blew, for the lovely flimsy old house, with slipping tiles and dry-rot in the beams, was fast tottering to decay. . . . It would be a very suitable place in which to transcribe for Stella, by the light of the moon and the candle in the brass candlestick, the story of the lovers of Gentian Hill.

## II

The Abbé wasted no time. The very next morning he presented himself at Newgate prison, joining the pitiful crowd of prisoners' friends watching at the felons' door. Owing to his respectable appearance he was the first to be admitted and was ushered straight away into the ante-room where the visitors were searched. He submitted to this process with cold distaste, even though in his case his clothes were not stripped from him and only his pockets were examined.

"What do you expect to find upon me?" he asked the turnkey who was dealing with him.

"Poison or a bit of rope, Sir," was the answer. "You'd be surprised how smart the relatives of prisoners can be in providing them with the means of doing away with themselves. And that though they know they'll be flung into gaol themselves if anything of the sort is found on 'em."

The Abbé looked grimly round the dirty dark room where he was standing. It was guarded by blunderbusses mounted on movable carriages and the walls were hung with chains and fetters. "Hell above ground" they called this place. He knew how cruel the penal laws of England were at this time, and for what slight offences men and women were tortured and hanged. He had a pretty shrewd idea of the dreadfulness of the scene he would look on in a moment, and he knew that it would bring back all the horror of the past that he had tried to forget. Then abruptly he remembered the view from Beacon Hill on Christmas Eve, Stella in the small green parlour and the mummers coming through the garden gate in the moonlight. That too was England, and life.

He went down a stone passage to a door which a second turnkey, keeping guard beside it, unlocked and unbolted. Passing through he found himself in a long narrow passage, its walls formed of iron bars. On one side was a yard, round which the prison was built and where the prisoners were exercised, and on the other, behind a double grating, was the first of the prison wards.

It was even worse than he had thought, and it brought back the past more sharply than he had thought it would. Involuntarily he stepped back a few paces, his back against the bars that surrounded the courtyard. A wave of nausea swept over him and he did not see very clearly for a moment or two. There was a roaring in his ears, like the sea, and he felt deathly cold. Then he controlled himself, and stepped forward, just as the door opened again and the first of the crowd who had been waiting at the felon's gate surged through it, shouting to the men shut in behind the double grating, pressing against him, knocking him against the bars so that he had to cling to them to prevent himself being swept off his feet.

Breathing like a man in pain he forced himself to look steadily at the inmates of the dreadful cage. Most of them looked inhuman and many of them were only half clothed. The dirt and overcrowding, the noise and stench were horrible. Many of the men were sodden with drink, for by the proceeds of their begging they could purchase liquor in the prison. The begging had started already; they were thrusting wooden spoons on long sticks through the double grating, and their visitors, many of them almost as ragged as they were, were putting in their few pitiful pence. But only the strongest could keep their pence, for each man had to fight to keep what he was given. Many were too weak even to try, and these did not come to the grating. There were young boys among those weak ones and it was among them that the Abbé searched for Zachary, his eyes going slowly from one gaunt face to another. But he could not find Zachary, and with relief he turned away, pushed through the crowd of visitors and found again the turnkey who had let him in.

"Are these condemned men?" he asked.

"Yes, Sir. Men condemned to the hulks or Botany Bay."

"For what offences?"

The turnkey shrugged. "Smuggling in rope to a prisoner, maybe. Hiding a thief or receiving stolen goods. Some minor offence."

"Have they been here long?"

"Months, Sir, some of 'em, waiting for trial, and then waiting to be sent to the hulks."

"Where are the men condemned to the gallows?"

"In cells, Sir. You can't see those."

"And the untried men?"

"Round the other side of the yard, Sir."

The Abbé walked slowly round to the other side, noticing as he went the military sentinels posted on the roof. He imagined that the hour for exercise was near and that they would shoot if there was lawlessness. Once again he fought down his nausea. In France he had witnessed scenes more terrible than the one he had just left, but those scenes had taken place during a civil war, they had not been part of the normal life of a country at peace within its own borders. It was the organised horror of this wild beast show that shocked him as nothing in his life had shocked him yet.

He came to the other side, where was the ward of the untried men. The scene here was much the same but not quite so terrible because the men had not been here so long and many still had some hope. Yet it was bad enough, and if this was the scene Stella had seen in her dream he thanked God for her sake that dreams, remembered on waking, lose a little of their sharpness of horror or joy. Once more he pressed himself against the double bars, his anxious gaze going from face to face of the crowd who were pressing against them on the other side. But though he stayed there for what seemed to himself an interminable time he could not see Zachary. The depression of his weariness and horror engulfed him. It had all been for nothing. The boy was not here.

He was on the point of moving away when the pallid ravaged faces, the surging movement, the noise, reminded him of something. . . . The sea. . . . It was a sea of misery that was breaking against the bars only a few feet from him, as the waves had broken on the beach the other night, white and torn in the glare of the lightning. The dreadful sea came nearer, reared itself up, crashed over his head. He was drowning in the darkness, sucked down in that horror. Mon Dieu, was he losing consciousness? With all his strength he exerted his will, swung back again towards that from which he had swung away, clutched the bars tighter. Was he a squeamish woman, an untried boy, to be so overwhelmed by dreadful sights? He remembered the legend of the storm and the drowning boy saved from it; and vividly he remembered Stella's courage in the face of storm, her offered fear. He stayed his ground. His vision cleared and through a sudden gap in the crowd, as though a wave had toppled and parted, he saw a picture that he never afterwards forgot.

Under a grating high in the wall a wooden washtub had been set and four or five men were gathered about it attempting to wash their clothes. The water in the tub appeared filthy, the rags they were wringing out of it scarcely less so, yet the Abbé found the sight incredibly heartening; for here were a few men struggling after decency; men who were not yet wild beasts like the rest. One of them, stripped to the waist, had his back to the Abbé. He was a tall boy with dark tumbled hair and a thin brown back upon which the ribs showed starkly. He half-turned, wringing out his shirt, but before the Abbé could see his face the gap in the crowd had closed again and he was hidden. It might have been Zachary, or it might not, but the Abbé was not going to leave this hell above ground until he knew.

During the next twenty minutes he passed through one of the oddest experiences of his life. As he moved up and down before the bars, trying ceaselessly for another sight of that boy, he began to recognise some of the faces that came and went in front of him. One hulking brute of a fellow had the bluest Irish eyes he had ever seen. Another, a boy, with the face of a depraved old man, had a mouth as sensitively cut as Stella's own. A third, hunchbacked and deformed, had a pock-marked face that startled the Abbé by suddenly splitting into a grin. He noticed other eyes, other mouths, other gallant attempts at cheerfulness. Occasionally, when he slipped a coin into a wooden spoon, his eyes would meet the eyes of the poor devil who held it, and he had the sensation that the trivial act was not trivial at all but an actual entering in of himself into the being of the man before him. He was recognising as though these men were not strangers and giving as though to his friends. When the appalling sea had broken over his head he had as it were passed through the breakers into the calmer water beyond. But he was in the sea now, part of it, no longer an isolated spectator on the shore. With a sudden sensation of sheer panic he knew he would never get back to the shore. Then came the calm knowledge that he did not want to. And all through the twenty minutes he was praying as he had never prayed before, every atom of himself poured out like water for those men behind the bars, but especially for one of them.

Quite suddenly he saw him again. He had finished his bit of washing and hung it on a nail to dry, and now he was leaning against the wall, shivering without his shirt. He was Zachary, but so changed that for a full moment the Abbé was not quite certain. Then, in this haggard young man leaning against the wall, his eyes dull and sombre with his hopelessness, ugly lines of exhaustion scored heavily on his face, he recognised some lingering remnants of the beauty that had so touched him in the King's child. Some of the colt-like grace was there, the mouth was the same, and the nostrils of the aquiline nose still flared like those of a startled thoroughbred. But Zachary, if like the young man in the legend he had travelled forth into the world to gain knowledge, had certainly gained it; too quickly and too much.

He was not looking at the Abbé and the turnkeys were coming down the passage, shouting that the visiting hour was over. The Abbé called "Zachary!" but his voice did not carry to where the boy stood, and then the turnkeys were among them, seizing the visitors by their shoulders and pulling them roughly away from the bars. The Abbé in his desperation remembered their meeting in his sitting-room after the wrestling match, and how quick had been their response one to the other. Nothing that had happened since had had any power to destroy the instant liking that had been like a bridge between them. It must still hold. He did not shout again but with his eyes on Zachary he set himself to cross it. It was not difficult, for in the last twenty minutes he had issued forth from the citadel of himself as never before. Zachary turned his head and their eyes met just as a turnkey's hand descended on the Abbé's shoulder and he was pulled from the bars. It did not matter. Almost unbelieving joy shone over Zachary's face, and from the Abbé's came that gleam of light, like a rapier flashing in the sun, that had so startled Zachary at their first meeting. The Abbé, pushed backwards like the rest, a turnkey's stave against his chest, could see tears pouring down the boy's face, but only the tears of a child awaking suddenly from nightmare. . . . Zachary knew now that he was not forgotten in the pit into which he had fallen. . . . The Abbé waved his hat, turned, and made his way back into the outer world.

III

The Abbé had all the aristocrat's power of getting what he wanted with the minimum of difficulty. Priest though he was his old arrogance was by no means dead in him, he still had the habit of command, a caustic tongue and a most intimidating presence. The various letters of introduction which he needed were soon in his possession and three days later the governor of the prison allowed him an interview with Zachary. They were locked in one of the cells where condemned criminals were imprisoned before a hanging, and sitting together on a stone bench the Abbé listened attentively to Zachary's carefully told story. They had very little time and could waste no words, but dazed and stupefied though he looked Zachary had the facts of the case quite clearly in his mind. He knew exactly what he had done and not done, and what were the alternatives before him. "If I killed Mike I'll be tried for manslaughter; if I did not kill him only for assault. But I'll have to wait months for my trial. You do here."

"I can see to it that you are committed for trial quickly. But first I must find out what happened to Mike."

"I should like to know that I did not kill Mike," said Zachary. He spoke quietly but the Abbé was aware of his misery.

"Alive or dead he has not the stain of murder on his soul," said the Abbé.

"No," said Zachary. That fact was the only comfort that he had; that and the fact of the Abbé here beside him. "The doctor—my father—" he went on, and then stopped.

"I will write to him tonight. He will be proud of you."

"Will it be a matter for pride to have his son hanged for manslaughter?" asked Zachary with bitterness.

"In the circumstances, yes," said the Abbé tersely.

"And Stella," said Zachary, and then stopped again. He could not go on with the subject of Stella.

"There are few things that are not understood by that small girl," said the Abbé. "She is a child only in years."

And then he told Zachary the story of Stella's dream; not forgetting Granny Bogan, the rue and the Pisgies' Well. To him these three were mere incidental additions, but he liked to speak of them in this terrible cell. The fairy world might have no existence in actual fact but the thought of it purified the air. Zachary suddenly laughed delightedly and tenderly, and the laugh startled the Abbé nearly out of his wits, for this was surely the first time that any man had ever laughed in this cell.

"She's a white witch!" chuckled Zachary. A shaft of summer sunlight, piercing the high grating, touched the opposite wall with a pencil of light. It drew for him a picture of the wise old tree, the cold water of the Pisgies' Well bubbling up beneath it, the clear pool fringed with forget-me-nots, and Stella and Hodge sitting there in the gold dust of the sunset. He remembered how a handful of this same brightness had floated through the prison grating on the evening of his first day there and how his whole soul had cried out in anguish to Stella. He thought the little white witch must have heard.

The key grated in the lock and the Abbé thanked heaven that he had just had time to admit the fairies to Newgate prison.

## CHAPTER VI

### I

The Abbé now passed his days tramping through the streets of London toiling for Zachary, and his evenings withdrawn far above it in a green nest, translating Stella's book into English for her. Daily too he attended mass and daily he said his offices. The darkness of squalor and wretchedness, the twinkling colours of fairyland and the clear white shining of his steadfast faith were woven by the passing days into a strange tapestry. Yet this was the stuff of life in the world, he told himself, and from henceforth he would accept the whole of it, neither shunning the darkness nor despising the small twinkling coloured lights. He was not yet ready for the white light only, for he was still a sinner and a man of dreams.

After anxious search and enquiry he found the officers of the watch who had arrested Zachary. He discovered that in England at this date method in the maintenance of order was as conspicuously absent as justice in the administration of law and sobriety in the officers of it. The men vaguely remembered that a dark young fellow had killed another young fellow with red hair, and they had taken one to prison and the other to the mortuary. The Abbé's stern eyes upon them, his questions rapping at their muddled wits, they became uncertain about the mortuary. They owned, when pressed, that they had not been too sober at the time. After deep cogitation they suddenly remembered that the corpse had shown signs of life before it reached its destination and that they had switched it over to the 'orspital. What hospital, the Abbé demanded? It might, they thought, have been Guy's. Then one of them, visited by a sudden brilliant flash of memory, felt in his pocket and produced two curiously shaped bits of wood, with a length of cord wrapped round them. "Found it on the cobbles where the lads had been fighting," he said. "Picked it up and kept it out of curiosity like."

"What is it?" asked the Abbé.

"Couldn't tell you, Sir. Never seen such a thing. Looks like it might be a sort of top."

The Abbé in his turn pocketed the toy. . . . It might come in useful. . . . Then slipping a gold piece into each grimy palm he reminded them that they would be called upon to give evidence and hoped their report of the prisoner would be favourable He left them assured that it would.

He went immediately to Guy's Hospital and found the wards there only slightly less terrible than those of Newgate. The dirt was appalling, the smells as bad and the heat insufferable. And again he was sickened by the way in which suffering humanity was put on show. The doctors, top-hatted and wearing the dirty frock coats which they kept for hospital use only, went their rounds followed by hordes of medical students. Each patient was displayed and lectured upon as though it were an insentient specimen beneath a microscope. The feet of the students were loud upon the bare floors and their voices and laughter were strident. If consideration and compassion formed any part of their make-up they were kept well hidden. The Abbé could not imagine how the suffering wretches in the dirty beds could be expected to get well. Probably they were not expected to. They were here not to be healed but to be observed and experimented upon. Fury boiled in the Abbé. Horror rather than fury had predominated when he entered Newgate but a change had taken place in him since then. He was no longer a spectator on the shore. He had plunged into the sea and these men were his friends.

There was no Michael Burke upon the hospital books. The porter had cheerfully remarked to the Abbé that not every young ragamuffin brought in from a street accident was in a state to remember his name—if he had one—but the gentleman was perfectly at liberty to look round the place and see what he could find there. And so for an hour the Abbé tramped through the wards, stopping at every bed that had a red-headed boy in it and asking if his name was Michael Burke. Some of the red-heads were unable to answer him, and among those was a lanky boy with bewildered unfocused green eyes, an arrogant child's mouth and a bandage round his head. When he had had a look at every man and boy in the hospital the Abbé returned to the green-eyed boy. He liked his ugly face. There was breeding about it. He sat down on the bed and asked him again if he was Michael Burke. There was no answer but the green eyes turned in his direction and suddenly focused upon his face with a distinct expression of pleasure, as though a man marooned for weeks with wild beasts on a desert island should suddenly meet one of his own kind. The Abbé took the bull-roarer from his pocket and held it out on the palm of his hand. The boy smiled, his green eyes lighting up with the delight of a child who after a long and painful parting is reunited with his favourite toy. The Abbé put the thing in the huge red hand lying on the dirty blanket, the boy's fingers closed upon it and he fell asleep.

The Abbé sighed in exasperation but remained where he was, sitting patiently upon the bed, until the visiting was over and an irritable ward attendant requested him to remove himself at once.

"What are his injuries?" asked the Abbé.

"Bruises, a few teeth knocked out, concussion and a cut head. Must have been in a street fight and fallen on a sharp stone. Regular bruiser, he looks, but got the worst of it for once. Time's up, Sir, and I'll trouble you to be moving."

"Will he live?" demanded the Abbé, immovable.

"Live!" The attendant snorted contemptuously. "Skull of an ox and a hide to match. In another three or four days he'll remember all about himself."

The Abbé rose. "I shall return in three days," he said briefly, and left the hospital.

But he was satisfied that this was Mike, and with Zachary cleared of the charge of manslaughter he proceeded at once to pay a few visits upon persons of importance in the legal world. His letters of introduction, his own distinction and air of frigid authority, won him instant admittance and attention, and two evenings later, after an excellent dinner he found himself sitting with a learned judge in his library, and after receiving a promise that Mr. Midshipman Anthony Mary O'Connell should be sent up for trial and subsequently liberated with all possible speed, remained in conversation with him until after midnight.

A curious state of affairs was revealed to him. His host and his kind were not, he found, altogether indifferent to the squalor and lawlessness of London, nor to the appalling confusion and misery in the prisons. They were awake to the fact that the officers of the watch were few and incompetent. They deplored the cruelty of the law and knew that many of its victims were convicted in error and innocent of the crimes for which they died. But what could be done? It was the English way to let things alone to develop as they would until they got to such a pass that public opinion was awakened. English public opinion was a sleepy sort of giant and it took a good deal to awake it, yet once awake it could be powerful.

"Any signs of awakening upon the matter of the prisons?" asked the Abbé dryly.

The judge shrugged. "We are at war. England is still fighting for her life and the government are too much occupied with foreign affairs to pay much attention to reform at home. But the citizens of London are not easy in their minds. I have known many cases of humane men who have let a thief go free when they could have handed him over to justice, because they would not have it on their conscience that they had sent a fellow human being to the gallows. Officers of the watch often connive at escapes. Juries seize upon extenuating circumstances to return a verdict of Not Guilty, and judges incline to the side of mercy. If it were not so, with the English law as it at present stands, with death as the penalty for most offences, we should have about four hangings a day, with the Old Bailey alone furnishing a hundred victims every year. Public opinion is stirring, undoubtedly, but it wants leadership. We want men and women with the courage to visit the prisons, immerse themselves in the horrors there, inform themselves thoroughly as to conditions and then shout about what they have seen from the very housetops. But such people are not easy to come by. Those who have never suffered torture are extremely sorry for the tortured but as a general rule they content themselves with compassionate feelings. Those who have themselves endured great suffering, who know it from the inside and not as mere spectators, belong for the most part to the ranks of the uneducated and the inarticulate and are powerless."

Both men were silent. It was late and there was no sound in the room but the distant rattle of a home-going coach over the cobbles and a whisper of wind in the trees in the judge's garden. Charles de Colbert was a man who had suffered. He knew many kinds of torture from the inside. But it was not the making of a decision that was keeping him silent; almost unconsciously that had been made already, at the moment when the waves broke over his head; he was silent because he was marvelling that he had delayed so long. . . . To have suffered, and then to have crept up to his lonely safety on the shore while other men were still drowning. . . . A faint red tinged his cheekbones and the Judge, looking at him curiously, saw his face as that of a man most deeply shamed.

II

During the next few days of waiting he visited Zachary at Newgate and Mike at Guy's Hospital. Conversation with Zachary was practically impossible but he had been able to shout the information that Mike was alive and recovering, and that freedom was only a matter of time and patience, and he put little packets of food into the wooden spoon that Zachary thrust through the double grating, food which Zachary hid hastily in his pocket and would not eat before him. He looked more like a scarecrow every day, and his body was covered with bruises and sores from the perpetual scrimmaging that went on in the ward, but now that he knew about Mike his eyes were peaceful. There was no trace of cringing or depravity in his face or bearing and if he did not wash his shirt now that was only because he no longer had it. The Abbé was anxious lest he should fall sick, but that was his only anxiety. The boy had discovered, apparently, how to live amidst foulness without being defiled, and if before he came here there had been any kind of fear that he had not met and mastered he had faced and conquered it now. And never, after this experience, would he, like Charles de Colbert, crawl up to the shore and leave other men to drown. The Abbé knew quite well where the food went and where the shirt had gone; to the other fellows. That proved it. Charles de Colbert, at his age and in his place, would have wolfed the food himself and fought like a tiger to keep his shirt upon his own back. Most humbly reverencing this boy, he wondered if the isolation in which he had encased himself would ever have cracked if the doctor had not carried Zachary into his sitting-room that autumn day at Torre. It might be that he owed his immortal soul to the prisoner behind the bars.

Mike recovered rapidly. The dirt, noise and stench of the hospital did not worry him at all but his own inaction drove him wild, and he was so profane and furious a patient that the Abbé was given permission to remove him at the first possible moment. The evening before he fetched Mike from the hospital he went to the inn where Zachary and Mike had stayed when they first reached London, to pay their bill and see if their belongings were still in existence. The landlady, an honest woman, guessing at the kind of disaster that had overtaken the two boys, had packed up their things and kept them carefully.

Alone in his green-panelled room the Abbé laid out Mike's things ready for him but Zachary's he put away in the press with his own. He smiled at the contrast between Mike's rags and Zachary's neatly mended shirts and socks, and at the means of recreation with which each boy had provided himself for use in the intervals of battle and storm. Mike's rags were folded round various instruments for making a noise picked up in foreign parts, a mouth organ from Spain, a concertina from Italy, and a bird-scarer's clapper from Corsica. Zachary's shirts were wrapped round his few and precious books. With the reverence of a passionate book-lover the Abbé laid them gently with his own, then picked up the little Shakespeare again to take a look at the type and paper. His action was automatic. As a lover of children must touch the bright hair so a lover of books must take a look at the type and smooth the page with his finger. The summer breeze, blowing through the open window, took a slip of paper that was between the pages and carried it to the floor. He picked it up, glanced at it, and instantly the room spun round him.

"Love is the divinity who creates peace among men and calm upon the sea, the windless silence of storms, repose and sleep in sadness. Love sings to all things which live and are, soothing the troubled minds of gods and men."

First Stella's locket and now this. He pulled himself sharply together. There was nothing at all in the juxtaposition of the two. The locket that he had bought for Thérèse had been of the same pattern as many others. There were a thousand men who loved these words from the Banquet. He recognised Dr. Crane's vigorous handwriting. The doctor had written out these words for the son he loved even as he had written them for the wife he loved. He put the scrap of paper back between the pages from which it had fluttered, and his eyes caught some words that Zachary had faintly underlined. "Fear and be slain." He felt as he had done when standing in the dark garden he had looked through the window and seen Stella sitting sewing in her green bower—ashamed of himself.

He put the book back and looked about him at his own green bower. He had become deeply attached to this austere, green-panelled room. He wondered if he would be able to rent it permanently when he had said goodbye to Devonshire, and come back to London again to work until he died for those whom the doctor had described to him as "the dirty, the ignorant and the wicked, the thieves, murderers and harlots; who so often turn out upon intimate acquaintance to be the best of us all." It was ironic that having at last found in Devonshire love, friendship and delight he should immediately plan to leave it. But there was nothing else he could do. The sky was peach coloured behind the gables across the way and it was already dusk in his room. He lit his candle and sat down once more to his work of translating and transcribing Stella's fairy-story.

III

The next day he fetched Mike in a hackney coach and put him to bed in his own four-poster with the maroon curtains. As there was no vacant bed in the house he himself slept on a palliasse on the floor. Mike protested furiously but found his fury no match for the iron determination of his host. And the Abbé assured him that he slept extremely well under these circumstances.

"I saw foreign service in the army," he assured the astonished Mike, who like all the young was incapable of visualising any of these elderly scarecrows as having once been as young and dashing as himself. "And I went through the revolution. I've learned to sleep in a ditch, behind a haystack or on a bare floor—anywhere. It is merely a question of training. The amount of time you spend in sleep is also a question of training."

The Abbé had apparently trained himself to do with the minimum of rest. When Mike went to sleep the last thing he saw was his host sitting writing at the window, a lighted candle beside him. When he woke the Abbé had already gone to mass and he would lie patiently waiting for him to return with the fresh rolls and butter he always bought on his way home, and then their landlady brought up strong hot coffee and they broke their fast together in the quiet green room.

Though he had been so wildly impatient in hospital Mike was the reverse here, even though he was consumed with longing to get to Zachary. The quiet room soothed him, the Abbé's great kindness, and the dawning knowledge that his friendship with Zachary had reached a new stage that was altogether good.

The fact that Zachary had half killed him had roused in him not resentment but a deep respect. Any fellow who could half kill him, Mike Burke, in fair fight, was the devil of a fellow. And but for Zachary he'd have murdered that poor bastard who'd gone off with the bull-roarer and his purse. Zachary had seen that. He knew what he was when the drink and his devil of a temper had got hold of him together. Zachary had saved him from doing a good many detestable things in the course of their friendship but never from any act quite so hateful as that would have been. The hugeness of Zachary's service, of his own gratitude, the hell of a time that he had had in the hospital, that Zachary was still having at Newgate, had so toughened the fibre of their friendship that now it seemed to him a rock upon which he could re-build his hitherto chaotic life. He vowed that in future he'd try his damnedest to do what Zachary wanted him to do, see things as he saw them. The fellow's way of thinking had the same sort of graceful rightness that his manners had.

And this old dry stick of an Abbé was the same; unerringly wise and courteous. Yet nobody is born that way, Mike knew. That sort of ease only came after such battles as gave him the horrors even to think of. After much unaccustomed thought he came to the conclusion that such victors were, and would always be, very rare birds, but that the rest of the world would not do so badly if it could recognise them for what they were, not such fools as they appeared, and have the humility to attend to what they say. . . . He'd chuck away that bull-roarer, and he'd go to Gentian Hill.

But the Abbé insisted that he should visit his guardian first, as was his duty. Before he left he took him to see Zachary in Newgate, smiling at the way the two held to the bars and stood there roaring cheerful insults to each other. Mike leaped at the bars like a dog hurling himself upon his master, and the agitation of his stern almost created the illusion that he had a tail there. Zachary's gaunt face shone with such happiness that the horrors of the place seemed almost to disappear in the light of it, like mist sucked up by the sun.

Two days later Mike climbed upon the coach for Bath, the mouth organ, the concertina and the clapper carefully packed among his shirts but the bull-roarer left behind in the landlady's kitchen fire.

Five days later the Abbé's four-poster once more had a boy in it and this time the boy was Zachary. The Judge had been as good as his word. After a mere formality of a trial, at which the officers of the watch had given most favourable evidence, Zachary was set free.

For three days and nights he slept constantly, rousing only when the Abbé shook him awake to feed him. He was so dazed and drugged with sleep that he did not quite know where he was. He seemed to think that he was in his room at the doctor's house at Gentian Hill, with Tom Pearse, and was blissfully happy. But he was no less happy, though slightly startled, when he came to himself, and found where he was and who was looking after him.

"I can't sleep in your bed, Sir," was his instant reaction.

"You will sleep where I tell you," said the Abbé shortly. "Mike did what he was told and so will you."

Zachary smiled and went to sleep again and the Abbé went out to buy mutton and vegetables for the landlady to make nourishing broth. She had been exceedingly put out by the introduction of yet another sick boy into her attic and he had had to take the marketing upon himself to pacify her, as well as the sweeping and dusting of the green-panelled room. He smiled grimly to himself as he went along the sunny street with a marketing basket on his arm, and for a brief moment imagined the roar of laughter with which the doctor, could he see him now, would greet him.

Yet though he smiled he was slightly annoyed with the doctor, whom he thought should have appeared upon the scene to relieve him of his duties before this. He had been obliged to apply to Sir George Carey for leave to prolong his holiday, and though another priest had once more been found to undertake his duty, Sir George had assented with no great willingness. He had told the doctor this and kept him well informed of all that occurred, and he had answered that he would come at the first possible moment but that he had several patients dangerously ill and could not leave them, and a little irritation was doing Sir George no harm. Meanwhile he knew that everything that could be done for Zachary was being done by the Abbé with a far greater skill and efficiency than his own, and he enclosed a letter to be given to his son as soon as that was possible.

The doctor had expressed himself charmingly and gratefully, and with obvious impatience to be done with his patients and on his way to

London, and yet there was an undercurrent of amusement in his letter that suggested that the thought of the Abbé acting as sick nurse to two boys was giving him keen and slightly malicious pleasure. The Abbé's grim smile developed into a chuckle, the first for a very great number of years. Well, it was giving him pleasure too. He had not known he had it in him to be so expert at washing and feeding the young, sweeping, dusting and shopping, and his own efficiency had warmed the cockles of his heart. And so had the boys' trust in him and reliance upon him. Long ago he had looked after Thérèse in her illness, and helped her care for the child, but he thought that he had lost the trick of the old tenderness. Apparently not, and its reappearance was like the resurgence of spring. Standing with aloof distaste before the butcher, and withering that worthy with the coldness of his eye (for no matter how domesticated he became his fastidious taste would never approve raw meat) he suddenly remembered the day at Torre when he felt that the ice of his winter was cracking. . . . It had gone now and he was alive. . . . He clapped the meat in the basket and strode off home to Zachary, who by this time would have woken up and be starving again. He could not endure to leave him for long. He was like a blackbird who had but the one leggy fledgling squawking for food in a green nest.

## CHAPTER VII

### I

THEY were amazingly happy together. "Like Elisha and the son of the Shunamite woman must have been after the boy woke up," thought Zachary that same evening. He lay with his arms behind his head, watching the Abbé. The dusk was blue outside the window and ten minutes earlier the candle had been lit. It illumined the Abbé's bent white head, his absorbed face and his fine hand guiding the quill pen over the paper, but left the rest of the room in shadow.

Zachary sighed luxuriously. He had eaten a large supper, gone to sleep again and awakened to the most extraordinary sense of well-being. For a brief moment body, mind and spirit were so gently at rest, so in tune with the hour and the place, that he felt a sense of liberation that was like that of a floating spirit. The Abbé's candle-flame was like a star, and there were others in the evening sky above the tree-tops. The small green room was so high above the world that he might have been drifting among the stars, enclosed within his own airiness like light in a soap bubble; if he had not been so lazy he could have stretched out his hand

and picked the near star like a flower. He shut his eyes, trying to hold the perfection of the moment. But the effort to keep it destroyed it. The soap bubble vanished, and he fell abruptly out of it, down into that sense of utter futility that for earthbound mortals must needs snuff out the heavenly moments almost as soon as born. Memories of Newgate flashed before him, and the pangs of indigestion once more attacked him. . . . He had eaten too much again. . . . He turned his head away from the light, fighting a ridiculous desire to cry, and sneezed instead.

" 'And the child sneezed seven times and the child opened his eyes'," quoted the Abbé, and put the cork in his ink bottle.

Zachary laughed unsteadily. The two of them had achieved so close a friendship that the thought of one often echoed the thought of the other.

"I'm not presuming to liken myself to the prophet Elisha," continued the Abbé, "it's merely the meagre furnishings of this apartment —a bed, a table, a chair and a candlestick—that reminded me of that little chamber on the wall."

Zachary was visited by a vivid memory of the evening when the Abbé had brought him home here, when he had been very ill indeed. " 'And he shut the door upon them twain and prayed unto the Lord'," he said, and somehow he managed to make of the quietly spoken words an expression of gratitude so heartfelt that there would never be any need for another.

The Abbé got up and touched the boy gently on the shoulder: it was the perfect gesture of acceptance. "I had no idea you were so observant that first night," he said lightly.

"I think I'm always observant," said Zachary. "It's a mistake."

"Why?"

"It's harder, afterwards, to forget."

"You appear low in your mind," said the Abbé.

"And a moment ago I was a floating star," said Zachary bitterly.

"Convalescence," commented the Abbé, and pulled the table, the candle and the chair beside the bed. "I've finished transcribing this story of Stella's. I've translated it into modern English, as simple as I can make it. Easy for her. Would you like to hear it?"

Zachary flushed with pleasure, yet hesitated. "Ought not she to hear it first?" he asked.

"It's as much your story as it is hers."

"My story?"

"And mine," said the Abbé, trimming the candle wick. "Now possess your soul in patience, for the first part of this story will be already familiar to you."

II

It was the story of the hermit's rescue from shipwreck by the monks of Torre, familiar and yet strange, because told now from a new angle, told by the hermit himself. He described his fear in the dreadful storm, his prayer for deliverance and his vow made under the impulse of his fear, just before the waves swept him from the ship and darkness came upon him. He described the awaking from the darkness, to find himself a sick man in the Abbey of Torre. He spoke a little of the suffering of mind and body that he endured at that time, of the great goodness of the monks and of his slow recovery. Then he described the despair that came upon him when he remembered the vow that he had made. "For I was a man of this world," he wrote, "a great sinner, a man of little faith, and that prayer for deliverance in the storm had been almost the first prayer of my life. Who was I that I should dare to offer my worthless soul to a God Who through all my life had been consistently insulted by my unbelief and sin? How was it possible that I could spend the rest of my life in prayer for others who had as yet prayed scarcely at all, and then only for myself? How could I endure the loneliness of a hermit's life, the dereliction and the pain, I who had lived softly all my days, who had known pride of race, honour and fame, and could know them again if I would? I could not do this thing. It was impossible."

In much torment of mind, he said, he went walking one day in one of the meadows that stretched between the Abbey and the sea, and weariness overtaking him he sat upon a rock to rest. The beauty of the world about him, the deep blue sky high spread with silver clouds, the sea, dancing with light, the rippling meadow grass, suddenly became intolerable to him, like a mockery of his distress, and he shut his eyes against the green, the silver and the blue. But it was the season of larks and he was not able to stop his ears against their singing. He put his fingers in his ears but the gesture seemed to him so paltry, so childish, that he removed them again, and in that moment the soaring music seized him, lifted him up. He felt himself transfixed, captured, nailed by his vow to the hard wood of the impossible thing that he had to do. He sat there rigid, as though he were indeed nailed, and fear worse than he had known in the shipwreck put a foul taste in his mouth, and sent the sweat trickling down his back; for that had been the fear of death, a thing soon over, and this was the fear of life. He was only forty-five years old, and the impossible life that he had vowed he would live might last for a very long time.

If there could be vouchsafed to him some sign, he thought, some voice or touch or heavenly vision to inform his struggling faith with certainty. A man could not face the impossible in cold blood. There must be some word spoken. . . . Something. . . . He waited and there was nothing at all

But the cold iron was still transfixing him and something of its hardness entered into him. Very well then, let there be nothing; only his vow and the hard wood behind his back.

He opened his eyes and they were dazzled by a flash of heavenly blue. Bewildered, he shut them and opened them again. What was it? Only a patch of gentian growing there beside the grey rock, like a bit of sky fallen down upon the earth. It must have been there all the time, though he had not noticed it. Gazing stupidly at the flowers he became aware of some one with him, standing beside him. It was Brother Thomas, a very old lay brother who had once cooked for the community. He was too old to do anything now but sit on a bench outside the Abbey walls, his hands on his knees, and blink at the sun like a cat; and occasionally, as now, stroll out into the meadows and take a look at the sea.

But it was not at the sea that he was looking now but at the patch of gentian, and there began in his throat that strange rumbling that now in his old age always preceded the few difficult words that he occasionally spoke.

" 'The eternal Word leaped down from heaven out of His mighty throne'," he croaked, and turning round ambled slowly off towards the Abbey again.

The other man stayed where he was, staring at the gentians. Down from the height of heaven to the lowest depth of his need had come this word of assurance. What more did he want? Nothing else. It was enough.

It continued enough, and supported him through the long, hard weeks of the building of the chapel, and the even harder years of prayer within it. Of what he endured, learning the life of prayer, he spoke to no one. For a man of his temperament it was a grim life that he lived alone on his hill-top. It had its rewards, but of these he could not speak either. Yet he was glad when some twelve years later he fell ill and the monks of Torre carried him down to the Abbey to die. He was not yet sixty but he looked an old man, white-haired, with a white beard flowing to his waist.

For two weeks he lay dying in the Abbey infirmary, but he was no longer absorbed in his devotions, as the monks had expected him to be, but intently watching all that went on around him. From his bed in the corner he watched the Infirmarian and his assistants at work. He saw sick men and women and little children come and go, watched the brothers bandage them, dose them, advise and comfort them. Many of them had homes to go back to, and families to care for them, but others, vagabonds, strolling players, travelling tinkers and friendless old men, had not, and these were put to bed in the infirmary and lay there around him, his brothers in pain. And watching all this there swept over the hermit a flood of bitter misery because he himself had never laboured with his body for the sick and suffering. Forty-five years of his life had he wasted in consideration only of himself, serving his king and country bravely, it was true, but with an eye to his own fame and honour far more than theirs, and the short span of twelve years that he had given to God had been spent entirely in prayer. It was true that he had spent himself in prayer for the suffering, for as time had gone on he had seen his vow to pray for those in peril of storm as something that embraced not only storms at sea but the storms of sorrow and pain and temptation as well, but with his own hands he had not served them and that to him in his death was a great sorrow.

Lying awake at night he thought of all the men who perhaps in their dying had felt, or would feel, as he did. He thought of the Crusaders fighting for the holy places, with little time for prayer and perhaps no aptitude for tenderness. He thought of the scholars and teachers whose preoccupation with the things of the mind had made them poor bunglers at everything else. He thought of the Infirmarian himself, who had told him one day that when the time came for him to say the offices with the other brothers he was often too tired to keep his attention upon the words he said. And then he thought of some tragic lives he knew of in which there had been nothing at all but pain. And for them all he grieved. In one life only had the fighting, the healing, the teaching, the praying and the suffering held equal and perfect place, and that life could never on earth be lived again. For some dying men, he thought, there would have been comfort in the old belief that a soul comes back to earth again and again, the fighter returning to pray and the teacher to heal. Once he had half believed that himself but now he could not. Once only had the perfect life been focused in a human body. He had not returned. Why should he? The Word now taught and healed, fought and suffered, through the yielded wills of other men.

And thinking this there gradually came to him complete and utter comfort in the thought of the one-ness of all men with each other and their God. Of all the illusions which torment the minds of men one of the worst is the illusion of separateness. Increasingly, through the last week of his life, the hermit knew that. Watching the Infirmarian bathing the sores of a sick child he knew it was his own hands, lying inert upon the blanket, that were at work; and that held within his own prayerful soul and one with it the soul of that wearied and harassed man was pouring itself out in prayer.

And then considering the special avocations of men and women in this world he perceived another sort of unity between them that was of a more human sort, held within the other that was larger and more Godlike, the unity of temperament and circumstance. He thought of the company of the martyrs described in the Apocalypse, those who ride upon white horses, clothed in fine linen, white and clean. The army is one but there are many companies of horsemen within the army. Those who have deeply suffered in some particular way are welded together in an understanding incomprehensible to those who have not so suffered; young lovers understand each other, and the men of prayer; and their unity is no hindrance to the larger unity but an enrichment of it, like the gems set in a king's circlet.

During the last hours of his life the hermit was thinking of the men who in centuries yet to come would kneel where he had knelt in the Chapel that he had built upon the hill; men of prayer even as he had been, men of the same company. He prayed that they would waste fewer years in the service of self than he had done, and that their hands as well as their spirits would be active for their God. He was one with these men in the last hour of his life, and the last movement that he was seen to make was the lifting up of his hands, as though he offered them to another to take and use.

III

The Abbé stopped reading and pinched the candle wick again, but Zachary did not speak. It had not seemed to him that the Abbé had been reading some old fairy-tale but telling him about himself. When a man has been telling you his own history you don't find much to say; reverence keeps you silent.

"The first chapter was dated," said the Abbé, "the date was 1274; that is, I suppose, roughly about a hundred years after the founding of the Abbey. The hermit continues his story in 1582."

Zachary opened his mouth to protest. That was more than three-hundred years later. It could not be the same man. Then he shut his mouth again, remembering in what sense it was the same man.

"That first chapter was of course retrospective," said the Abbé. "The whole story was actually written at the same time, in 1582."

Then he turned a page and began to read again.

"I, Brother Johan, Infirmarian of Torre Abbey at the time of its dissolution, have been a fugitive now for many years," he wrote. "Yet a fortunate one, for in this small tower room of Cockington Church I have found once more a cell to dwell in, I can earn my bread by the craft of basket making, in which I have taught myself to be proficient, and the faithful in their goodness bring me many gifts to help me on my way, candles to burn and wood for my fire, so that I live in a comfort that seems to me at times almost sinful. Yet in these long dark winter evenings, when my work is finished, I sometimes find the time hang heavy on my hands, and so I tell myself stories like a child, and as a child does sometimes I write them down and draw little pictures round the margins of my tales. This book in which I write belonged to Brother Simon at the Abbey, and in it he had intended to inscribe a new copy of the psalter. After the king's men had driven us away from the Abbey I came back one day and found it still within his desk, and I took it, together with a few pens, pigments and brushes. I took these treasures of his that I might have some remembrance of him, for he had been my friend, but I have always secretly longed for leisure to practise the art of the scribe and illuminator, and now I have my wish.

"I will not write much of the dissolution of our Abbey, for even now after the passing of so many years it is a memory too bitter to dwell upon. The fair church and library despoiled, the children driven from the school and the sick from the infirmary, the brothers sent away into exile —I cannot write of it. Suffice it to say that of all the White Canons of the Norbertine Order I only remain here a fugitive. I might have escaped to a monastery abroad, as many of the brothers did, I might have gone back into the world as others chose to do, but I remained here, and I had three reasons for my choice.

"The first was the vow that I had taken as a young man. 'I, Brother Johan, do give myself to the Church of Torre.' I gave myself then not only to God, not only to the church, but to this spot of earth as well, and here I belong until I die. And my second reason is the great love that I have for the men and women who live in the fishing hamlets along the coast and in the villages among the round green hills. I have seen them come as children to the Abbey school. I have watched them grow up. I have cared for them in the infirmary. They are my children and I cannot leave them either. Living here I can still go to them when they are in trouble, comfort them, nurse them, teach them and pray for them. I have now more leisure for prayer, and though I can no longer pray in the Abbey Church there still remains the Chapel of St. Michael where three centuries ago the hermit lived and prayed for twelve long years. Why do I write of him in that detached and distant way? He has become to me so much a part of myself that at the beginning of this story I wrote of him as though he was indeed myself. It is because of him, too, that I stay here. He is my chief reason for remaining. His spirit that is part of my spirit is also a part of the life of this fair and gracious plot of earth, is in union with all the men and women who live here and will be until the end of time.

"I became acquainted with his story when I first came to the Abbey as a young novice, for a brief outline of it had been written down by one of the monks after his death, and when I had read the record there came to me instantly the knowledge that this man was my friend. It was because of my sense of friendship with him that when the time came for me to take my vows I took as my name in religion the name that he had taken when he became a hermit—Johan. Then as the years passed the sense of friendship deepened into a mysterious feeling of identity. My imagination, dwelling upon the outline of the story, rounded out the bare bones of it into living flesh and blood. And yet was it only imagination? When I found the gentian that he had carved in the chapel I knew instantly what it commemorated; I saw that patch of living blue beside the grey rock in the meadow, heard the words spoken by old Brother Simon, and there leaped into my heart the same living assurance that had given strength to the hard years of his prayer. And it was the same when I read of his preoccupation with the work going on in the infirmary, when he lay dying there, and of the lifting of his hands. I knew of the reason for both. His hands had been given to me and I must use them as he wished. I told the Father Abbot of the compulsion laid upon me and he made me Infirmarian.

"This work was not at first easy for me, for I am naturally a scholar, and I found it hard to give learning the second place in my life, but I was comforted by the knowledge that others would attain to the learning for which I had no leisure, and that in their striving all men are made one. Perhaps there will one day come to this place a servant of God who will feel himself caught into union with the two men that I am, and in his life, perhaps, the learning that I missed will find equal place with the healing and the prayer. If this is so, may God's blessing rest upon him, and if he reads this book may he think of me as his brother and his friend.

"And John and Rosalind, will they too have close friends among young lovers in the years to come? Without doubt they will, for the company of the young knights who ride out into the world to suffer and to learn is a close-knit company, and so is that of the maidens to whom the slow years teach their patience. Another young man will sing the chant of the plough over the hills, where John sings it now in the years of his fulfilment, and another woman will come to the farmhouse door in the twilight as Rosalind does, a child held upon her hip, the firelight streaming out behind her, and listen for the footstep of a man returning home.

"It was in the Chapel of St. Michael that I first saw John, and I laugh when I remember that he thought I was a dream and I thought he was a vision. Young men and old men dream dreams and see visions and often they are truer than they know.

"Through all these years it has been my habit upon the vigil of the nativity of St. John the Baptist, whose name my friend and I both took when we renounced the world, to visit the Chapel of St. Michael and pray there through the night. And because it is a joyful occasion I take two lanterns, that I think of as two souls, and set them burning in the two niches in the northern wall, that there may be brightness and light around me as I pray. . . . Though often the short June night has been so bright with moon and stars that the radiance of the lanterns has been almost dimmed.

"But upon a certain vigil only a few years after the dissolution of the Abbey it was not so, the night though warm was clouded and dark. After I had entered the Chapel I could see nothing at all, and I had to grope my way to the niches. As I stood thus, lighting the two lanterns, there came to me the knowledge that I was not alone in the chapel; but the sense of being not alone comes to me very often in that holy place, and so I did not look about me but turned at once to the rough-hewn altar of grey stone and kneeled down to pray.

"I do not know for how long I prayed, for perhaps an hour or more, and then I was disturbed by a slight movement behind me. This time I did look round and saw a beautiful boy standing in the glow of the lantern light. He was tall and slender, yet strongly built, dark-eyed and fine-featured with rough dark hair. He stood very erect and he had a sheep-skin slung about his shoulders. Even so, in many old pictures, the young St. Johan stands watchfully behind the figures of Our Lady and the Child. For a moment we looked at each other and his eyes were wide with wonder, but he did not move.

" 'Your name, young Sir?' I asked him. Even as my lips formed the words I marvelled that I dared to speak; yet I had to know.

" 'John,' he answered gently.

"And then I bent my head before the first heavenly vision that had ever been vouchsafed me.

"Yes, they are from heaven, these visions, even though when we look more steadily at the blinding loveliness we find it to be of earth. A patch of blue gentian, a young boy's beauty, a wild swan flying, what are they but the Word?

" 'Sir!' he said, 'Sir!' and it was the human distress in his voice that made me look up again and see him for what he was, a rather scared young lad who thought of me too as some vision of the night. And perhaps I was rather a frightening figure, for my beard and my hair had gone white and I wore my tattered old monk's habit with a rope round my waist. I went to him and gave him my hand, that he might feel it warm flesh and blood, and we sat down together upon the old grey rock that thrusts itself through the Chapel floor.

" 'Why are you here, my son?' I asked.

" 'I came to pray,' he said.

" 'Are you troubled, my son?'

"He did not answer and his mouth set a little obstinately. I did not question him further, for youth has many tumultuous troubles of which it cannot speak to age, and which age can ease only by prayer. I said, 'And when you had prayed, you slept?'

" 'Yes,' he said, and then smiling at me with that same wonder, as though the grasp of my hand had not convinced him that I was flesh and blood, 'I had doubted the truth of it.'

" 'Of what?' I asked him.

" 'The story of the man who was rescued from the storm and who built this chapel and prayed here for those in peril at sea.'

" 'He lives,' I said, 'and you may yet be grateful for his prayers.'

"He looked at me again and the wonder in his eyes was clouded with sleep. 'You are only half awake, my son,' I said. 'Lie down and finish your rest.'

"He lay down and in a moment he was asleep. I wondered that he could sleep so easily in this strange place, with only his sheep-skin coat to protect him from the hard rough floor; but youth, utterly wearied out, will sleep anywhere. I watched him for a little, marvelling at his beauty, and I saw that by his side there lay a small carved huntsman's horn with a silver band round it. Towards morning, after I had prayed again, I extinguished the lanterns and left the chapel. The boy was still asleep. I knew that when he woke he would think me only a dream.

"More than a year passed before I saw John again, and then it was once more at the chapel. It was early December, mild and warm, as the month so often is in the West Country, yet already in the cottages and farms the children were beginning to chatter of Christmas, to make their gifts and hide them away in secret corners, and string berries together as Christmas decorations.

"One late afternoon, just as twilight was deepening to night, I went to the chapel to pray. I was weary and sad that day and toiled up the path slowly, with bent head. When I was nearly at the top I stopped to get my breath, and looked up, and the sight that I saw was so lovely that weariness and sadness dropped from me like a cloak. A fairy-tree, I thought, a fairy-tree trimmed with celestial light. But it was only the old storm-twisted yew tree that in those days grew beside the chapel door, transformed by the witchery of the hour to a thing of beauty. Behind its dark branches was a sky of cool deep green, deepening to gentian blue, and the few stars that twinkled there shone through the branches like silver lights hung upon them. The sickle moon hung upon a branch too; or so I thought until I looked again and saw it was a bugle hanging there. Beneath the branch where the bugle hung stood a young boy and girl, the girl hardly more than a child. A lighted lantern set upon the ground beside them illumined the delicate beauty of their grave faces and the flowing colour of the fairy-tale clothes they wore. I thought that her dress was of rose and silver, and his jerkin of pale green belted with scarlet, but I could not be sure, for there was a transparency about those two figures, a gossamer lightness, that escaped the clumsy grasp of my clogged and earthly senses. They were the spirit of youth itself there beneath the tree, fragile, innocent, gone as soon as seen, like a rainbow or the flash of a kingfisher's wing beside a stream.

"Yet their faces I did not forget, for the bewildered first grief of the young is a thing that age, witnessing it, can scarcely endure. The girl's elfin face was blanched with sorrow under the dark cloud of her hair. Her cheek was laid against her lover's breast, her face turned a little towards me so that I saw the poignant droop of her child's mouth, her wide dark woman's eyes tearless but clouded with selfless fear. The boy's arms were about her, her hands clung to his shoulders, but had he let go of her she would not, I think, have fallen. Though the lissom curves of her body, of her gown that flowed about them both, were all grace, there was a hint of strength in her figure. I had less fear for her in this sorrow of parting than for the boy. He was John, grown older, but still, I thought, a dreamer of dreams upon whom the stark realities of life would fall with a brutal force. Her face had the stillness that lies over reserves of strength like ice over deep water, his the strained intensity of strength that is taxed to the utmost. He began to whisper to her. 'I will come back. I will come back. Do not forget, Rosalind. Do not forget.' She did not answer but she turned to look up at him and lifted her hands with the gesture of a mother to pull his face down to hers. Shame woke in me. What was I doing here? I turned quickly that I might not see them kiss and made my way back the way I had come. I had meant to keep vigil all night in the chapel, I kept it instead here in my tower room, and it was the first of many that I kept for the boy and girl beneath the fairy-tree."

## IV

"It was three years before I saw them again, and once more it was December, but bitterly cold this time, with a wild wind racing in from the sea. Yet I went to the chapel at nightfall, for all day I had been restless and full of dread, aware of the storm that was coming and tormented by a dream I had had in which I had seen John's body rolling limply in the trough of a huge towering wave of green fire. The wave had had a devilish look about it, and had been white-fanged like some monster. When it had reared itself over John's unconscious face I had woken up in my tower room crying out loud in horror and rage. The hours of the day were leaden, but at nightfall, with my lantern alight in one of the niches and my body in stillness before the altar, the hermit and his peace were with me and his prayer aflame in my soul was a flame of power.

"It was strange that the sound of her light footstep could reach me through the sound of the rising wind, yet I did hear it, and turning I saw her standing framed in the doorway. How fair she was, this Rosalind! Tall now, and grown from a child to a maiden, yet still with the same elfin face, the same strength that gave to her slim body a look of resilience, like a silver birch that bends but will never break in the storm. The wind had whipped a faint colour into her cheeks and the hood of the blue cloak she wore had fallen back from her dark hair. Under her cloak her full skirts were deep crimson and in the hollow of her neck a jewel glowed. Her tanned skin showed her country bred but she was no peasant girl. She stood for a moment as a queen might do, then curtsyed and bent her head.

There was awe and bewilderment in her eyes when she rose from her curtsy and I wondered if she too, like John that first night, thought me a vision or a dream. But I could not wait to tell her who I was, for at sight of her there had come to me instant knowledge of what we must do.

" 'The storm that is coming tonight will be the worst since this chapel was built,' I said, 'and John's ship will soon be out there in the bay. Have you the courage to come down to the shore and face the storm with me? His safety depends on you.'

"She did not ask me how I knew this, nor could I have told her if she had asked. She merely nodded and turned round again towards the storm from which she had come. I followed her and we climbed down the hill together.

" 'John has been at sea, fighting the Spaniards,' she said. 'He has been away three years.'

" 'And you have not forgotten him.'

" 'He is unforgettable,' she answered proudly.

"Then the fury of the wind caught us and we did not speak again. Clinging together we fought our way down to the shore. The waves were pounding thunderously on the beach, the blown spume stung our faces like fire and it was bitterly cold. The clouds were like phantom horses in full gallop, trampling the stars as they fled across the sky. We found a little shelter behind an outcrop of rock, and now and then, in the intervals of watching the sea, we crouched there and talked a little.

" 'Down under the sea there is a forest buried,' said Rosalind. 'The fishermen bring up the musons of harts in their nets. It is quiet down there, but the water is swaying a little now because of the storm above, and the bell of the church in the forest is ringing. We should hear it if the wind were not so loud. Once huntsmen rode through those woods, winding their horns, as John did once in the Berry Pomeroy woods.'

" 'There is a castle built upon a hill deep in those woods,' I said.

" 'I live there,' she answered.

" 'And not far from it I have seen a farmhouse set among orchards. Its windows look upon a green hill where sheep are folded.'

" 'That's John's home,' she said. 'And before he went away he kept the sheep on that hill.'

"There in the darkness of the storm, partly from what Rosalind told me and partly from the exercise of my own imagination and intuition, I pieced together the story that I now set down. Later I verified some of it from the talk of the countryside, yet it came to me that night in a series of pictures so vivid that I could not doubt their truth any more than I had been able to doubt the truth of the picture of Johan opening his eyes to the vision of the gentians.

"The first picture that I saw was that of a young girl leaning out of a window high in a castle tower. Beneath her shimmered the spring green of the woods, and down below the sea of leaves she could hear the hunt go by. She propped her chin in her hands and looking down at the swaying green tree-tops, with here and there the spire of a blossoming wild cherry tree reaching up to the light, she thought them like tumbled green waves, foam-flecked and beautiful. . . . And down below in the depths of the sea the hunt went by. . . . The sun was warm on her face and perhaps she dreamed a little, for the sound of a horn startled her awake. It was silvery clear and near at hand, and its music was like a stab of pain at her heart. Who was coming up the hill? A merman from the depths of the sea, riding upon a white horse? A fairy huntsman? The prince who had ridden through the wood to awake the Sleeping Beauty in her bower? Her cheeks were flushed and her eyes bright as she watched and listened. The leaves parted and he rode up out of the green sea, a sunburnt boy riding a dappled pony. He wore a sheep-skin coat and a horn was slung over his shoulder. He was singing as he rode up the green slope beneath the castle wall, but he did not look up. On the window-sill beside Rosalind was a bowl of spring flowers, gentians, star-of-Bethlehem, campion and bluebells. She took them out of the bowl and just as he rode beneath the window she dropped them on him. He shook his head as a young colt might do as the wet flowers fell about him, pulled his pony to a standstill and looked up laughing. But when he saw the girl at the window he did not laugh, and neither did she. For a full minute they looked at each other in silence, and then he asked her, 'What is your name?'

" 'Rosalind.'

" 'My name is John.'

"That was enough. With just the telling of their names to each other they plighted their troth.

" 'Do you know Bowerly Hill?' he asked her.

" 'Is that the hill with the broken stone wall at the top? Someone is building a little house with the stones.'

" 'I am building a shepherd's hut,' said John. 'I'll be there tomorrow at sunset, with the sheep.'

"A handful of gentians and star-of-Bethlehem were scattered over his pony's mane. Without looking at her again he made a little posy of them and stuck them in his sheep-skin coat, and then he rode away, down once more beneath the sea of green leaves, and she heard the sound of his horn dying away in the distance.

"She went to Bowerly Hill the next day at sunset, just when the gulls were flying home to the sea, and hidden by the grey stone wall of the shepherd's hut that he was building they talked for a little, and then they kissed each other. That kiss gave them courage and after that they rode about the countryside together, he on his dappled pony and she on her chestnut palfrey. They were both of them motherless children and their preoccupied fathers knew nothing of what they did. If others saw them they kept their counsel.

"They had two favourite meeting-places, Bowerly Hill and the Chapel of St. Michael, where John believed he had once seen the old hermit in a dream. He had always loved this chapel. He had found it first when he was quite a small boy and had run away from home after his hard and unloving father had given him a beating for no just cause. He had had a vague idea that he would run away to sea, but when he reached the coast at Torre he had seen the chapel on the hill and had climbed up there to see what it was like inside. It had been peaceful and quiet in the chapel and he had sat there and rested, and out of the quiet there had somehow come to him the knowledge that the time to go to sea was not yet. It would come later. Now he must go back and just endure his father's injustice and his unloving home. And he had gone back, and had endured grimly, until the finding of Rosalind filled his life with joy.

"Because it was one of their meeting-places he loved the chapel more than ever, and the shepherd's hut that he was building on Bowerly Hill out of the stones of the old wall, ostensibly for the lambing season, became in his mind another chapel, and himself another hermit building it. To make it as like the other as he could he dug up a young yew tree from the Weekaborough garden and planted it there, and to make it holy, like the churchyard yews, he cut the sign of the cross on its bark. And again to make it like the other chapel he cut a gentian on one of the stones.

"It was about this time that he began to trim the garden yews into fantastic shapes. He was skilled in topiary, as in all garden crafts. His father cared nothing for the garden and did not mind what he did in it. He was the gardener, the bee-man, the shepherd, and the singer of the ploughman's chant over the hills, and his father attended to the cattle, the crops and the business of the farm.

"A year passed and the joy of his love for Rosalind began to turn to pain and bewilderment. She was still hardly more than a child but he was growing up, and he saw clearly that soon they would have to do one of two things, either part from each other or get married. But how could he marry her, when he was a farmer's son and she a great lady? His mother, too, had been a great lady, who had run away from home to marry his father, and he had her blood in his veins, and the lovely hunting horn which had been one of her heirlooms; but still, he was only a farmer's son.

"He went up to Bowerly Hill one warm summer night of moon and stars and sat down outside the half-built hut. Behind him his sapling yew stood like a tall spear planted in the ground, and in front of him a line of silver that was the quiet sea stretched along the horizon. And here he fought his battle and made his decision. He would do what he had tried to do as a young boy; he would go to sea. England was at war with Spain and had great need of seamen. He would go to Plymouth and join a ship there. If they doubted his usefulness he would tell them he was an expert drummer. He was. His father's father had sailed to the Indies and back as ship's drummer and his drum was now in the Weekaborough attic, and almost since his babyhood John had practised upon it. If he stayed here, sheltered within these green hills like a sheep in its fold, he would never be anything but just a dreaming shepherd boy, but if he went to sea, and fought, and saw the world, he might perhaps come back a man whom Rosalind would be allowed to marry.

"Though he was a humble boy he was aware of latent powers within him. He knew that through his mother there had come to him a sensitiveness that his father could not begin to understand, and the capacity for fine manners and clear thought. It had occurred to him on rare occasions, when he looked in the mirror in the green parlour, that perhaps she had given him a little of her beauty too. And so he must go away, step outside the peaceful blindness of his fold and see life as it is in the place where the skies rip open and men see death in all its terror and courage in all its might. But it was not an easy decision to make for he loved this spot of earth passionately, and the thought of parting for years from Rosalind, a very young girl who might easily forget him, was almost unbearable. And he was not very brave either. The fold was more to his taste than the unclosing skies. And so the battle that he fought on the hillside was the hardest of his life.

"The countryside had been used to the sound of John's horn sounding over the hills, but for a little while after this those going home late would hear the sound of distant drumming, and wonder where it came from. It came from Bowerly Hill, where John was practising the ancient art of the Devon seamen.

"Then he said goodbye to Rosalind and sailed away to the other side of the world, and for years endured a life that for most of that time was exactly his idea of hell. But in the intervals of battle and storm, wounds, fever, hunger and thirst, he learned a good deal more besides courage and the arts of war and seamanship. He sailed under a fine captain who was much attached to him and finally made him his secretary. There was a chaplain on board who brought him books to read when he was ill and admitted him to the joys of scholarship. When he sailed away from Devon he was drummer-boy and messed with the crew. When he sailed home again he was dining with the captain, and he had learned the manners of gentlemen and their way of thought. Yet he still wanted to be a farmer; only the kind of farmer whom Rosalind would be allowed to marry. But after three years had she forgotten him and married another man? During the last weeks of the journey home the thought that he might have lost her was like a mounting nightmare, that reached its culmination on the last night of all, when within sight of England their battered unseaworthy ship was caught in a storm. Then the thought of loss suffered a sea change. As he fought with the rest of the crew for the life of the ship he was tormented by the thought that she was faithful but that he, within a few miles of her, was deserting love for death and in so doing would bring grief upon her.

"And now I bring my narrative back once more to the storm-swept beach at Torre. Fishermen, and all folk who live close to the sea, develop a strange extra sense by which they know when a ship is in distress even before they hear the boom of the gun, or catch through the flying spray a glimpse of the wounded hart being hounded to death by the white horsemen of the sea. And so it was no surprise to me, a little later, with no distress signals to be heard or seen, to find that Rosalind and I were no longer alone on the beach. Several men were there, uneasy, straining their eyes to see what as yet could not be seen. Rosalind and I joined them and it was she who first saw the stricken ship. A groan went up from the men on the beach when they saw her too. Her mainmast had gone and she was rolling helplessly. The tide was coming in now and the wind rising all the time. The moon was at the full and to our right we could see large rollers dashing against the sea-wall in front of Torre Abbey, shooting up in masses of spray and then falling into the meadows beneath the elm and ash trees. If any men managed to leave the ship their rescue in that terrible sea would be almost impossible. Yet more men, and women too, came hurrying down to the shore, and the old fight that all knew so well started yet again. Rosalind and I were separated now but I caught sight of her working as hard as any there, helping to drag the boats down the beach as though she had a man's strength. But only a few boats got away from the shore; the rest were swamped and we were hard put to it to rescue the rescuers.

"I do not remember now how many men were saved from the wreck but I know it was very few. But I do remember how Rosalind saved John, for it seemed to me then that his rescue was miraculous, and I think so still. I saw her running along the shore towards Torre Abbey. The beach had disappeared now for the sea was right in the meadows. In the bright moonlight I saw the gleam of her blue cloak flying back from her shoulders like wings, the green grass, the flying silver spray, and the sight was beautiful and strange. I followed her, but the wind was so fierce that I could scarcely make headway against it; and yet she ran as though the strength of her wings was greater than the wind's power. There are so many old stories of little children who have fallen from high places and floated down gently as though upon wings, and others of the saints who have travelled from one place to some other where they were sorely needed with the speed of birds, as though they anticipated powers which do not belong to man while he remains in this earthly body but which may be his hereafter. I had disbelieved all these stories until that night.

"I fought my way at last to the end of the meadow, where it adjoined the park of Torre Abbey, and there was her blue cloak lying on the grass, as though it were not her wings that she was needing now. Though I stood upon grass, ripples of sea water were washing round my feet and waves were breaking only a few feet from me. The moon came out from behind a cloud and I saw her again, up to her waist in water, looking like some wild sea-maiden with her skirts floating about her on the water and her dark hair streaming in the wind.

"A huge wave was gliding in towards her with smooth but terrible speed, a great curve of green fire soaring higher and higher, crested with foam. In another moment it would soar up to the apex of its arch and break in thunder. She bent a little towards it, her arms outstretched, and I knew what she saw within its curve, for it was the wave of my dream. I tried to fight my way towards her through the lesser waves, but I was like a man in a nightmare, my feet weighted with lead and my heart pounding with fear. She would not be able to keep her feet. It would not have been possible for even the strongest of men to keep his feet when that wave broke. It soared up over her head and the thunder all along the shore deafened me and the flying spray blinded my eyes as I fought my way through it. When I could see again she was still on her feet, her arms gripped tightly round the body of the man who would have been dashed to death on the shore had she not been there to save him.

"I reached her and we dragged him to the meadow together. I looked at his face and scarcely recognised the beautiful boy whom I had seen last under the yew tree by the chapel in the lantern light, but I did not say 'He is dead,' for I knew myself in the midst of a miracle that was not yet ended. Rosalind said nothing at all but acted as though the speed of her flight was still with her. She opened the gate that led from the meadow into the park and then spread out the blue cloak on the ground. We laid John on it and carried him up through the park to the Abbey, as once long ago the monks must have carried Johan. The wind was roaring through the trees and behind us the waves pounded against the sea wall. Now and then gleams of moonlight revealed groups of terrified deer huddled together, their antlers shining as though made of silver, and ahead of us the lights of the Abbey showed us the way we must go.

"It seemed a long way to me, so exhausted was I by the carrying of so heavy a burden, and when we reached the great hall of the Abbey it seemed to me all a strange confusion of lights and hurrying figures, for John was not the only half-drowned man to be brought to the Abbey that night, and the fight that had begun on the beach was being continued in the great hall. I was overwhelmed, too, by being once more in this place where I had lived long ago as a monk, and finding it now not a monastery but a private house. Relieved of my burden I think that I sat down in a corner, my head in my hands, to recover my wits and my strength. When I looked up again I saw John lying on the floor not far from me, a strong and skilful fisherman at work upon him. Rosalind knelt beside him, intently watching his unconscious face that was turned towards her. I got up and went to her, touched her on the shoulder and spoke to her, but she did not hear or see me. There was nothing more just now that I could do for those two and so I turned away to do what I could for others.

"The first grey light of dawn was coming through the tall windows when I went back to them again and found John conscious and warmly wrapped in blankets, with Rosalind caring for him. All was well with them both and they were absorbed in each other. Thankfully I made the sign of the cross over them and turned to go home.

"But at the door I lingered a moment, looking back, for they had become like my children to me and I did not like to leave them, and then I saw Rosalind coming after me. She curtsyed to me, as she had done in the chapel, and then she took my hand and said a little breathlessly, 'You have helped us so much. Why? Who are you?'

" 'Johan,' I said. 'He helps and comforts all who come to the chapel. He will always do that, while the chapel stands.'

"I blessed her again and went away into the dawn, which was peaceful and beautiful now that the storm had ceased. I looked back once more and she was leaning against the door, rubbing her knuckles in her eyes like a tired and bewildered child. I knew that I would never see her or John again, though I would hold them within the circle of my prayer for ever, they and all those whose lives in succeeding generations would follow the pattern of their own. And I knew that until the end of their lives they would think of me as a visitor from Paradise, sent to help them in their need; or at least Rosalind would think that, John would perhaps reserve his judgment. But they would not forget Johan, they would reverence him and teach their children to reverence him, until they died, and through them his legend would live on beyond their death. And that was what I wanted.

"And now years have passed and I am a very old man indeed, and near my death, and it had been as I expected and I have not seen them again, though I have heard of them and of their happiness. After the storms of their youth they have, as the old fairy-tales say, lived happy ever after. And now my story is finished and I shall put the book away in the cupboard in the chimney. If it is right that it should be found one day, then it will be found. If not, it will remain unread. I am contented either way. And I am contented, too, at the thought of my approaching death. My spirit will follow the spirit of the hermit to Paradise, but Johan will never leave this spot of earth between the green hills and the sea."

V

When the Abbé had finished reading, the candle had almost burnt away to nothing, and he and Zachary were both silent until a fresh candle had taken its place and had burned up brightly.

"Like this fresh burning up, in our day and time, of the old story," said the Abbé quietly.

"It's beautiful, but very strange," said Zachary.

"Why strange? That story is deep-rooted in that spot of earth. It is right that it should spring up again, and perhaps yet again, as the gentians do. And then, Zachary, the experience of each one of us is not as unique as we think it is. We learn as our fathers learned, suffer much as they did."

"It explains many things," said Zachary. "If my love for Stella is a new flowering of an old love then I need not wonder any more that it came so instantly."

"My instant liking for you is also explained," said the Abbé. "And so is the echo of the hunting horn over Bowerly Hill, and the rolling of the drum."

"Rosalind and John lived out their lives at Weekaborough," said Zachary with satisfaction. "Those two old graves in the churchyard, with gentians carved upon them, must be their graves."

"Possibly. . . . And now do you feel like sleep?"

"Sleep? After that story? No."

"Then tell me how you found Stella."

Zachary told him, and then the talk drifted to love and its mystery. "Love sings to all things which live and are, soothing the troubled minds of gods and men," murmured Zachary, stifling a yawn, for contrary to his expectations he was beginning to feel sleepy.

"Contained in a passage written on a scrap of paper in your Shakespeare," said the Abbé. "It fell out when I was putting the book away."

"The doctor wrote it out for me when I went to sea," said Zachary. "He thought I'd like to have it because it was written on a scrap of paper in Stella's locket."

He was murmuring as a child does who is half asleep, and this time he yawned hugely. He was lying as a child does, curled up on his side, his cheek buried in the crook of his arm, his dark lashes casting huge circular shadows on his hollowed cheek. He looked all hollows and curves, utterly relaxed, drifting into unconsciousness. Then suddenly he tensed, lifted himself on his elbow, as wide awake as he had ever been in his life. What had happened? The Abbé had pulled his chair to the window again and was sitting with his face in shadow, but he had not moved or spoken. There had been no movement at all in the room, no sound, yet it was vibrant with feeling so intense that Zachary felt it pressing upon him, almost unbearably, like that fear that had half stifled him before Trafalgar. He sat up in bed and pity welled up in him. He knew what it was to feel intensely. His extraordinarily mature sympathy reached the man in the chair like a breath of revivifying air. Their positions were suddenly reversed. It was Zachary, still and patiently waiting, who seemed the elder of the two.

The Abbé moved at last and leaned forward with his clasped hands between his knees. "Did the doctor tell you anything about Stella when he gave you that scrap of paper?" he asked. His voice was light, dry and precise, and Zachary's was equally light as he answered across the width of the room, "He told me how she came to be adopted by Father and Mother Sprigg." Yet so unifying a thing is the presence of perfection that each voice seemed to the other to be speaking inside his own soul, as though they had become fused by the need of the one and the perfect response of the other's answering sympathy.

"Tell me all you know about that adoption," said the Abbé.

Zachary told him. He was still completely in the dark, yet aware that each of his gently spoken words, as quietly and evenly uttered as the ticks of a clock, were ageing the Abbé like so many years. For the impact of great joy can in the first moments be as anguishing as the impact of grief; perhaps more so for it has not the benumbing quality of grief. For in the depths of his soul man expects happiness sometime, somewhere, somehow. Suddenly drenched in light he is not stunned by unbelief as he is when the heavens darken and the floods descend. Zachary knew it was joy to which the story that he told was leading; he was aware of it serenely and steadily reaching up through the turmoil of the first anguish. He finished his story and waited, but not to be told anything, only to see what he could do next. It was good to serve this man, who had so selflessly served him.

The Abbé moved, unclasped his hands, stretched out his arms and let them fall with a gesture of release over the arms of his chair. "Years ago I had a wife and child," he said to Zachary. "I thought that I had lost them both in the wreck of the *Amphion*. Now—I think—that I still have a child."

The light of moon and candle together seemed to Zachary most extraordinarily bright. It half blinded him. He shut his eyes and then opened them again. The Abbé had moved in his chair so that the moonlight fell full upon his face. But Zachary did not see it. Instead he saw Stella's face in the moonlight, her chin propped upon the top of the gate. "What a fool I've been," he said softly. "Only you and Stella have such dark grey eyes, set like that, bright, hard to look into steadily. And the shape of your hands, and—so many things." He paused, aware of what he had to do next. "The night is nearly over, I think. You told me once that you liked being out of doors when the dawn came."

The Abbé got up abruptly. That was what he wanted. To be out, striding through the streets alone. But first he crossed to the bed and stood looking down at Zachary. "There is no one," he said, "not even your father the doctor, whom I would rather have had tell me this piece of news than you."

He was gone in a flash, closing the door soundlessly behind him, but Zachary just heard what he was saying to himself as he went out " '. . . she lives. . . . It is a chance which does redeem all sorrows that ever I have felt.' "

He had been lying on the Abbé's study table after the wrestling, he remembered, when he had first heard him quote those words. How much there was to think about! Yet alone now to think about it he found himself quite too extraordinarily tired to think about anything. He turned over on his other side, cradled his cheek in the crook of his arm again, and was instantly asleep.

## VI

He was awakened hours later by the smell of coffee and the clink of china, but when he turned round expecting to see the Abbé's tall, sword-straight black figure outlined against the window he saw instead the rugged head and bowed sagging shoulders of the doctor.

"Father!" he almost shouted.

The doctor grunted an acknowledgment of the greeting but did not turn his head. "One thing at a time, now," he said. "I'm busy with this coffee. I've taken a look at you while you were asleep. You'll do."

Zachary smiled. The richness and warmth of the doctor's deep voice seemed to bring all the splendour of the English countryside tumbling about him, the hot glow of the cornfields, the hum of the bees, the smell of the clover. "You'll do." It was England speaking. He'd loved her and served her. She was pleased.

The doctor finished preparing breakfast, crossed to the bed and stood looking down again at Zachary. "Awake, you'll still do, my son," he said, and the warmth of his voice deepened to a husky tenderness. His eyes twinkled brightly and his weatherbeaten, tanned, ugly face was irradiated with his pride. Then his tone changed abruptly. "Get up, you lazy hound! Breakfasting in bed like a lady of fashion! If you call this breakfast. Coffee and rolls. Dammee, I could do with a couple of fried eggs and a slice of ham."

Grinning, Zachary got out of bed. His legs buckled under him as he crossed to the press where the Abbé had put his clothes, and the doctor steadied him with a grip of iron above the elbow. The grip suddenly put more strength into him than all the Abbé's cossettings. "Yet, by gad, he was good to me," muttered Zachary. "But he was not you."

With one arm round his son the doctor opened the door of the press and pulled out Zachary's clothes. Then he helped him to dress, pushed him into the chair and perching on the window-sill poured out the coffee.

"I came as soon as I could," he said. "You know that. I got in too late last night to do anything but tumble into bed at the inn. Coming along this morning I met Monsieur de Colbert outside the baker's. After a few moments' conversation we turned about and made for the inn again. A west-country coach leaves this morning. He just caught it. In the inn yard I took the rolls and he took my bag. It had a few necessaries for the journey in it, a razor and so on. Also a book on diseases of the liver which won't interest him. I must now make do with his razor, and his breviary, which won't interest me."

"Stella's fairy-story will interest you," said Zachary softly. "He told you about Stella?"

"Yes. Between the baker's shop and the coach he told me a good deal. I will say for a Frenchman that reeling though he may be under whatever shock of joy or grief, and after a sleepless night, he remains a sustained and generally coherent conversationalist."

"You were surprised about Stella?"

"Immensely surprised, naturally, to find the Abbé possessed of a daughter, for I had not suspected him of matrimony. But not surprised to find my Stella a princess. Well, not quite that perhaps, but I understand that the little thing could have called many a dead prince cousin."

Zachary's faced blanched.

"Tired?" asked the doctor.

"No, Sir."

The doctor regarded him steadily. "Got those dead princes on your mind? You've the blood of Irish kings in your veins, my son. You're alive, too. That's an advantage in a husband."

Zachary laughed. "You're making great haste," he said.

"She's making great haste to grow up—the white witch," said the doctor. Then he grew suddenly sombre. "Poor Mother Sprigg," he muttered. "I wish I could be there to soften the blow when the Abbé tells her. Poor Mother Sprigg."

## CHAPTER VIII

### I

"STELLA?" asked Mrs. Loraine, glancing up at the Abbé as they stood together in her parlour. "Must you see her at once?"

"I would like to see her as soon as it is conveniently possible, Madame," said the Abbé. "She is at Torre, I know, for I have just come from Weekaborough and they told me she was with you today."

"You have been at Weekaborough so early in the morning?"

"I had business with the worthy couple there." He spoke with a studied courtesy that only thinly veiled his wild impatience. He looked like a heron poised on one leg ready for flight, she thought. But looking again at his face she saw a sudden look of youth flash across it that for the brief moment of its passing made her heart miss a beat and her cheeks flush. Suddenly, overwhelmingly, she remembered what it was like to be passionately loved by a man, and put a hand on the mantelpiece to steady herself. That she should remember like this, remember so vividly in her old age! It was that look on his face, gone now. Had he been such a lover as the man she remembered? She sat down in her chair, her knees shaking slightly. She lifted her hands and looked at them, surprised to see them so withered. The fires of youth are not dead in old age, she had just discovered, only banked down.

"Stella?" repeated the Abbé.

"She went with Araminta to the almshouses. We heard that old Granny Bogan died in her sleep last night. Stella wished to take a bunch of flowers to lay on her bed. I gave Araminta strict injunctions, of course, that the child should not be allowed to see the body."

"It would not disturb Stella if she did see it," said the Abbé. "She is a country-bred child and would see it for what it is, an empty husk with the living grain gone from it."

He made the sign of the cross and said a wordless prayer for Granny Bogan. He remembered the day when they had met and reverenced each other. Then he crossed his arms on his breast in an effort to still the impatience there.

"You know so much about Stella," said Mrs. Loraine a little wistfully.

He bent, took her hand and kissed it with the ceremonious courtesy that was expected of him. "It is because of your great kindness that I know it, Madame," he said. "I should have known nothing had you not given your workbox to a little girl for a Christmas present. Later, Madame, I shall have so much to tell you. Will you excuse me now?"

She smiled and withdrew her hand. "You'll meet her on her way home with Araminta."

From one of the windows of the parlour she saw him striding along Robber's Lane, and was reminded no longer of a heron or a man in love but of the giant who wore the seven-league boots.

II

He went so fast that he encountered Stella and Araminta in Cockington park, not far from the church. Under Araminta's severe eye he and Stella greeted each other with a very correct bow and curtsy. He looked at her once, hungrily, and then away. No wonder her smile had so stabbed him at their first meeting, for it was Thérèse's own. She had his mother's eyes, that she had handed on to her sons. There was race in every line of her body, and in her slim hands. She would be tall when she was full grown, tall and very slender. Though he was looking away from her he saw her still.

He turned to Araminta. "Will you go back to your mistress, Araminta? I have her permission to greet your young charge after my return from London."

He turned to Stella and offered his arm. She took it sedately but it was with a child's eagerness that she looked up at him. "Shall we go to the church, mon Père? I want to show you the birds there."

Araminta curtsyed and departed homewards in high dudgeon. Birds in the church indeed! There were no birds in the church so far as she knew. Bats in the belfry, perhaps. She'd always doubted if the man had the full possession of his wits. Treating the child like a princess in the way he did. He'd turn her head. She returned to Torre and worked off her wrath pummelling the feather beds.

"Will Zachary be home soon, mon Père?" asked Stella eagerly, as soon as they were alone.

He managed to walk very slowly towards the church, and to talk about Zachary. He even stood still and attempted to admire the view, talking about Zachary. He did not find it impossibly hard. In the years to come, out of his own experience, he would understand how she felt about Zachary better than anyone else. They did not walk on until there was nothing more that she wanted to say to him about Zachary.

"You took your flowers to Granny Bogan, Stella?" he asked when they were at last walking up the path towards the church.

"Yes. Araminta took them in for me and I stayed in the herb garden. All the herbs were smelling nice, but especially the rue. That's for clear sight, you know."

"I have often thought that the awakening after death must be like the opening of the eyes of one born blind," said the Abbé.

Stella nodded and they went into the dim, musty-smelling church and up the aisle to the screen. "Granny Bogan did not know what the birds meant," said Stella. "Please, mon Père, will you tell me what they mean?"

Luckily he had been to the Church before and had informed himself about it. "The bird with the grape in its beak is the penitent soul of man feeding on the true vine. The bird attacking the caterpillar is the strengthened soul of man fighting evil. The singing bird is the soul that has overcome praising God. You take them in that order, Stella."

Stella's eyes went from the singing bird to the carving of the Madonna and Child just below it. "She is crowned like a queen," she said.

"That's because this church was built long ago in the days when the people of this country still held the old Catholic faith, and worshipped the Mother of God as the Queen of Heaven."

"The old faith—that's yours and Zachary's."

"And yours, for you were baptized into it."

He had wondered how he would begin to tell her, and now the beginning had come so easily. Her hand trembled on his arm, and then slipped from his arm and into his hand, where it went on trembling as though one of the birds from the screen had taken refuge there. They went into the Mallock family pew and sat down on the cushioned seat. The high walls towered about them, so that they could see nothing beyond. They were shut away in a secret world of their own.

"Stella, once I told you a story about my boyhood. Now I am going to tell you one about myself grown-up."

"Yes," said Stella, and moved a little nearer to him. She did not know what it was that had suddenly happened between them, but it had made her tremble with the same sort of happy awe that she had felt when as a small child she had lain in bed on Christmas Eve, knowing that the front door was set wide to welcome whoever might come. She had lain listening for a step on the stairs. Would Gabriel come mounting very swiftly, his wings brushing against the panelling? Would it be Saint George, climbing from stair to stair slowly because of the weight of his armour? Or the Mother of God herself, her step light as leaves falling? Who came now? When she had said goodbye to the Comte de Colbert on the night of the storm she had known that when he came back it would be as someone different.

"When I was a younger man, before I became a priest, I had a wife and baby daughter. I had to go to Ireland and leave them in England to follow me later. They tried to follow me, but the ship on which they embarked was wrecked at Plymouth before ever she put to sea, and nearly all the people on her lost their lives. I came back to Plymouth and they told me that my wife and child were dead. I went back to Ireland in great grief, and I became a priest there. Just lately I have found out that the baby girl was saved."

"What was the name of the ship, mon Père?" How practical she was, how blessedly practical, like Thérèse.

"The *Amphion*. My child was brought to Gentian Hill and became the adopted child of Father and Mother Sprigg."

How abruptly he had spoken! What a fool he was, he thought. He dared not look at her. She lifted his hand to her lap and held it in both hers, and now hers were warm and steady while his was cold and trembling. At last he turned to look at her, and she was looking up at him with a warm and glowing face, and her eyes were as compassionate as though she was his mother.

"I am glad it is you who have come," she said. And then abruptly she began to cry, quietly, and he took her in his arms to comfort her. But he soon discovered that it was not from shock that she was crying.

"You've been such a long time without my mother," she sobbed.

"Do you remember anything at all of your mother?" he asked her.

"Only how tight her arms were when there was all the noise, and fire and black water," she said, and began to tremble again.

He got up and with her still in his arms strode out of the dim church into the park, where the dappled deer were moving in and out of the pools of sunshine and the sky was the colour of turquoise above the murmuring trees.

"Forget the noise and fire and dark water," he said almost sternly as he sat her down. "It passed quickly. All earthly life passes quickly and then we open blind eyes."

They walked slowly towards Torre, hardly speaking but happy. The Abbé felt their two spirits moving towards each other, reaching out for the new adjustments, touching, taking hold. And with each movement, each touch, surety grew. He knew that his love for his daughter, as hers for him, would be all joy until the end. Blind? Yes, that was true. Yet earthly love was a foretaste of light that could dazzle the eyes.

At Mrs. Loraine's gate Stella stopped and looked up at him. "Father," she said with sudden urgency, "I must go at once to Mother and Father Sprigg." Her voice dropped. "It was so quiet in the garden when Father Sprigg brought me home, and Mother Sprigg's arms felt so comfortable."

"After we've seen Mrs. Loraine I'll get a chaise and take you there," he said. He had never loved her so much for anything as for this.

III

At Mrs. Loraine's suggestion Stella stayed on at Weekaborough for the harvesting; partly for the harvesting, partly for the comforting of Mother Sprigg and partly to keep Old Sol company during his last days on earth. For Sol had not died when Dr. Crane expected him to; he had apparently decided to see the harvest safely gathered in first; but they all thought that he would die when the corn was safely stacked.

The comforting of Mother Sprigg had not been easy (Father Sprigg had not needed so much, so delighted was he to find his Stella a lady of such quality) but Stella and the Abbé had achieved it between them. The finding of her real father had increased, not lessened, Stella's love for her fosterparents. If, like all children, she had taken their devotion rather for granted, she did not do this now. Her intuition told her that the depth and mystery which she felt in the Abbé's love for her was a part of the depth and mystery of nature; she had been fashioned from his being as flowers are fashioned from warmth and rain and soil, and his love flowed to her as naturally and powerfully as showers and sunshine to the flower. But Father and Mother Sprigg's love for her and care for her through her life was not such a natural thing, it was a rare gift to her, an outflowing of their own selfless generosity, and her gratitude caused a fresh burgeoning of her love. After the first few bewildering days she seemed to become more their child than ever, and she managed to make it clear that she always would be.

And the Abbé managed to make it clear that he was not going to take her away from them. He was a priest now and had no right to home or family. And as soon as possible he was leaving Torre and going to fresh work in London. He would come to see Stella as often as he could but until she married her home would be with them and Mrs. Loraine as before.

"And if she marries Zachary," Father Sprigg said privately to the Abbé, "her home will always be here. I've no near kin of my own and I'll make them my heirs. I like the lad. Weekaborough means more to him than it does to any of my own distant kin. It's odd, Sir, how he cares for the place. Might have been born here."

The Abbé smiled. He had come up this morning to see Stella, and Father Sprigg had taken a short time off from work to sit with him in the little green parlour, which was used more often now in his honour, and looking out at the garden he seemed to see a tall figure moving lightly among the yew trees. Not Zachary, but like him.

"Will she marry the lad, do you think, Sir?" continued Father Sprigg.

"I think that she will," said the Abbé.

"In another two years, maybe," mused Father Sprigg. "Fifteen is a good marriageable age. My own wife, she was seventeen when I married her, but I was sorry I'd not had her earlier. She was a bit set upon her own way by that time. The younger they are, Sir, the easier brought to heel. It's the same with a colt or a pup."

The Abbé smiled again. He could not visualise Zachary bringing Stella to heel. It was more likely to be the other way round.

"And she must be a Papist, Sir?" went on Father Sprigg a little wistfully.

"I'm afraid that she must. She comes of a Catholic family and was baptized a Catholic. And Zachary is a Catholic." He paused, seeking for comfort for Father Sprigg. "The men who built this home of yours were Catholics, you know, and so was your ancestor whose hunting horn hangs there on the wall."

"That's so," agreed Father Sprigg. "And the chant of the plough, they say that came from the old faith. And the yule log and the wassailing, they're older still. And the harvest maiden—she comes from a long way back."

Puffing at his pipe, he was looking out of the window, and the Abbé followed the direction of his eyes. The reapers were busy in the wheat field to the right of Bowerly Hill. The Abbé watched them with delight. The reaping hook, larger and broader than the common sickle, was held in the mower's right hand and his left arm gathered the standing corn. The swing of the hook, the encircling movement of the left arm, the bend and rise of the body, had the rhythm of music, and the curve of the golden hill against the blue sky was part of it.

"Well, I must be getting back to work in the field," said Father Sprigg, knocking his pipe out of the window. "You'll find Stella in the walled garden, Sir, she always hides there while the reaping is on. Can't abide to see the rabbits knocked on the head. But she'll watch the binding up of the sheaves and the arish-mow."

The incredible age of it all, thought the Abbé, walking with Father Sprigg down to the garden gate. Arish must come from the Latin aridus. It was from their Roman conquerors that the British had learned how to collect their sheaves of corn in stooks in the field that it might dry and harden before it was housed, with the heads turned inwards in the form of a pyramid to shoot off the rain. He leaned on the garden gate for a moment or two, watching the scene, and then made his way through the vegetable garden with its narrow winding paths and trim box hedges, and lifted the latch of the green door under the stone arch that led to the walled garden.

Stella was sitting on the bench that stood against the wall just inside the door sewing her sampler, her workbox beside her, and the sampler was nearly done. She jumped up when she saw her father, curtsyed and bent her head for the blessing that he always gave her now. Then they sat down together and the Abbé stretched out his long legs and sighed contentedly, while Stella continued to stitch silently. Their companionship was already so tested and welded a thing that resting themselves upon the fact of being together they could be silent when they wanted silence, and yet be speaking to each other in their hearts. The Abbé liked the walled garden better than any other place at Weekaborough; though he had come to love the whole of it, and Father Sprigg's decision to make Zachary and Stella his heirs had given him joy. His two children would eventually live here, and he would have a share in their home. He supposed that when he was too old to work any longer for his vagabonds he would live out his last years here, sitting blinking in the sun on this very bench perhaps, with one of Stella's little girls sitting beside him sewing her seam. He would tell her stories of his boyhood, he supposed, for by that time his mind would be doddering about between the two extremes of his earthly existence, focused upon the two points of entry and departure, and he would have forgotten the time between.

The high old walls of the small garden were patched with moss and crowned with pink and white valerian. Peach and nectarine trees grew against the south wall and in one corner was the old mulberry tree and in another an ancient fig tree. The six beehives stood facing them on a square of green turf, and not far away was Mother Sprigg's herb garden with its mystic herbs. Here and there were flowers and bushes that the bees especially loved, a buddleia with its purple tassels, a few rose bushes and clumps of michaelmas daisies. It was a fragrant and cloistered place and when you were within it time stood still. There was never any sound here except the humming of the bees.

"The autumn bees are being born now," said Stella. "The summer bees live only for six weeks, but the autumn bees live till the primroses come. They have to look after the queen their mother, you see, through the long winter. They comb her, smooth her wings and offer her honey on their outstretched tongues, and they always keep their heads towards her because they love her so. When it is warm again she comes out and flies into the sunshine, up and up as far as she can, following the larks. She meets her love high up in the sky, and they look down together on the great world. Then she comes back to the hive and unless she takes her children to a new home she does not leave it again. I'd like to do that. I'd like to see the kingdoms of the world with my lover, and then come home for ever and ever. Father Sprigg says the queen can have two million babies in three years, but I think that's a bit many. I'd rather just have two in three years. She is like a goddess, she goes on living from generation to generation. Bees are another sort of fairy I think. They eat the nectar of flowers and drink dew, just like the fairies, and they have diaphanous wings. They can fly backwards, too, as the fairies can; the birds don't do that. They are very wise. They know their bee-master. Father Sprigg can lay his hand in the entrance of a hive and they will run over his hand and never sting him. They never sting a child they know, either. They never sting me. But when the bee-master dies they must be told at once. The new master must go from hive to hive and say, 'Bees, your old master is dead and now I am master.' But he must say it very politely and bow to each hive. If he does not do that they will all fly away and never come back."

The Abbé had seen John moving among the yew trees but looking up now it was Zachary whom he saw moving among the hives, pausing at each one with bent head.

IV

After tea Stella and Hodge went up to Sol's room and watched from his window the binding of the sheaves and the arish-mow. Early in the morning his bed had been moved so that he could see all that went on, and he had spent a happy day. The neighbours had gathered soon after seven o'clock and at eight had eaten a huge breakfast in the kitchen. The farms of the district did their reaping by turns, all of them helping each other. Work began quietly but after eleven o'clock, when the first pitchers of ale and cider had been brought out to the fields, there was laughter and jokes and songs. The twelve o'clock dinner of meat and vegetables was carried out to the fields, and after that there was more ale and cider and everyone was very merry indeed. By five o'clock the cutting of the wheat was over and they all sat in the shade of the trees and ate the special harvest cakes that Mother Sprigg had baked for them, washed down with yet more liquid refreshment, and then the binding of the sheaves went on until the evening.

Stella found it all a bit too wild and noisy when she was down in the fields with them, but she loved watching from Sol's window. Now that the tragedy of the rabbits was over she discovered that she was very happy. Last night, in her sleep, she had been in the far place again and its peace was still with her, and out of it a deep joy was building up, a shining thing coming slowly into being as the stooks in the field were coming into being, like tents of cloth of gold fit for Sultans to live in.

There was no doubt about it. A great joy was building up for her, and another for Sol, and the songs the reapers were singing, softened and sweetened by distance, made her think of the song the birds sing in the spring just before dawn, when the first lark has told them that he has seen the sun.

"They've finished!" she cried. "Look, Sol! Father Sprigg is making the Maiden."

Sol gave a grunt of satisfaction and she fetched another pillow and propped him up higher so that he could see better. Father Sprigg had bound up a little sheaf in rough imitation of the human form and set it upon the central stook. This was the harvest goddess, Demetra, though none of the reapers knew that. The doctor, had he been present, would have quoted Theocritus. "Ah, once again may I plant the great fan on her corn-heap, while she stands smiling by, Demetra of the threshing floor, with sheaves and poppies in her hands." When she was in place the reapers flung their sickles up in the air towards her and the sun glinting on them made them look like half moons falling about her. "We ha in! We ha in!" they yelled, and the triumphant shout echoed over the hills to tell the countryside that yet another farmer's corn was safely stacked. Then cheering and singing they tramped towards the farmhouse, where they would eat and drink and enjoy themselves until one in the morning.

Stella helped Sol to lie flat again, and with Hodge at her feet sat beside him holding his hand and talking to him softly about the creatures on the farm, the dogs and cats, the sheep, the pigs, and cows and horses. This was how she had talked to mon Père, telling him about the bees, drawing him into the charmed circle that was the kingdom of Weekaborough, and she felt now that she must talk to Sol in the same way. It was like wrapping someone up in a familiar old cloak before they set out on a journey, so that they should feel warmed and comforted during the first strangeness. Yet she was not sure if Sol heard. His eyes were shut and he was smiling, but it might not have been at what she was telling him. His hand in hers felt light and dry and brittle like an autumn leaf.

"He's asleep," she said, when Mother Sprigg came in with a bowl of bread and milk for him.

Mother Sprigg looked at the old man and sighed. She was glad that he looked likely to pass from sleep to death, with as little trouble as a man can have in his going from this world, but she would miss him after all these years.

"Have the bread and milk for your supper, my honey," she said gently to Stella. "And you'd best keep out of the kitchen tonight. They are very merry, for it's been a good harvesting, and they'll get merrier, for there's plenty of ale left yet."

She went out, shutting the door quietly behind her, and Stella went on talking to Sol, while the golden light lay level across the harvest fields and the first fresh breath of the coming night deepened the colour in the sky, lifted the heads of the drooping flowers and set the leaves faintly rustling. But gradually she left off telling him about the animals and began to say other words, that seemed to come to her without any choice of her own. It was as though Sol was speaking through her, taking his leave of the earth.

"It is a land of hills and valleys, and drinketh water of the rain of heaven. A land which the Lord thy God careth for. The eyes of the Lord thy God are always upon it, from the beginning of the year ever until the end of the year. . . . Blessed be the Lord for the precious things of heaven, for the dew, and for the deep that coucheth beneath. And for the precious fruits brought forth by the sun, and for the precious things put forth by the moon. And for the chief things of the ancient mountains, and for the precious things of the lasting hills. . . . As thy days so shall thy strength be. . . . The eternal God is thy refuge, and underneath are the everlasting arms."

The sunset light was brimming the world like wine in a transparent cup, and then it seemed to drain away and the cool twilight was very blue and clear. Sol was still breathing quietly yet Stella felt that something in him had drained away with the golden light. She withdrew her hand, knowing he did not want it any more, and she and Hodge sat so quietly that a mouse ventured out and ran across the boards. Presently the owls began to call and a square of moonlight lay upon the floor. Then Mother Sprigg came in again and kissed her and told her to go to bed, and she went away and left Mother Sprigg to continue the watch with Hodge.

V

But she did not go to bed. She went down into the small green parlour where for so many years the dead had lain in state, and the babies had held their court after their christenings, and the brides and bridegrooms had kissed each other, and she lit the two candles. She was not quite sure why she did it, unless they were one for Sol and one for herself, in honour of the joys building up for them both. Then she looked out of the window and saw the corn stacks shining in the moonlight, and they were no longer golden tents for Sultans to dwell in but silver pavilions for the fairies. She could fancy a door in each one and a sentry standing there on guard. Leaving the candles burning in the parlour she ran out into the garden and across the lane to the fields. It was a still and lovely night, almost as bright as day with the light of the moon and stars. Warmth was still breathing from the sun-soaked earth but the air was cool with the dew. There was no sound but the distant singing in the Weekaborough kitchen and the soft crackle of the stubble beneath her feet as she ran in and out between the pavilions of the fairies. Before the central one she stopped and dropped a curtsy to the Maiden, and then ran on through the gate that led to Bowerly Hill.

Here on the green grass among the sheep, with above her on the hill-top the old yew tree stretching its arms up to the stars, her mood changed and a deep awe was added to her dancing joy. She did not run now, she walked slowly up the hill, sedately like a grown lady, lifting her flowered linen skirts in both hands above the dew. The moon was bright in the sky, just to one side of the yew tree, and she could see the man in the moon with his bundle on his back. At sight of him she stopped and an almost unbearable longing swept over her. "Zachary!" she cried. "Zachary!" and did not know that she had cried aloud. A tall figure moved out from beneath the yew tree, across the face of the moon. He stood there as though he had come from the moon, and called to her.

"Stella! Stella!"

She thought later that she must have flown up the hill, because she did not know anything more until she found herself beneath the yew tree in his arms.

Gradually she became aware of things again, of the feel of his coat beneath her cheek, of his shoulders beneath her clinging hands. The yew tree above her seemed spangled with stars, like a Christmas tree, and the bit of the moon that was showing through the branches was the shape of a silver horn. The sheep had gathered about them and down at the foot of the hill she could see the candle-light shining from the small green parlour. Then she stood on tiptoe and lifting her hands from Zachary's shoulders pulled his face down to hers. It was a strangely unchildish gesture, and her lovely gentle kiss was not a child's kiss. Zachary, as he lifted the little girl off the grass into his arms that he might carry her down the hill, knew that he would not have very much longer to wait before she was a woman and his wife.

## CHAPTER IX

It was a summer evening in Torbay and the sunset light was streaming over the hills, filling the leafy valleys with light, edging the ripples of the calm sea with gold, and the wings of the gulls as they flew back from their inland feeding grounds to the rocky islands off the coast where they slept at night. There had been much coming and going that day along the coast, at Torquay and Torre, Livermead and Paignton, and quite a traffic in the deep lanes with men and women and children coming down from the villages in the hills to see the ships in the bay. Seldom had there been so many of them, sloops and frigates and ships of the line, with all their colours flying and their paintwork and gilding brilliant in the sun. It had been a day of excitement and rejoicing, for Waterloo had been fought and won, the war was over, and out there in the bay, on board the *Bellerophon*, was Napoleon, a captive.

All day the fishermen had been doing a brisk trade taking sightseers out in their boats to cruise around the *Bellerophon*, in the hope of seeing "the Monster" in his green coat with the scarlet epaulettes and his chapeau-bras with the tri-coloured cockade. Only because it is the nature of the English to take a fallen foe immediately to their hearts he was now no longer "the Monster" but an ill-looking little man for whom they were all extremely sorry. They were ashamed, too, because of the restrictions put upon him and the contemptuous refusal of the government to treat him as England's guest. Many of the women wore his emblem, the red carnation, and when they saw him pacing on deck the men took off their hats.

Yet their sympathy was not sufficiently severe to cloud their joy. . . . The war was over. . . . The long, dragging, weary war that had seemed to end so many times, only to break out afresh, was over at last and a long vista of peace stretched in front of them. They could sleep easily in their beds now and have no fear for their children. All day, both on board the ships in the bay and in the villages along the coast, the joy had been extremely vocal, but now at sunset there had come a hushed silence, imposed perhaps by the extraordinary beauty of the moment, or by the slow rhythmical beating of the gull's wings overhead, or perhaps by the deeper realisation of peace that had come with the dropping of the wind and the ebbing of the tide. The men on shore looked out to sea and marvelled at the splendid beauty of the great ships in the evening light, and remembered that the men upon them no longer went in danger of their lives, and the men on board looked at the woods held in the folds of the green hills, and at the white-walled cottages in their gay gardens, with the smoke curling up from their chimneys, and remembered their own homes and were glad.

Into this moment of peace came sailing three frigates. They glided slowly into the bay, and it was evident from their dim paintwork and generally battered appearance that they had come from far. Yet they had great beauty. The slight breeze filled their sails and they dipped proudly through the gold-flecked blue water, as though conscious of duty well done.

The young captain of the first frigate stood as still as a statue on his poop, but his face was not quite as rigid as his body. Nothing moved in his face, yet something passed over it like a flash of light on water as the village of Torquay came into sight, with behind it the sweep of of the hills that he knew as well and the valleys brimming with light. It had not changed much in eleven years; there were a few more white houses scattered over the seven hills and more shipping in the harbour than there used to be, but that was all; the beauty of the place was still untarnished. It had seemed like the vision of another world to Mr. Midshipman O'Connell, spreadeagled in the rigging, and it seemed the same to Captain O'Connell motionless upon his poop. Then, he had been enduring a sailor's life with detestation, and now he was leaving it with sadness in his heart. The war was over, he was returning from his last voyage, and he was sorry. For so many years he had longed for the last moment of his last voyage and yet, now, he was sorry. He supposed it was always that way. A man looked forward to the ending of a way of life that had been hard and difficult, and then when the end came he felt regret. That particular way had moulded and enriched him and so was a friend, and goodbyes to friends are not easy.

Yet the new way opening before him was a good way and far more congenial to him. It would have its difficulties too, as well as its deep and satisfying joys. It would not be a soft life, and its hardness would befriend him. Resolutely he turned from regret and opened his mind and heart in welcome to all that was to come, from this golden moment right on until the end. How lovely was this land towards which he sailed, how inexpressibly dear. Through the years of danger he had known her a land to die for with peace and content, now he knew her a land to live for with a gladness rising afresh with the sun of each morning and the moon and the stars of each night. Gliding steadily nearer to her he felt with an intensity that shook him, made his body tremble a little as it had trembled when he had been spreadeagled in the rigging. Then he suddenly relaxed and smiled, as though a hand had touched him. Stella down in the cabin had known how he was feeling and had put him to rights. He did not allow her to be with him on the poop, it was bad for discipline, and on board his ship, though nowhere else, she always obeyed him. But it never seemed to make much difference if they were apart, for she knew what he was thinking just the same.

Ever since her twentieth birthday she had been going to sea with him whenever she could, and he had been much censured for allowing a lovely young wife to undergo such hardship and danger. But it was not a question of allowing, for if it was possible for her to go she would not stay behind. Although he had married her when she was fifteen, the age at which Father Sprigg considered a man can be certain of capturing a wife's obedience, Stella retained her smooth shining determination to go her own way, from which scoldings slithered to oblivion like water off a duck's back. And her adventurous spirit had welcomed life at sea with a joy that had communicated itself to Zachary. Because Stella liked being a sailor he began to like being one too. Her passionate delight in the old and lovely cities and harbours of the world had enriched them with new beauty for him. Now, in sight of home, their four years of journeying done, he knew they would never forget those journeys. Their love for their own country would be deepened because they had learned to love the whole world too.

They were drawing near to the harbour now and his thoughts went to those who loved them and waited for them at home. His father, who seemed to become more truly his father with every year that passed. Father Sprigg, grown old now and glad to have Zachary come home and take the burden of the farm off his shoulders. Mother Sprigg, grown older too but not changed very much. Stella's father, still toiling in London for his suffering poor but never forgetting them, seeing them whenever he could, loving them deeply and praying for them at night in that small green room that was like Elisha's chamber high upon the wall, and in St. Michael's Chapel upon its hill-top. And for these four they would have great news when they got home, for Stella's first child would be born in the spring.

He heard a light step behind him and the rustle of a woman's skirt. Stella, just this once, had disobeyed him and come to him upon the poop. He did not move, and when she reached him she did not speak, for the crew could see them. She stood beside him, her shoulder lightly touching his, for she was as tall as he was now, tall and very slender. Yet how strong she was both in body and spirit. The very touch of her shoulder put iron into him. He did not need to turn his head to know exactly what she looked like for he knew every line of her face by heart and almost, but not quite, as much of her mind as she knew of his. She was happy now, he knew, with a flush on her sunburnt cheeks and her grey eyes full of light, and she was holding her head high so that the hood of her cloak had fallen back and her short dark curls were blowing about her face. The hills and the sunlit valleys drew a little nearer and the first breath of the land came to them, fresh and flower scented. High over their heads the gulls passed, their white wings lit with gold. Stella fitted her shoulder more comfortably against her husband's and their warm hands touched as they swung together to the rise and fall of the ship. Somewhere on land a bell tolled the hour. It was eight o'clock and in a world at peace they had come home.

*The following books by Elizabeth Goudge are also published by Hodder Paperbacks*

## The Scent of Water

*The Scent of Water* is a gentle and compassionate story of country life, of a woman who goes back, one warm spring, to the village she last visited forty years before. There Mary Lindsay takes up an inheritance, finds a new way of life and acquires a fresh sense of peace and tranquillity.

"The story is told with all Miss Goudge's unrivalled charm and deep sincerity." *Church Times*

## A City of Bells

A novel of a quiet cathedral town, of an orphan who finds a new home, of two people who fight to separate themselves from the ghost of a man whose mystery has cast a spell that only his return can break, of a dream that can only end with a new dawn. But mainly the story of Henrietta . . .

## The Dean's Watch

"About the novels of Elizabeth Goudge there is always something of the fairy-tale, and *The Dean's Watch* is full of the enchantment of goodness—it has that timelessness which marks the author's best work." *The Scotsman*

## Green Dolphin Country

A magnificent epic of love, courage and selfless devotion, set in the Channel Islands and New Zealand in the nineteenth century, written with Elizabeth Goudge's inimitable feeling for the intricacies of human emotions.

"Breathtaking. . . . A long vista of undulating story, with here and there peaks of volcanic excitement." *Daily Telegraph*

## The Herb of Grace

The story of an old country inn, near to Damerosehay, the heart of the Eliot family; and of David, the grandson, disillusioned and unhappy, who has still to find his bride.

"Quality of writing, breadth of vision, humanity. . . . What more could you expect in a novel? In *The Herb of Grace* you get all these qualities and more." *Aberdeen Press and Journal*